THE LIGHT WITHIN US

Cornwall, 1891. Talented painter Edith Fairchild is poised to begin a life of newlywed bliss and artistic creation in the inspiring setting of Spindrift House, freshly inherited by her charming husband, Benedict, and overlooking the stunning harbour of Port Isaac. But when her honeymoon turns sour, her dreams are all but dashed and after a moment of madness and desire she finds herself pregnant with another man's child. Edith swears never to tell her secret and devotes herself to her art. Joined at Spindrift House by her friends — Clarissa, Dora and the secret father of her child, Pascal — together they turn the house into a budding artists' community. But despite their dreams of an idyllic way of life creating beauty by the sea, it becomes clear that all is not perfect within their tight-knit community . . .

CHARLOTTE BETTS

THE LIGHT WITHIN US

Complete and Unabridged

CHARNWOOD
Leicester

First published in Great Britain in 2020 by
Piatkus
An imprint of Little, Brown Book Group
London

First Charnwood Edition
published 2021
by arrangement with
Little, Brown Book Group
An Hachette UK Company
London

*A catalogue record for this book is available
from the British Library.*

ISBN 978–1–4448–4747–5

Published by
Ulverscroft Limited
Anstey, Leicestershire

Printed and bound in Great Britain by
TJ Books Ltd., Padstow, Cornwall

This book is printed on acid-free paper

To the memory of my mother
Dorothy Spooner

1928–2019

1

September 1891

Spindrift House, Cornwall

In the darkest hours of the night, a storm thunders inland from the sea, carrying with it the sharp tang of salt and seaweed. It howls over the rocks and buffets the Bronze Age standing stone on the cliffs. Blustering across the grounds of Spindrift House, it batters the slate-roofed outbuildings and slams the garden gate against the wall. Russet leaves whirl through the air, twisting and turning like a flock of migrating birds, and the branches of the great copper beech dance wildly in the tempest, reaching out in the dark to scrape and tap the farmhouse's windows.

The stone house creaks and groans in its sleep, bracing itself against the storm. Wind moans down the chimneys, rekindling the embers in the hearths. Whistling through the attic windows, it flurries down the staircase, sighs along the passages and mingles with distant echoes of the tears and laughter of people long gone.

Upstairs, widowed Hester Tremayne, who has lived at Spindrift House for over four decades, is dreaming of happier times.

1

The wind of change is blowing through the house. Dark times may be coming but Spindrift House is reawakening, waiting for the light.

★　★　★

The harsh cry of a seagull scattered Hester's dream.

She lay with her eyes shut, clinging to her memory of a golden sunset over a murmuring sea, the touch of his hand in hers and the sand gritty beneath their feet. She caught her breath on a sob, aching to hear his voice again. That perfect day had been half her lifetime ago. Thirty-five years since they were young together: skimming stones across the shining sea, laughing as they ran through the waves. There had been so much shared laughter over the years and the sheer joy of their love had sustained them against all difficulties.

A sudden gust rattled the window, dashing it with rain as hard as pebbles. Hester eased herself out of bed to draw the curtains, her heartbeat skipping irregularly as it often did nowadays. Great black clouds raced across the lowering sky and the sea sounded angry, roaring as it smashed against the rocks in the cove below. She stared at the handsome mansion up on the headland. Cliff House. The house where her beloved Jago's body now lay, waiting to be conveyed to the churchyard at St Endellion.

She wondered how she'd find the strength to go on. Her fingers shook as she twisted her thin plait of white hair into a knot but she resisted the urge to creep into bed and bury herself under the eiderdown. When she was dressed, she stiffened her spine and went downstairs to the warmth of the farmhouse kitchen.

Mrs Gloyne, her ancient housekeeper, lifted the teapot off the range, the swollen joints of her fingers trembling under the strain. 'I'll warrant you'll need a good brew to get you through today, Mrs Tremayne. Sit you down.' She poured the tea, strong and bracing, into Hester's rose-patterned cup.

'Sit with me awhile?' said Hester.

Mrs Gloyne lifted the teapot again, filled a plain white cup and sat at the opposite end of the table. 'Shall you go?' she asked.

'I've changed my mind a dozen times,' said Hester.

'You'll regret it if you don't.'

'I daresay.'

Mrs Gloyne drained her cup. 'Best get on. I've a fruitcake to bake before your nephew comes tomorrow. And I'll make chicken soup. You don't want to catch a chill.'

★ ★ ★

The rain had thinned to a fine drizzle by the time Hester arrived at the churchyard. The sexton was laying lengths of sacking around the freshly dug grave in a vain attempt to conceal the mud. Hester waited to one side of the church, back ramrod-straight. Her mind whirled with memories of Jago; their first breathtaking kiss, their passionate arguments and the love that had

3

lit them from within, right to the end. Bowing her head, she bit the insides of her cheeks, staving off tears. Once she wept, she'd never stop.

The mourners began to arrive and then came the grinding of carriage wheels. Hester peered out from beneath the brim of her bonnet to see a pair of jet black horses drawing up by the gate. The hearse was glass-sided and her stomach clenched when she saw the velvet-draped coffin within. How could her Jago, once so full of vigour, now lie cold and still inside that narrow box?

She pressed her back to the wall while the pall-bearers hoisted the coffin onto their shoulders. Jago's wife, Morwenna Penrose, heavily veiled and leaning on her son's arm, took her place behind the coffin and headed the procession into the church.

Fighting back nausea, Hester waited behind a yew tree. After what felt like an eternity, the mourners came out of the church and gathered around the grave. The wind snatched away the vicar's words but she watched the coffin being lowered into the ground. First Morwenna and then her son threw a handful of soil into the grave. And then it was over. Hugh and his mother led the funeral party towards the waiting carriages.

The wind whisked Hester's silk scarf up into the air and she reached out to catch it as Jago's widow walked by. Morwenna lifted a corner of her black crepe veil and stared directly at her. The malevolence in her glare made Hester quake.

Once the carriages had rolled away, Hester hurried to the graveside, her heart thudding. Opening her reticule, she withdrew a crimson rose plucked from the gazebo at Spindrift House where she and Jago had often sat. Inhaling its rich fragrance, she kissed the velvet petals, then dropped it onto the coffin. 'Goodbye, my love,' she whispered.

The sexton, spade in hand, walked towards her. 'Has the funeral finished, Missus?'

Hester gave the crimson rose a last, lingering look. 'Yes,' she said, 'it's finished.'

★   ★   ★

By the following morning the stormy weather had blown itself out. The air was warm and moist when Hester climbed down the rocky steps to Tregarrick Cove. They were too steep for her these days and the effort made her breathless. She meandered along the sand but Jago would never come here with her again and she couldn't bear the thought. Stumbling down to the water's edge, she wanted to scream and rage and tear her hair. The sky was overcast and sullen, while the sea, a threatening steel grey, rumbled its discontent and slapped choppy waves onto the rocks. How long, she wondered, would it take to drown if she walked into the water? Perhaps not long, if she didn't fight it.

Abruptly, she turned her back on the siren-song of the waves and walked unsteadily towards the steps.

5

Hester had composed herself by the time
Benedict arrived. Her favourite nephew was tall
and broad-shouldered; he filled the spacious
drawing room with his amiable presence.

'Dear Aunt Hester!' He enfolded her in a
hug and planted a smacking kiss on her cheek.
Her drooping spirits lifted a little. 'Father and
Mother send their best wishes,' he said. Too
restless to sit, he rested one elbow on the great
stone mantelpiece while he chattered about the
family.

Throughout his childhood, he'd exasperated
his father, Hester's youngest brother, not only
with his lack of intellectual rigour but by the way
he cheerfully flitted from one interest to another.
Schooled in Truro, Benedict had frequently
spent his holidays with Hester. She finally
captured his attention by sharing with him her
love of painting and now he was studying at the
Slade School of Art.

'And what were you doing this summer that
meant you had no time to visit me?' said Hester.

'There were so many invitations to balls and
parties, I barely spent an evening alone.'

'I imagine a young man such as yourself would
be very popular.'

'I've never lacked for dancing partners,' he
said, a gleam in his hazel eyes. His expression
grew serious. 'But there's a girl who's different
from the others. One morning I was outside the
Slade when a hansom cab hurtled through a
puddle, splashing me with mud . . . '

'How unpleasant!'

'It would have been, if a vision of loveliness with ebony hair and the most glorious green eyes hadn't offered me her handkerchief.'

'Does this paragon have a name?'

'Edith Hammond, a fellow student. Father once told me there are two kinds of girl: one for fun and the other for marriage. Aunt Hester, I'm going to marry Edith.' Benedict raked his fingers through his curls. 'I went to see her father but he sent me away with a flea in my ear, insisting I wait until I'm earning enough to support her.'

'Quite right, too!'

Benedict groaned. 'But how long will that be? I shan't graduate until next summer.'

'All the more incentive for you to work hard and start earning.'

'But Edith's such a prize, some other fellow will snap her up before then.'

'She'll wait for you, if she loves you enough.' It wasn't the time to tell him she'd left him everything she owned, including Woodland Cottage. Much as Hester loved her nephew, his mother had spoiled him. He must learn patience and self-discipline.

Benedict was on his second slice of Mrs Gloyne's fruitcake when Hester told him that it might be his last visit to Spindrift House. He stared at her. 'But why? My happiest childhood memories are of this house.'

'I doubt I'll be able to extend my tenancy. My landlord has died,' Hester said, attempting to steady her voice.

'Jago Penrose? Oh, Lord! I'm sorry to hear

7

that,' said Benedict. 'I liked him. I remember him looking at my sketchbook and helping me when I couldn't get the perspective right.'

Hester nodded. 'He was an architect so he knew about perspective. He built Cliff House and then rented this one to your Uncle Cador and me.' She closed her eyes, remembering how, newly married, she'd fallen under the welcoming spell of Spindrift House at first sight: the stone walls clad in Virginia creeper, the stately copper beech and the hydrangeas bordering the lawn that undulated down towards the sea. But more than anything, the moment she went inside and walked through the rambling, sunlit rooms freshened by sea breezes, she'd known it was destined to be home to her. Widowed young, she'd stayed on, finding comfort within the sheltering walls of Spindrift House.

'I believe Jago's widow will wish her son to reside here, now Hugh's family is growing,' Hester said.

'But you can't leave!'

She glanced at the panelled walls, the bookcases crammed with her favourite books, the seascapes she and Jago had painted, and on the mantelpiece the china dogs he'd brought her from Truro. These things were impossibly dear to her but she couldn't take them all with her. 'There's a little cottage in the woods where I might go.' She blinked back the hot tears that stung her eyelids.

Benedict hurried over to hug her. 'I thought you looked glum. I wish you'd told me earlier, instead of letting me rattle on.'

She clung to him. 'It's been a shock to lose my old friend. I wish to sit quietly for a while. Why don't you go and unpack?'

After he'd gone upstairs, she leaned back in her armchair and stared out of the window at the lush green fields, the huge Cornish sky and wide expanse of sea. She'd bought Woodland Cottage years ago, as a secret bolt hole where she and Jago could snatch a few precious hours together whenever they could, but of necessity it had been secluded and there were no views. Overwhelmed with heartache, she closed her eyes.

She must have dozed because she started when the doorbell jangled. Mrs Gloyne's footsteps tapped along the passage and a moment later the drawing-room door burst open. Hugh Penrose, a fair, stocky figure, stood on the threshold, fists bunched.

'I'm sorry, Mrs Tremayne,' said Mrs Gloyne, peering around him. 'He pushed right past me.'

Hester stood up. 'Thank you, Mrs Gloyne. It seems Mr Penrose has something urgent to say.'

'Damn' right I do!' He stepped into the room, a muscle twitching visibly in one cheek. 'My mother is in a state of such distress we've had to call the doctor. She might have had an apoplexy. It would have been your fault if she'd died!'

Hester's pulse began to race. 'Perhaps you should explain . . .'

He thrust his chin towards her. 'That's rich, coming from you! As if you didn't know . . . Well then, I'll *explain*, shall I?'

She stared at him, experiencing a terrible premonition.

'But of course you must already know about

9

Father's new will,' he said, through gritted teeth.

Heavy footsteps clattered down the stairs.

An ache blossomed in Hester's jaw and she couldn't catch her breath. 'But I didn't . . . '

'Shut up! When the will was read, my poor mother fainted dead away. Now she's had to tell me the truth, the painful truth she's borne with great dignity and in complete silence for over thirty years.' Hugh's face was flushed an angry red.

Benedict strode into the room. 'Aunt Hester?'

Hugh ignored him. 'As if it wasn't bad enough to discover you were my father's whore, you persuaded him to leave you Spindrift House and a significant portion of his wealth, all of which should have been mine!'

A crushing pain in Hester's chest made her sink down onto her armchair. 'I *didn't* ask him . . . ' Jago had said he wanted to leave Spindrift House to her but she'd utterly forbidden him to do so.

'Don't lie to me!' shouted Hugh. He made a visible effort to compose himself. 'Much as it sickens me, I've come to appeal to your better nature, if you have one. I'm asking you to forfeit my father's bequest to you, in favour of my mother who has been so sinned against.'

'I didn't ask or want your father to . . . '

Hugh bent over her, hands planted either side of her on the arms of the chair. 'You're lying!'

'You don't understand,' gasped Hester.

'On the contrary, I understand perfectly.'

Benedict stepped forward. 'Leave her alone, Penrose!'

10

'You've destroyed my family, you old bitch!' Hugh's voice rose. 'You wheedled your way into Father's affections for your own financial gain.' His angry face was so close to Hester's that spittle sprayed her cheeks. 'You cheated Mother out of her husband's love.'

'I never intended . . . '

Hugh jabbed his forefinger at Hester. 'I will make it my personal mission to have your name dragged through the mud at every possible opportunity,' he said, his voice low and malevolent now.

'Penrose, stop this!' Benedict gripped Hugh's arm and pulled him away.

He shook himself free and glared at Hester. 'There won't be a soul left in the neighbourhood who will pass the time of day with you, none of the shops will allow you credit and, by God, you'd better keep your doors locked at night.'

Frightened by the hatred in his eyes, she cowered away, her hands pressed to her ears.

'How dare you terrify and insult an old lady?' Benedict shouted.

Taking no notice of him, Hugh continued to harangue Hester. 'You will visit my father's lawyer tomorrow and return what is rightfully ours. And when you've done that,' he sneered, 'why don't you take a walk into the sea and never come back?'

'Enough!' bellowed Benedict. 'Get out of this house!'

Hugh pushed him against the wall. 'It's my house!'

Benedict barged Hugh with his shoulder.

11

Grunting with the effort, the two men wrestled each other, knocking over a side table and sending a vase of roses crashing to the floor.

Benedict forced Hugh's arm up behind his back, making him yell in pain. 'It's quite different now the boot's on the other foot, isn't it, Penrose?' he said. 'Aunt Hester, I'll escort this piece of filth off the premises and then we shall report the matter to the police.'

'It is I who will be reporting you!' shouted Hugh. He struggled violently, lashing out and kicking Benedict's shin.

Hester heard them go, scuffling and cursing their way along the passage, with Benedict eventually dragging Hugh outside. The front door crashed back on its hinges and bounced against the wall.

Mrs Gloyne hurried to Hester's side, her toothless old mouth trembling with shock and outrage. 'Thank goodness Mr Benedict was here. Look at you, bone-white and your lips all blue! Shall I fetch the smelling salts and a nip of brandy?'

Gradually, the pain in Hester's chest eased but still she trembled.

Benedict returned, brushing his hands together. He gave Hester a grim smile. 'He won't bother you again.'

Hester wasn't so sure.

Mrs Gloyne removed herself to the kitchen and Benedict refilled his aunt's glass and poured a brandy for himself. 'Well, aren't you the dark horse, Aunt Hester?' There was more than a hint of amusement and admiration in his voice.

Unable to look him in the eye, she rubbed at the pins and needles in her arm. Although her love affair with Jago had been secret, it had never felt sordid to them, only pure and beautiful. 'It wasn't how Hugh thought it was,' she said. 'I was already widowed and his parents lived separate lives before Jago and I became close. And I told Jago my husband had left me well provided for. I didn't want the Penrose money.'

'Well, Hugh doesn't deserve any of it, not after the way he threatened you.'

'He was such a sweet child, once.' She remembered her delight on meeting him with Jago in the cove one day when he was small, a breeze ruffling the child's fair hair and his face alive with excitement when he showed her a sea anemone in his long-handled fishing net.

'You look done in, Aunt Hester,' said Benedict. 'I'll help you upstairs to rest.'

She sighed. 'Perhaps everything will look better tomorrow after I've seen the solicitor. I shall, of course, make sure Spindrift House is returned to the Penroses.'

Benedict supported her up the stairs but dizziness overwhelmed her and she clung to the banisters. She felt herself being lifted up in her nephew's arms and leaned gratefully against his chest. He laid her upon the bed and tucked the eiderdown around her.

'I'm worried about you,' he said, an anxious frown on his forehead. 'I'll fetch the doctor.'

'Don't leave me,' she said, her breath coming in harsh gasps. Turning her head on the pillow, her gaze sought out Jago's watercolour of

13

Tregarrick Cove that had hung on her bedroom wall for twenty-five years. How she loved that picture! The sea shimmered under a cerulean sky and a man and a woman watched a small boy with a fishing net peering into a rock pool exposed by the retreating sea.

'I *must* fetch the doctor,' said Benedict.

She was tired, so very tired, and all she wanted now was to sleep. 'It's too late, my dear,' she whispered. She gazed again at the painting, remembering the smell of the seaweed glistening in the sun, the love in Jago's eyes and the little boy's excitement. How blissfully happy she had been on that day.

'Aunt Hester?'

But the darkness was already crowding in and Jago was waiting for her. 'I'm coming, my darling,' she murmured.

And then there was only peace.

2

July 1892

Kensington

On the morning of her wedding, Edith stood in her nightgown before the looking glass, wondering what Benedict would look like, naked. Over the past three years she'd seen many naked men but none of them had been young and some had been positively peculiar. There had been that nameless sailor whose entire body was inked with writhing sea serpents and then there was the hunchback with the sad, beautiful eyes. Once she'd overcome the shock of so much nakedness, she saw those men only in terms of light and shade, their skin merely draping the muscles, bones and sinews beneath, while her charcoal raced over the paper to capture their images.

A naked Benedict, however, would be an entirely different matter from the artists' models at the Slade. A foot taller than herself, well-built and with curly bronze-coloured hair, he'd only to look at Edith with laughter in his sleepy eyes to make her melt. From the first day she met him, he'd dazzled her. Showering her with compliments, flowers and small presents, he'd made her feel special and beautiful. Her family never made her feel like that. Mindful of her mama's warnings, Edith hadn't allowed him to take any liberties, apart from a few stolen kisses, but her self-control didn't mean his presence left her unaffected. Her friend Clarissa had whispered that Edith's new husband would expect her to remove her nightgown in the marital bed. Shocked, she hadn't believed it, even though Clarissa assured her it was true.

Slowly, Edith loosed the ribbons of her nightgown, exposing her breasts. She believed they were a good shape. Although full, they didn't sag like those of some of the models in the Life Class.

There was a tap at the door and, without waiting for permission, Mama swept into the room, followed by the maid carrying a breakfast tray set for two.

Edith hastily retied the ribbons at her neck. Heat flooded her face but her mother didn't appear to have noticed.

'Good morning, Edith.'

She pulled on her dressing gown as the maid set the breakfast things on the round rosewood table and discreetly left the room.

'I wanted a word with you,' said her mama, sitting down and spooning kedgeree onto Edith's plate. 'Are you still sure you wish to marry Benedict? You made such a fuss until Papa allowed you to attend the Slade that I imagined you'd want to follow your artistic ambitions for a while before becoming a wife. You must understand that in sickness and in health, *until death parts you*, marriage is for life. Once the wedding has taken place, there's no going back. Ever.'

'Of course I'm sure! I thought you liked my

husband-to-be? Even Papa is happy with the match now that Benedict has his inheritance from his aunt.'

'He's charming and it's a relief he'll take you on. I'd been worried you were so set on painting you'd remain a spinster for evermore. Marrying another artist is probably the best outcome for you.'

'I could never have married a man who didn't understand that I *must* paint.'

Mama sighed. 'I always expected my darling Amelia would marry first.'

Edith didn't want to talk about her elder sister, not on her wedding day. A gifted pianist with the singing voice of an angel, Amelia had taken three years to die of consumption. Her memory haunted the house, leaving their mother still grieving eight years later, and it seemed impossible for Edith ever to live up to the level of perfection Amelia had acquired in Mama's eyes. Benedict's proposal had opened up the promise of a new life, one where Edith would be cherished and loved for herself. If she worked hard and achieved her dream of having a painting exhibited in the Royal Academy, perhaps then Mama would love her as much as she had her elder daughter.

'Eat your kedgeree. We can't have you fainting in church.' Mama stared out of the window overlooking Bedford Gardens, her fingers restlessly tapping the table. She glanced at Edith and looked away again. 'Normally I'd never dream of discussing such a delicate subject but, after my own honeymoon, I vowed that, if I had

17

daughters of my own one day, I'd counsel them before the event, no matter how awkward it was.'

Edith put down her fork.

'A bride may find her wedding night a little . . . ' Mama hesitated momentarily before continuing ' . . . *surprising*.'

'In what way?'

Edith's mother twisted her wedding ring around her finger. 'A bride must expect her husband to . . . ' Her cheeks became suffused with pink. 'To touch her. Remember, there's no shame in this. On the contrary, it's her duty to do her husband's bidding, however unusual his wishes may seem.'

'I shall always do my duty to Benedict.' Edith suppressed a shiver of longing as she imagined his eager kisses.

Mama rose to her feet, leaving her own breakfast untouched. 'I'm glad we've had this chat. I shouldn't have wanted you to imagine afterwards that some outrage had been committed upon your person.'

Edith frowned at this baffling statement and watched her mother close the door behind her. The bride ate her breakfast, including all the kedgeree. Her mother was quite right; it wouldn't do to faint in church.

★　★　★

Tightly laced, Edith lifted her arms while Colette, Mama's maid, tied her petticoat ribbons. Outside, the sun shone. She sighed, yearning to be at the church already with Benedict at her side. In a

18

few hours' time they would be properly alone for the first time. Imagining his embraces then, given without any need for restraint, made her feel quite overheated.

'Miss Edith?' Colette held out the cream silk wedding dress. She hooked together the mother-of-pearl buttons down the back of the bodice.

'*Et voilà!*' said the maid. 'I will inform Mrs Hammond you are ready for the veil.'

Edith slipped her feet into new satin shoes and inspected herself in the mirror. The wide leg-of-mutton sleeves emphasised her narrow waist and the heavy silk of the bell-shaped skirt clung to her hips before it flared out into an elegant train at the back.

Mama, wearing a vast hat adorned with feathers, entered the room with the veil laid over her outstretched arms. Even on Edith's wedding day she'd chosen to wear lavender silk, half-mourning in memory of Amelia.

'Grandmama's Brussels lace veil,' she said. 'I'd always imagined darling Amelia would wear it next.'

The bitter disappointment in her voice made Edith feel second best again. It irked her even more since Amelia hadn't always been as saint-like as Mama imagined.

Her mother arranged the veil over Edith's dark hair and secured the coronet of wax orange blossoms with pearl-topped hatpins. She studied her through narrowed eyes before nodding approval.

Edith's mouth was dry. She followed Mama along the passage and paused at the top of the stairs. Papa and Uncle Toby waited for them in the hall below.

19

Mama called down, 'Edward!'

Papa and Uncle Toby looked up expectantly.

Mindful of her long train, Edith carefully descended the stairs.

'Enchanting, my dear,' said Papa, kissing her cheek. 'The carriages are at the door,' he said. 'Shall we?'

The servants lined the hallway and bowed or bobbed as Papa led her outside. Mama set off with Uncle Toby in the first carriage, while Papa handed Edith into the second.

'We'll drive in the other direction, around Kensington Gardens,' he said. 'It wouldn't do to arrive early and make young Benedict think you're overeager. Keep him on his toes!' He reached for Edith's hand. 'Nervous? You'll soon settle into the way of married life. Though I could wish Cornwall were a little closer. Still, I daresay you'll write to your mama and let us know how you go on.'

Edith rarely spent any time alone with her father and lapsed into awkward silence, hardly knowing what to say to him. The Bayswater Road was teeming with carriages and their progress was slow. She gripped her bouquet of pink roses and white freesias and prayed they wouldn't be late.

Her corset pinched and she felt nauseous; perhaps it hadn't been sensible to eat Mama's breakfast as well as her own. Staring out of the carriage window, Edith kept her gaze fixed on the park, watching the horses and the nannies wheeling perambulators. To take her mind off her nervousness, she imagined how she'd capture the scene in watercolour, concentrating on the vibrant shades of green and the patterns the sunlight made filtering past the park railings.

Before long they were drawing up outside St Mary Abbots. Clinging to her papa's arm, Edith stepped down from the carriage.

Benedict's little nieces, adorable in frilled dresses with pink sashes, waited by the church door with their governess. She chivvied her charges into position, one holding Edith's train and the others ready to strew rose petals at her feet.

Edith's knees trembled as an echo of Mama's voice reverberated in her head: 'Once the wedding has taken place, there's no going back.'

The organ music swelled and Papa guided Edith out of the sunshine and into the shadowy cavern of the church. The air inside smelled of freesias, incense and mould. Faces turned to stare as they made stately progress down the nave and Edith glimpsed Clarissa, chic in sky blue, and dear Dora, her freckled face smiling encouragingly.

And then there was Benedict, standing before the altar painted with a kaleidoscope of cobalt and crimson from the light slanting through the stained glass. Tall and impossibly handsome, he was waiting for her. Edith's momentary uncertainty evaporated like mist in the sun.

★ ★ ★

Later, she hardly remembered the ceremony at all, except for the scent of freesias and Benedict's

21

hazel eyes looking into hers as they made their responses.

Then they were in the carriage together with rose petals and rice on their shoulders.

Benedict pulled her against him and kissed her until she had to turn aside to catch her breath. 'What a shame it's such a short journey to Bedford Gardens,' he murmured, his hand caressing her waist.

Edith straightened her coronet, her pulse skipping. This was the beginning of her new life. No more failing to live up to Amelia's perfection. She'd spend the nights in her husband's arms, whispering words of love, and during the days they'd paint, side-by-side. Wonderingly, she touched Benedict's cheek. 'I love you so much,' she whispered.

He gave her a dazzling smile and kissed her nose.

The carriage halted outside Edith's home in Bedford Gardens. No longer my home, she thought, as her husband led her inside. Her home now was Spindrift House in Cornwall, a place she'd never seen except in drawings in Benedict's sketchbook.

Both sets of parents waited to greet them. Edith's mother-in-law's eyelids were pink from weeping. She had an exceptional fondness for Benedict, her last, very late baby. He made no secret of the fact his mother had indulged him, allowing him to study art instead of following his father's footsteps into Harley Street where he was a renowned surgeon. Just as well, Benedict had said, because he loathed Latin and the sight of blood made him queasy.

The afternoon passed in a blur of congratulatory speeches, an endless meal of several rich courses and Champagne bubbles fizzing in Edith's nose. And, all the time, Benedict was at her side, his knee pressing against hers under the starched white tablecloth, his arm draped along the back of her chair, his fingers making her shiver when they caressed the nape of her neck.

Clarissa, Dora and Wilfred, fellow students from the Slade, came to hug her and offer Benedict their congratulations. Wilfred shook his hand.

'You look so beautiful today, Edith,' said Dora. She blushed, the expression in her grey eyes suddenly worried. 'Not just today, of course — you're always beautiful.'

'Positively radiant,' said Clarissa, amusement at Dora's awkwardness written across her face. 'Now, Benedict, don't forget,' she pressed one manicured finger to his chest, 'our boat train leaves Victoria at ten o'clock sharp tomorrow morning. There'll be no time for lingering in bed.'

'But there's every reason to linger, don't you think?' He gave Edith a smouldering glance and a tremor of anticipation tingled down her back.

'Isn't it exciting?' said Dora, wide-eyed. 'I've never been to France.'

'So you've told us, at least, oh . . . ' Clarissa tapped her cheek and pretended to look puzzled ' . . . twenty times today.'

'Don't tease her,' said Edith.

Soon it was time to change into her

going-away outfit of pink silk. Mama came to supervise and clasped a string of pearls around Edith's neck. 'My father gave these to me upon my marriage to your own father,' she said.

'Thank you, Mama.' Edith kissed her cool, perfumed cheek, knowing she'd intended them for Amelia.

'Your luggage has been sent on to the Savoy and the doorman will arrange for a cab to take you to Victoria tomorrow morning.' Her mother sighed. 'I still find it odd that you and Benedict wish to take your friends with you on your honeymoon.'

Edith hadn't been happy about it either, at first, but he'd promised her they'd have plenty of time alone together at Spindrift House later on. 'Benedict says it will be a summer-long party. Wilfred's cousin Pascal is an artist, too. His parents will be away so we'll have the house in Nice to ourselves.'

Downstairs, Benedict escorted his wife to their carriage and the wedding party gathered in the street to wave them off.

Mrs Fairchild clutched her son's hand through the carriage window, smothering it with kisses. 'Look after my precious boy, Edith!'

'Of course, Mrs Fairchild.'

Impatiently, Benedict loosed his mother's grip. The carriage rolled away amongst a flutter of handkerchiefs and a chorus of goodbyes.

'That was the most wonderful day of my life,' Edith said, sinking back against the seat cushions.

'It isn't over yet.' Benedict gave her a sideways

glance and kissed her again.

The Savoy was bright and new and unimaginably luxurious. A dignified porter escorted them to the electric lift and Edith's eyes widened as it sped them upstairs to the honeymoon suite, where flowers, exotic fruit and more Champagne awaited. She ran from light switch to light switch, flicking them on and off, and exclaimed with delight at the marble bathroom with its shiny taps and constant hot water.

'Why don't you have a bath?' called Benedict from the sitting room. 'I'll open the Champagne.'

A short while later, the bathroom was full of steam and Edith slid into the perfumed water. It was such a relief to be free from her corset, even though she'd have to put it on again for dinner. The bath was so vast her toes didn't reach the end.

A sudden draught made her glance over her shoulder. Water sloshed over the side of the bathtub as she reared up in shock, clasping her knees in an attempt to conceal her nakedness. Benedict stood behind her, wearing only a silk dressing gown.

'I've brought the Champagne.' He placed two glasses and a bottle on the marble bath surround.

She glanced at her *peignoir*, hanging on the bathroom door and impossible for her to reach.

'Don't be shy,' he said. He lowered the window blind to dim the light. 'Shift forwards and I'll climb in behind you.'

She hesitated, then remembered Mama saying

it was a bride's duty to do her husband's bidding, and wriggled towards the bath taps. Out of the corner of her eye she saw Benedict's dressing gown drop to the floor. He got into the bath and extended his legs, one either side of her hips. She stared at his calves, all covered with hair, and his feet, so large beside her small ones. There was a great deal about being married that Edith must become accustomed to.

He shifted and water slapped the rim of the tub. 'Lean back against me.'

Tentatively, she rested against his chest. His bare chest.

Gently, he lifted one of her tightly folded arms away from her breast and placed a glass in her hand. 'Better?'

She nodded and tried not to flinch as he laid one hand across her stomach. She gulped her Champagne but the bubbles made her choke.

Benedict took the glass until she'd recovered. 'You're nervous,' he said, pouring more wine for her, 'but I'm not going to hurt you.'

After her third glass Edith became drowsy and stopped worrying. 'I think,' she said carefully, 'perhaps I've had a bit too much to drink.'

Benedict chuckled. 'I think you'll find you've had just the right amount.'

Lazily, she watched drops of condensation running down the tiles and listened to the slow dripping of a tap in the peaceful, steamy silence. She giggled as Benedict stretched out a foot and turned on the hot tap with his toes.

Caressing her shoulders, he dropped tiny kisses on the nape of her neck while Edith sighed with pleasure. One by one he removed the pins from her hair until it tumbled down her back and floated upon the water. He buried his face in her dark curls. 'I've waited a long time for this.'

'Have you?' she whispered.

'You nearly drove me mad imagining it.' His hands stroked her throat and lightly brushed her breasts, making her gasp. 'You were always so prim and proper but I guessed there was a sensual little heart beating somewhere under all that tight-lacing,' he murmured.

Edith closed her eyes and, when he rolled one nipple between his finger and thumb, there was a sharp, sweet ache inside her. She wondered for a moment how he knew exactly where and how to touch her, to make her melt. His fingers stroked over her stomach and then reached lower, towards her private place. Involuntarily, she pushed his hand away.

'Don't think!' whispered Benedict, gently loosening her grip.

She closed her eyes again and allowed herself to relax while he stroked her. It was quiet, except for the sound of their breathing and the gentle lapping of the water between her thighs. The bathroom was a warm, steamy sanctuary far away from the rest of the world and what happened in it was their private business. Time didn't exist anymore and the tingling inside her grew stronger until she was taut with longing. She held her breath, knowing something momentous was going to happen. And then a great heat exploded within her and she cried out in astonishment as wave after wave of exquisite sensation washed over her.

Benedict lifted her out of the bath, her wet hair clinging to his chest as he carried her into the bedroom and laid her on the bed. Hurriedly, she dragged the eiderdown over their nakedness. He lay beside her, his hands sliding over her back and breasts as he kissed her, his mouth hot and urgent. After a while, he turned her on her back, threw off the eiderdown and kneeled between her thighs.

She caught her breath in shock. The loins of the Life Class models had always been muslin-draped and Benedict's manhood didn't look anything like that of the classical statues she'd studied. It certainly wouldn't fit behind a fig leaf.

'I'll be careful, Edith,' he whispered.

Careful or not, he did hurt her but it was only momentary and his rising excitement aroused her again. She clung to him, wrapping her legs around his waist and surrendering herself entirely to the intensity of their pleasure. Finally, he gasped and shuddered to a climax.

Afterwards, he kissed the tip of her nose. 'Well, Mrs Fairchild,' he said, 'now you are truly my wife. And I was right, wasn't I?' He ran a finger-nail down the swell of one breast and circled her nipple. 'Your demure exterior conceals a wonder-fully passionate nature. We shall suit each other well, you and I.' He yawned and closed his eyes. A second later he was asleep.

Disappointed he didn't want to talk about such an extraordinary happening, she studied her husband's face, learning every handsome contour and plane of it, while her heart ached

28

with love for him. She had given him her trust, relinquishing all modesty and shame, and he had made her truly his forever. Edith smiled to herself. Mama had been right; her wedding night had been most *surprising*.

3

A fly bumbling against the windowpane awoke Clarissa. The carriage of the Méditerranée Express was stiflingly hot and the hills and valleys outside a parched ochre in the harsh sunlight. It had been a long journey south from Paris and her companions' excited chatter had dwindled as the heat grew more intense. One by one, the train rocked them to sleep.

Edith was encircled in Benedict's arms, her head nodding on his chest with every lurch of the carriage. Clarissa noted the dark shadows beneath her eyes. The poor girl was probably short of sleep but at least she hadn't seemed too shocked after her wedding night. She'd gazed adoringly at Benedict ever since they'd arrived, late, at Victoria. Idly, Clarissa wondered if it was Edith's undeniable innocence that had so inflamed Benedict's lustful infatuation with her that it had driven him to the surprising step of taking her to the altar.

Clarissa contemplated his sleeping face, remembering their own brief affair two years before. Her aunt Minnie, with whom she'd lodged while she studied at the Slade, was a New Woman and had afforded Clarissa a great deal of freedom. Benedict hadn't been her first, not by a long chalk, but she'd discovered he was an ardent and skilful lover. It had taken her aback, however, that unlike most of the men she'd amused herself with, he hadn't fallen in love with her.

'We're too alike, you and I,' he'd said, when she'd quizzed him about it.

Of course, they weren't alike at all. He'd been seeking sexual adventure, while she . . . Clarissa didn't want to think about that.

The train juddered to a standstill.

Wilfred yawned and unfolded his lanky figure. He leaned out of the window, a breeze ruffling his fair hair. 'Not long now,' he said. Sitting down again, he eyed the creases in his linen trousers with disfavour and attempted to smooth them flat. Even in his painting smock, he always took trouble to appear immaculate.

Dora blinked awake like a startled baby owl and knuckled sleep from her eyes.

Edith disentangled herself from Benedict's embrace and stretched as elegantly as a cat. 'I'm hungry,' she said.

Dora rummaged in her basket. She offered a piece of shortbread to Edith and passed the rest around.

'How frightfully resourceful of you, Dora,' said Clarissa.

Dora glanced at her, clearly wondering if she was being teased, which she was.

The train emitted a piercing whistle and a great hissing cloud of steam, before jolting on its way again.

Benedict plucked the last morsel of Edith's shortbread out of her fingers and kissed the crumbs off her mouth when she protested.

31

Half an hour later, they arrived at Nice.

The platform was crowded and everyone had to bellow over the noise of the engines, wailing children and chattering passengers.

'Look out for my cousin Pascal,' shouted Wilfred. 'He has dark brown hair.'

Since almost all the Frenchmen visible had dark hair, Clarissa didn't find that particularly helpful.

'There he is!' Wilfred waved wildly. Then the two men were shaking hands and slapping each other on the back. A moment later Wilfred drew Pascal over to meet the rest of them.

Clarissa held out her hand. Pascal kissed it and, with a flash of his dark eyes, said how enchanted he was to meet her. Of medium height, he was still tall enough for Clarissa to look up at him from under her eyelashes. He had a narrow face with interestingly high cheekbones and an aquiline nose. Rather disappointingly, he turned away to greet Dora and showed her exactly the same courtesy. Lastly, he greeted Edith. Clarissa thought he held her hand slightly longer than necessary.

Pascal shepherded them out of the station, followed by a porter who complained as he pushed their overladen trolley. Outside, Pascal flipped a coin to a boy holding the reins of a horse hitched to a wagon.

'How delightfully . . . rustic,' said Clarissa, making a face as she climbed into the wagon. It looked as if it had been used to transport dung-matted straw.

Benedict swung Edith up off the ground and

onto the bench beside Clarissa. Wilfred directed the porter, in perfect French, to stow the luggage in the cart he'd hired to follow them.

'Where's Dora?' said Edith.

Clarissa sighed and shaded her eyes against the sunshine. 'Surely she can't have got lost already?'

'There she is!' Wilfred waved and Dora dashed towards them, holding onto her hat.

She squeezed herself down on the seat next to Edith. 'Sorry. I had to pay a visit,' she mumbled. Her sandy hair had come loose and Edith helped her to tuck it back under her hat.

Half an hour later, they arrived at Bellevue, Pascal's family home in the hills above Nice.

A young woman opened the wrought-iron gates for him to steer the wagon onto the forecourt's neatly raked gravel.

Feeling pleasantly surprised by their destination, Clarissa studied the house. Colourwashed a soft pink, it had green shutters and terracotta roof tiles. The sun-warmed courtyard was shaded by chestnut trees and the path to the front door lined with billowing clouds of fragrant lavender, humming with bees.

'It's charming, isn't it?' said Edith.

'And much grander than I'd expected after being conveyed here in a pig cart,' whispered Clarissa.

Pascal linked his arm through the young woman's. 'May I present my sister Delphine.'

Clarissa shook her hand. Delphine was pretty and shared Pascal's dark colouring but she was a fraction too plump and her mouth was sulky.

33

Wilfred kissed her on both cheeks in the French fashion. 'Still enjoying married life, Delphine? How is Édouard?'

She shrugged, pouting a little.

They followed her into the drawing room where they refreshed themselves with glasses of lemonade.

'The maid will show you to your rooms,' said Delphine. 'Dinner is at eight o'clock, when my husband returns from the office.'

'Then there's time for a little nap first,' said Benedict, eyeing Edith with a wolfish grin.

Clarissa and Dora shared a room with a view over the garden. Clarissa kicked off her shoes and flopped down on one of the beds.

Dora hummed as she unpacked her small case. Placing a bible and her sketchbook on the night table, she gave a contented sigh. 'We're going to have such a lovely time here, I can tell.'

★   ★   ★

It was dusk when Clarissa joined her friends in the loggia for dinner. The heady perfume of jasmine scented the air and warmth still radiated from the flagstones. Glasses and silverware glimmered in the candlelight.

Dora was chatting to Wilfred at one end of the table. Neither of them had quite fitted in at the Slade but during their studies there the baker's daughter and the aesthete had formed an unlikely friendship.

Edith sighed in contentment. 'The air is as soothing as a warm bath,' she said.

34

Benedict laughed softly. 'I do so enjoy a warm bath.' He nuzzled Edith's neck and she flushed bright pink and fiddled with her bracelet.

Clarissa guessed he'd used that old trick to deflower his bride, then. She seated herself opposite Pascal since he was the most interesting man at the gathering. 'Wilfred tells us you trained to paint in Paris,' she said.

'Yes, I attended the École des Beaux-Arts there.'

'And did you spend your student years drinking and carousing, like some I know?' She glanced at Benedict, who raised his glass to her with laughter in his eyes.

'Some carousing was essential, *bien sûr*,' said Pascal. 'Afterwards, I worked in a number of *ateliers* in Montmartre.' A mischievous smile illuminated his face. 'That was a completely different education.'

'We stopped in Paris,' said Benedict, 'and watched the artists painting in the open air.'

'These are interesting times for artistic expression,' said Pascal. 'Once, the Impressionists shocked the traditional art world. Now,' he shrugged, 'Impressionism itself is *passé*.'

Clarissa sighed. She'd hoped for a little flirtation, not a sermon on new movements in art. Benedict, also clearly bored, juggled with three pieces of bread, and she covered her mouth to disguise a smile when he winked at her.

'I wanted to see one of the entertainments at the Moulin Rouge,' said Benedict, 'but Edith wasn't keen.'

'*Naturellement*,' said Pascal. 'They are not suitable for a lady.'

'There were some posters for the Moulin Rouge by an artist called Toulouse-Lautrec,' said Wilfred. 'Startlingly original, I thought.'

'That one will achieve great things,' said Pascal, 'if he does not drown in absinthe first.'

Édouard Caron arrived then, mopping his face with a silk handkerchief. His waistcoat buttons strained across his prominent stomach, his hair was neatly pomaded and his shoes highly polished. 'I apologise for my tardiness,' he said. 'I had important matters to attend to in the office.'

Clarissa disliked him instantly. She never could abide pompous men and he reminded her far too much of her father.

Pascal introduced the guests and Édouard made a small bow to each of them. Delphine, unsmiling, offered her cheek for his kiss.

As soon as he was seated, the maid carried in the soup.

'We were talking about changing fashions in art, Édouard,' said Pascal, speaking in French.

'Isn't there something more interesting to discuss? Pass the bread — I'm ravenous.'

Clarissa raised her eyebrows at Edith, who met her glance with a shrug. Dora merely stared at her plate.

The soup was followed by an excellent duck stew, a platter of cheeses and grapes, coffee and Armagnac.

Benedict topped up the glasses. 'So, what are we planning for tomorrow?'

'We could go into Nice and walk along the Promenade des Anglais,' said Wilfred.

'All I want,' said Clarissa, 'is to sit quietly in

the sunshine. I have absolutely no intention of working for at least a week.'

Benedict raised his glass to her.

'I must begin the sketches for Mr Rosenberg,' said Edith.

Dora turned to Pascal. 'Edith's end-of-year exhibition was marvellous. She was approached by a Mr Rosenberg on the very first day. Tell him, Edith!'

'He was very complimentary about my work,' she said, eyes modestly cast down. 'When I mentioned I was visiting the South of France, he said he'd like to see my sketchbook when I returned.' She glanced up and her eyes shone. 'If he likes one of my sketches, he'll commission a painting.'

'Bravo!' said Pascal.

'My wife is extremely diligent,' said Benedict, 'and also talented. She's far better than any of us mere mortals will ever be.'

Clarissa looked at him over the rim of her glass. 'Do I detect a trace of jealousy, Benedict?'

'Don't be ridiculous,' he said, with no trace of humour whatsoever in his voice.

'He might not like any of my ideas,' said Edith, glancing anxiously at her husband.

'Of course he will!' said Dora.

Benedict yawned. 'Shall we have an early night?' He pulled his wife to her feet.

'You look tired, Edith,' said Clarissa. 'Do try to get *some* sleep tonight.' She gave Benedict a knowing look and his lips twitched in amusement.

'Love's young dream,' said Clarissa, noting

how Pascal's gaze followed the couple as they went indoors. 'Still, there's plenty of time for them to settle down into uncomfortable domesticity. I believe the glamour wears off after a year or two.'

Delphine shot a glance of pure dislike at Édouard.

So that was how the land lay, thought Clarissa.

'That's a horrible thing to say!' said Dora. 'You only have to look at them to see how in love they are.'

Clarissa sighed, suddenly tired and dispirited. 'You're a much nicer person than I, Dora. Really, I wish them every happiness.'

'And you, Dora?' asked Pascal. 'What will you do tomorrow?'

'I'll take my sketchbook into the garden for inspiration. Like Wilfred, I hope to be an illustrator.'

'Dora and I have very different styles,' he said, 'but we advise each other on where we're going wrong.'

Édouard drained his glass and pushed back his chair. 'All this talk of art! I'm going to bed. Come, Delphine.'

Lips pressed together sullenly, she followed him.

Wilfred yawned and stood up. 'Goodnight, all.'

'So that leaves the three of us.' Clarissa reached for the Armagnac. 'A nightcap, Pascal?' Her voice was husky and she hoped Dora would toddle off to bed and leave them alone together.

He shook his head. 'I must work tomorrow.'

Disappointed, Clarissa pushed the bottle away

and they went inside.

Later, Dora's sleeping breaths were steady and even in the adjacent bed. Clarissa lay staring into the dark, too warm to sleep. Voices murmured through the wall from Edith and Benedict's room, soon followed by a rhythmic knocking. She heard Edith cry out and then all was quiet again.

4

Sunlight was creeping through the gaps around the shutters when Dora woke up. Clarissa was still asleep with her forehead resting on one slender arm and a waterfall of flaxen hair flowing over the edge of the bed. Dora sighed. She'd never have Clarissa's sophistication or Edith's beauty. When she was younger, Ma had always said she was 'perfectly serviceable' and that, once she'd grown up, she'd blossom into a beautiful swan. Well, now she was grown up but her reddish hair still went frizzy in the damp and her face, prone to blushing and freckling, hadn't changed at all.

Tiptoeing across the floorboards, she eased back the shutters. Beyond the garden wall was a hodge-podge of terracotta roofs and cypress trees on land that sloped steeply down towards the sea.

Carefully, Dora closed the shutter again so the light wouldn't wake Clarissa. She dressed, pinned her hair into some semblance of tidiness, then collected her sketchbook and went downstairs.

The aroma of coffee drifted towards her and she saw Pascal crossing the hall with a bundle of baguettes under his arm.

'Good morning, Dora! Will you join me for breakfast?'

He poured her coffee as black as sin and the

hunks of crusty bread, thickly spread with butter and apricot jam, were the most delicious things she'd ever eaten. She didn't speak a word of French so they chatted in English while they looked out over the garden.

'May I see your sketchbook?' asked Pascal.

Slightly embarrassed, Dora pushed it towards him. 'I bought it especially for coming to France.'

She watched him closely as he leafed through the pages, studying her sketches of Victoria Station, alive with porters and passengers. There was a cartoon of a guard, his cheeks puffed out as he blew his whistle. He smiled at a drawing of Edith in the railway carriage, fast asleep in Benedict's arms. 'You have caught her likeness exactly.'

'Benedict woke up before I had time to draw any more than his outline,' she said. It wasn't true, though. Edith had looked so sweet, all rosy with sleep, that she hadn't thought of including Benedict at all.

'Ah! La Tour Eiffel. What did you think of it?'

'It's taller than Notre-Dame. That feels . . . sacrilegious.'

'But the view from the top is magnificent, don't you agree?'

'We didn't go up,' said Dora. 'Most of our time in Paris was spent in the Louvre.'

Pascal returned her sketchbook. 'You are an illustrator?'

'I hope to find work with a publisher or a magazine but I have to expand my portfolio first,' she said, experiencing again that familiar niggle of worry about the future.

He nodded. 'It's a precarious life, making a living as an artist, especially for a woman. Do you live with your parents?'

'I have to, until I can earn enough.' She was desperate to escape from the cramped terraced house in Lambeth. 'My father wants me to paint the pictures they use on biscuit tins.'

Pascal laughed. '*Biscuit* tins?'

Dora tipped up her chin. 'I'm not like the others. My family isn't wealthy. Pa's a foreman in a biscuit factory.' She expected Pascal to react scornfully but he simply waited for her to go on. 'When I was fifteen, Pa found me a job in the office. Filing, making the tea, running messages and the like. I'd always been ever so interested in drawing, right from when I was no more than a tiny tot. One day the owner caught me sketching when I should have been dusting the ledgers.'

'Was he angry?'

'That was the strange thing. He looked at my sketchbook and said I should have lessons. I was that shocked, I didn't know what to say. Anyway, he said I could join his daughter for her art studies. The drawing master taught me for two years and then said I should go after a scholarship at the Slade.'

'I see you have a natural talent,' Pascal said.

Dora was unable to hide her delight. 'Pa didn't want me to take up the place at first because the expenses — materials and the like — were too much. But then my nan gave me some money. She said she was going to leave it to me in her will but it'd be more use to me to have it before she'd gone. She died last year.' Dora sipped her

42

coffee abruptly, the pain of Nan's loss still sharp.

'But you finished your training?'

'I did.' She didn't say how nerve-wracking she'd found it to be amongst a group of posh students who never had to think where the next tube of paint or stick of charcoal was coming from. But making friends with dearest Edith and, later, Wilfred, had changed all that. She'd even grown to like Clarissa, though she had a tongue as sharp as a knife, because surprisingly enough Dora felt a little sorry for her. She never seemed quite happy.

'To be here in France is beyond anything I dreamed of,' she said. 'Pa couldn't understand why I wanted to come. But stepping outside what's known and safe makes the colours seem brighter and my heart beat faster. Fear spurs me on to find out who and what I am.' She stopped, uncomfortably aware she'd blurted out things she'd never said aloud before.

Pascal nodded, as if he understood. 'I stayed with my parents' friends while I studied but I wanted to see the other side of Paris. That is why I went to Montmartre. My mother, always so elegant and with such cultured tastes, would be shocked if she knew my friends there were alcoholics, artisans and,' he hesitated, 'dance-hall girls.'

'Most mothers would be shocked,' said Dora.

'I met an artist called Suzanne Valadon,' said Pascal. 'Her mother was a laundress. She never knew her father, left school at eleven years old and was working in a circus as a trapeze artist at fifteen. She had a child when she was eighteen

43

but no husband. Suzanne earned her living as an artist's model but she taught herself to paint.'

'Was she any good?'

'Excellent. She learned by watching artists while she modelled for them. She let nothing stand in her way.'

'Perhaps there's something for me to learn from your Suzanne Valadon,' said Dora. 'My family is working-class but I never ran away to join a circus and I haven't been an artist's model, never mind had a child . . . ' She broke off. Would Pascal think she was vulgar for saying that?

'*Exactement!* You have been taught to draw, you come from a respectable family and have the desire to succeed. You're halfway to success already!'

'From now on,' said Dora, 'I shall think of Suzanne and count my blessings.'

He nodded. 'She will be an inspiration to us both.'

Dora chewed contemplatively on her last crust. What a very kind man Pascal was to take the time to encourage her, almost as if he knew how bothered she was about what the future would bring.

★   ★   ★

Edith's hand moved steadily over the page, sketching Benedict while he dozed. Sunshine filtering through the shutters touched his hair with gold and there was umber stubble on his jaw, stubble that had grazed her mouth and breasts a short while before. His breathing was

44

deep and even, his full lips parted to expose slightly crossed front teeth. He often fell asleep after they'd made love, while she remained wide awake, fizzing with energy and pulsating with the aftershocks of their loving.

The days, and especially the nights, since their wedding had rendered Edith dazed and astounded. She'd had no idea that this wonderful, secret side to married life existed. Why did no one ever speak of it? She was sure the others must have noticed she was different, transformed and radiant. How did other married couples conceal the bliss that the union of two souls created? Perhaps it was only that she'd not known what to look for — the complicit smiles, the touch of a hand that made you shiver with desire?

In the passage outside, the door to Clarissa and Dora's room closed and footsteps tapped along the landing.

Benedict stirred and Edith kissed him. His lips smiled under hers. 'The others have gone downstairs,' she whispered.

He groaned.

'We can always take a nap after lunch,' she said, getting out of bed.

He reached out to slap her naked bottom. 'Still not satisfied, you shameless wench?'

'Perfectly, thank you,' she said, smiling sweetly. 'For the moment, that is.'

He gave a shout of laughter and pulled her back into bed.

Later, they hurried downstairs hand-in-hand to find their friends already seated around the breakfast table.

45

'What shall we do today?' asked Pascal.

'I vote we follow Clarissa's suggestion and sit in the garden,' said Benedict, licking jam off his fingers.

'Pascal,' said Edith, 'may we see what you're working on?'

'But of course!'

Delphine, who lived in a separate cottage in the garden, waved to them from an open window as they passed.

In the stable yard, a groom was brushing a chestnut mare and Pascal called out a greeting to him. 'Poor Marchal!' he said to Edith. 'I've taken possession of half his tack room and most of the covered work area.' He sighed. 'I cannot live with my parents forever. I must find a studio of my own before the winter.'

An easel draped with muslin stood in one corner of the tack room. Edith caught her breath when Pascal pulled back the cloth, revealing an explosion of colour. The painting depicted a gnarled olive tree silhouetted against yellow wheat under a fiery sun. A peasant girl trudged across the field and the brooding sky above was a deep purplish colour, as if there was going to be a flash of lightning and a crack of thunder at any moment.

Clarissa leaned over the canvas, her head close to Pascal's. 'Very pretty,' she said, looking up at him from under her eyelashes.

A flash of irritation made Edith tighten her lips. Did she have to flirt with every man she met?

'Pretty?' Pascal pretended to be outraged and

46

took a step back from her, one hand pressed to his heart. 'Have you no higher praise than that for a work created from the depths of my tormented artistic soul?'

'Clarissa is such a tease,' said Benedict. 'Take no notice of her.'

Edith moved closer to the canvas. The smell of fresh turpentine and oil paint was heady in the warmth. 'There's such tension in the sky,' she said, conscious of the intensity of Pascal's gaze upon her.

'You feel it?'

'How could I not?'

'The colouring is wonderfully vibrant,' said Wilfred.

Pascal propped up half a dozen other canvases against the stable wall. 'I attempt to capture details characteristic of Provençal landscapes; fields of lavender, pines bent and hardened by the wind, ploughed meadows with parallel furrows leading the eye into the distance. I want to express the strength of Provence, tempered by Nature.'

'I've never fancied painting landscapes, myself,' said Benedict, lighting a cigarette. 'I prefer the female form in all its glorious variety.' He blew out a stream of smoke and looked at Edith through narrowed eyes.

'What a surprise!' said Clarissa.

'We'd better let you get on, Pascal,' said Dora. 'Shall we go and sit under the chestnut tree with our sketchbooks, Edith?'

Clarissa groaned. 'Don't you want a holiday?'

Edith frowned. 'I'm never going to see my

47

paintings in the Royal Academy if I don't keep honing my skills, am I?'

Clarissa tucked her arm through Benedict's. 'Let's have a gossip in the sun.'

He dropped a perfunctory kiss on Edith's lips. 'I know better than to stand in my wife's way when she has her paintbrushes out.'

Watching them walk away, Edith wondered if there'd been an acid edge to Benedict's tone or if she'd imagined it. She sat on the grass with Dora, working in silence. Frequent peals of laughter rang out from the other side of the garden, where Delphine had joined Clarissa and Benedict.

After a couple of hours Edith showed Dora her studies of the others drinking wine and chatting in the garden. 'I'm pleased with these,' she said. 'I'll make some more and then choose two or three to work up into something more finished.'

Dora studied the sketchbook carefully. 'You've caught the carefree spirit of the moment beautifully,' she said.

'I want to develop this one of Clarissa into a portrait, too.' Smiling, Edith said, 'In future years, these drawings will remind me of my idyllic honeymoon among dear friends.'

Dora chewed at her lip. 'Edith, I can't thank you enough for making it possible for me to come here. I could never have afforded the train fare by myself.'

'It wouldn't have been the same without you.' Impulsively, Edith hugged her. Dora was entirely free from artifice and Edith had grown very fond of her. It wasn't her fault her family didn't have

48

two pennies to rub together.

Dora bent her head over her work again and Edith started another sketch.

★ ★ ★

Edith hadn't believed it was possible to be so happy. The languorous days slipped by in a haze of sunshine, wine and laughter, while the nights with Benedict were charged with the intensity of their passion. She'd wondered if she ought to show more restraint but he was delighted by her joyful and enthusiastic response to his love-making.

They made excursions to Cimiez and explored its Roman remains and the monastery. In Nice they drank coffee overlooking the harbour, enjoyed the sea breeze as they walked along the Promenade des Anglais and explored the narrow streets of the Old Town. On one blisteringly hot afternoon, Benedict and Edith lagged behind the others until they were out of sight. There was a wicked glint in Benedict's eye when he pulled her into a doorway in an alley and kissed her until her knees turned to jelly. If an old woman clutching a shopping basket hadn't opened the door, she'd have let him take her in the shadows there and then. They ran off hand-in-hand, laughing, as the old woman chased after them, waving her basket over her head.

Mostly, they stayed in the garden. Edith painted Clarissa relaxing in the sunshine with her flaxen hair loose over her shoulders, like a river of light. She enjoyed working beside Pascal.

49

He had a curved mouth that looked as if it was always on the edge of a smile. A calm presence, his eye was unerring if she made a misjudgement in composition. Sometimes she wondered if he had a secret fancy for her because, quite often, she'd glance up and find his gaze upon her.

Benedict pestered her to pose naked for him but she laughingly refused; she had her own work to do. Some days he lolled in a deckchair in the garden, eyes half closed and dreamy while he smoked his favourite Moroccan cigarettes. She, however, worked feverishly, alight with enthusiasm while she sketched her friends picnicking on the grass or gathered around their easels. Every morning she was impatient to finish breakfast and set to work.

Delphine often brought them a pitcher of lemonade and, sometimes, madeleines warm from the oven. When they included her in their conversations she lost her sulkiness and became pretty and animated. She was flattered when Benedict asked her to sit for him — fully clothed, of course.

In the evenings they congregated in the loggia to display their canvases and sketchbooks in an impromptu gallery. Passionate, even vehemently argumentative at times, their discussions stimulated new ideas. As darkness fell and moths began their evening dance around the candle flames, they dined, drank wine and talked about art into the small hours.

Then Benedict would hold out his hand to Edith and they'd retire to the private sanctuary of their room. After they'd made love, she would lie in his arms, tired but elated and with her heart full of gratitude.

51

5

In the late afternoon, they gathered beneath the chestnut tree. The mid-August heat had been unbearable all day, sapping Edith's energy until it was an effort for her to move. The humid air weighed upon her as she flopped onto the grass next to Benedict, feeling irritable and out of sorts. He rested a heavy arm around her shoulders and pressed a moist kiss on her cheek.

'You look worn out, Edith,' said Dora.

'It was too hot to sleep last night.' There was a dull ache in the pit of her stomach and, despite her sun hat, she had a headache.

'Let's see what you've all been doing today,' said Benedict.

'Yet again, I've nothing to show you,' said Clarissa. 'I'm simply not in the right frame of mind to paint.' Her tone was brittle, almost as if she was spoiling for a disagreement.

Wilfred showed them his disturbing pen-and-ink illustrations of semi-naked women in flowing drapes with Medusa-like tresses writhing against stark white backgrounds. Terrifying goblins and mythical winged beasts with forked tails leered out of the shadows. 'These represent the decadence of our times,' he said.

'You've surprised me, Wilfred. I'd no idea you moved in such depraved circles,' drawled Clarissa.

He blushed scarlet to the roots of his hair.

'I think they're tremendous,' said Dora, giving Clarissa a fierce look.

Benedict picked one up, amused. 'You hardly put women on a pedestal, do you, Wilfred?' He handed it to Edith.

'I can't say I care for the subject matter,' she said, 'but they're beautifully detailed. You'll be sure to find a market for these in one of the more avant-garde magazines.'

'And you, Edith?' asked Pascal. 'You've been in another world these past days.' There was a smile in his dark eyes. 'You must have filled many sketchbooks?'

'I'm determined to have plenty of ideas to show Mr Rosenberg.' She passed her drawings around the group. 'I want to start on the watercolour studies this week and I need advice on narrowing my selection.' She watched their faces, searching for signs of which sketches they liked or disliked.

'Why so many?' asked Benedict. 'You could have started the studies by now.'

'It isn't about finishing quickly,' she said, taken aback to discover he didn't understand. 'You know as well as I do that first ideas are often banal. I must discard those to arrive at something original.'

He raised his eyebrows. 'I don't find that.'

'Perhaps you don't feel the hunger to develop your skills that I do?'

Frowning, he said, 'For God's sake, Edith, do you always have to be so serious?'

'My work is important to me.'

'You're suggesting mine isn't?'

His jaw tightened and she decided not to argue the point.

'So many have possibilities,' said Wilfred, bending over Edith's sketches. 'The composition of this one is particularly good, though the background is dull.'

Pascal peered over Wilfred's shoulder. 'Perhaps the Roman amphitheatre would be a more interesting setting instead of the garden?'

'I *knew* there was something missing!' said Edith. 'There's still great interest in classical landscapes. Using the arena as a backdrop is an excellent suggestion.'

'Let me show you what I've been working on,' said Benedict. He propped a half-finished portrait against the garden wall and stood back. 'What do you think?'

It was the first time Edith had seen it and she was disappointed. He'd caught Delphine's likeness but the pose was wooden.

No one commented.

'Of course, it's not finished,' said Dora, filling the awkward silence, 'but it's obviously Delphine.'

'Obviously,' said Benedict, sarcasm heavy in his tone.

Dora flushed and sat back, silenced.

'I expect Delphine is pleased with it,' said Pascal.

'She certainly is,' said Benedict. 'She's so excited she can't sit still and keeps getting up to see what I'm doing.'

Edith massaged the back of her neck. The

portrait was lumpen and heavy but the worst thing was that Benedict didn't realise it. 'It's lifeless,' she said. 'Perhaps the pose is too formal? And look at the hands; the drawing leaves something to be desired.'

Benedict glared at her.

'It needs work,' she said, 'but I'm sure you can make something of it, if you're prepared to make the effort.'

'You're criticising my portrait?'

'Isn't that what we're meant to be doing here? Trying to help each other?' She noticed the frozen expressions on the others' faces and floundered. 'None of us will progress if we don't aspire to something greater.'

Benedict's nostrils flared. 'Well, your little scribbles on scraps of paper can hardly be counted as masterpieces, can they?'

'Not at present,' she said, flushing at his sneering tone, 'but I'll make the effort to improve them.'

'Do you have something to show us, Dora?' asked Pascal.

Grateful to him for breaking the tension, Edith gathered up her drawings. 'I shan't be a moment,' she murmured to Clarissa.

She walked back towards the house, still agitated by her *contretemps* with Benedict. The garden was quiet, disturbed only by the hum of the bees on the lavender. In the bedroom, the shutters were closed against the heat and the dim light was soothing as she changed her dress.

She still had a stomach ache and went to the lavatory, where she was dismayed to discover

55

blood between her thighs. Hurrying back to the bedroom, she rummaged in her suitcase for her bag of sanitary rags. She hadn't considered the implications of her monthly visitor now she was a married woman. Although Mama had said it was her duty always to do her husband's bidding, she hadn't advised what Edith should do when she was bleeding. How on earth could she explain such an embarrassing event to Benedict?

By the time she returned, the others were seated for dinner. Thankfully, Benedict appeared to have recovered his good humour and was joking with Wilfred.

Edith sat down and the maid placed a tureen of beef stew on the table.

The conversation flowed as freely as the wine and she relaxed a little, even though Benedict still didn't address her directly. As the light faded, the chirruping song of the cicadas grew louder and jasmine perfumed the warm breeze.

'Isn't this divine?' said Clarissa. 'Wine and good company. I don't know how I shall bear to return home to Father.'

'Is he really that awful?' asked Dora.

'I've avoided him while I was at the Slade by staying with Aunt Minnie.' Clarissa rubbed her temples. 'The sad truth is that I'm simply not talented enough for Fine Art. If, by the time I return home, I haven't worked out how to make best use of my training, Father will make my life a misery. He's an arrogant bully. Once, when I dared flout his wishes, he threatened to have me put away in a lunatic asylum.'

'He couldn't have meant it!' Edith was

shocked that any father would say such a thing.

'No?' Clarissa stared into the depths of her wine glass.

'I don't want to go home either,' said Dora. 'My family couldn't care less about art and I'll really miss being with all of you. I'll have to work in the room I share with my three younger sisters.'

Benedict drained his glass. 'But why does this have to end?' he said. 'You must all come to stay with me in Cornwall.' He beamed. 'Let's continue the party at Spindrift House!'

Appalled, Edith attempted to catch his eye. Benedict had wanted to spend their honeymoon with friends but had promised they'd be alone together afterwards in Cornwall. She caught hold of his sleeve. 'Benedict, I'll be working on my commission when we return.'

Unsmiling, he said, 'Then, since you're so ready to find fault with other people's work, you'll be grateful for advice from our artist friends, won't you?'

Edith stared at him. So that was what this was about; he hadn't forgiven her for criticising his portrait of Delphine.

Benedict turned back to the others. 'Come for several months,' he said, opening his arms expansively. 'The light is incredible and there are big skies and wide horizons.'

'Cornwall is excellent for painting, no?' said Pascal.

'I'm sure it is,' said Edith. 'It's only that I haven't seen Spindrift House yet. Benedict inherited it from his aunt and tells me it's old-fashioned and shabby. There'll be a great deal to do before it's fit for visitors.'

'No one here cares if it's crammed with Aunt Hester's things,' said Benedict. 'We'll throw them on the bonfire!'

'You won't want guests while you're setting up home,' said Dora, echoing Edith's thoughts.

'Why not?' asked Benedict. He raised his glass. 'Pascal, you must come, too, of course. Here's to our artistic success!'

'*Peut-être*,' said Pascal, 'you and Edith should discuss it first?'

'No need,' said Benedict, smiling expansively. 'She's my wife and, naturally, she wants what I want.'

Edith gulped her wine, trying not to choke at the sudden rage that seethed inside her. She'd never find time to work if she had a houseful of guests. Even though Mama's servants ran her house like clockwork, she always said hosting a house party utterly exhausted her. And that was only for a Friday to Monday.

'It's a *wonderful* invitation,' said Clarissa. 'I'm delighted to accept.'

Edith pushed her plate away. Benedict had left her with absolutely nothing she could say without looking unfriendly and inhospitable.

'You'll love Spindrift,' enthused Benedict. 'It's a rambling old stone farmhouse overlooking the sea.'

Dora clasped her hands to her breast. 'I've always dreamed of living near the sea!'

'There's a story behind my inheritance,' said Benedict. He leaned forward to whisper. 'Strait-laced Aunt Hester was a bit of a dark

58

horse. I'd always imagined she was as respectable as the Widow of Windsor until I happened to be there when the cat jumped out of the bag.'

Clarissa reached for the wine bottle. 'Do I detect a whiff of scandal?'

'Rather more than a whiff!' he said. 'Gather round, children, and I'll tell you a story.'

Edith pressed her lips together. It wasn't right for him to discuss private family matters like this.

'Aunt Hester was widowed young and rented Spindrift House from her neighbour, Jago Penrose. Last autumn I was staying with her when Hugh, Penrose's son, came storming into the house and threatened her. Obnoxious little oik!'

'But why?' asked Wilfred.

'It turned out Hester and Jago had been lovers for years and, when Jago died, he left Spindrift House to her. Hugh was apoplectic. He yelled at Aunt Hester that the house should have come to him and not to his father's whore.'

'Benedict!' said Edith.

Dora pressed her fingers to her mouth.

'What a vile man!' said Clarissa.

Benedict puffed out his chest. 'I threw him off the property. Aunt Hester was terribly distressed. She intended to see the solicitor in the morning and tell him to give the house back to Hugh.'

'But she didn't?' asked Pascal.

Benedict shook his head. 'She died that evening. Later, I discovered that, barring a small bequest to her housekeeper, she'd left everything to me. And by then, of course, that included Spindrift House. It was a stroke of good fortune for me but I do miss the old biddy.'

'And you didn't follow your aunt's wishes and give the house back?' said Dora.

'Hugh Penrose can whistle for it,' Benedict said, cracking his knuckles. 'He burned his boats when he frightened Aunt Hester into a heart attack.'

'But how priceless to discover a prim old lady had a secret lover!' said Clarissa. 'I can hardly wait to see the scene of such debauchery.'

Edith couldn't bear to listen to any more. She rose abruptly to her feet, her chair legs scraping over the stone flags. 'Excuse me, I have a headache.'

'Poor Edith!' said Dora. 'Shall I fetch you a headache powder?'

She smiled mechanically. 'I have some but thank you.'

Pascal stood up and opened the door for her. '*Bonne nuit*, Edith.'

Benedict refilled his wine glass. 'The night is young. Does anyone fancy a game of cards?'

★   ★   ★

It was over two hours later when Edith heard voices on the stairs and then Benedict opened the bedroom door.

'Not asleep?' he asked.

She sat rigidly upright in bed. 'As you see.'

He undressed rapidly, dropping his clothes on the floor, and climbed into bed.

'Benedict, you didn't ask me if I wanted them to stay with us.'

He raised his eyebrows. 'They're your friends as much as mine.'

60

'But you know I was looking forward to being alone with you while we make Spindrift House into our home.'

'It *is* our home and we're alone together now. If you must, tell them you don't want them to come. I didn't realise you were such a killjoy, Edith.'

'I'm not! But can't you see we should have discussed it first? If I tell them now that I don't want them to stay, they'll think I'm most disagreeable.'

'Well, you would be. Anyway, I want them to come.' He trailed his fingers down her breast.

She pushed his hand away. 'You should have asked me,' she insisted. Anger made her voice waspish.

'Should I? In my family, a husband expects support from his wife, not to be publicly humiliated by her before their friends.'

'I was trying to help you improve your work!'

'Funny way of doing it.' He turned off the lamp and reached for her in the dark.

He ran his hand up her thigh but she moved away. In any case, she couldn't let him touch her there when she was wearing sanitary rags.

'Playing hard to get, Mrs Fairchild?' He cupped her breast.

His complacency infuriated her. 'Don't!' she said, moving away. 'I don't want to tonight.'

'But I do.' He snatched at the hem of her nightdress.

She wrenched it out of his fingers and dragged it over her knees.

'For God's sake, Edith, what's come over you

to turn you into such a shrew?'

'Don't I have *any* say about anything? Let me get some sleep in peace for once!'

Abruptly, he released her. 'If that's what you want.' His voice was cold. 'I shan't touch you again until you beg me.' He turned his back on her. 'And Spindrift is my house, not yours. I shall invite whomsoever I wish.'

She stiffened, too shocked by his cruel tone to argue. What had happened to them? For years she'd stood in Amelia's shadow and it had felt like walking out of an icehouse and into the sun when Benedict declared his love for her. In a matter of moments, her absolute confidence in his love for her had vanished. She felt sick. Was she wrong to have expected him to discuss the invitation with her first? Was she an undutiful wife to refuse him his marital rights?

Beside her, Benedict let out a deep rumbling snore.

6

All sound was muffled by the oppressive heat and sultry air. Edith had found a patch of shade under an olive tree in the ruins of the amphitheatre where she set up her easel, but the sun had moved again. The heat was so fierce that the paint dried too quickly for her to lay down the watercolour washes evenly. Dazzled by the light, she squinted at the ruins of tiered steps and stone arches.

Back in Roman times, the arena would have reverberated with the cheers and taunts of five thousand spectators as the gladiators circled each other in a fight to the death. She pictured sunlight flashing off their swords as they slashed at each other, muscles rippling under oiled brown skin, while the crowd roared in approval. By sunset the sand on the arena floor would have been soaked with the lifeblood of the dead. Imagining the coppery stench of it, she shuddered and dabbed perspiration from her top lip. She'd never envisaged she and Benedict could ever be like those circling gladiators, each searching for a vulnerable place where cold steel would do the other most damage.

Two weeks had passed since they'd argued. She'd tried to talk to him but he'd ignored her, except to say he was waiting for her to apologise. With their friends, he was his usual jovial self,

63

talking about Cornwall and what a fine time they'd all have there, whipping up their enthusiasm for the plan just to goad her. Each night he came to bed late and turned his back on her while she lay awake and unyielding beside him.

The previous day, when they'd gathered for lunch, Benedict had made a point of ignoring her when she spoke to him. Humiliated, she'd made some excuse and fled the table, leaving her sketchbook behind. Later, she'd returned to collect it and heard raised voices. Lurking in the drawing room, she'd eavesdropped while Pascal berated Benedict for his unkindness. Benedict had laughed it off, accusing their host of making a fuss about an unimportant tiff.

'In that case,' said Pascal, 'it will be simple to make up your differences.'

'Since you have no wife, Pascal,' Benedict had responded, 'you have no understanding of how unreasonable a woman can be.'

Edith had heard Benedict stride off over the gravel and then Pascal walked into the drawing room before she could escape.

He saw her and shrugged.

In that moment she felt a great affection for him. 'Thank you.'

He bowed his head and left.

Now, Edith caught a movement out of the corner of her eye as Clarissa descended the arena steps.

'We're going to visit the monastery gardens,' she said. She glanced at Edith's watercolour on the easel and pulled a face. 'Not up to your usual standard, is it?'

'I can see that for myself!'

'No need to bite my head off — I'm not Benedict! Really, Edith, the atmosphere between you two is thick enough to cut with a knife. It's upsetting us all. You should have been less open with your criticism of his portrait of Delphine.'

'How will he improve if he doesn't realise the truth?'

'Some men don't like the truth.' Clarissa shrugged. 'Still, he's started another portrait of Delphine, though he's not letting anyone see it.'

'He refuses to speak to me.'

'Is it because he invited us to Cornwall?' Clarissa gave a brittle laugh. 'I wondered at the time if you weren't enamoured of the idea. I was so dreading the prospect of going home, I jumped at the offer without asking if you minded. And Dora is equally desperate to avoid ending up working in the biscuit factory.'

'He should have asked me first,' Edith said. 'Now I don't want to be alone with him in this mood so I really want you all to come to Cornwall.' She rubbed at her eyes. 'Our quarrel blew up out of nowhere. I was tired and had a headache . . .'

'So that's it!' said Clarissa with a knowing smile. 'Men don't like it if you're tired,' she said. 'They expect you to be endlessly sunny-natured and available. Benedict will go on sulking unless you make a herculean effort to overcome your pride and chivvy him out of it. For goodness' sake, put us all out of our misery! We're going home soon so give him a kiss and say you're sorry.'

'It's not that simple.' Edith twisted her wedding ring. The heat had made her fingers swell and it was too tight.

Clarissa sighed. 'It'll get worse if you let it fester.'

'I suppose so.' She knew so. And however galling it was to beg Benedict to forgive her, when he was the one at fault, they couldn't go on like this.

'Thank Heavens for that! Then I'll see you later.'

Now she'd made the reluctant decision to swallow her pride, Edith's despondent mood lifted. She packed up her easel and paints and trotted along the road so fast her feet stirred up eddies of dust. In the interests of harmony, she'd swallow her misgivings and apologise. And, later that night, she would lie in Benedict's arms again. Visualising their reunion, she felt a tremor of pleasure. She'd missed the physical delights of the marriage bed and there was a yearning ache deep inside her.

The house was deserted and she ran upstairs to put her easel away. She dabbed eau de cologne behind her ears and went to look for Benedict.

Pascal was working at his easel in the garden. He looked up with his usual welcoming smile.

She paused to look at his landscape, an arresting view over the hillside. 'Your work is going better than mine. Have you seen Benedict?'

'My sister said she was going to sit for him today.'

The front door of Delphine's cottage was ajar.

The hall with its flagstone floor was invitingly cool and shadowy after the sweltering heat outside. Edith was about to call out to Delphine when she caught a glimpse of her in the sitting room.

She blinked as her eyes grew accustomed to the gloom. There was a long moment of stillness while she attempted to make sense of what she saw. The picture was neatly framed by the doorway, painted in Paris Green. Delphine, wearing nothing but stockings and a black velvet choker, sprawled on her back on an overstuffed daybed. One arm was raised above her head, exposing a tuft of dark hair beneath. Her forearm shielded her eyes against a shaft of sunlight coming through the window.

Then she made a small noise, a breathy sigh or a moan, and Edith snapped out of her trance.

Now there was no mistaking what she saw and the corrosive image of it would be forever painted on the canvas of her mind. There, nestled between Delphine's thighs, was Benedict's head, moving slowly up and down.

Edith opened her mouth to speak but there was absolutely nothing she could say that would erase the image or undo what was happening. She backed away, slipped out of the front door and hurried down the path, her breath coming in great gasps.

Then she was running, running as fast as she could to escape. Hurtling around the corner of the stables, she heard a shout and then footsteps pounding after her. Sobbing, she plunged into the shrubbery, fighting her way through bushes that clawed at her hair and snagged her clothing until she came to a small clearing.

Twigs snapped behind her, followed by a muffled curse.

Hands seized her shoulders and she turned and pounded his chest, thrashing and kicking to escape his restraining grasp. And then she realised it wasn't Benedict.

'Stop!' ordered Pascal. He imprisoned her wrists in a fierce grip until the white-hot heat of her tumultuous rage and anguish abated.

She collapsed against him. Her eyes squeezed shut to eradicate the unspeakable image of what she'd witnessed.

'Edith?' His voice was low. 'What happened?'

Her legs shook and she shivered, despite the heat. 'Benedict.' Her teeth chattered and it was hard for her to form words. 'Delphine. Together.' She heard Pascal's sudden intake of breath and his arms tightened around her. 'I thought he loved me . . . ' Her voice cracked and the tears came then, great hot tears that scalded her cheeks and soaked the front of his shirt. 'He doesn't love me. It was all a lie!' She gasped for breath, incoherent with anguish.

Pascal wiped her tears away with infinite gentleness. 'Benedict is a fool. If you had been my wife, I should not have treated you so badly. We will go back to the house and I will pour a glass of wine to fortify you.'

Benedict had thrown her aside. The recollection of that perfectly framed picture of his head nestled between Delphine's thighs rose up before her again and a tidal wave of agony and fury nearly knocked Edith sideways. She felt degraded and rejected. Clinging to Pascal, she looked up into his face at the very moment he bent to kiss her cheek. Their lips met by accident.

They both froze.

A shaft of desire, as sudden and intense as a bolt of lightning, ran through her entire body, leaving her trembling. He touched her shoulder and she read his answering hunger in the dilated pupils of his eyes.

There was a moment when she could have pulled away and pretended nothing had happened between them. But she didn't. The sudden, desperate craving to hurt Benedict, to lash out in revenge, was too powerful to resist.

She slid her arms around Pascal's neck, their lips still touching.

He made a small sound of protest and moved his head back.

She pressed herself against him. Benedict didn't want her but she could feel that Pascal did. 'Love me,' she murmured.

After a moment of frozen stillness, his mouth came down hard on hers and he kissed her, not as a friend but as a lover.

Passion ignited as swiftly as a burning brand in a summer haystack. The heat of his hands on her back scorched through the fine muslin of her dress and an intense stab of mounting pleasure made her gasp. He swept her into his arms and laid her on a bed of leaves, covering her face and neck with frenzied kisses. She tore at his buttons and he dragged up her skirt in a foam of lace petticoats. His fingers searched out her secret places, stroking her until she was almost fainting with ecstasy.

She moaned and he raised himself over her. It was a hasty, desperate coupling and in only a few moments she arched her back and they both cried out as their frantic passion was sated.

Still joined together, they lay facing each other under the canopy of leaves. As their breathing steadied and the fever of lust faded, he touched her cheek, his expression full of remorse. 'I'm so sorry, Edith,' he whispered.

She pressed a fist to her mouth. 'Pascal,' she said, 'what have I done?'

7

The leaves were turning russet in Berkeley Square when Edith and Benedict arrived at his parents' townhouse. Travel-stained and weary after the long journey from Provence, they'd both stared silently out of the carriage window since saying goodbye to their friends.

A maid let them in and then the drawing-room door burst open and Benedict's mother erupted into the hall.

'My darling boy!'

Benedict swung her into his arms, lifting her feet off the floor. 'Dearest Mother!'

Laughingly protesting, Mrs Fairchild smothered his face in kisses. 'I've been waiting by the window all afternoon,' she said. 'And how is my boy's lovely bride?' She pressed her powdered cheek briefly against Edith's.

'I hope we find you well, Mrs Fairchild?' Edith murmured.

Her mother-in-law studied her face. 'You look a little pale.'

'Edith doesn't travel well,' said Benedict with a slight curl of his lip. 'The motion of the train upset her digestion.'

Immediately, Mrs Fairchild's inquisitive gaze moved to Edith's waist.

A hot, tingling sensation swept up her throat, rendering her speechless with embarrassment.

She folded her arms over her stomach.

'Perhaps you'd care to tidy yourself before tea? Travelling is so tiresome, isn't it?' Mrs Fairchild directed the maid to take Edith upstairs and then hooked her arm through Benedict's. 'Come and tell me about your adventures.'

Edith retreated to the guest room, where clean towels were ready by the washbasin. She splashed her face and hands and perched on the bed, wondering how long she could delay before making an appearance downstairs. Her mother-in-law's prying glance had made it clear she was wondering if a honeymoon grandchild was on the way. But surely that was impossible?

There was a sudden sour taste in the back of Edith's throat and she wanted more than anything to curl up on the bed and close her eyes. Benedict, meanwhile, was probably spinning his adoring mama some tale about how ill humoured his bride had been while they were on their honeymoon.

During their last days in France, he had finished his new portrait of Delphine, naked except for her stockings and velvet choker, eyes half closed in sated bliss. When Edith saw the canvas, she'd barely stifled a moan, sure Benedict intended it to distress her. Sighing, she lifted her drooping head and forced herself to rise.

She endured the remainder of the afternoon in near silence, her thoughts fluttering like a bird beating its wings against the bars of a cage, while Mrs Fairchild listened with rapt attention to Benedict's account of their sojourn in Provence.

'But now you must stay here for a month or two,' she said.

Benedict shook his head. 'I'll write to Mrs Gloyne tomorrow to prepare the house and arrange for us to be met at the station.'

'*Must* you go, dearest?'

'I'm dining with an old school friend on Tuesday but we'll travel the following day.'

'You'll see your family before you leave, Edith?' said Benedict's mother.

'Tomorrow. And I have an appointment with a client on Monday.'

Her mother-in-law's eyes widened. 'You won't continue painting now you're married, will you?' she asked. 'Surely you wish to make Spindrift House into a comfortable home for your husband? Besides,' she glanced at Edith's waist again, 'you may be busy with . . . other things.'

'Benedict has invited our friends to stay for several months,' she said. 'We'll all be travelling down to Cornwall together. I can't undertake renovations while we have guests.'

Mrs Fairchild raised her eyebrows. 'Might it not be better to wait until the house is ready, Benedict?'

'Not at all, Mother.' He sent Edith a belligerent glance. 'It's necessary for me to be surrounded by those who understand my artistic temperament. Together, we'll make greater advances in our chosen creative fields.'

'I see,' she said, her tone uncertain.

'And I agree wholeheartedly with Benedict's decision,' Edith said, watching amazement spread across his face. 'Since we already know the congenial dispositions of our friends, I've no hesitation in supporting my husband in his wishes.'

'How very dutiful, Edith,' said her mother-in-law. 'I certainly shouldn't have liked that for myself as a new bride.'

At six o'clock, Edith and Benedict retired to rest before changing for dinner.

She removed her dress and lay on the bed.

'What brought about your change of heart?' asked Benedict, unbuttoning his shirt. He sat down heavily on the bed to unlace his shoes.

She opened her eyes, surprised he'd initiated a conversation. 'I reconsidered and agree it will be beneficial to have our friends close at hand. Since you rebuffed me every time I attempted to speak to you, we haven't been able to discuss it as yet.'

He dropped his trousers and shirt on the floor and lay beside her. 'If there's no disagreement between us, why are you still going about looking as miserable as a box of wet cats?' He turned to face her, his hazel eyes only inches away. 'I know what's been making you look so sour-faced!' Smiling, he rested a hand on her breast.

Her body momentarily betrayed her by yearning to yield to him but his conceit enraged her. Abruptly, she sat up. 'Don't!' she said.

He sighed. 'Isn't it time we stopped all this nonsense?'

'I wanted to,' she said, the anger that had simmered just below the surface of her misery suddenly rising to the boil. 'When we were in France I came to you, prepared to beg you to let us be reconciled, but . . . .' Her chest rose and fell as she struggled to remain calm.

'But what? Come on, Edith,' he cajoled, trailing his fingers down her arm.

'Benedict, I saw you with Delphine.'

His fingers stilled and something, remorse perhaps, flickered in his eyes. 'Of course I was with Delphine. I was painting her portrait, for God's sake. You slated the first one so I had to start another.'

'You know that's not what I meant.' Edith turned away so that he wouldn't see her gathering tears. 'I trusted you and you betrayed me! I thought our love was so very special, such a beautiful thing . . . ' She swallowed a sob. 'And then I saw you with her, your head between her thighs. You'd persuaded me there was nothing shameful in that between married couples who really loved each other. You said it would always be our most secret and private pleasure.' Her voice cracked and she scrubbed away tears with her palms. 'I gave you my body and my soul and you were unfaithful to me, on our *honeymoon*!'

He pulled her into his embrace.

Angrily, she thrust him away.

'It didn't mean anything,' he said. 'I didn't love Delphine.'

'Then why did you do it?' Her cry of anguish reverberated in the air between them.

'Shh!' Benedict glanced over his shoulder at the door. 'Mother might hear you! A man has needs, Edith, and you, my wife, denied me.'

'Once! I said I was too tired only *once*. I'd been your willing and loving partner every single

75

time before. How *dare* you say it was my fault?'

Shrugging, he said, 'Look, I'm sorry for what happened. Can't we put it behind us?'

She bowed her head, tears dripping off her chin. 'Again and again I remember seeing you together, framed by the doorway like some hideous painting.' Then she was tormented anew by the memory of what she'd done with Pascal and hated herself for it. But it would never have happened if Benedict hadn't betrayed her first.

'Let's start afresh. Neither of us wants to be trapped in an acrimonious marriage.'

'I can't forget seeing you with Delphine. If we're going to repair our marriage, you must destroy her portrait.'

He sighed heavily. 'If it's so important to you, it shall be done.'

'Promise me?'

'I promise.'

This time, when he encircled her in his arms she clung to him, remembering how happy they'd once been. Delphine was the snake in their Eden. But then there was her own terrible guilt. She desperately regretted that fierce urge to feel the heat of another man's passion, the need to feel loved and desired again. All she wanted now was to forget it had ever happened.

Benedict kissed the top of her head. 'Edith?'

She allowed him to stroke her back and nuzzle her neck but when he touched her breast, she stopped him. 'No, Benedict. I can't. Not yet.'

Slowly, he withdrew his hand. He tipped up her chin and kissed her unresisting mouth. His breath fanned her cheek as he studied her face, as if he were seeing her for the first time. 'You're so beautiful, Edith, even when you're weeping.'

She rested her head on his chest, listening to the thudding of his heart while consciousness of her own iniquity nearly suffocated her.

8

Clarissa opened the envelope that was waiting for her on the breakfast table. 'It's from Edith,' she said.

Aunt Minnie, her blonde hair immaculately dressed as usual, glanced up from her newspaper. Clarissa's aunt was the archetypal merry widow. Her husband, considerably older than she, had left her enough to live on comfortably in a smart mansion flat in Devonshire Place.

'Edith and Benedict are travelling to Cornwall tomorrow, as planned,' said Clarissa, 'but she's asked the rest of us to follow at the weekend.'

'I imagine they want a few days alone,' said Aunt Minnie. 'Besides, that will give you a little longer to recover.'

Clarissa had been forced to retire to bed the previous day with the debilitating pain that often overwhelmed her during her monthlies. 'I'm better today,' she said. 'Perhaps the newly-weds will have made up their differences by then.' She'd been dreading a strained atmosphere in Cornwall but even that would have been an improvement on returning to Weybridge to live with her mother and father. 'May I stay until Saturday?'

'We'll take in a matinee and have lunch at Claridge's.' Aunt Minnie glanced at the clock. 'I've an appointment with my dressmaker this morning.'

Clarissa's stomach clenched. 'Will you be back before Father arrives?'

Aunt Minnie picked up her hat from the sideboard and peered into the overmantel mirror to skewer it into place with a pearl-topped hatpin. 'Probably.'

'He'll be angry when I tell him I'm not going home.'

'Sebastian always liked his own way, even as a boy. Why don't you come with me, Clarissa? He'll just have to wait if we're late back. Run along and put on your hat.'

Half an hour later, Clarissa sat on a small gilt chair while her aunt had final fittings for a crisp white blouse with leg-of-mutton sleeves, a wool crepe skirt and an evening gown of sapphire velvet.

Clarissa admired the dressmaker's showroom while she was waiting. Decorated with crimson moiré wallpaper, fringed silk curtains and an Aubusson carpet, it exuded restrained sophistication. She was particularly interested in a glass-topped counter displaying tempting costume jewellery: a brooch in the shape of a cat with green glass eyes, a variety of bracelets, drop earrings with topaz stones and pretty velvet chokers.

Madame Monette, the French dressmaker, chatted easily with Aunt Minnie about the latest fashions and what she might require for her wardrobe for the coming season. Once the hem of the evening dress had been pinned up, Aunt Minnie withdrew to the dressing room to change.

'And you, *mademoiselle*,' said Madame

Monette, 'is there something you require? A walking costume or an afternoon tea gown, perhaps?' Her dark hair was coiled into a chignon and she was as small and neat as a wren.

'I'm spending the winter with artist friends in Cornwall. I expect to be wearing a painting smock most of the time.'

'What a pity! You have the same slender figure as your aunt. It is always a pleasure to dress her.' Madame Monette regarded the young woman through narrowed eyes. 'Work clothes need not be ugly. I could make you a flattering dress for when you are painting that allows freedom of movement.'

'Haven't you heard about the Rational Dress movement, Clarissa?' asked Aunt Minnie, emerging from the dressing room.

'Of course. Once, I saw a woman on a bicycle wearing a divided skirt. All the men were laughing and calling out.'

'There's always resistance to change,' said Aunt Minnie. 'It's detrimental to a woman's health to be tight-laced simply to conform to the male idea of beauty. A corset makes a woman delicate and therefore weak and subservient to men. Liberation from tight-lacing enables women to move and work more easily, allowing them more independence.' She laughed. 'Of course, men don't care for that idea at all!'

'I can imagine what Father would say if I removed my corset,' said Clarissa, 'but I'd like to be comfortable while I'm painting. What a shame there isn't time to make me a painting dress before I leave.'

Madame Monette shrugged. 'I will take your measurements and the cut will be loose so a fitting is not essential. I will post the finished garment to you next week.' She fetched a pattern book and Clarissa decided on a simple shape with a round neck to be made in a jade cotton with a subtle print of peacock feathers.

'Visit me again in the spring, *mademoiselle*,' said Madame Monette, 'and I will make something beautiful for you.' She turned to a satinwood display case and removed a wool shawl in a beautiful azure blue. 'This is the colour of your eyes. Perfect for the country where it is always so cold.'

The shawl was downy soft against Clarissa's cheek.

'You simply must have it, Clarissa,' said Aunt Minnie. 'My little gift to you! Add it to my account, Madame Monette.'

★ ★ ★

Clarissa was relieved to arrive at Devonshire Place in time to remove her hat and compose herself before her father arrived. She held her back ramrod-straight when she heard his voice booming in the hall.

'Sebastian, how lovely to see you,' said Aunt Minnie. 'And you've brought dear Lydia with you.'

'She took the opportunity to take the train up to town with me today,' he said. Although shorter than his wife, Sebastian Stanton exuded self-confidence. He always made Clarissa think of a bantam cock strutting about the farmyard.

She greeted her mother dutifully, noticing her fair hair had faded so much it almost exactly matched the washed-out dove grey of her costume.

'Prettier than ever, my dear!' Father squeezed Clarissa's arm. She submitted to his kiss, waiting until he'd turned away to wipe the corner of her mouth where his ginger moustache had prickled her.

'So you're back from your travels,' he said. Hands clasped behind his back, he rocked backwards and forwards on his toes. 'And now you will return to the fold.' He spoke as if it was *fait accompli*.

Clarissa's mouth was dry. 'Actually,' she said, 'Edith and Benedict have invited me to Cornwall.'

He frowned. 'Out of the question! I was indulgent enough to allow you to go to France for the summer but now it's time to come home.'

'We must look for a suitable young man for you,' said Mother in her colourless voice. 'Time is passing and I fear it will become more difficult . . . '

'Don't be absurd, Lydia!' said Father. 'There's no need to rush the girl into marriage yet.'

Mother silently folded her hands.

'I have no desire to marry,' said Clarissa.

'Plenty of time for that, eh?' Her father smoothed his moustache. 'Besides, I want the pleasure of your company for a while.'

'It would be too dreadful if you were to find yourself on the shelf, Clarissa,' said her mother, gaze downcast.

'The idea of a husband is repugnant to me.' The sulky tone of her own voice irritated Clarissa. Why did her parents always make her feel like a wayward child?

'If you've a mind to be a spinster,' said Father, 'you'll be company for me in my old age.'

Clarissa repressed a shudder. 'I intend to make my own way in the world.'

'Hah! And how do you intend to do that, miss? You'll not get far without either a husband or my allowance, will you? I indulged your nonsensical whim to attend the Slade but, frankly, daubing a few pretty pictures won't even keep you in pin money.'

The familiar wave of despair always engendered by her father washed over her.

'Sebastian, many young women do support themselves these days,' said Aunt Minnie.

'Mill workers and shop girls? I hardly think that's suitable for *my* daughter.' He turned to Clarissa, triumph all over his face. 'So, how is it you plan to make your fortune? Do tell me, because apart from being ornamental, I can't think what else you're useful for.'

At that moment, neither could she. She stared at Aunt Minnie's carpet while the silence became more and more strained. All summer she'd struggled to find an answer to the question she'd known he'd ask. The prospect of bowing to his will again made her nauseous.

The jewel tones of the Persian carpet swirled before her unfocused eyes, reminding her of Madame Monette's display of earrings with topaz stones, dress rings with semi-precious jewels and a brooch in the shape of a cat with green glass eyes. She gripped the arms of the chair as her mind raced to order her chaotic thoughts.

'Well?'

She lifted her head. 'I shall design costume jewellery,' she said, her voice brimming with sudden confidence. 'And I'm going to create my first collection while I'm in Cornwall.'

9

It had been Benedict's suggestion that he and Edith should travel to Cornwall before their friends joined them.

'We shall have some time alone together,' he'd said. 'Perhaps you'd like to walk along the headland and picnic on the beach?' He'd lifted her hand to his lips. 'I want you to love Cornwall as much as I do.'

She'd smiled faintly and withdrawn her hand. How strange that, once, all she'd wanted was to be alone with him at Spindrift House but now the prospect alarmed her.

A hired carriage had been waiting for them at the newly opened station at Tresmeer and they'd trundled through Delabole an hour since. Edith stared silently out of the carriage window, the mile upon mile of undulating fields rolling away to either side of the narrow lanes only increasing her rising sense of unease. And then there was the other terrible worry that gnawed away at her, the one she avoided thinking about.

Out of the corner of her eye, she noticed Benedict watching her again. Ever since she'd told him she knew about Delphine, his manner had been conciliatory. Before they left London, he'd escorted her to a successful meeting with Mr Rosenberg and then acted every inch the devoted husband when they dined with her parents. Since then, the more she denied him and the more distant she became, the more attracted to her he seemed to be and the more she struggled with her guilt.

'Nearly there!' he said.

Despite her misgivings, she felt a stirring of interest.

After a few minutes, Benedict banged his fist on the roof of the carriage. It ground to a halt and he jumped down. Clasping Edith's hand, he pulled her along the lane.

The high, mossy banks were studded with feathery ferns and pink and white flowers like tiny stars. A soft breeze carried the faint smell of cows, rich and earthy in the warmth of the early October sunshine. They reached the brow of the hill and the view made her catch her breath. The land sloped gently downwards and there, in the distance, was the shining sea.

'As a boy, whenever I stayed with Aunt Hester, we always stopped here for our first glimpse,' said Benedict.

She gazed at the soft greens and blues of the landscape, the serenity of the scene alleviating some of her anxiety. 'It's beautiful, Benedict.'

He draped an arm around her shoulders. 'Let's go home.'

Ten minutes later, the carriage rattled around a bend in the lane. 'Spindrift House,' he announced, opening the carriage door almost before they drew to a halt before a pair of stone gate pillars.

Edith glimpsed a three-storey stone house set square on to the road with a great copper beech to one side. Benedict's sketches had given her no idea it was a property of such distinction.

She waited by the gate while Benedict tipped the coachman to carry the luggage inside. The property was set around a paved courtyard. There were two wings, each at right angles to the façade of the main house and all clad in an autumnal blaze of Virginia creeper. To their right, behind a hedge, she glimpsed another large slate-roofed building.

'What's that?' she asked.

'The barn. There are more outbuildings, too.'

They walked up the flagstone path to an elegant centrally placed Georgian portico. Before Benedict could lift the brass knocker, the door opened.

A diminutive old woman stood in the hall, very upright and dressed in a rusty black gown of ancient design.

Benedict grinned. 'You look the same as ever, Mrs Gloyne!'

'Welcome, Mr Benedict. Oh, begging your pardon, sir! I should've said Mr Fairchild, now you're the master.'

'I'm happy to remain Mr Benedict to you.'

She bobbed a curtsy and scrutinised Edith with sharp black eyes. 'Welcome to Spindrift House, Mrs Fairchild.'

'Mrs Gloyne always baked me vast fruitcakes for my school tuck box,' said Benedict. 'They made me extremely popular with the other boys.'

The old woman smiled, exposing almost toothless gums.

She led them through a slate-floored hall and opened the door to a spacious drawing room.

Once she'd sent the coachman on his way, she said she'd bring the tea. Her footsteps pattered away down the rear passage.

Despite the unfashionable furniture, the room was charming with lofty ceilings and a double aspect. Edith was immediately drawn to the large sash windows that filled it with light. At the end of the undulating lawn was a gazebo. Set atop a small hillock, it made a perfect place to look out over the fields that curved down to the sapphire sea beyond. She couldn't wait to explore.

Benedict stood behind her and rested his chin on her head.

She slid away from him and perched on an armchair beside the great stone fireplace.

'Mrs Gloyne will show you the rest. And I,' he said, 'will burn Delphine's portrait.'

Edith nodded, relieved he'd remembered his promise without being reminded.

He slumped onto a sagging sofa with thread-bare arms. 'So how do you like Spindrift House?'

'It's lovely. Far larger than I'd imagined.' She ran her fingers through a bowl of dried rose petals on a side table, releasing the fragrance of summer past. A bubble of excitement rose up inside her at the realisation that she was now the mistress of this wonderful house. It was a little shabby but there was something so welcoming and comfortable about it that, even without having seen the rest, she knew she was going to love it.

The rattling of cups and saucers in the hall heralded the arrival of the tea tray, which Mrs Gloyne placed on a table beside Edith.

'Splendid!' said Benedict, rubbing his hands

together at the sight of a richly fruited cake.

'After we've had our tea, Mrs Gloyne,' Edith said, doing her best to emulate Mama's voice when she gave instructions to the servants, 'I'd like you to show me the house.'

A little while later, Mrs Gloyne guided her through a dining room with its red flock wallpaper and a vast mahogany table; a morning room; a sitting room with an ancient piano and untidy bookcases; and finally, a sizeable study. Edith was disconcerted to notice festoons of cobwebs and a layer of dust everywhere. She supposed the housekeeper was too ancient to keep the parlour maid up to scratch but was daunted by the prospect of having to speak to her about it. It was alarming to be responsible for managing a household and Edith determined to write to her mama for advice. There was a passage leading to the domestic offices but she didn't feel it necessary to inspect those. She'd send for Cook the following morning and trust she'd make suitable suggestions for the menus.

Upstairs, the fraying stair carpet gave way to a narrow piece of drugget along the landing. Pretty watercolour seascapes were displayed on the whitewashed walls and a mahogany grandfather clock ticked slowly into the quiet.

The master bedroom was large and light. Late-afternoon sunlight streamed through the window. Outside, elongated shadows slanted across the lawn. The end of the garden was bounded by a stream and then the fields inclined steeply down towards a grassy headland with the sea beyond.

'The view is wonderful!' said Edith, a pulse of excitement throbbing in her veins. The linen curtains were sun-faded but somehow they suited the sprigged wallpaper and plain cotton bedspread. She ran a finger over the mahogany dressing table and wiped the furring of dust from her fingertip. 'We have four guests from London arriving at the end of the week for an extended stay.' She was rather proud of how confident she sounded, as if she was used to giving such orders to servants every day.

'Guests?' A puzzled expression settled on Mrs Gloyne's face. 'We live very secluded here at Spindrift House.'

'Nevertheless,' said Edith in her firmest voice, 'I shall decide today which bedrooms our guests will occupy, to give the maids plenty of time to prepare for their arrival.'

'There are no *maids*, Mrs Fairchild, only myself. Mr Benedict was so kind as to keep me on temporary, to air the house and so on, after Mrs Tremayne passed on. And, in case Mr Benedict has forgot, I'm going to stop with my sister from this evening.'

Edith's mouth fell open in dismay. So that explained the air of neglect. 'But we shall need at least a kitchen maid to assist Cook.'

'The mistress always did cook for herself.'

Edith swallowed. 'There's no cook?'

Mrs Gloyne shook her head. 'As I said, we lived simply. Still, if you have need of servants, there are two dormitories in the attics and rooms off the kitchen for a cook and a housekeeper.'

'I see,' said Edith, her heart sinking. She'd

have to speak to Benedict straight away about employing staff.

Mrs Gloyne showed her four additional double bedrooms and a box room and then paused for a moment before opening a door at the end of the landing.

The faded wallpaper was decorated with a design of overblown cabbage roses and there was a threadbare rug on the polished boards. A pink eiderdown covered the bed and a folded nightgown rested neatly on the pillow. The curtains were half-drawn and a table and a chintz-covered armchair were placed before the window.

'I've kept the mistress's room just as it was,' said Mrs Gloyne in a low voice.

Edith sniffed the fresh roses in a vase on the mahogany dressing table. There were no dusty cobwebs here and the brass bedstead shone. 'Mrs Tremayne was a good mistress?'

'The best.' The old woman's mouth trembled.

Edith drew aside the curtain. She saw an imposing house in early Arts and Crafts style on the high peak of a neighbouring headland. 'I'm surprised Mrs Tremayne didn't choose the master bedroom with the sea view,' she said.

'She and her husband used to sleep there but, after she was widowed, she took this room.'

'Perhaps there were too many memories for her there?'

Mrs Gloyne folded her hands in silence and Edith remembered what Benedict had said about his Aunt Hester taking a married lover. Perhaps it hadn't been grief but guilt that made her decide to move to a different room. She picked up a slim volume of poetry from the table by the window. The calfskin binding was velvety-soft and the place marked with a pressed pansy. On the flyleaf was inscribed in a firm hand:

To Hester
Love Eternal
J

'Mrs Tremayne loved to sit there by the window,' said Mrs Gloyne.

Carefully, Edith replaced the book on the table.

'I expect you'll be wanting to unpack before preparing the dinner?' said Mrs Gloyne.

'Yes, I suppose so,' she said. She'd not been in a kitchen since she was a little girl and had watched Cook baking gingerbread.

'There's some cold ham and potatoes,' said Mrs Gloyne with a pitying smile.

* * *

After Edith had unpacked, she visited the lavatory. A comparatively recent addition, Mrs Gloyne had been full of pride when she showed it to her, explaining Mrs Tremayne had installed it, together with the adjacent bathroom, only the previous year.

Sitting on the polished mahogany seat, Edith recalled visiting her parents before travelling down to Cornwall. She and her mother had left the men to enjoy their port after dinner, retreating to the drawing room. Mama had wasted no time in making searching enquiries about her health. 'It wouldn't be at all unusual to find yourself in an interesting condition by now.'

Edith's cup had rattled when she replaced it on the saucer. 'Oh! I'm sure that isn't the case.'

'Have you had your monthly recently?'

She'd nodded, her face scarlet, and remembered that terrible night she and Benedict had argued.

Mama had persisted. 'If you miss once, it's likely you're in the family way but if you miss twice, you can be sure of it. Especially if your digestion is unsettled.'

Edith had missed one monthly. The next was overdue and there was still no sign of it. She'd been queasy all the time on their return from Provence. There was no avoiding it any longer; she must be expecting. She moaned and buried her face in her hands. Clearly, she hadn't been in the family way when she and Benedict had argued and they'd barely spoken to each other since, never mind had any marital relations. She was pregnant and, try as she might to expunge her guilty memory, she had allowed — in fact encouraged — Pascal to make love to her. The baby could only be his.

She hurried back to the bedroom and delved into the drawer where she'd secreted her diary amongst her petticoats. Sitting on the bed, she went back over the dates, counting the days with shaking fingers, and confirmed her worst fears. She couldn't begin to imagine Benedict's anger when he discovered she was carrying another man's child. He'd be perfectly within his rights to cast her out into the street and Mama would disown her for the shame she'd brought down upon them all. Even if she was devious enough to pretend to Benedict that it was his baby, at some point or other he'd discover a woman is unlikely to remain with child for ten months or more. The expanding knot of terror in her chest nearly choked her.

The sound of running footsteps came along the landing. 'Edith?'

She stuffed the diary back into the drawer as Benedict opened the door.

'I want to take you down to the cove before sunset.' He held out his hand and, too guilty to meet his gaze, she reached out to take it.

They hurried outside, crossing the lawn and taking the gate into the fields beyond. The sun was low and the sky was painted with vivid brushstrokes of Rose Madder and Naples Yellow. Benedict laughed as they ran over the tussocky grass.

A narrow rock, taller than a man, loomed out of the ground, silhouetted darkly against the marbled sky. Edith pulled on Benedict's hand to make him stop.

'It's a Bronze Age standing stone. Spindrift House used to be called Tregarrick, which means farm by a rock.'

'So why isn't it called Tregarrick now?'

'Jago Penrose changed it when he sold off the land and moved to Cliff House. Come on!'

They turned onto the coastal path, thick with gorse bushes, and he led her to steps hewn from the rocky cliff face. He went down first and she followed, clinging onto a fraying rope handrail while the breeze tugged at her hair.

At the foot of the steps she was enchanted to discover they were in a sandy cove. The sea, touched gold from the setting sun, was calm in the sheltered inlet, making a soft shushing sound as it frothed onto the strand. Edith drew in deep breaths of briny air, inhaling a little calm with each one.

'Except by boat, the only access here is from Spindrift House and Cliff House,' said Benedict.

She followed his pointing finger to the mansion on the headland and was transfixed by the sight of amber sunlight reflected on its windows, making it appear as if Cliff House was on fire.

'Aunt Hester used to pack a picnic when we came here and I'd pretend to be a smuggler. Do you see the cave behind the rocks over there?'

She looked at the dark cleft in the cliff and imagined what an excitement that would have been for a boy.

'We used to bring our paints and sometimes Jago Penrose came down with his sketchpad, too.' He gave a mischievous grin. 'Of course, I didn't know then he was Aunt Hester's lover.'

'I pity his poor wife,' Edith said. 'He must have known the pain he inflicted on her by his adultery.'

Benedict's smile faded. 'Morwenna Penrose is a hard woman and Aunt Hester was the gentlest of souls.'

Edith was overcome with remorse. It had been hypocritical of her to make such a statement.

The sin she'd committed against Benedict was far, far worse than mere adultery. Another man's child would be a living and unforgivable reminder of her immorality. Full of self-loathing, she drew in a deep sobbing breath.

They stumbled over pale sand that slipped and shifted beneath their feet. Wandering along the water's edge with the music of the gentle suck and hiss of the sea in their ears, they peered into rock pools and discovered shrimps, crabs and jellyfish. Benedict guided Edith to an outcrop of rock and they sat there in silence, watching the golden light shining on the sea as the sun slipped below the horizon.

She didn't resist when he put his arm around her and, after a moment, rested her head against his shoulder. Once he knew her shameful secret he'd never hold her like this again. He took her face between his hands. 'I want all to be well again between us,' he said, his hazel eyes serious.

She glanced away, her remorse and loss of innocence sharp in her breast. If only it were possible to go back to that idyllic time before their quarrel. If only she'd overcome her embarrassment and explained why she hadn't wanted him to make love to her.

'This is our new beginning.'

How she wanted that! But she'd ruined everything. She might, in time, forgive Benedict but she didn't know if she could ever forgive herself.

'A new beginning,' he said, and kissed her mouth with a feather-soft touch.

She leaned a little closer, wishing that everything could be as it was before.

He must have taken the small movement for acquiescence and gathered her into his arms, his lips brushing her neck.

A sudden tremor of desire made her shiver. She'd missed their lovemaking desperately but nothing changed the fact that she was pregnant with another man's child. An innocent child she'd condemned to be an outcast even before it was born. Closing her eyes while her husband pressed kisses on her throat, her thoughts raced. If he made love to her now and she concealed her pregnancy for a while longer, he might accept the child as his own, as an apparently seven- or eight-month baby. The prospect of taking such a risk made her pulse gallop. It would be wicked of her but there was the baby to think of now. If she made every effort to be a perfect wife to Benedict, perhaps it would make the sin a little less heinous?

'Sweet Edith, please won't you let me love you?'

The plea in Benedict's voice reminded her of how it had once been between them and she clutched his arm and let out a painful sob of regret.

'Shh!' he whispered, smoothing her hair.

She clasped her arms around his neck, her tears of shame and sorrow falling onto his shoulder.

Then he kissed her, gently at first but, as dusk fell and his passion rose, she made no attempt to stop him when he laid her gently on the sand and lifted her skirt.

10

Clarissa, Dora and Pascal arrived at Tresmeer station on a damp October morning and hired a carriage to convey them to Port Isaac. Swirling mist and narrow lanes bounded by high banks made it impossible for them to see much of the countryside. The little that Clarissa could see was mostly green and the uncertainty was having a dispiriting effect upon her formerly buoyant mood.

'Whatever shall we do with ourselves in the country?' she said. 'There's nothing but trees and fields.'

'We'll have the sea,' said Dora.

'And we will paint,' said Pascal. 'The new landscape will be an inspiration.'

If life in the sticks was too boring, thought Clarissa, there was always Pascal. She studied him through half-closed eyes. His thick dark hair curled onto his collar and his high cheekbones were so attractive.

'It's awkward though, isn't it?' said Dora. She rubbed at a smut on her sleeve, spreading the stain. 'Edith didn't really say how long we can stay.'

'Benedict will tell us soon enough when he wants us to leave,' said Clarissa.

'I hope they've made up their quarrel. They were so much in love before.' Dora sighed. 'I wish Delphine hadn't modelled for him. That portrait seemed rather vulgar somehow and it upset Edith.'

'My sister should not have agreed to sit for Benedict,' said Pascal, his mouth set in a grim line.

Delphine must have been bored, thought Clarissa, with a pompous husband like Édouard. She wouldn't be at all surprised if Delphine and Benedict had gone far beyond mere flirtation. 'The honeymoon was certainly over by the time we left Provence,' she said. She glanced outside as mizzle began to form droplets on the window. 'And so, it seems, is the summer. I'm looking forward to a hot bath and a good dinner.'

Before long, the carriage rounded a bend and lurched to a halt before a pair of stone gateposts.

Dora clutched Clarissa's arm. 'Can this really be Spindrift House? It's so grand.'

Pascal and the coachman unloaded the luggage onto the grass verge.

The front door opened and Edith flew down the path towards them. She hugged Dora and Clarissa, her eyes shining, though her face was pale. 'Did you have a good journey?' She looked around. 'But where's Wilfred?'

'He couldn't come, after all,' said Dora. 'I've brought you a letter from him. His mother is ill again.' She sighed. 'If you ask me, she's putting it on because she wants to keep him at her beck and call.'

'According to Maman,' said Pascal, 'my Aunt Sylvie often invented mysterious illnesses for herself, even as a child.' He kissed Edith on both cheeks. She stiffened and blushed before turning away from him.

Clarissa narrowed her eyes as Pascal also stepped back. There had been an unusual formality between Edith and him while they were travelling back from Provence and she'd wondered if they might have had a tiff. 'One day Wilfred will have to learn to refuse his mama's demands,' she said, 'if he's ever to have any life of his own.' It was easier said than done, of course, to oppose a parent, but she had stood up to her own father in the end. She'd even persuaded him to continue her allowance for the coming winter, though she'd been forced to accept his condition that she'd return home if she couldn't support herself.

'Benedict's gone to the village,' said Edith. She picked up one of the cases and set off down the path, followed by Pascal with the easels and Dora carrying an armful of boxes.

Clarissa stared at the stack of luggage, wondering if they were supposed to carry it themselves. Perhaps that was usual in the country? Reluctantly, she picked up a carpet bag. Benedict and Pascal could fetch the rest later.

Inside, Edith put the case down at the foot of the stairs. 'Unfortunately, the housekeeper only stayed until we arrived. We don't, at present, have any servants.'

'But however will you manage?' asked Clarissa. The news didn't bode well for a hot bath and a good dinner.

'We need a cook so I've written to Mama for advice.' Clarissa saw now that Edith's bright smile didn't match the shadow of anxiety in her eyes. 'Meanwhile, we'll have to slum it.'

'I shall fetch the luggage,' said Pascal.

'Tea?' said Edith. 'I've managed to keep the range alight today and, miracle of miracles, the kettle's hot. Would you like it in the drawing room? Though the kitchen's warmer.'

'The kitchen,' said Dora.

Soon they were ensconced around a scrubbed pine table in a spacious room with a high, beamed ceiling, a slate floor and a dresser stacked with blue and white china. If they had to slum it, thought Clarissa, this wasn't a bad way to do it.

Pascal, sitting next to Clarissa, fidgeted with his knife, laying it perfectly straight on his plate. He cleared his throat. 'Edith,' he said, 'how was your meeting with Mr Rosenberg?'

A smile flickered across her lips. 'I've been dying to tell you all. I have my first commission! It's for an oil painting of the scene in the arena. If he likes it, he'll ask me for a companion painting. I can hardly believe I'm going to be paid for doing something I love.'

'That's wonderful, Edith!' said Clarissa.

Dora jumped up to hug her.

'I'm sure it will be the first of many commissions,' said Pascal.

The kettle on the black-leaded range whistled. A moment later, Edith set a brown teapot and a plate of saffron buns on the table.

'Will you be Mother?' asked Dora.

Edith drew in her breath sharply and snatched her hand away from the teapot.

'Did you burn yourself?' said Pascal.

'Oh . . . ' She rubbed her little finger. 'It was hotter than I thought,' she murmured.

'Shall I do it then?' Dora set out the cups.

The front door slammed and a moment later Benedict hurried into the kitchen. 'Welcome to Spindrift House!' He held up a parcel wrapped in newspaper. 'Supper.' He dropped the parcel on the table and unwrapped it, revealing six glistening herrings.

Edith grimaced. 'But, Benedict, they've still got their heads and tails on! And what about the entrails? For goodness' sake, put them in the scullery!'

'I really couldn't face cold ham and burned potatoes for another night.' He made a comical face at the others. 'My wife has many talents but cooking isn't one of them.'

'I've never had to cook before,' said Edith, 'and neither did Mama.'

'I can gut the herrings,' said Dora.

'Can you really?' asked Edith.

She nodded. 'We'll fry them in a bit of flour or oatmeal and they'll be delicious.'

'Thank heavens! We shan't starve, then,' said Benedict, drawing up a chair beside Edith and kissing the top of her head. 'Pass me a saffron bun, there's a good girl.'

Amazed, Clarissa watched Edith push the plate of buns towards him. She felt a tiny pang of unease. Of course, she was happy if the lovebirds had made up their quarrel but she hoped it wouldn't mean their visit might be curtailed if Edith no longer needed her friends' support.

102

'Where's Wilfred?' asked Benedict.

'His mother didn't want him to come,' said Dora.

'We're outnumbered by women, Pascal,' said Benedict, making a comical grimace. 'No doubt we'll be henpecked to boot if we don't take a firm stand!'

Pascal gave a Gallic shrug.

'Spindrift House is very handsome, Benedict,' said Clarissa, imagining how wonderful it would be to have a house and a private income that allowed you independence.

'Fallen on my feet, haven't I?' He grinned, his mouth full of bun. 'I passed Hugh Penrose in the village. He stuck his nose in the air and crossed the road. As if I cared!'

'How ill-mannered,' said Clarissa.

'He's an ignorant oaf, full of puffed up self-importance.' Benedict licked his forefinger and dabbed at the last crumbs on his plate. 'We'll give you the grand tour in a moment. Edith's been like a whirling dervish, preparing for your visit.'

'Mrs Gloyne hadn't done any cleaning for years,' said Edith, 'and I had to make up the beds.'

'We could have done that,' said Dora.

Edith laughed. 'You may wish you had! I'd never made a bed before and got the sheets in a tangle. And it never occurred to me dusting was such hard work.'

'I wouldn't have had the first idea where to begin,' said Clarissa.

The girls cleared the table while Benedict

brushed crumbs from his knees onto the floor. Pascal picked up as much luggage as he could and Edith led the way upstairs.

'Dora, I've put you in this room next to ours,' she said. She drew back the drapes, making the brass curtain rings rattle. 'There's a sea view. You said you dreamed of living by the sea.'

'Oh, I do!' She clasped her hands to her chest, her freckled face lit by happiness.

They returned to the corridor and Edith opened another door. 'Clarissa, this used to be Aunt Hester's room.'

'Very comfortable,' said Clarissa. The rose-patterned wallpaper and the rug were faded but there was a large wardrobe and a pleasant outlook.

'See Cliff House on the headland?' said Benedict. 'Aunt Hester's lover lived there. Do you think she used to sit here, pining for a glimpse of him?'

Clarissa laughed. 'Perhaps he'd put a light in the window to signal an illicit meeting?'

'Close the sash, Benedict,' said Edith.

Clarissa turned to look at her, surprised by her sharp tone.

'There's a draught,' she said. 'Pascal, now Wilfred isn't coming, you can choose one of two rooms. They're at the opposite end of the house and both have a view of the harbour. And then I want to show you all something I think will please you.'

She took them to a narrow staircase up to the attics. 'Servants' dormitories,' she said, when they reached the landing.

Through open doorways, Clarissa saw there were two large rooms with vaulted ceilings and exposed beams.

'See how light they are!' said Edith. 'Don't you think they'll make ideal studios?'

Pascal laughed. '*Magnifique!*'

Clarissa noted the light from the rows of dormer windows on both sides of each whitewashed room. The pine floorboards were thick with dust and a number of metal bedsteads, miscellaneous chairs and small chests of drawers were piled into a corner.

'I couldn't have dreamed of anything better!' said Dora. 'After trying to work on my illustrations at the kitchen table last week, with brothers and sisters squabbling underfoot and wet washing draped everywhere, well, it's grand to have all this space!' She glanced up at the ceiling. 'Or it will be once we've got rid of the cobwebs.'

'It's perfect,' said Clarissa. 'I've struggled all summer with wondering how to earn my living. I've never kidded myself I'm good enough for Fine Art and I dreaded telling Father I'd wasted my time at the Slade. Then, at the last possible moment, I realised what it is I want to do and I'm so excited!'

'And what is this wonderful idea?' asked Pascal.

'I've decided to design jewellery.' She laughed. 'Don't look so surprised! They won't be heirloom items,' she said, 'but pretty, affordable things. Modern designs for the independent New Woman who, perhaps, works in an office and doesn't have, or want to wear, her grandmother's rubies.'

Pascal nodded thoughtfully. 'You have an eye for fashion. This is an excellent choice for you.'

'*Can* a woman be a jeweller?' asked Benedict.

'Why not?' said Clarissa, irritated by his tone.

'It's an excellent idea,' said Edith, frowning at him. 'How will you go about it?'

'I don't know yet,' Clarissa confessed. 'After I've designed a collection of suitable pieces I'll find out how they can be made up. I've frittered away the summer but now I can't wait to begin.'

'I'm so happy for you,' said Dora.

Her genuine pleasure and the warmth in her voice almost brought tears to Clarissa's eyes.

'Meanwhile,' said Edith, 'Dora and I have an appointment with some herrings if we want any dinner tonight.'

11

The following morning Edith slipped out of bed without disturbing Benedict. They'd all stayed up late the night before talking about Art — always Art, drinking wine, explaining British politics to Pascal and discussing the death of the Poet Laureate, Lord Tennyson. Benedict received a standing ovation from the rest of the party after his dramatic recitation of 'The Charge of the Light Brigade'. When Edith and Benedict finally retired to bed, he'd kissed her, his breath tainted by cigarette smoke and wine, and slid his hand inside her nightgown. Although exhausted after preparing for their friends' arrival, she made an effort to welcome his advances.

Since they'd arrived in Cornwall, Edith had felt like an actor upon the stage, smiling and pretending a contentment she didn't feel. Benedict was oblivious to the deep emotional wounds he'd caused her and she was drowning in guilt. She dressed and crept downstairs, dreading the daily battle with the range. Astonished, she paused in the kitchen doorway. The kettle was steaming away, the kitchen was warm and the aroma of coffee was in the air.

'Good morning, Edith.' Pascal, reading yesterday's newspaper at the table, stood up to greet her.

She'd avoided being alone with him ever since

the day her world had irrevocably changed and she didn't want to be alone with him now. She forced herself to smile. 'How clever of you to light the range.'

He poured her some coffee and, hesitantly, she sat down.

Glancing at the open door, he said, 'Edith, since that time we . . . '

'No!' she said, sensing he intended to discuss what had happened.

'There has been no opportunity for us to speak alone but I must apologise . . . '

She held up her hand, warding off his words. 'Please, I don't want to talk about it!' She gulped at the coffee and burned her tongue.

'I must assure you . . . '

She clattered the cup onto the saucer. 'Don't!' she said. 'Forget it ever happened. I was deeply distressed and hardly knew what I was doing.' That wasn't the whole truth, though, and she knew it. The memory she'd carefully packaged away of how he'd caressed her so tenderly was completely at odds with his untamed wildness at the height of their passion. It had surprised and moved her. She'd never again be able to look at him without remembering the lightning bolt of desire that had sparked between them.

Pascal sighed.

As long as he remained at Spindrift House there was a risk he might say something to Benedict. Her stomach churned, the smell of the coffee suddenly making her queasy. She breathed shallowly, hardly daring to move, and prayed she wasn't going to be sick again.

'I have no wish to cause you anguish. I shall not mention it. Not to anyone.'

A little of the tension loosened inside her. 'Thank you.' Her voice was no more than a whisper.

Voices drifted down the staircase and she was relieved when Dora and Clarissa joined them, chattering about plans for the day.

★   ★   ★

Later that afternoon, Edith leaned on her broom and admired their new studio. Benedict and Pascal had heaved the dozen or so bedsteads out to the barn and carried upstairs trestle tables they'd discovered in one of the outbuildings. Dora and Clarissa had helped her wash down the chairs and chests of drawers and arranged them into separate work spaces.

Dora, her hair wrapped in a scarf, stretched up with her broom to sweep away the last cobweb dangling from the beams. Clarissa hummed to herself while she set out her paints on a trestle table.

Edith slumped onto a chair and yawned. She ought to work on the Rosenberg painting but she was too drained. Still, the drizzle had ceased and pale sunlight shone through the newly polished windows. 'Since the men have gone to the public house, perhaps we should have a half-day holiday, too?' she said.

'Shall we go down to the sea?' Dora's face wore an eager expression and Edith was happy to indulge her.

A short while later they climbed down the cliff steps and trudged through the shifting sand and clumps of marram grass. Small clouds scudded across the milky sky and white-crested waves sailed upon the sea. Dora, laughing like a child, ran off to chase a seagull.

Edith turned her face into the bracing breeze, the salty tang reviving her.

'I'm pleased you've made up your differences with Benedict,' said Clarissa. She was wrapped in a lovely blue shawl and the wind had whipped roses into her cheeks. 'Are you happy again?'

Edith hesitated. 'I will be,' she said, wondering if the joy she'd once felt in their love would ever return. 'Benedict thinks I am. I'm determined to be a good wife and I'm learning how to go about that, I think.'

'Be careful, Edith.'

Her insides gave a little somersault. Surely Clarissa couldn't know her shameful secret? 'What do you mean?'

'Benedict behaved abominably with Delphine.'

Edith caught her breath. 'How did you know?'

Clarissa gave her a searching look. 'I didn't,' she said, 'until now. But her portrait made me guess he might have had an affair with her.'

'It's over,' Edith said.

'Nevertheless, if you try *too* hard to be a good wife, always compromising and appeasing, you'll lose the essence of yourself,' her friend said. 'Girls are brought up to believe they're inferior to the male sex and men take it for granted that their needs and wants are paramount.'

'Men are stronger than us.'

Clarissa's face looked pinched as she said, 'And sometimes they use that physical strength against us.' She sighed. 'Women aren't less intelligent than men, unless we choose to live up to the accepted view that it's unfeminine to think for ourselves.' She drew Edith's arm into the crook of her elbow. 'I'd hate you to become the same sort of wife as my mother: subdued, always afraid to speak her own mind . . . '

'It was because I wasn't compliant that difficulties arose between us,' Edith said.

'Never forget how beautiful and talented you are and how fortunate Benedict is to have you as his wife.'

Edith pressed her hand. 'I'm fortunate to have you as my friend.'

'We're very different, you and I and Dora.' Clarissa's expression was thoughtful. 'Maybe it's because we're different that we complement each other. We're stronger together than we are individually.' She shook her head. 'I never imagined I'd be so thrilled by the prospect of spending winter in the country, but I can feel excitement at our exploring new ideas together bubbling inside me. We women are capable of much greater things than we know and I believe times of great change are coming for us.'

'Times of great change,' Edith echoed. Oh, yes, change was on the horizon for her, all right. Probably not the one Clarissa was envisaging.

Dora was waving wildly at them and pointing to something on the sand.

'Come on,' said Clarissa, 'let's see what she's found.'

At the water's edge the beach was rippled by the outgoing tide and strewn with seaweed, cuttlefish and driftwood. Glistening black rocks edged up from the hard sand, blistered with barnacles and clothed in seaweed.

Dora's find was a large crab that must have been dead for a considerable time. 'Isn't it beautiful?' she enthused. 'I'm going to paint it.'

'You'd better sit at the opposite end of the studio from us, then,' said Clarissa, wrinkling her nose. 'It smells ghastly.'

'There are so many interesting things,' said Dora, poking the flotsam and jetsam with a piece of driftwood. 'Look at these pearly shells!'

They strolled along the beach, buffeted by the wind and collecting little treasures.

Clarissa picked up a piece of sea glass. 'I love the colour of this.' She turned it over. 'It's a sea jewel. I wonder if . . . '

A movement caught Edith's eye. A woman with a baby in her arms and a little boy trotting along beside her was walking towards them. A black dog gambolled in the surf nearby and ran to drop a ball at Dora's feet. She threw it back into the waves and he raced after it, barking excitedly.

'Your dog is enjoying his exercise,' she said as the woman approached them.

The baby was about eighteen months old and bounced up and down in his mother's arms. Plump and rather plain, she laughed as she tried to restrain him.

Dora tickled the baby under his chin. 'What a fine little fellow!'

'This is Timmy,' said the woman. She kissed his wind-blown curls and set him down on the sand. 'Go and find the bow-wow, Timmy!' A determined expression on his face, he toddled off. 'And this is Noel.' The boy, aged about two and a half, regarded them from the safety of his mother's skirts.

'Shall I fetch Timmy?' asked Dora, as the toddler picked up speed towards the sea.

'Thank you,' said his mother. 'He's so quick now.'

The wind ruffled her shawl, moulding it to the curve of her belly, and Edith realised she was expecting. Before long her own waist would thicken. She closed her eyes briefly at the thought. What kind of a mother could she be to a child she didn't want? Every time she attempted to visualise caring for a baby her thoughts skittered away, as slippery as the seaweed under her feet.

Dora snatched up the toddler just as he reached the water. Singing 'Tom, Tom, the Piper's Son', she carried him back.

The dog, dripping from his swim, pranced in circles and then shook himself vigorously.

Clarissa squealed as drops of sandy water splattered her skirt. 'Oh, for Heaven's sake! I'm drenched.'

'I'm so sorry,' said the woman. 'Here, take my handkerchief.'

Edith felt obliged to fill the awkward silence while Clarissa was mopping at her skirt. 'We've been collecting shells for inspiration for our paintings,' she said.

113

'You're artists? How interesting! My father-in-law used to paint. We have some of his seascapes in the drawing room. Do you live nearby?'

Edith nodded. 'At Spindrift House. I'm Mrs Fairchild.'

The other woman became very still. 'Benedict Fairchild's wife?'

'That's right. I suppose talk of newcomers travels quickly through the local community?'

She narrowed her eyes. 'You'll find everyone hereabouts knows of Mr Fairchild. I'm Mrs Hugh Penrose,' she said. 'I'm sure your husband has boasted to you about how he stole my husband's inheritance?' She lifted her chin as if spoiling for a fight.

Dora gasped.

'It wasn't like that, Mrs Penrose,' Edith protested.

'It was exactly like that! But then, I'm hardly surprised by your husband's dishonourable behaviour, given he was Hester Tremayne's nephew. It would have been difficult to find a more conniving and immoral woman in the whole of Cornwall. And you,' she looked Edith up and down, her small grey eyes as unyielding as flints, 'are no more welcome in the locality than your thieving husband.'

Edith caught her breath and stepped back.

'How unkind!' said Dora.

Clarissa proffered the borrowed handkerchief to Mrs Penrose. 'It's wrong of you to judge Mrs Fairchild by the conduct of a woman she never knew. Or indeed by the actions of her husband.'

'The facts speak for themselves,' said Mrs

114

Penrose. 'Moreover, any friends of the Fairchilds' are unwelcome here. Keep the handkerchief; it's tainted by your touch.'

Clarissa laughed. 'Now you're being ridiculous!'

'Get out of my sight! Better still, leave Cornwall, the whole lot of you!'

Timmy's chin quivered at the anger in his mother's voice. He buried his face in her neck and wailed.

Dora patted his back. 'Don't take on so, little man!'

'Don't touch my son!' Mrs Penrose wrapped her arms around the howling toddler and caught hold of Noel's hand. 'All of you, keep away from my family!'

'Well,' said Clarissa, 'that's a nice welcome to Cornwall.' Her tone was amused but her blue eyes were as cold as charity as Mrs Penrose hurried away.

'I'd never have hurt Timmy,' said Dora, her cheeks blazing. Her fingers shook as she picked up the dead crab by one of its pincers.

'Of course you wouldn't,' said Edith. 'Let's go back.'

They walked in silence towards the cliff steps, all the pleasure drained out of the day. Edith couldn't help wondering if they'd ever be able to make peace with their nearest neighbours.

12

Dora sighed as Benedict rummaged about on Edith's worktable, muttering under his breath. When he found a pencil, he cursed because the lead was broken and, after he'd sharpened it, dropped the penknife with a clatter. He made a sketch of Edith, then flung the book on the table with a thud and clattered downstairs.

Able to concentrate again, Dora delicately added a final highlight to her illustration of the crab. Watercolour washes of salmon, mushroom and ochre glowed pleasingly against the crisp lines of black ink and she nodded in satisfaction.

What a relief it was to paint in the studio instead of hugger-mugger with her family. So much depended on building up her portfolio. She already had some good drawings from the Slade but she wanted to add livelier, more colourful illustrations, to show the breadth of her skills. Her next effort was going to be of a wonderful piece of bleached driftwood, scoured bone-smooth by the sea to reveal the swirling grain of the wood. But first, she must dispose of the crab. It smelled worse than the communal privy in the yard behind her family home in Lambeth. Wrinkling her nose, she wrapped it in newspaper and carried it downstairs.

She went outside into a yard surrounded by outbuildings, past the barn and into the walled kitchen garden. Once upon a time it might have been productive but now the ground was choked with weeds. She buried the crab in the ashes of the kitchen bonfire, along with the mackerel heads. They'd have to set a fire soon or all the cats in the neighbourhood would visit.

Before she returned inside, she couldn't resist catching a glimpse of the sea. The air was laden with moisture and the grass wet as she set off across the lawn, soaking her boots. She climbed the hillock to the gazebo and found Pascal had set up his easel there, facing the view.

'I wondered where you were,' she said.

He waved his brush. 'Look at the soft greys and blues of the sea and sky today. The mist blends them together so that you cannot tell where one begins and the other ends.'

'It's quite different from the harsh sun and intense colours of Provence, isn't it?'

Pascal nodded. 'So I must see it through different eyes. Perhaps watercolour is more suited to this climate than oils. I shall make some experiments. And you, Dora, how is your friend, Monsieur le Crabe?'

She laughed. 'In his funeral pyre in the kitchen garden.'

'And did he make a good painting?'

'I think so. It will be the first of a collection I'll call *Seashore*.' She sighed in contentment. 'Isn't it lovely to be here with the time to paint in peace?'

'But I do not forget that I must sell my work if I am to put bread on the table.'

Dora shivered and rubbed her hands together.

'I can't bear the thought of having to give up painting to work in a factory or a shop.'

Back at the house, Dora found Edith sweeping the kitchen floor. 'It's dirty yet again,' she said, 'and I need to be working.' She ran her hand over the table, gathering scattered crumbs. 'I never knew what a lot there is to do in a house. And Benedict mentioned he's out of clean shirts.'

'Perhaps you could ask Mrs Gloyne if she knows of a good washerwoman? The washing takes Ma and me the best part of two days every week, longer if it's wet. And then there's the ironing.'

'Oh, Lord!' Edith rested her head on her hands. 'I've never done laundry.'

'Aren't you the lucky one!' Fond of Edith as she was, irritation made Dora's tone vinegary. Rich people had no idea how hard their servants worked simply to keep their betters clean, warm and well fed. 'Anyhow, I'm going back to the studio now to set up my next painting.'

'Aren't you the lucky one!' echoed Edith.

Her voice was so full of doom that Dora laughed out loud.

A smile spread across Edith's face. 'I love to hear you laugh,' she said, leaning the broom against the wall. 'It takes away your worried expression and makes you pretty. Come on, we'll go to the studio together.'

Edith thought she was pretty! Smiling, Dora followed her upstairs.

★ ★ ★

118

The following Sunday, Dora put on her hat and coat ready for church.

Clarissa was downstairs already, dressed in the classy blue costume she'd worn for Edith's wedding.

'Don't you look posh!' said Dora. 'And is that rouge?'

'Only a touch. It's important to look our best in case we're introduced to some of the locals, isn't it?' said Clarissa, peering into the hall mirror. 'It'll be such a long winter if we're not invited to any dances or card parties.'

'But that isn't why we go to church!' said Dora, shocked.

'Isn't it? I always find it most agreeable to see who has a new hat and to catch up on the latest gossip. Occasionally there might be a sermon that doesn't send me to sleep.'

'Reminding myself that I'm a part of Our Lord's family is what matters to me. It's . . . ' Dora floundered, trying to find the right word. 'Comforting.'

'I can't say the Church has ever given me any comfort when I needed it.'

There was such a bleak expression on Clarissa's face but, still, Dora didn't care for it when she spoke like that.

'You simply cannot wear that awful hat, Dora,' said Clarissa, plucking it off her head. 'It looks like something a fisherman's grandmother might wear. Wait here.' She hurried upstairs and returned with a navy straw hat decorated with silk ribbons and a swathe of velvet roses.

'Oh, but I can't . . . '

119

'Of course you can.' Clarissa placed it carefully over Dora's hair, tilted it to a rakish angle and then turned her to look in the mirror.

Dora caught her breath, hardly recognising herself. She looked like somebody who was somebody.

'Pretty, isn't it?' said Clarissa. 'Keep it; it suits you.'

Dora mumbled her thanks as the others, all dressed in their Sunday best, came clattering down the stairs.

'Everybody ready?' said Benedict.

'We'd better hurry,' said Edith, doing up the buttons on her coat. 'We don't want to start off on the wrong foot.'

Dora thought she looked wan and distracted. 'Are you all right, Edith?'

She nodded. 'I didn't feel very well this morning.'

Pascal offered his arms to Dora and Clarissa and the small procession set off up the steep hill and along narrow lanes to St Endellion church.

Half a dozen smart carriages and various pony traps and dog carts passed them but Dora noted many of the pedestrians were working men and women in their Sunday best. She made sure to nod and wave.

They reached the stone church, with its squat tower at one end. Edith and Benedict went to pay their respects at Aunt Hester's grave and then they all entered the church together. They slipped into a pew in one of the side aisles.

Dora said her prayers then looked around. She liked the church's simplicity; a slate floor, wide aisles, oak-beamed and vaulted ceiling, and plain glass in the windows. Edith knelt beside her, head bent over clasped hands as she prayed. A strand of dark hair peeked out from her hat and curled over the nape of her neck. Dora studied her covertly, wishing she had her sketchbook.

The service began and Dora felt the familiar sense of peace envelop her as she made her responses and sang the hymns. Clarissa sang in a clear soprano, whilst boldly studying the congregation. During a rousing sermon on the subject of God's wrath, Edith nudged Dora and nodded towards a pew on the other side of the aisle.

She noticed the small boy first, recognising him by his fair hair. Timmy sat on Mrs Penrose's lap with young Noel at her side. They were flanked by an older lady and a man of perhaps thirty years of age. The memory of that upsetting meeting in the cove made Dora fidget.

After the final hymn the congregation filed outside. Dora, feeling very grand in her borrowed hat, was chatting brightly to Pascal as they walked towards the church gate when she realised the Penrose family were standing directly in their path. Mrs Penrose was definitely in the family way.

'It looks as if our delightful neighbours from Cliff House wish to exchange pleasantries with us,' murmured Clarissa.

The older lady, dressed in deepest mourning, stood proudly erect and glared at Benedict as they approached. 'I don't know how you have the nerve to visit the House of God after what you've done,' she hissed.

Benedict raised his hat to her without slowing his pace.

The man Dora assumed was Hugh Penrose stepped in front of Benedict. 'I'll thank you not to come to this church again or allow your friends to distress my family.'

'Still moaning, Penrose?' said Benedict. 'As for your wife, you ought to keep her under better control. Without any provocation whatsoever, she was unspeakably offensive to my wife and guests.'

Mrs Penrose gasped and her plump cheeks flooded scarlet.

'No provocation?' Mr Penrose's voice rose and he clenched his fists. 'After your aunt humiliated my mother and you stole my inheritance, you dare to say that?'

People were turning to stare and Dora could have curled up and died from embarrassment.

'Don't be a bore, Penrose,' said Benedict. 'Now do get out of my way, there's a good fellow.'

'Or what?'

Benedict took a step closer, looking down at the other man from his superior height. 'You know perfectly well what will happen. I shall forcibly remove you, like the time you terrorised my aunt into the heart attack that killed her. I should have had you locked up then.'

Pascal came to stand at Benedict's side. 'Perhaps we should go home, *mon ami*?' he said.

Mrs Penrose placed a hand on her husband's arm. 'Don't stoop to the level of this despicable man.' Her lip curled. 'After all, it won't be long before anybody who is anybody will refuse to receive him — or his wife and friends, for that matter. We'll make quite sure of that.' She smiled in grim satisfaction, the feather on her hat bobbing in self-righteous indignation.

Edith's face paled.

'What a nasty, spiteful person you are, Mrs Penrose,' said Clarissa. 'Did your mother never tell you that an outburst of bad temper on the part of an expectant mother may affect her child adversely?'

Mrs Penrose glared at her. 'Our friends and neighbours have only to glance at Mr Fairchild's artist friends, all tricked up in cheap finery and with their faces painted like actresses or worse . . . *paint* for church, mind you . . . to know what sort of degenerates they are. Heaven only knows what immoral acts you get up to out of the sight of decent people!'

Several parishioners darted scandalised glances at them, whispering amongst themselves.

Clarissa raised her eyebrows. 'A word of advice, my dear Mrs Penrose. Though a woman may have the misfortune to be born with the face of a pug, making jealous and unfounded accusations, to those so much more attractive than herself, will render her charmless as well as ugly.' She swept past the Penroses with her head held as high as a duchess's.

Benedict snorted with laughter. 'Well said, Clarissa!'

Dora couldn't help noticing Mr Penrose's avid gaze as he watched Clarissa's retreating back.

Edith swayed and Dora hurried to support her, anxious her friend was going to faint, but Benedict reached her first.

'I'm warning you, Penrose,' he said, 'any more malicious threats on your part, or that of your womenfolk, and this will become a matter for my lawyer.'

Dora's knees trembled and she was relieved when Pascal tucked her hand firmly in the crook of his elbow. Her neck and shoulders remained rigid as they walked past the Penrose family. Their hostile stares made her feel as if the skin on her back were crawling and she didn't relax until they were back at Spindrift House.

13

Clarissa arose at first light and wrapped up warmly to go down to the cove. The chilly November breeze teased her hair as she walked along the strand, searching for pebbles and pearly shells to make into necklaces and earrings. She'd surprised herself by how enthusiastically she'd taken up the idea of designing jewellery and, for the first time, had an inkling of the passion behind her friends' artistic aspirations.

A dull turquoise gleam nestling amongst a clump of seaweed caught her eye and she pounced upon it with a cry of triumph. Rubbing away grains of sand, she held the sea glass up to the light. She tucked her prize into her collecting bag and continued her search.

Before long, her stomach growled for breakfast. Wending her way towards the cliff steps, she paused. A man was throwing a ball for a black dog. Hugh Penrose. Clarissa's enjoyment of the morning was ruined by the anticipation of another unpleasant scene. Her eyes narrowed as she watched Hugh playing with his dog. The contempt his wife had shown towards her, insinuating she was little more than a whore, had been utterly humiliating and, despite giving that spiteful woman a good set-down, her comments had struck home. Burning with indignation at the memory, Clarissa climbed up the steps.

At the clifftop, she glanced down at the beach. Hugh was staring at her, his hand shading his eyes against the light. She stared back, determined not to move until he looked away. Her resolve was about to break when he bent to pat the dog's head.

The sound of laughter and the aroma of toast and freshground coffee greeted her as she let herself in by the kitchen door. Her friends were sitting around the table and Benedict was recounting a risqué story about a bishop and an actress. Dora's hand was pressed over her mouth to suppress a giggle. Edith sipped her tea with a faraway expression on her face.

'Where were you, Clarissa?' said Benedict, crunching into his toast and marmalade.

'The cove.'

Edith cut a slice of bread and offered it to her on the point of the breadknife. 'We were too hungry to wait for you.'

Pascal picked up an envelope from beside his plate and slit it open. 'Delphine writes with happy news,' he said, a moment later. 'She is to have a child.'

'That should keep her out of mischief, then,' said Clarissa.

Edith's face blanched and she glanced at Benedict. He spooned more marmalade onto his toast but Clarissa noticed his expression was thoughtful as he stared at his plate.

'And the postman has brought you a parcel, too, Clarissa,' said Pascal.

She reached for the package and untied the string, all the while wondering if Benedict might

126

have fathered Delphine's child. Perhaps it was best not to know. 'This is from Aunt Minnie's dressmaker,' she said, folding back the brown paper and lifting out the jade green dress. Holding it up against herself, she said, 'What do you think? The loose cut means I don't have to be tight-laced and can move freely when I'm painting.'

'What a marvellous idea!' said Edith. Her voice was determinedly cheerful.

'I don't know about you, Pascal,' said Benedict, 'but I like a woman to show off an hourglass figure.'

'I'm sure you do,' said Edith, 'but if you were so tightly corseted you were nearly cut in two, you'd know how difficult it is for a woman to breathe, even when she's not exerting herself.'

Pascal's glance lingered over Edith's waist. 'Perhaps it is not necessary for a slender woman to be so uncomfortable?'

'Exactly,' she said. 'I'd very much like a painting dress, Clarissa. Would your aunt's dressmaker sew one for me?'

'There's no need,' said Dora. 'It's a simple shape. If you buy the material, I could make it for you, Edith.'

'How clever of you! After breakfast, Benedict and I are going to visit Mrs Gloyne,' said Edith. 'I'll see if there's a draper's in the village.'

'I'll walk with you,' said Clarissa.

The lane into Port Isaac meandered past the school and down a steep hill towards the sea. The Platt, the harbour foreshore, was bustling with activity. Fishermen disgorged their catch

127

into the fish cellars and men loaded Delabole slate onto shallow-hulled coasters, while others unloaded the coal brought in from Wales. Pigs rooted amongst the seaweed on the stony beach. Above the harbour were close-packed terraces of higgledy-piggledy whitewashed or slate-stone cottages.

Benedict and Edith went to call on Mrs Gloyne, agreeing to meet Clarissa later at the Golden Lion on the harbourside.

Left alone, Clarissa explored the steep lanes and interconnecting alleys, peered into shop windows and bought saffron buns for tea. The cold wind numbed her fingers and, when a fine drizzle began to fall, she returned to the harbour. Too early to meet her friends, she took shelter inside the Golden Lion.

The innkeeper took her order for tea and directed her to a small parlour. A short while later a young barmaid with eyes as dark as sloes brought in the tea tray.

Clarissa warmed her hands on her teacup and watched raindrops running down the window-panes, while her thoughts returned to pudding-faced Mrs Penrose. The other woman had probably been jealous of her but the memory of her mortifying accusations made Clarissa's cheeks burn again. Out of habit, she ran her fingers over her inner forearms, seeking out the fine scars that crisscrossed the delicate skin. Over the years she'd learned to shut her ears to Father's cruel comments and had found other ways to redress the balance of power between herself and other men like him, but she'd never before encountered such hostility from a woman.

A shadow fell across the table.

Hugh Penrose stood with his legs set apart, holding a tankard of ale and looking arrogantly down his nose at her.

There was a pugnacious set to his jaw and she wondered if he was going to make trouble. She glared at him.

'You were in the cove this morning,' he said. 'You don't often see flaxen hair like yours in these parts.' He sipped his ale. 'It's very striking.'

A little of Clarissa's tension drained away. Now she was on familiar ground and felt confident she could, with a little investment of her time, prick the bubble of this man's self-importance. Perhaps, in so doing, she might also make his wife pay for her malicious words. And so the game began again. She leaned back against the settle and gave him a slow, welcoming smile.

Uninvited, he sat down beside her, as she'd guessed he would.

'I don't see why you and your wife are so hostile to me,' she said. 'I understand you might feel animosity towards Mr Fairchild but the rest of us had nothing to do with whatever occurred before. And, you must agree, your wife was perfectly vile to me.'

Hugh Penrose stroked his moustache. 'I can't deny Jenifry has a sharp tongue.'

He was too stocky for Clarissa's taste but nevertheless fairly good-looking. Or he would be if he lost that sulky scowl. 'Is that why you're drinking instead of working at this time of the morning?' she asked.

He sighed. 'She makes such a fuss over the children that it's impossible to have a proper conversation; she speaks in baby talk half the time.' He shook his head. 'I never knew having children dissipated what little wits a woman has.'

Clarissa gritted her teeth against the sharp retort she wanted to make about men having fewer wits in the first place. Lightly, she patted his hand. 'In my opinion, children are vastly overrated, with their whining and constant demands.'

'All I ask is for a sensible conversation once in a while.'

'Sometimes,' Clarissa sighed deeply, 'my friends can be very immature. Perhaps . . . ' She waited.

'Perhaps what?'

'I like to walk on the beach in the early mornings. There's never a soul about. Perhaps we might run into each other there and enjoy some adult,' she moistened her lips and glanced up at him from under her eyelashes, 'conversation?'

He glanced down at her hand, still resting on his wrist. 'Tomorrow?' he said.

Got him! She removed her hand. 'But you'd better go now. Mr Fairchild will be here at any moment. Best to avoid a *contretemps*, don't you think?'

He nodded and rose to his feet. 'Tomorrow morning then, Miss . . . '

'Stanton. Clarissa Stanton. I shall anticipate our meeting with great pleasure.'

After he'd gone, she was unable to decide if she was excited by the prospect of another chase or if it sickened her.

Edith arrived soon after, her cheeks pink from the cold and her arms full of packages.

'Where's Benedict?' asked Clarissa.

'In the public bar.' Her friend delved into her basket. 'Look, I've bought this length of garnet moleskin for my painting dress and another in olive green, which will be perfect for Dora. And I've a basket of fresh eggs, new-baked bread, and mutton, onions and carrots for a stew.' She frowned. 'I do hope Dora knows how to make mutton stew because I certainly don't.'

'She appears to be perfectly at home in a kitchen.'

'But she's a guest and I can't keep asking her to cook our dinner.' Edith sighed. 'I do hope Mama will find a cook for us soon.'

Benedict strolled through the doorway, followed by the sloe-eyed barmaid carrying a tea tray. 'This is Tamsyn,' he said. 'She's agreed to pose for me tomorrow afternoon.' He briskly rubbed his palms together.

Clarissa looked at the girl's plump pink lips and curvaceous figure and hoped Benedict didn't have any plans for her other than as his model.

He studied the girl with his head on one side. 'Just some sketches at first.'

'I'll spare you three hours between morning and evening trade,' said Tamsyn, setting out the cups. 'And I want paying at the end of each sitting.' She nodded at Benedict and sashayed back to the public bar.

'I didn't know you were looking for a model,' said Edith.

'I wouldn't be, if only you'd let me paint you,' he said.

'I can't take time away from my work! At least, not until Mr Rosenberg's canvas is finished.'

'So you've told me. Several times,' said Benedict. 'So Tamsyn will have to do. There's a certain insolence about her that intrigues me.'

'Hopefully, then, you'll stop distracting the rest of us by prowling around the studio and breathing over our shoulder every five minutes,' said Clarissa.

Benedict shrugged. 'I've been unsettled. Tamsyn will begin a new chapter for me.'

'Coming to Spindrift House is the start of a new chapter for all of us,' said Clarissa. She banished her unease about her intentions towards Hugh Penrose and his unpleasant wife, and talked instead of her plans to design a collection of jewellery to be known as *Sea Glass*.

★   ★   ★

The following morning, Clarissa woke early after a night broken by dread-filled dreams of her childhood. She sat on the edge of the bed having second thoughts about encouraging Hugh Penrose, wondering if the euphoria of seducing and then ditching him would be worth the effort. She removed her nightgown and stared at the myriad silvery lines on the inside of her thighs; old scars from where she'd cut herself again and again when she was younger. In some peculiar way the act had relieved her terrible distress. For a while anyway. Sighing, she washed and dressed.

A short while later, she went to the cove and was almost relieved to find it deserted. She strolled along the strand, her gaze fixed on the flotsam and jetsam, searching for a pair of shells she might fashion into a locket or fragments of sea glass to embellish hatpins. Her sketchbook was full of designs now but she was pondering how on earth she might actually make them when she heard a shout.

Hugh was clambering over the rocks by the foot of the steps to Cliff House. She waited while he sprinted over the sand towards her, planning to knock the conceit out of him by telling him he was too late and she was about to leave.

'I couldn't get away,' he said, when he reached her. His eyes were bright and his fair hair ruffled by the breeze. His hopeful smile made him appear younger and more attractive.

'Two more minutes and I would have left,' she said.

'What have you there?' He nodded at her collecting bag.

'I was searching for sea glass.'

'I used to collect that when I was a boy. What do you want it for?'

'To make into jewellery.'

'Aren't you a painter like the others?'

She nodded. 'I was. Designing costume jewellery is a new venture for me. I'm going to write to some jewellers in London to ask for advice on how to make up my designs.'

'Why don't you visit the jeweller's shop in Wadebridge?'

She was surprised by his helpful suggestion. 'I haven't been to Wadebridge yet. In fact, I don't know Cornwall at all. Tell me about Port Isaac.'

He shrugged. 'It's a fishing village and there's farming all around but little mining anymore. Of course, smuggling used to be a busy trade hereabouts.'

'But not now?'

'The Golden Lion had . . . probably still has . . . a secret passage down to the harbour. The brandy was hidden in the cellars. There are any number of caves along the coast where the smugglers hid their contraband.' He pointed at a shadowy cleft in the cliff face behind them. 'Including that one.'

'Are you teasing me?'

He regarded her speculatively. 'I'll show you.'

They scrambled over the rocks and he put his hands around her narrow waist to lift her down onto the sand. He didn't release her immediately but leaned towards her as if he intended to kiss her.

Laughing, Clarissa wriggled out of his grip. Looking back provocatively over her shoulder, she walked away. She wasn't going to make it that easy for him.

The cave stank of rotting seaweed and the walls trickled water.

'Do you see the wide fissure in the rock there?' Hugh said, peering into the shadows. 'Smugglers squeezed through into a larger cave behind and stored the goods there. It's underwater here at high tide but the rear cave is higher so the contraband remained dry.'

Clarissa shuddered at the thought of slithering between the two great slabs of rock into a pitch-black cavern with the weight of the cliff above. 'Did you ever go in there?'

'As a dare, when I was a boy.' He grinned at her. 'I dropped my lantern and had nightmares for weeks afterwards, imagining the ghosts of smugglers from long ago were throttling me so I wouldn't tell their secrets.'

She shivered. 'It's cold. Shall we go?'

'Not just yet.' Reaching out, he caught a strand of hair that had escaped from the knot at the nape of her neck and ran it through his fingers. 'It's so silky. I want to see it loose.'

'Do you now?' She pulled the tress away from him. 'You know a lady never wears her hair down in public. That's only for the privacy of the bedroom.'

'I'm sure it could be arranged.' Suddenly, he lunged at her, pressing her back against the seeping rock, and covering her face in hot, moist kisses.

His moustache prickled her top lip and she recoiled, a wave of fear and disgust overwhelming her. His mouth was on her neck now and his hand clutching at her skirt. Breathing shallowly, she forced herself to remain calm. This was what she'd planned. It was a means to an end but she must remain in control. 'Hugh!' Firmly, she lifted his hand off her hip.

'What?' His eyes were glazed.

135

'You forget yourself!' She fixed him with an unsmiling and haughty gaze.

He blinked and then bit his lip. 'I thought . . . '

'You thought what? That I was a common tart who would expect no more than to be pushed up against a wall?'

'But you came to meet me . . . '

'For the purpose of conversation. What do you think your wife would say if she knew how you'd behaved?'

He stepped back as quickly as if he'd touched burning coals. 'I apologise unreservedly, Miss Stanton. I completely misunderstood your intentions.'

Clarissa bit the inside of her cheeks to stop herself from smiling as she watched him squirm. 'You certainly need lessons in how to please a woman. You cannot simply run at her like a bull at a gate. Now, come here.'

He stared at her, his eyes wary.

She cupped his face in her hands, as tenderly as if she loved him, and kissed him. Sliding her arms around his neck, she pressed herself against the length of his body, her lips never leaving his. 'Now you may kiss me,' she whispered.

Tentatively, he returned her kiss.

She leaned back to look at him, her arms linked behind his neck. 'There, that was so much better. Lesson one: if lovemaking is pleasurable, a woman will want more.' She moistened her lips. 'Perhaps once again, before I have to leave?' This time she kissed him with simulated passion and felt him grow hot against her.

She disentangled herself. 'I must go.'

'Go?' His cheeks were flushed.

'Shall we meet again tomorrow?'

'Yes.' His voice was hoarse. 'Yes, please.'

'Don't be late, then.' She pecked his cheek and led him out of the cave.

14

Christmas Eve 1892

Rain lashed at the studio windows and a dazzling flash of lightning rent the darkening sky. A thunderclap made Edith jump and a blob of paint dropped from her brush.

Pascal left his easel to watch the storm from the window. 'What a painting that would make!' He smiled at her, his eyes glittering.

She went to stand beside him. Forked lightning lit up the sky, closely followed by a crack of thunder. 'How dramatic,' she murmured. She caught a hint of his bay rum hair oil, rich and spicy, and had to deny an impulse to lean towards him. His presence made her uneasy, reminding her of that time he'd held her so intimately in his arms. She'd half hoped he'd return to France for Christmas. At least he'd remained true to his promise and hadn't attempted again to discuss what had happened between them.

She returned to her easel but her concentration had fled. Mr Rosenberg's canvas of the amphitheatre was so nearly finished it would be foolhardy to risk spoiling it now. She and Benedict were to travel to London the following week to deliver it. Dora would accompany them and visit her family for a few days. She'd been corresponding with Wilfred and was very excited because he'd made an appointment for her to meet the editor of a magazine that might be interested in her illustrations.

Edith massaged her shoulders to relieve the tension that had never released its grip on her in the past weeks. Anxiety over whether the canvas would be finished in time had been intensified by her dread of telling Benedict she was expecting. She'd waited until sufficient time had passed so that he'd assume the child was his but then her courage had failed her in case he read the terrible lie in her eyes. Her waist was thickening and, even though it was disguised beneath her painting dress, she could delay no longer.

There was another crash of thunder and Benedict laughed in the adjacent studio when Tamsyn Pengelly let out a shriek. The smoke from his Moroccan cigarette drifted on the air, pungent and earthy. It pleased Edith he was working again and, though she thought Tamsyn a pert little creature, there was no doubt she was the muse Benedict had needed to inspire him. He'd already finished some creditable pastel drawings and an oil portrait and was working on another.

She tiptoed into the other room to see his progress. Tamsyn, wearing only a chemise, sat on the edge of the iron bedstead with her chin on her knees and her arms wrapped around her shins. She flicked a glance at Edith.

'Keep still, Tamsyn!' commanded Benedict.

She sighed heavily. 'Aren't you finished yet? I'm frozen, sitting here almost starkers! Poke up the fire a bit, will you?'

Ignoring her, he said, 'What do you think, Edith?'

He'd captured Tamsyn's dark looks and sly expression very well. 'It's good,' she said. 'You're back on form, Benedict.' It mattered to her that he was taking his work seriously again, rebuilding her damaged opinion not only of his painting, but also of his dedication to it.

Smiling, he kissed the top of her head. 'I'll take these with me when we go to London and try my luck at some of the galleries.'

'The storm has ruined my concentration and I'm finishing for the day.'

'And I need to get back to the Golden Lion,' said Tamsyn. 'Old Curnow will skin me alive if I'm late for my shift, what with it being Christmas Eve. All the reg'lars'll be in.' She scurried behind the screen to dress.

Benedict dunked his brushes in a jar of muddy-looking turpentine.

Edith went downstairs and found Dora and Clarissa hanging home-made paper chains in the drawing room. A fire crackled in the grate and they'd decorated the Christmas tree with gold bows and lanterns of scarlet paper.

'I haven't had so much fun cutting and sticking since I was in the nursery,' said Clarissa. 'At home we have mouth-blown glass baubles on the tree, 'specially imported from Switzerland. Father would be very scathing about our efforts but it looks very jolly, doesn't it?'

Dora laughed. 'My pa would have a fit at the expense of using coloured paper. We always use newspaper for our paper chains. Still, we've made a wreath from holly and ivy out of the garden, so that wasn't dear.' She sighed. 'It's going to seem strange being away from home on Christmas Day.'

'I feel as if I've been reprieved by *not* being at home,' said Clarissa.

Edith glanced at her, taken aback by the bleakness of her tone. 'It's beautifully festive,' she said. 'There wouldn't have been any decorations if it had been left to me.'

'Mrs Jenkins was looking for you,' said Dora.

Reluctantly, Edith set off for the kitchen. Despite Dora's lessons on gutting fish and making scones, she'd found cooking to be fraught with pitfalls and an exceedingly tiresome distraction from her work. To her great relief, Mrs Jenkins, cook-housekeeper, had arrived a month since, interviewed in London by Edith's mother. There was no doubt they were all eating better since Mrs Jenkins's arrival but she was determined to make it clear at every possible opportunity that her new situation wasn't at all what she was used to after working for a titled lady in Hanover Square.

The kitchen was filled with the aroma of cinnamon and oranges and Mrs Jenkins sat at the table in the midst of a cloud of feathers, plucking the goose that was to be the centrepiece of the Christmas dinner. The room was warm and Edith almost regretted they no longer ate scratch meals of fried mackerel or bread and cheese at the kitchen table but now dined in formal splendour in the chilly dining room.

141

'You wished to speak to me, Mrs Jenkins?' she said.

'I did, madam.' Her mouth was pressed together in a thin line and her narrow figure was taut with disapproval. Edith's heart sank. 'This goose isn't the size I ordered,' the cook said. 'I'll be hard pressed to feed five people with it, never mind have any leftovers for my own dinner. I complained to the butcher's boy but he said it was the last bird left in the shop. All the good ones had been spoken for.'

'I see.' Now it was denuded of its feathers, the bird did indeed look rather scrawny. 'Can't we have some extra roast potatoes or bread sauce to make up for it?'

'That's hardly the point, madam.'

'Isn't it?'

'I have my reputation to think of.' She shook her head. 'I don't care to have the word put about that people leave my table unsatisfied.'

Ten minutes of dreary conversation ensued after Edith offered to reprimand the butcher and Mrs Jenkins took offence because she imagined her mistress was suggesting the cook wasn't capable of tearing him off a strip herself. Edith apologised and listened to a litany of other grievances ending in 'This would never have happened in Hanover Square', before she was able to escape.

Pascal and Benedict had finished work and there was much merriment as they hung over the banisters tying an ivy garland up the stairs. Edith placed sprigs of holly over the pictures and joined in the fun but all the time she was fretting over telling Benedict about the baby. It was impossible, however, to catch him alone for even a minute. After they'd finished hanging the decorations and had their tea, he went off with Pascal to the Golden Lion. Mrs Jenkins was complaining about the dinner growing cold by the time they returned, full of Christmas spirits and clutching a bunch of mistletoe. After dinner, Benedict opened a bottle of port and refused to hear of the ladies retiring to the drawing room.

Edith reflected on how much she'd changed from the horror-struck bride who'd so wanted Spindrift House to be perfect before they invited guests, that it had instigated a terrible quarrel. Now, she loved having them to stay and felt as if they were a new family. None of them cared a jot the house hadn't been decorated; they were far too immersed in their work.

Clarissa put a hand over her mouth to suppress a yawn and reached out with a languid hand for the decanter. 'I can't tell you how relieved I am we've given up changing for dinner. It's unthinkable the amount of time I used to waste at home, changing clothes several times a day.'

Edith giggled. 'If Mama could see us now, she'd be utterly shocked at our lack of regard for the social niceties.' She picked a clump of dried paint off her sleeve. 'All that seems so frivolous these days, doesn't it?'

Benedict poured himself a second glass of port and lit a cigarette.

'One of my favourite things about staying here,' said Dora, 'is that no one tells me I'm being selfish because I want to draw instead of scrubbing the front step.'

Benedict laughed. 'I promise never to ask you to scrub the front step, Dora. Do you know what I'm looking forward to most of all tomorrow?'

She shook her head.

He blew out a series of perfect smoke rings, pleased with himself. 'Enjoying Christmas dinner without having to be polite to my father's tedious business acquaintances, ancient great-aunts, crusty old generals and the odd bishop or two. Here we make our own rules. We shall drink wine, sing carols round the piano, play charades and have a lovely lazy time without anyone to disapprove.'

It was late by the time Edith and Benedict retired upstairs. He pulled off his clothes and climbed into bed but Edith fiddled about taking longer than usual to brush her hair and fold her clothes, while she summoned up the courage to tell him her news.

'For goodness' sake, Edith, come to bed!' He threw back the eiderdown.

She'd no sooner joined him than Benedict wrapped her in his arms. She took care to respond to his kisses with apparent enthusiasm. In truth, as long as she blotted out that deeply ingrained picture of him with Delphine, their love-making was physically satisfying. Emotionally, however, she was always left wanting. It was impossible for her to respond to Benedict's advances with the same uncomplicated joy she'd experienced in their first weeks of marriage.

Afterwards, they lay side by side, listening to

the ticking of the grandfather clock on the landing. It began to make the slight grinding noise that prefaced chiming the hour.

'Midnight,' murmured Benedict. He kissed her nose. 'Merry Christmas! I'm going to give you your present now.' He reached under his pillow and took out a small box.

She opened it and lifted out a pair of tiny pearl earrings. 'Oh, Benedict! They're beautiful.' She kissed him, touched he'd made the effort to find her such a lovely present. 'There's something for you too, but it's under the Christmas tree.' She swallowed and seized the moment. 'I have another present for you, though. One I hope you'll love forever.'

'Intriguing,' he said. 'Where is it, then?'

She lifted his hand and placed it upon her stomach. 'Here,' she said.

There was a long silence and her heart was thudding so hard she thought he must hear it.

His hand grew heavy and the heat of it seemed to sear her skin. At last, he said, 'A baby?' His voice was hoarse.

She nodded then turned out the lamp in case he saw the fear and guilt in her eyes.

He pulled her back into his arms. 'I'm going to have a son!'

'It might be a daughter.'

He shook his head. 'It will be a boy.' He kissed her, not passionately but with great tenderness. 'When we arrived back from France, Mother asked me if you were expecting. She was sure of it but I thought it unlikely because we'd had that argument.'

145

Edith remembered her mother-in-law's questioning glance. That was when she'd first realised she might be pregnant. 'That day we arrived at Spindrift House, on the beach . . . '

He laughed. 'So the baby will be a lasting reminder of our new beginning.'

A lasting reminder of her shame and guilt. But, for the baby's sake, she had to put that behind her. The child would belong to her and Benedict.

Tenderly, he stroked her hair. 'I love you, Edith.'

She rested her head on his shoulder. 'I love you, too,' she said. And in that moment of great relief at unburdening herself of the secret that had tormented her for so many weeks, she did love him again. Gradually, his breathing grew deeper and she sent up a prayer of thanks that she and the child had been reprieved, together with a solemn promise to be the very best wife she could to him from now on.

* * *

Benedict announced their news at the breakfast table on Christmas morning.

Dora squealed in delight. 'Edith, that's wonderful!'

'Isn't it?' she said, studiously avoiding looking at Pascal.

'A baby?' said Clarissa.

The news appeared to have shocked her but it really wasn't so surprising that a bride of five months should be expecting.

Pascal pushed away his unfinished plate of eggs and bacon. 'Congratulations, *mes amis*,' he said. 'But now, perhaps you will wish your house guests to leave at such a happy time as this?'

His smile didn't reach his eyes but it quelled Edith's fear he might suspect the child was his. The timing of the announcement gave him no reason to believe that. He was probably more concerned about the possible disruption to his work that a baby might bring. 'Of course we don't want you to leave,' she said, her tone bright and cheerful. 'Besides, the baby isn't due for ages yet, not until late June.'

'But, Edith,' said Dora, 'what about your painting?'

'What about it?'

'You won't be able to paint if you have a baby, will you?'

'Not for a week or two, perhaps,' she said, 'but nothing will ever stop me completely. We'll have a nanny, won't we, Benedict?'

'Whatever you wish, my sweet.' He stretched for the butter. 'And I shall order a case of Champagne to celebrate.'

All at once Edith was ravenous. Her morning queasiness had vanished, along with her apprehension. She spread marmalade thickly on her toast. 'I'd better speak to Mrs Jenkins,' she said, 'and see if she has any queries about our Christmas dinner before we leave for church.'

'Must we go?' said Benedict. 'It's misty and cold outside but so cosy beside the drawing-room fire.'

'Of course we must,' she said firmly.

147

Dora chattered about the baby all the way to church, advising about the layette that would be needed. She was so excited that Edith let her run on but, when her friend talked of weaning, napkins and teething rashes, it brought home to her some of the more inconvenient aspects of becoming a mother. Not least that the baby growing inside her was a small person with his or her own personality. The thought unnerved her. Perhaps her blithe assumption that she'd resume painting a week or two after the birth was a little over-optimistic.

'Shall we walk ahead, Pascal?' said Clarissa. 'I can't abide all this talk of babies. The little creatures are always screaming and invariably damp at one end or the other.'

Edith felt Pascal's gaze on her and tucked her hand in the crook of Benedict's elbow.

'My son will be different,' said Benedict, full of confidence. 'I'll put his name down for my old school as soon as he's born and, once he's out of petticoats, I'll teach him to swim and paint.'

Dora smiled up at him. 'You'll be a wonderful father, Benedict. Isn't it exciting?'

Edith hoped she was right, on both counts.

The church was prettily lit with candles and decorated with boughs of holly, ivy and yew. They settled, as usual, into a pew as far as possible from the Penroses. It had been a relief to Edith on previous Sundays that, apart from some sharp looks, there had been no further distressing incidents.

During the sermon, her thoughts drifted to the following week when she and Benedict would

148

stay with her parents. It felt odd not to be with them for Christmas. She hoped her mother would be pleased about the baby. She remembered past Christmases, long before Amelia became ill, and recalled squabbling with her over who had the biggest helping of plum pudding and of crying when her sister pulled the arm off her new doll. She wondered if her parents would raise their glasses in a toast to her this year or only to Dear Departed Amelia.

The sermon finished, they sang the final carol. Outside, Mr Mellyn, the farmer whose land ran alongside that of Spindrift House, shook their hands and bade them a Merry Christmas. His wife, a fresh-faced country girl, proudly showed them Tom, the new baby she carried wrapped in a shawl. Edith gazed at his little face and wondered what it would be like to hold her own baby in her arms.

The Penrose family were standing beside the porch talking to an elderly gentleman. There was no other option but to walk past them. Benedict linked his arm through Edith's and led the way. It annoyed her that she lived in dread of an unpleasant scene every time they attended church. She hoped that, over time, they might build bridges with the Penroses. Her footsteps faltered; there was no time like Christmas Day to begin.

She faced them with a nervous smile. 'A Merry Christmas to you,' she said.

Hugh Penrose and his wife remained stony-faced and silent.

Embarrassed by their lack of response, Edith

149

bent to speak to young Noel. 'Don't you look smart today in your sailor suit?'

Jenifry glared at Clarissa and Edith sighed, sad that her effort to break the stalemate hadn't made an iota of difference.

Benedict tugged on her arm. 'Don't waste your time,' he murmured.

But then an odd thing happened. Jenifry Penrose laughed softly. 'Season's greetings,' she said. 'I do hope you all enjoy your little Christmas goose.'

'I'm sure we will,' Edith replied.

Jenifry glanced back over her shoulder at them as Hugh led his wife firmly towards the waiting carriage.

Puzzled, Edith watched the Penroses walk away. There had been something very odd about Jenifry's expression and it took her a minute or two to recognise it as amusement.

15

January 1893

Dora wriggled her fingers through the letterbox and smiled as she fished out the familiar string with the key tied to it. She let herself in and the smell of boiling cabbage and fried onions greeted her, the smell of home.

Ma was at the range stirring a pot and Dora's youngest brother, Alfie, was sitting at the table tearing newspapers into squares for the privy. His eyes widened but she put a finger to her lips, tiptoed across the room and tapped her mother on the shoulder.

Ma spun around, her careworn face lighting up at the sight of her. 'Dora, love!' She pecked her daughter's cheek. 'I was getting worried.'

'The omnibus's horse threw a shoe so it was Shanks's Pony for me the rest of the way.'

'Take your coat off and I'll bring you a cuppa.'

Dora tried to kiss Alfie but he squirmed away. 'Too old to be kissed by your sister now?' She laughed. 'It won't be long before all the girls'll be chasing you and then you won't be running away.'

A guttural grunt came from the corner of the room.

'Grandma?' said Dora, going to hug her. 'I didn't see you there.'

'Grandma's come to live with us,' said Ma. 'She had a funny turn and can't speak anymore.'

It upset Dora to see her grandmother's face all twisted down on one side. She'd already lost Nan and couldn't imagine a future with sharp-tongued Grandma Cox struck silent.

She hung her coat in the scullery and washed the dirt of the journey from her hands. Her nose wrinkled at the sight of the bar of soap, blackened and cracked. She'd become spoiled with the lovely scented soap at Spindrift House.

Ma placed a cup of tea on the table. 'Sit down and make yourself useful. Roll out the pastry for the pudding, will you?'

'I've finished,' said Alfie, stacking the pile of newspaper squares. 'Can I go out, now?'

Ma nodded. 'But don't be late for tea.'

In the corner, Grandma began to snore.

'There's no room, Ma,' Dora whispered, nodding at Grandma. 'How will you manage?'

Ma sighed. 'Pa wouldn't hear of her having the parlour for her bedroom. He said he'd go mad if he didn't have somewhere to sit and read the paper in the quiet of an evening. So Ivy's followed Lizzie into service. It's a live-in situation and now there's only Annie left.' She pulled a face. 'Grandma wets the bed, poor thing, so Annie sleeps on the floor.'

Rolling out the suet pastry, Dora tried to ignore the panicky flutterings in her stomach. She'd often grumbled about the cramped conditions at home but had never imagined there might be no longer be a place for her there. Grandma might go on for years. A hot coal of anger at Pa burned in Dora's chest. 'It can't be right,' she said, 'for Pa to push Ivy out of the house so he can read his paper. She's only fifteen. Besides, it must be a job to get Grandma up the stairs every night. She'd be much better off in the parlour.'

'It's your pa who pays the rent so what he says, goes.' Ma suddenly gripped Dora's wrist. 'How many times have I told you — if you bash away at the pastry like that it'll be heavy as lead?'

Dora glanced at her face and knew it was no good arguing.

'Did you have a good Christmas with those fancy friends of yours?' asked Ma.

'It wasn't the same without all of you.'

'Had a rich man's Christmas dinner, I expect?'

'There were plenty of trimmings but only a tiny portion of goose.' She decided not to mention the whole Stilton cheese, the vast roast ham studded with cloves, the chocolate truffles, the plum pudding bursting with fruit and flamed with brandy or the fine wines and bottles of port to follow.

'I'm surprised your friends were mean with the goose,' said Ma.

'They weren't.' Dora sighed. 'Benedict made enemies of the neighbours and it turned out they threatened the butcher to take their custom elsewhere if he let the Fairchilds have a decent bird.'

'Fancy that!'

'But then,' Dora said, 'on Christmas Day, Edith told us she's expecting.'

'Well, that was happy news then.'

153

'Yes.' Dora frowned. 'But I hope it doesn't mean we'll have to leave Spindrift House.' The thought made her feel hollow and sick but she couldn't remain as a guest there forever. None of them could. Her hands were floury so she blew a wisp of hair off her forehead.

Ma spread a mixture of cabbage, onion and bacon over the pastry. 'Roll that up and I'll fetch the pudding cloth.' When she returned from the scullery, she said, 'I'm sorry love, but you can see there's no room for you here. You can make up the trundle bed by the range tonight. You're going to have to find lodgings when you leave Cornwall. Perhaps Lizzie could help you find a live-in place?'

'I'm not going into service and I'm not going to work in the biscuit factory!' Dora drew a deep breath. 'I'm an artist. I've worked so hard and I won't give up now!'

Ma shrugged. 'You wouldn't be the only one to have to give up your dreams.' Her voice was flat. 'Thanks to Nan, at least you've had some time to indulge yourself. Money you could have put away for when you get married.'

Dora glanced at her mother, seeing again how worn out she was. In truth, marriage was the last thing Dora wanted for herself. But she wasn't going to get into that old argument again. She lifted the sagging roll of pudding onto the cloth and tied it up neatly with string. 'I posted some of my illustrations to Wilfred,' she said. 'He showed them to the editor of a periodical called *Nature Review* and he's asked to see me.'

'You think you can sell them?'

'I hope so.'

'Don't get your hopes too high, will you? Selling a couple of drawings won't bring in enough to keep you.' Ma lowered the pudding into the waiting pan of simmering water.

Dora slumped over the table, picking sticky lumps of flour from under her fingernails. Ma was right; she'd been lucky Nan gave her the money for the Slade and perhaps she was spoiled now. It was only by grace and favour that she lived at Spindrift House. It couldn't last.

* * *

The train was already at the platform, wreathed in clouds of steam, when Dora arrived at the station late and out of breath. She spied Edith waving at her out of a compartment at the far end of the train and sprinted towards her. Benedict jumped down to lift her case into the carriage and Dora scrambled aboard. An elderly gentleman and two ladies shuffled along the bench seat to make room for her.

'I thought I was going to miss it,' Dora panted. 'Grandma had a fall as I was about to leave and I missed the omnibus.'

Edith enfolded her in a hug. 'Was she all right?'

'Shaken and bruised.'

The engine's whistle shrieked and the train juddered into motion.

Benedict closed the window and placed the case on the luggage rack.

'I expect your parents were pleased to hear

155

your happy news,' Dora said.

'Benedict's mother was thrilled,' said Edith. 'She says she'll send us the biggest perambulator she can find.'

Dora wondered if Edith's mother had been thrilled, too, but the closed expression on her friend's face meant she didn't like to ask. 'I've been dying to hear,' she said, 'did Mr Rosenberg like your painting?'

'He did,' said Edith, beaming. 'And I have a commission for two companion pieces.'

'You never saw such unladylike behaviour,' said Benedict. 'She insisted on negotiating a higher price for them.'

'Benedict had a success, too,' said Edith.

'A gallery took two of my portraits on a sale or return basis,' he said, lighting a cigarette. 'And Mother bought another one for a very good sum.'

'But what about you, Dora?' asked Edith. 'How is Wilfred and was your meeting successful?'

'Wilfred was well, and I met the editor of *Nature Review*. He liked my *Seashore* illustrations though he couldn't use them at present. Anyway, he said if I did some wildflower paintings, he'd like to see them.'

'Well done, Dora!' said Edith. She yawned behind her hand. 'Sorry. It's been a busy few days and I'm going to close my eyes for a while.'

It was all very well, thought Dora, but unlike the other two, she hadn't come away with either money in her pocket or a definite commission, only the knowledge that she couldn't return

home. She was on her own and her future felt
horribly uncertain.

★　★　★

Clarissa continued her meetings in the cove with
Hugh but wasn't sure of him until the cold, grey
morning when he handed her a small velvet bag.

'A present?' she said.

His expression was tense. 'A mere trifle but I
wanted you to have it.'

She pulled apart the drawstring closure and
tipped a handful of sea glass onto her palm.
'Your childhood collection?'

He nodded. 'It meant a great deal to me once
but I'm sure you'll make good use of it.'

'Why, thank you, Hugh.' She was annoyed
with herself because she was touched by his
gesture. That wasn't in the plan at all. 'These will
give me a very good start towards my first
collection.'

He lifted her hand to his lips. 'Our meetings
are important to me, Clarissa.' He sighed. 'In
fact, they're the only bright spot in my day. My
wife is always easily irritated but it's worse when
she's pregnant. This morning she accused me of
not being attentive enough.'

'But you mentioned she frequently denies you
in the bedroom?'

'She says if I were more attentive, she'd be
more forthcoming.' He scratched his cheek.
'Blowed if I understand a woman's mind.'

Well, that was a blessing, thought Clarissa.

'I haven't been able to stop thinking about

157

you,' he said. 'Not for a minute. You've bewitched me.'

Exultation pulsed through her veins. She'd nearly snared him now. Softly, she touched her lips to his.

He kissed her and she didn't stop him when he pressed himself against her. 'You're driving me mad,' he whispered. 'I want to see your hair loose around your naked shoulders.'

She schooled herself to remain aloof. 'You don't imagine I'd let you have your way with me here, in a *cave*?'

'No . . . no, of course not.'

She suppressed laughter at the disappointed expression on his face.

He hesitated and then said, 'I had an idea.'

'Mmm?'

'I have to visit a client in Wadebridge next week.'

'A client?'

'I took over my father's architectural practice a few years ago. I'm drawing up plans for a townhouse there.' Hugh spoke quickly, barely able to suppress his excitement. 'I wondered if you'd care to accompany me? You could visit Trewin's the jeweller's while I deliver the plans to my client. There's a hotel where we could take lunch and . . . ' he caressed her cheek ' . . . rest for an hour or two before we return. What do you say?'

It was a great temptation to accept the offer of transport to the jeweller's. Perhaps the time was right to bring her scheme to its conclusion. Clarissa looked up at him through her eyelashes.

'How thoughtful of you. A lovely lunch in a hotel and then . . . ' She smiled. 'A delightful idea.'

★ ★ ★

Clarissa left Spindrift House after breakfast and walked into the village to wait at the junction of Rose Hill and Dolphin Street. Within minutes a carriage jolted into view and, almost before the wheels stopped turning, Hugh jumped out.

'You look ravishing,' he said as he handed her inside.

She noticed he'd parted his wavy hair neatly and flattened it down with pomade. His suit was well-cut and his shoes so shiny he could probably see his face reflected in them. 'I'm looking forward to our little adventure,' she said. 'Though I did wonder if your coachman might inform your wife that you were accompanied by a young lady on your visit to Wadebridge?'

'I thought of that!' Hugh said, looking inordinately pleased with himself. 'Mother always takes our carriage on a Thursday to visit a friend so I hired this one.'

'How clever of you!' said Clarissa. Her desire to prick his balloon of self-importance reasserted itself. She'd half-hoped Jenifry Penrose would discover their liaison after Clarissa finished with Hugh but perhaps it would be even better if she retained a more enduring control over him. She might then be in a position to prevent future discord with the Penrose family.

Hugh fidgeted during the journey. His fingers drummed a tattoo on his knee, he wiped the

159

condensation from the window every few moments and glanced frequently at Clarissa. Eventually he came to sit beside her. 'I want to kiss you,' he said.

She gave him a slow, considering look. 'I know.'

'May I?'

'Well, let's see,' she teased. 'Perhaps just one?'

Carefully, he took her in his arms and kissed her as if she was made of glass. When she didn't pull away, he risked showing a little more passion and held her tighter, his tongue exploring her mouth.

She relaxed a little; it seemed she'd taught him well and he was unlikely to force himself on her now.

They reached the outskirts of Wadebridge and soon they were driving into the courtyard of the Molesworth Arms.

'I wrote in advance, asking the landlord to reserve a private suite for our luncheon,' said Hugh, 'but first I shall accompany you to Trewin's.'

★　★　★

The jeweller's shop was situated in nearby Trevanson Street. There were two bow windows, each displaying fine pieces carefully arranged on midnight blue velvet.

Once inside, Clarissa hesitated. It was a very traditional shop and she wouldn't be able to bear it if Mr Trewin laughed at her idea. She stiffened her spine. If she were unsuccessful here, she'd simply have to find a more suitable jeweller's.

An elderly man sporting a magnificent set of mutton-chop whiskers came forward to greet them. 'May I be of assistance?'

'Miss Stanton wishes to discuss a matter of business,' said Hugh.

'Business?' Mr Trewin raised his bushy eyebrows. 'Do you have an item to sell, madam?'

'Indeed not! I am enquiring about commissioning several pieces of jewellery to be made in your workshop.'

'A matching set of earrings, necklace and bracelet suitable for evening attire?' His manner was obsequious. 'Sapphires and diamonds, perhaps?'

'Not today,' Clarissa said. 'I design costume jewellery suitable for the young independent woman.' Mr Trewin's eyebrows rose again. 'I intend to sell the pieces in London, where there's a market for them. May I show you my sketchbook?'

'I don't think . . . '

'I'm not suggesting you sell these pieces,' she said. 'I require only someone to make the items for me.'

He leafed through Clarissa's sketchbook. Shaking his head, he said, 'I cannot work with shells, pebbles or sea glass.'

Clarissa took from her reticule Hugh's velvet bag of sea glass to which she'd added her own small collection. She tipped them onto the mahogany counter, hoping to persuade him.

Mr Trewin picked one up and laid it on the palm of his hand. 'Your drawings are pretty, madam, but my skills lie in more traditional and valuable pieces.'

161

Disappointment made her sigh.

'However,' he continued, 'my assistant may be able to help.' He drew a curtain behind the counter. 'Mr Lobb, will you attend this lady, please?'

A gangly young man with auburn hair and a neat beard and moustache appeared, buttoning up his jacket.

Mr Trewin explained what was required, opening the sketchbook at random to show his assistant one of the illustrations and handing him the samples of sea glass. 'Perhaps you will take Miss Stanton into the workshop?'

'In that case,' Hugh said to Clarissa, 'I shall return shortly.'

The shop bell jangled as he left and the jeweller's assistant ushered her beyond the curtain.

A long workbench was situated under barred windows and a variety of pincers, small saws and hammers hung upon one wall. Reels of gold, silver and copper wire were ranged like books on shelves and two large safes were bolted to the floor.

Mr Lobb pulled out a chair for Clarissa and they sat at a table. 'May I see your drawings?' He took a pair of gold-rimmed pince-nez from his pocket and bent over the sketchbook. The pages rustled as he turned them but he remained silent.

Clarissa gripped her hands together as the minutes passed.

At last, Mr Lobb looked up at her. 'These are very appealing,' he said. He removed his pince-nez and his pale blue eyes gleamed with interest. 'Not Trewin's usual line of work, of course.'

'I'm a designer, not a jeweller,' said Clarissa, 'but I believe these pieces will be popular with young women. They don't all want to wear jewellery like their mother's; it's too expensive and too staid. Fashions in dress are changing and my jewellery will complement the new less formal styles.'

Mr Lobb nodded. 'Your difficulty may lie in the pricing. Will these items be affordable for the younger woman?'

Clarissa shrugged. 'The sea glass and pebbles are free, except for my time spent looking for them, but there'll be the cost of the other materials, and of making them up. And then I shall have to take them to London and sell them through existing shops, who will take a percentage.'

'I suggest the best course of action would be to make up half a dozen sample items and see how many orders you can obtain. You might consider using silver or copper for the settings, rather than gold. That would be cost-effective and perhaps also more in tune with modern ideas?'

Two hours later, after a most satisfactory discussion, they'd selected six designs. Mr Lobb promised to post a quotation within the week for supplying the necessary materials and making up the prototypes.

'I do hope we shall do business together, Miss Stanton,' he said, shaking her hand vigorously. 'It would be a most refreshing change for me to work on a project such as this.'

★ ★ ★

Hugh was already pacing up and down outside the shop, waiting for her. He offered her his arm for the short walk back to the Molesworth Arms. He chattered nervously about nothing in particular while Clarissa thought about her meeting with Mr Lobb and where it might lead. They arrived at the inn and were ushered to a suite with a private dining room on the first floor. The door to the adjoining room was slightly ajar and Clarissa glimpsed a four-poster bed hung with damask drapes. It appeared Hugh had been rather too sure that she was ready to be seduced.

The waiter, a young man with pimples, couldn't take his eyes off her and, just to annoy Hugh, she fluttered her eyelashes at him.

Hugh frowned and reprimanded the waiter when he spilled a drop of wine on Clarissa's sleeve.

'Really, it doesn't matter at all,' she said, looking up at the young man with a smile so dazzling he blushed crimson.

They were served mulligatawny soup, Dover sole and a delicate lemon mousse. Hugh dismissed the waiter, saying they'd call if they required anything further.

Clarissa enjoyed everything placed before her, keeping up a flow of bright conversation.

Hugh toyed with his lemon mousse, watching her while she ate. Several times he opened his mouth to speak, glanced at the bedroom door and nervously smoothed his moustache. He gulped down three glasses of wine.

She took her time, eating only tiny spoonfuls of mousse. She'd taken to earnest Mr Lobb. His respectful manner was unlike that of so many of the young men she met. Even Hugh had been well behaved today and she realised she'd lost her appetite for putting him down a peg or two.

Finally, she dabbed her mouth with her napkin. 'That was delicious,' she said. 'Aren't you going to finish your mousse, Hugh?'

His forehead was shiny with nervous perspiration. 'We'll have to leave within twenty minutes,' he said, his voice full of desperation. His glance flicked towards the bedroom door again and he cleared his throat. 'Shall we retire to rest in comfort?'

'But we haven't had our coffee yet. Such a lovely luncheon but it would be spoiled if we didn't finish it with coffee, don't you think?'

'Yes, of course,' he said. The light of hope died in his eyes and his shoulders drooped.

Clarissa bit the inside of her cheeks to stop herself from laughing aloud. Hugh really had no idea what a lucky escape he'd had. His disappointment because she'd avoided going to bed with him was absolutely nothing compared to the humiliation he'd feel if she had.

16

Edith's son, Jasper Arthur George, arrived in time for lunch in the third week of May. Her pains had started early the day before and Dora sent for the midwife, while Benedict took himself off to the Golden Lion. Edith laboured through the night, all the while panicking that the baby would resemble Pascal.

Dora remained steadfastly at her side. She wiped the sweat from Edith's brow and encouraged her near the end when she thought she would split in two. Moments after it seemed inevitable she would die in agony, Jasper thrust his way out of her battered body and into the world, yelling loud enough to burst their eardrums.

Exhausted, Edith sank back, shocked to the core by the discovery of how primitive and bloody an act it is to give birth.

The midwife wrapped the baby in a towel. 'This one's a lusty lad with a good pair of lungs on him for an eight-months child,' she said, placing the swaddled infant in Edith's arms. 'It's a good thing he was early or you'd have had a far more difficult time. Are you sure about your dates?'

'Absolutely,' she said. 'My husband is tall and big-boned, though.' Hurriedly, she pulled back the shawl with trembling fingers. The baby screamed, waving his fists in the air. His hair was dark and thick and his squashed little face was scarlet. She kissed his forehead and, surprised, he stopped howling and squinted suspiciously at her. His eyes were a slatey blue, not brown like Pascal's or green like hers. It was impossible to judge if he bore facial similarities to any one of his forebears.

Tears of relief rolled down her cheeks and she rocked her son against her chest, breathing in the new-born smell of his hair and skin, learning to know and love him. 'Welcome, little one,' she whispered.

'He's beautiful,' whispered Dora.

Benedict appeared large and out of place when he tiptoed close to the bed, white-faced and reeking of ale, his hair dishevelled. 'Are you all right, Edith? I heard you yelling.'

'Everything is well now,' she said. 'Will you say hello to our son?'

He puffed up his chest. 'See, I told you I'd have a boy!' He stared at the baby for a long time without moving or saying another word.

Edith's stomach clenched. Could he discern Pascal's features in the baby's face?

Her husband cradled one of the tiny feet in his palm and kissed each little toe. 'He's so perfect.'

The tension drained out of her in a long sigh.

Benedict kissed her cheek. 'It's frightening, the responsibility, isn't it? Nothing will be the same again. Will we be good parents, do you think?'

'We must be,' Edith said. Her voice was firm but, inside, she was scared, too.

The following day, after Jasper's morning feed, Edith came downstairs to the drawing room in her dressing gown. Benedict held her arm since she was still unsteady and Dora followed behind, carrying the baby. Gingerly, Edith settled herself on the sofa.

'I'll tell the others you're here,' said Dora, placing Jasper in her arms.

Edith's mouth was dry. Since Jasper had arrived, apparently early, might Pascal have guessed that he was the father? And, if so, would he say anything? The damage he could inflict if he said anything to hint at it was too awful to contemplate.

Benedict peered at the sleeping baby. 'He doesn't look so battered today,' he said. 'His hair is as dark as yours but I can see his likeness to me now.'

'He's going to be the image of you,' Edith said, crossing her fingers under Jasper's shawl. A few days before, Pascal had mentioned that his sister had given birth to a daughter. Edith wondered if Delphine was anxious her baby might not resemble Édouard. Best not to think about that.

'There are telegrams from our families,' said Benedict. 'Mother says she'll come and stay for a few weeks. Your mother says the same.'

Her heart sank. 'I'd rather get the baby into a routine first.'

Benedict grinned. 'What a relief! The prospect of the mothers descending on us for an extended visit isn't remotely appealing. We're so comfortable here and I couldn't stand all that *fuss* they'd make.'

168

'Mama would be horrified to discover we only have one servant and the house isn't as organised as she'd like it to be. We need a nanny, though,' Edith said.

Benedict raised his eyebrows. 'For one tiny baby who'll sleep most of the time?'

'I must get back to my painting. Mr Rosenberg won't pay me for the next canvases until they're delivered. Feeding the baby takes up so much time and there'll be his washing too. He'll need taking out for regular airings and . . .'

'There are enough of us to help out with that. Dora seems very useful in that way. Besides,' Benedict rubbed his nose, 'I'd expected my paintings to have sold by now. We can't afford a nanny as well as a cook.'

'But I don't know the first thing about babies! Mama always had a nanny for me and my sister. She couldn't possibly have managed without.'

'You'll have to. Besides, that sort of thing comes naturally to a woman, doesn't it? Once those galleries sell my paintings we might find a girl from the village to help.'

Edith couldn't say any more because Dora tiptoed into the room, accompanied by Pascal and Clarissa.

'Meet my son, Master Jasper Arthur George Fairchild!' said Benedict.

Clarissa leaned forward to look at the baby. 'They all look the same, don't they?' she said.

'I don't agree,' murmured Edith, hurt that Clarissa hadn't said something complimentary.

When Pascal drew closer, Edith kept her gaze fixed on Jasper's face, apprehension making her

169

tense. He stroked the baby's palm and Jasper curled a tiny hand around his finger. A sob burst up from within her but she disguised it with a cough.

'He is a very handsome child, Edith,' said Pascal quietly.

'He's going to be as handsome as his father,' said Benedict.

A shadow of a smile flickered across Pascal's mouth. 'No doubt,' he said. 'And you, Edith? You are well?'

His voice was so tender and concerned she couldn't bear it. 'I'm very tired,' she said. 'I think I must go upstairs to rest again.'

'I warned you, Edith,' scolded Dora. 'The midwife said you must have ten days' lying in.'

'Shall we wet the baby's head, Pascal?' said Benedict.

'Jasper's birth must certainly be celebrated.' Pascal gently stroked the baby's cheek with his thumb. 'And I shall raise a glass to my sister's daughter, too.'

Edith retreated to bed, more exhausted by the brief excursion downstairs than she could have imagined. Jasper slept in his cradle while she leaned back against the pillows, picturing her son's tight grip on his natural father's finger.

* * *

'I'm going into the village to post my latest designs to Mr Lobb,' said Clarissa at breakfast a fortnight later. 'Have you any errands for me, Edith?'

'May I walk with you?' she asked. 'Benedict promised Mrs Gloyne I'd take the baby to see her.'

'How exciting! Jasper's first outing in his perambulator,' said Dora. 'I'll come, too. Shouldn't we change out of our painting dresses?'

'My normal clothes are still too tight,' said Edith, 'but I can't imagine anyone in the village will care if we aren't in our Sunday best.'

It was a gloriously sunny day and even Edith and Dora's fussing over whether the baby would be warm enough failed to dispel Clarissa's good humour. She'd been working hard to complete her *Sea Glass* collection. Once Mr Lobb had made up the latest items, she'd taken them to London and Madame Monette had snapped them up.

The friends chattered together as they set off along the coast path, laughing when they had to lift the perambulator over some of the deeper potholes so as not to wake the baby. The hill down to the village was so steep Dora refused to let Edith push the perambulator on her own.

'You haven't fully recovered your strength,' she said, 'and we don't want any accidents.'

They called first on Mrs Gloyne but refused her invitation to tea.

'If I pick Jasper up now,' explained Edith, 'he'll need feeding again.'

Mrs Gloyne leaned over the perambulator and cooed at the baby. It never failed to amaze Clarissa what a to-do people made about such a small and, so far, uninteresting scrap of humanity.

'Childbirth is a dangerous time for a woman,' said Mrs Gloyne. 'I'm pleased to see you well but 'twas sad Mrs Penrose lost her babe.'

'I'm very sorry to hear that,' said Edith. She rested her hand protectively on her sleeping baby for a moment.

They waved goodbye and went to sit on the empty fish barrels down by the harbour, enjoying the sunshine and watching boys skim stones over the sea.

Jasper began to whimper.

Clarissa sighed. 'We'd better get to the post office before he starts yelling.'

Dora and Edith remained outside with the perambulator while Clarissa went in. There was a queue and she was obliged to wait a while before it was her turn. She was paying for the postage when she heard raised voices outside.

Jenifry Penrose was shouting at Edith and Dora, who clung, frozen-faced, to the perambulator.

'You brought your baby here deliberately to taunt me.' Jenifry's voice was hysterical. 'You *knew* I'd lost mine.'

'We heard your sad news only today but I promise you,' said Edith, 'we'd never do such a thing.'

Tears stained Jenifry's cheeks and her two small boys hid behind her skirts.

'Whatever's the matter?' asked Clarissa.

'You!' cried Jenifry. 'It's your fault.'

Clarissa caught her breath. Had someone seen her with Hugh at the Molesworth Arms? She hadn't been near him since then.

172

Jenifry pointed at Clarissa with a shaking finger. 'It's your fault. You ill wished me and killed my baby!'

'Don't be ridiculous!' Clarissa's voice was cold but her heart hammered.

Jenifry appealed to the women who were watching the scene. 'Can't you see? She's a witch! Just look at them, all dressed up in their heathen robes. They're witches, the lot of them!'

'You're touched in the head,' said Clarissa.

'How dare you? You *know* what you said to me outside the church.'

Clarissa frowned. 'Merely that an outburst of spleen from a pregnant woman might adversely affect her child.'

'You ill wished me!' shouted Jenifry.

Two of the watching women came forward to assist her and, sobbing uncontrollably, she sank into their embrace.

Another woman, carrying a pail of water from the pump, shook her head. 'You b'ain't from around here. You furriners had best get along home.' She stumped off down the street, the pail slopping water as she went.

In silence, Dora and Edith pushed the perambulator away.

Mortified, Clarissa walked beside them, her back very straight but her thoughts seething.

Edith sniffed and her chin quivered while tears poured down her cheeks.

Clarissa hated to see her so upset. Her baby's first outing should have been a proud day for her but instead it had turned out to be distressing. Jenifry was clearly unbalanced, her brain addled

173

by grief but, nevertheless, Clarissa wasn't prepared to allow Hugh's wife to get away with hurting her friends. She would take steps to right the wrong.

17

June 1893

It hadn't been hard for Clarissa to initiate another meeting with Hugh. She'd simply loitered along Rose Hill at the time she expected him to leave his office in the early evening. Once he'd closed the door behind him, she waited at the end of Dolphin Street and turned so smartly into Rose Hill as he passed that they collided. Hugh was obliged to catch her when she tripped.

'Oh!' she said, looking up at him with wide blue eyes.

'Clarissa.' He stared down at her upturned face and pursed his lips. 'Are you hurt?' He released her.

'Only a little shaken.' She clung to his sleeve. 'Thankfully, you saved me from falling flat on my face.' She gave him an angelic smile. 'Perhaps we might call into the Golden Lion for a restorative cup of tea?'

He shook his head. 'I must go home.'

'In that case, we'll walk up the hill together. It's so lovely to see you again.'

'Is it?'

She linked her arm through his. 'Of course it is.'

They walked in silence for a while and Clarissa glanced at him. He was frowning and smoothing his moustache.

'I was sorry to hear you and your wife experienced an unhappy event recently.'

'It's been awful. Since Jenifry lost the baby, you never heard such a wailing and a carrying on. She blames you. Thinks you're a witch.'

'You know that's ludicrous!'

He sighed. 'She can't seem to get a grip on herself. I daresay she'll have another baby but she never thinks of my feelings at all.'

'You need something to cheer you up. I know! It's an age since we went on that lovely visit to Wadebridge. What a shame it was all such a rush. If you have to go again, perhaps we'd have more time to linger after luncheon?'

He stopped walking. 'You want to go again?'

'I can't think of anything nicer.'

★   ★   ★

A week later, they were ushered upstairs to the private suite at the Molesworth Arms. The same pimply waiter as before served them. All through luncheon, Hugh complained about Jenifry's unreasonable behaviour. Clarissa rested her chin on her hand and gave him her whole attention, occasionally saying 'How awful!' or 'Poor Hugh!' She couldn't help thinking husband and wife were each as self-absorbed as the other.

After coffee, when he suggested they made themselves comfortable in the adjacent room, she allowed him to draw back her chair. Better get it over with.

He led her into the bedroom, which was

dominated by a four-poster bed.

She looked at the tapestry hangings and polished oak furniture and said, 'How lovely!'

'It's the honeymoon suite.' He certainly looked as nervous as a bridegroom. 'I wanted the best for you, Clarissa.' He took her in his arms and kissed her, carefully and slowly.

Keeping her gaze locked on his, she removed her hatpin and took off her hat. She loosened her hair and allowed it to tumble down her back.

Burying his face in the silky tresses, he fumbled at the buttons of her jacket. 'You're so beautiful,' he whispered.

Sighing inwardly, she helped him undo her shirtwaist and the various ribbons and laces of her underwear until she wore nothing but silk stockings and garters.

He scrambled out of his own clothes, nearly tripping over his trousers in his haste.

She held out a hand to him and drew him towards the bed.

'I've been dreaming of this ever since I first saw you,' he murmured.

Kneeling over him, she allowed her breasts and hair to brush his chest, touching and stroking him while he writhed beneath her, moaning with pleasure.

Panting and flushed, he turned her on her back and climbed on top of her. She closed her eyes so she didn't have to look at him while he pushed his knee between her thighs, clutching at her breast. She imagined, as always, that she was walking along the beach, breathing clean, salty air. The sea murmured its endless lullaby, the sound soothing away discomfort and fear. Mentally stepping into the foam, she began to swim, the salt water supporting her body so that she rose and fell with each passing wave. She lay on her back, eyes closed and drifting peacefully in the sunshine.

Something bumped her head and she blinked.

Above her, Hugh's sweating face was contorted in a grimace and his final thrusts banged her head against the headboard again. He groaned and collapsed onto the bed beside her.

She rolled over, facing away from him, trying to imagine herself floating on the sea again.

He rested a heavy hand on her hip and gave a contented sigh. A moment later, he began to snore.

After a while, she slid out of bed, gathered her scattered clothes and withdrew to the dressing room. Once dressed, she stood before the mirror, pinned up her hair and put on her hat. Dropping her hands to her sides, she stared impassively at her reflection. She hesitated a moment and then jabbed the hatpin deep into the ball of her thumb. Blood welled up into a scarlet bead and she let out her breath in a release of tension. Hugh and all the other conceited men like him thought they could take what they wanted from women but he'd find out he couldn't do that to her.

Returning to the bedroom, she shook him awake. He sat up hastily, his hair sticking out in tufts. 'Oh, Lord! I fell asleep.' He leaped out of bed and picked up his shirt. 'I promised Jenifry I wouldn't be late back. Luckily I paid in advance so we can make a quick escape.'

Clarissa let out a snort of laughter. 'Well, I suppose it is thoughtful of you not to be late home after you've spent the afternoon in bed with another woman. And it certainly isn't a good idea to upset Jenifry. I've seen what she's like when she's angry.'

Frowning, Hugh scratched at a mole on his buttock. Hastily buttoning his trousers, he slipped on his coat. A moment later, he stepped into the corridor. 'We'd better hurry.'

Downstairs, the hotel manager stepped from behind his desk. 'You're leaving, sir? Already?'

Hugh nodded and hurried towards the door.

The manager bowed to Clarissa. 'Was everything satisfactory to you and your *husband*?' His mouth curved knowingly.

She felt tawdry and cheap. Staring boldly back at him, she followed Hugh into the courtyard where their carriage waited.

Hugh reached for Clarissa's hand and kissed her fingers.

Flinching at the prickle of his moustache, she forced herself to smile. She almost felt sorry for Jenifry Penrose. Clarissa had intended to endure an affair with Hugh until he was so captivated by her that his devastation would be all the greater when she abandoned him, but suddenly the whole thing sickened her. The sooner she ended it the better. But she'd wait until the last possible moment before they arrived in Port Isaac, to minimise any opportunity for disagreeable behaviour on his part.

'Happy?' asked Hugh.

Enraged by his complacency, she pressed one

hand to her mouth as if to conceal a yawn. 'I've become quite sleepy,' she said.

'Wore you out, did I?' He preened his moustache. 'You have a little nap, my dear.'

She feigned sleep for the rest of the journey, pretending to wake only as they approached the outskirts of the village.

Hugh patted her knee. 'A most satisfactory afternoon! I'd thought you were such an ice maiden, enticing a chap almost beyond endurance.' He chuckled. 'But once I had you between the sheets, I roused the passion you conceal beneath that frosty exterior!'

Clarissa gave him a sideways look. 'Did you now?'

'I certainly did!' He trailed a finger over her breast. 'Do you know, I think I'm half in love with you already.' Peering out of the window, he banged on the carriage roof and it ground to a halt. 'You can alight here so no one sees us together. You don't mind a little walk, do you? We'll return to the Molesworth Arms next week.'

'Oh, I don't think so.'

'Sorry?' Hugh's expression was puzzled.

Clarissa gave a brittle laugh. 'Luncheon in a provincial hotel does not in any way compensate for an exceedingly boring twenty minutes in a four-poster.'

His mouth gaped like a mackerel caught on a hook.

'I was sadly disappointed. The best thing you can do, Hugh, is to go home to your odious wife.' She smiled sweetly. 'May I say, you're perfectly matched?'

180

'But . . . '

'I'm sure you wouldn't wish Jenifry to know about our little excursion today so it would be wise of you to curb any further unpleasantness, by either your wife or yourself, towards me and my friends at Spindrift House.'

Hugh remained silent but his complexion turned a sickly green.

The coachman opened the carriage door.

Clarissa fixed Hugh with a gimlet stare. 'Do I make myself understood?' She waited while he clenched his jaw and finally gave her a brief nod. Only then did she descend from the carriage.

She watched it drive away and all at once was deathly tired. As she walked along the lane she noticed a bloodstain on her skirt from where she'd pricked her thumb. She licked a finger and tried to rub it away but she knew with an aching heart that the rusty stain would remain forever.

★　★　★

September 1893

Dora worked hard all morning. She studied her finished illustration of Black Horehound through narrowed eyes. The deep pink of the flowers against the hairy heart-shaped leaves of dark green was very pretty. She'd built up a good collection of wildflower illustrations for her portfolio already but, now it was September, she had to forge on with it before the season ended. There was a creamy froth of Queen Anne's Lace growing in the lane nearby and she must catch it before it faded to brown.

On her way downstairs, she heard Jasper crying in Edith's bedroom. The poor little chap sounded desperate. She called out but there was no reply so she peeped through the doorway.

Jasper lay abandoned in the middle of the unmade bed, his face magenta with distress.

Dora hurried into the room, gathered him into her arms and walked him back and forth. 'There, there, little man,' she murmured. 'Where's your ma then?' His tiny body was damp with sweat and wracked with sobs.

There was a half-full bottle of his feed standing on the pot cupboard and he gulped it down, almost choking in his desperation. She rocked and sang to him until he sucked more slowly. It was a shame Edith hadn't been able to nurse him for long; a bout of milk fever had put paid to that, but it meant Dora sometimes had the opportunity to feed him and pretend he was her own.

Edith came in, still wearing her nightgown.

'Jasper was crying,' said Dora.

Edith sat on the edge of the bed and buried her face in her hands. 'I had to drop him and run,' she said. 'Oh, Dora, whatever am I to do?' She burst into noisy sobs.

'Don't worry! He's perfectly content now.'

'You don't understand.' Edith looked up at her with a tear-stained face. 'I've been ill every morning this week. I'm sure I'm pregnant again and Jasper isn't even three months old!'

Dora bit her lip. 'So soon?'

'Benedict won't be denied.' Edith's mouth trembled. 'He's already irritated because Jasper needs so much of my time. I was afraid he might look elsewhere if I wasn't accommodating.'

'Of course he wouldn't!' But Dora wasn't so sure. She remembered how he'd flirted with Delphine. Gently, she placed Jasper in Edith's arms. 'Look at his dear little face! When the new one arrives, you'll love it quite as much as Jasper.'

Edith sighed and kissed the baby's forehead. 'Benedict will have to let me engage a nanny now.'

Dora went downstairs.

Clarissa was curled up in an armchair in the drawing room with her sketchbook on her knee.

'Do you want to walk with me?' asked Dora. 'I'm on a hunt for wildflowers.'

'I might as well,' said Clarissa, yawning. 'I'm a bit out of sorts and so tired I keep dropping off.'

They set off along the lane, chatting about their work while Dora gathered a basket of Queen Anne's Lace, Gentian and Bladder Campion.

'I'll visit Madame Monette next month,' said Clarissa. 'Mr Lobb has sent me the new samples and I'll have finished designing the next collection by then.'

'Are you nervous?' asked Dora.

Clarissa grimaced. 'If she doesn't buy anything I'm in deep water. I've saved as much as I can but Father keeps writing nagging letters telling me to return home. I'm hoping Madame Monette will give me bigger orders in future and

183

I'll take my samples to show other shops too. I feel obliged to offer Edith something for my keep.'

Dora glanced at her. She was uncomfortably aware she'd not been able to offer their hostess anything. 'She was very upset this morning.'

'Did Benedict pick an argument again?'

'Not this time. She's suffering from morning sickness again.'

Clarissa came to a sudden standstill. 'Another baby?'

'It's far too soon for her to be in the family way again.'

'I hadn't thought about a baby.' Clarissa pressed her fingers to her lips. 'God in Heaven!'

Dora frowned. She didn't like it when Clarissa blasphemed. 'Benedict won't be happy, but it takes two.'

'I must go back to the house.'

'But we haven't finished our walk . . . '

'I need to pack. I have to go to London tomorrow.'

Dora's brow furrowed as she watched Clarissa hurry away towards Spindrift House. She knew her friend didn't care for babies but Edith's news had really ruffled her feathers.

18

It was dark and Clarissa was utterly exhausted by the time she arrived at her aunt's mansion flat in Devonshire Place.

'How delightful!' said Aunt Minnie, proffering her perfumed cheek to be kissed.

'I hope it's not too inconvenient at such short notice?' said Clarissa.

'Not at all.' Her aunt frowned. 'By the look of you, I'd guess you've been burning the candle at both ends. Or has your old trouble made you unwell again?'

'Not exactly.' Clarissa swallowed hard. She'd had nothing to do all day while the train jolted towards London except to think and, the more she thought, the more panicked she'd become.

'My dear! Whatever's the matter?' Aunt Minnie drew her niece down beside her on the sofa. 'Has something happened? A quarrel with your friends, perhaps?'

Clarissa shook her head, fighting back tears and failing. 'Aunt Minnie, I don't know where to turn.'

'A man?'

'Worse.' She drew a shuddering breath. 'Much worse. I'm pregnant.' There was a long, stunned pause while her aunt stared at her. Clarissa held her breath. Had she made a ghastly misjudgment in imagining there might be help available here?

185

'Are you quite sure?' Her aunt's voice was flat.

'I've missed twice. I've never been regular so I didn't think anything of it at first. Especially since a doctor told me the pain I have every month meant I'd never be able to conceive.' He'd said Clarissa had too much internal damage. She'd been deeply relieved she'd never have a child and it had left her free to have as many affairs as she wished. But now . . .

Aunt Minnie squeezed her hand. 'Will the father marry you?'

'No.'

'Already married, then?' Her aunt caught her breath. 'Not Benedict? I know you used to walk out with him.'

'No!' Clarissa scraped her thumbnails over the insides of her wrists, feeling the stickiness of blood as the fresh cuts opened up again. 'Please, Aunt Minnie, will you help me? I'm desperate. You're the only person I can ask.'

'Aren't you close to Edith?'

Clarissa pulled her cuffs over her wrists. 'I can't trouble her. She's unexpectedly pregnant only a couple of months after she gave birth to her son Jasper. I've heard there are medicines you can take . . . '

'Clarissa! That's dangerous. You must see a doctor. Perhaps it's a false alarm?'

'I've been sick before breakfast every day this week.'

Aunt Minnie wiped her face with her palm. 'Your father will be furious.'

'Don't tell him!' Clarissa gripped her aunt's arm. 'He'll kill me, I know it!'

'You're being melodramatic but, I agree, there's no point in telling Sebastian until we have to. He'd make life extremely unpleasant.' She drummed her fingers on the arm of the sofa. 'There are discreet places you can go to have a baby . . .'

'But I can't have one!'

'Calm yourself, Clarissa! We need to think.'

'I *have* been thinking. I've thought about nothing else since I realised.' She caught her breath on a sob. 'Once, a long time ago, Father threatened to put me in a lunatic asylum because I didn't behave as he wanted me to. He whipped me and told me then I was never to forget that if I became an inconvenience to him, if I ever shamed him, that's what would happen. And he said he'd make sure I'd never escape.' She hung her head. 'I'd rather die than be locked away in a madhouse to have this baby.'

'Please don't talk like that!' Aunt Minnie rubbed at her eyes. 'In the morning I'll send for my doctor. He's very discreet. Meanwhile, you shall have a light supper on a tray and I'll give you a sleeping draught.'

★   ★   ★

The following morning, Dr Bellweather attended, dapper in pin-stripe trousers and morning coat and bearing an aroma of eau de cologne. Clarissa lay, white-faced, on the bed while he examined her and the worst was confirmed.

'Please,' she whispered, 'can you get rid of it?'

'Certainly not!'

'I can't have a baby. Especially not *his* child.' She shuddered, remembering Hugh's complacency and self-satisfaction.

Dr Bellweather suddenly gripped her wrist. He examined the fresh cuts she'd made with her penknife and gave her a sharp look. 'Did he force you?'

Clarissa turned her face away, ashamed. Of course he hadn't forced her; she'd encouraged him.

'In that case, there are places that may be able to help you.'

She had no intention of explaining her culpability.

'I recommend a place in Yorkshire that takes in ladies in distress and, after the confinement, finds a home for the child.'

'No! I've told you, I can't have it.' She caught hold of his sleeve. 'I beg you! There must be something I can take?'

'Nothing that I can, or will, prescribe you.' Dr Bellweather closed his medical bag with a snap. 'Good day, Miss Stanton.' He strode from the room and shut the door firmly behind him.

Clarissa heard his muted voice in the passage outside, followed by her aunt's higher-pitched and urgent tones.

A moment later, Aunt Minnie opened the door.

'He refused to help,' whispered Clarissa. Despair tightened her throat. 'I have no money and nowhere to go.' She clenched her fists over her stomach. 'It sickens me to imagine it like some hideous little goblin growing inside me. I won't have it!' She pounded her stomach with clenched fists, wailing and striking herself again and again.

Aunt Minnie gripped her niece's wrists. 'Be still!'

All at once, Clarissa went limp and slid to the floor, her silken hair falling like a cloak around her shoulders. 'I wish I were dead!' She curled up on the rug and sobbed while her aunt tried to soothe her.

At last, she sat up and wiped her nose on the back of her hand. 'I've been a terrible trouble to you,' she whispered. 'I'll leave now.'

'Leave?' Aunt Minnie's tone was harsh. 'I love you dearly, Clarissa — you're the daughter I never had — but I'm frightened to take my eyes off you while you're like this. Where would you go? Home to your mother and father?'

Clarissa shook her head.

'No, I thought not. I will not sit by and allow you to harm yourself.'

'Dearest Aunt Minnie, you can't watch me all the time. My mind is perfectly clear.' Clarissa buried her face in her hands. 'I daren't ask Father to pay for me to go to the place in Yorkshire and I prefer not to live than to have this child and suffer the consequences.'

'You're overwrought. There is no other choice for you but to have the baby. It will go to a good home and you'll resume your life with no one but us any the wiser. You're not the first to be caught and you won't be the last. One day you'll look back and see matters weren't as desperate as you think they are now.' Her aunt stroked Clarissa's wrist.

'I'm never going to think that.' She was so

189

weary. 'I want only to fall asleep and never wake again.'

Aunt Minnie's brow wrinkled. 'You scare me, saying things like that. I'm going to give you another sleeping draught. Then I shall go out and make enquiries, to see if there is anything else that can be done.'

★ ★ ★

Clarissa lay in bed with her face to the wall all day. Her aunt's maid brought her a luncheon tray but she was too miserable to eat.

Aunt Minnie returned in the afternoon. 'I've been worried to death about you all the time I was out.'

'I'm sorry I've caused you so much trouble. Have you found a way to help me?'

'I spoke to someone I met through the Women's Suffrage Society. She's done a great deal to ease the plight of fallen women. We'd have to invent some tale to explain your absence to your parents but she tells me there's a place in Wales where the medical care is excellent.'

'No! I told you, it's impossible for me to ask Father for the money.'

'I could speak to him for you and offer to contribute to the cost?'

'Thank you but I'll jump off Tower Bridge first.' The breath was tight in Clarissa's chest as she fought down the rising waves of panic. 'I mean it, Aunt Minnie. I *have* to get rid of this baby.'

'If I weren't so frightened that you'd harm

yourself, I wouldn't even consider . . . ' Her aunt paced back and forth, wringing her hands. 'There might be another way. I've spoken to a woman who helps girls from the brothels when they find themselves in trouble.'

'Would she help me?'

'For a fee. But it's dangerous and illegal. Sometimes the girls die.'

Clarissa closed her eyes. 'I need to end this. I beg you to take me to her.'

★ ★ ★

The cab dropped them outside a terraced house in Kennington.

Mrs Collins, bone-thin and with her greying hair scraped back in a tight knot, waved them inside.

Aunt Minnie fumbled in her bag and brought out an envelope. 'I have the payment here.'

Mrs Collins didn't reach out to snatch it as Clarissa had expected.

'Not so quick,' she said. Her gaze raked over the younger visitor. 'You're not more'n three months along, dear?'

Clarissa shook her head.

'Come into the parlour.'

Heavy lace curtains made the room dim and the meagre fire sulking in the grate did little to warm it.

Mrs Collins sighed. 'I'll do what I can.' She took a bottle of whisky from the sideboard, poured a full glass. 'Drink this.'

Clarissa recoiled. 'No! I can't. Even the smell

191

of whisky turns my stomach.'

The other woman pinched her lips together. 'Do you want me to help you or not?'

Clarissa's heart raced as she took the glass and, gagging, gulped down the whisky. It wasn't smooth like Father's favourite.

Mrs Collins nodded her head in approval. 'It dulls the discomfort. Now we'll wait.'

Soon, warmth crept over Clarissa and her cheeks glowed. She was achingly tired and longed to curl up and sleep in the threadbare armchair.

Mrs Collins murmured something to Aunt Minnie, then helped Clarissa to her feet. She led her down the passageway and into the lean-to scullery behind the kitchen. She closed the door. 'Take off your drawers, dear.'

The scullery was bitterly cold. Shivering, Clarissa fumbled under her skirts.

Mrs Collins moved a cabbage and a handful of carrots off the table then covered it with newspaper and a ragged towel marked with rusty-looking stains. 'Lie on the table with your knees up.'

Clarissa lay on her back and stared at the cracks in the sloping ceiling while her skirt was folded back. Mrs Collins's hands were icy between her thighs and Clarissa tried not to think of the shame of it but, instead, imagined she was walking along a beach, listening to the sea and watching white seagulls circle against a blue sky. She felt a slight pinch as something was inserted inside her and moved about. She forced her thoughts back to the soaring seagulls and a briny wind tousling her hair.

About ten minutes later, she caught her breath as her stomach cramped.

'That should do it,' said Mrs Collins. She pulled a small mattress out from under the table, unrolled it and pushed it against the wall. 'Keep the towel under you. I don't want blood on my clean floor.'

Clarissa lay down and stared at the whitewash flaking off the brick wall. The cramps came in waves, deep down in her pelvis.

Mrs Collins brought her another glass of whisky. 'Drink it up, dear. You'll feel the better for it.'

Clarissa lay in a daze, jolted awake each time the spasms came.

Mrs Collins peeled the carrots, chopped the cabbage and pottered about in the larder. Every now and again she lifted Clarissa's skirt and peered between her thighs.

Clarissa dozed. When she woke the square of light through the scullery window had turned black. She was rigid with cold and her head throbbed. The cramps had faded to a dull ache. The scullery door was ajar and she heard Mrs Collins talking in the parlour.

A moment later Aunt Minnie leaned over Clarissa. 'There's a hansom outside and I'm going to take you home now.'

Clarissa blinked. 'Is it over?' Her mouth tasted sour.

'Not yet, dear,' said Mrs Collins, helping her to stand. 'I've done all I can. Sometimes these things take a little longer — even a week, sometimes. I'll give you a bundle of rags in case you bleed while you're in the cab.'

Swaying slightly as the whisky swilled around in her stomach, Clarissa frowned. 'Can't you make it happen sooner?'

Mrs Collins shook her head. 'I've told you; I can't do no more. Now get along home with you.'

Silently, Aunt Minnie took Clarissa's arm, led her down the passage and into the waiting cab.

★ ★ ★

That night, Clarissa barely slept. She stared into the darkness, waiting for something to happen, every nerve attuned to the slightest internal sensation. Her headache and nausea grew worse and she vomited into the basin beside the bed.

'Are you all right now?' whispered Aunt Minnie.

'It was the whisky, I expect.' Clarissa's teeth chattered. 'I've hated the smell of it for as long as I can remember. I feel awful. And it's so cold.'

Her aunt fetched another blanket and tucked it around her.

Eventually Clarissa fell asleep but her dreams were full of her father's angry whispering voice as he forced her to drink whisky from his hip flask while a terrifying little goblin with a baby's bald head shrieked with manic laughter and chased her down an endless corridor.

At first light she awoke, sweating and shivering, her mind confused by nightmares.

Aunt Minnie stroked the tangled hair off

Clarissa's forehead and rested her cool hand there for a moment. 'You're burning hot!'

The rest of the day passed in a blur. Clarissa's legs shook so much that when she tried to get out of bed they gave way. She dozed but when she awoke the walls pulsed in her peripheral vision and she couldn't remember where she was. And she was cold, so cold. It grew dark again.

Later, the light hurt her eyes and she was breathless, as if there was a cabin trunk pressing down on her chest, forcing every breath to rasp in her throat. A voice called her name but she couldn't move, too weakened even to open her eyes. There was a cacophony of discordant shrieks and cymbal sounds in her head and she dreamed the room was spinning around and around, faster and faster, sucking her towards a vortex. She screamed for help but her voice came out in a whisper.

Then, with the abruptness of a slammed door, there was only silence and complete darkness.

19

November 1893

Edith's back ached and she kneaded it with her fists. Pale sunshine came through the studio window and all at once she was tired of painting. Besides, Jasper would wake from his nap soon. She glanced at Dora, working nearby. 'Shall we take a turn in the garden before Clarissa arrives?'

Two months before, soon after Clarissa had made her hasty departure for London, Aunt Minnie had sent a note to say her niece was too ill to return to Cornwall. Edith wrote to Clarissa a few times during her convalescence but received only the briefest of responses, the last asking if she might visit them at Spindrift.

There was a cold wind but the sun was warm on Edith's face when she and Dora climbed the hillock to the gazebo. Dora took her friend's hand and laughingly pulled her up the last few yards.

Pascal, who'd set up his easel further along the boundary fence, waved to them.

Edith was happy to sit and catch her breath while they gazed out to sea from the shelter of the gazebo. She watched Pascal, leaning intently over his easel, eyes frequently flicking up to glance at the view and then back to his canvas. He intrigued her. Usually reserved, he sometimes caught her by surprise with flashes of humour and that wonderful smile that illuminated his face. She often watched him, driven by the fear that Jasper would grow to resemble him. Her future, and Jasper's, depended on Benedict never perceiving any likeness. At least she had no worries the new baby would take after Pascal.

She rested a hand on her stomach. Benedict had been pleased when she'd told him she was expecting Jasper but his reaction had been very different this time, almost as if she'd become pregnant to spite him. He liked the idea, but not the reality, of fatherhood. It was difficult enough for Edith to anticipate the new baby with any kind of pleasure without her husband's open antagonism.

'Look!' said Dora, rising to her feet and waving her arms.

Clarissa, wrapped in a caped coat, was hurrying towards them across the lawn.

Edith caught a hint of expensive perfume as her friend kissed her cheek. 'How was your journey?'

Clarissa pushed a strand of hair off her forehead and gave a tired smile. 'Long.' She had shadows as dark as bruises under her eyes.

'Are you better?' Dora asked. 'What was it, influenza?'

'Blood poisoning,' she said. She sat down, fingers clasped so tightly in her lap that her knuckles resembled a row of white pebbles.

'You still look peaky,' said Dora.

'But you're blooming, Edith.' Clarissa glanced curiously at the once-loose painting dress, now

197

moulded around her friend's thickening waist.

'Benedict's mother is ecstatic,' Edith said. 'Mama tells me I must give up painting.'

'But you won't?'

'Of course not. Painting is my life.' She saw Dora open her mouth as if to speak but then think better of it. 'Let's go into the warm.'

'Actually . . . ' Clarissa hesitated. 'There's something I need to say to you first. I'd prefer to talk about it out here.'

'How mysterious!'

'I've been planning all day how to tell you but now,' she shrugged, 'I can't remember any of it.' Slowly she unbuttoned her coat and held it wide open.

Edith stared. There was a distinct curve to Clarissa's stomach.

Dora gasped. 'You're having a baby?'

Clarissa held out her hand to show them a narrow wedding band. She lifted her chin defiantly. 'Despite the ring, I'm not married,' she said. 'However, I'm borrowing my mother's maiden name and calling myself Mrs Fitzgerald for the time being.'

Shocked, Edith didn't know what to say. After all, she was in no position to adopt the moral high ground over an illegitimate baby. 'But who . . . '

'He's long gone. It was a dreadful mistake. Dear Aunt Minnie has been an absolute treasure and helped me to conceal my condition from Father but I can't stay with her now I'm showing. There's her reputation to think of and if Father finds out . . . ' Clarissa's chin quivered and she swallowed rapidly.

'What are you going to do?'

'The child will arrive in March. I shan't keep it.'

'Oh!' Dora pressed her fingers to her mouth.

'I'd been told I could never have children and I've never wanted them. Nevertheless, I'm in a considerable predicament. If Father finds out he'll have me put away.' She clenched her fists. 'He threatened me with that before, even taking me to visit the asylum.' She closed her eyes. 'You can't believe how hideous it was.'

'What a brute!' Edith said. 'Of course you must stay here.' As soon as she'd uttered the words she regretted them. She should have asked Benedict first. He'd flown into a terrible temper when she'd told him she was pregnant for the second time and it would be too awful to fall out with him again. What if he had an objection to an unmarried mother living in his house and asked Clarissa to leave?

Sobbing, she threw herself into Edith's arms. 'Oh, thank you, thank you! I've been so frightened and I didn't know where to go.'

Edith remembered her own terror when she'd discovered she was expecting Jasper. Whatever Benedict said, she had no intention of letting their friend remain so fearful about her future.

★ ★ ★

Later, Edith climbed upstairs to the attics. When she reached the landing, she heard a peal of laughter coming from the studio. Tamsyn

199

Pengelly. She disliked that pert little madam but was relieved that the girl inspired Benedict to paint.

Tamsyn was busy dressing behind the screen, keeping up a flow of inconsequential chatter.

Benedict was cleaning his brushes, a cigarette hanging from the corner of his mouth.

'I need to speak to you,' Edith said.

'That sounds ominous.' He grimaced and wiped the turpentine off his brushes with a rag.

Tamsyn appeared, pinning up her hair. 'I'll be off then.' She clattered down the stairs.

'What do you think?' asked Benedict.

His portrait was technically competent but there was nothing new about it. 'It's good but perhaps it's time to find a new model?'

'Tamsyn suits me well enough,' he said. 'Besides, where will I find another girl with such interesting looks?'

'Does it have to be a girl? Some of the fishermen down in the village would make good character studies. Or the landlord's wife at the Golden Lion has strong features.'

Benedict stubbed out his cigarette on the corner of his palette. 'Horse-faced, you mean. I can't bear ugliness and prefer to surround myself with beauty.' He nodded at the swell of Edith's stomach. 'One of the things that first attracted me to you was your tiny waist. It's horrible to see you like this.'

She tried not to show the hurt his words caused her. 'Clarissa is back.'

'She's better, then?'

'Yes, but there's something I have to tell you.'

Edith took a deep breath, praying they weren't going to quarrel. 'I should have asked you first but she was so upset. I've said she can stay with us. At least until the autumn.'

'I'd always assumed she'd return. In any case, Dora and Pascal don't appear to have any inclination to leave and I like having them all with us, don't you?'

She nodded. 'The thing is, Clarissa's expecting a baby.'

His eyes opened wide. 'She's finally bagged herself a husband?'

'No.'

Benedict let out a shout of laughter. 'That's set the cat amongst the pigeons, hasn't it? I don't suppose her father's best pleased.'

'It's no laughing matter,' Edith protested. 'She's going to have the child adopted.'

'Good. We don't want any more screaming children here.' Benedict pursed his lips. 'She'd better stay away from the church and the village, though. The Penroses would be delighted to have visible proof of a fallen woman living at Spindrift House. That would confirm all their worst expectations of the unutterable vices of our community.'

'If anyone asks, we'll say Clarissa was married and widowed whilst she was in London. She's using her mother's maiden name.'

'No one will believe it.'

'Will anyone care? We don't have many friends amongst the locals. Anyway, Clarissa's offered to contribute what she can to the housekeeping and I think we should accept. Our household expenses are higher than I'd imagined.'

'I agree,' said Benedict. 'Especially since the Penroses have ensured the tradesmen won't give us credit.'

Edith returned downstairs, feeling relieved Benedict had taken the news so well. And, though she was sorry for Clarissa's distress, she was delighted to have her old friend back again. Pregnancy was more draining than Edith had imagined and the others couldn't be expected to understand. She and Clarissa would be able to compare notes about heartburn, fallen arches and even, perhaps, to laugh together about their frailties.

★ ★ ★

After dinner, the friends sat by the flickering firelight in the drawing room.

Benedict stubbed out his cigarette in the saucer balanced on the arm of his chair and lit another.

Edith was cradling Jasper in her arms while she gave him his bottle. 'I wish you wouldn't smoke near the baby, Benedict.'

Loose-limbed and heavy-eyed, he blew a stream of smoke rings towards the ceiling. 'Don't fuss! My father smoked and it never hurt me.'

Tight-lipped, Edith carried the baby to a chair as far away from him as possible. She worried that her husband was smoking more than ever these days and it seemed to make him even lazier than usual.

'What's been happening while I've been

away?' asked Clarissa.

'It's a slow business building up my portfolio,' said Benedict. He poured himself another glass of wine and passed the bottle to Pascal.

'It'd be a much faster business if you spent less time in the Golden Lion and more time working,' said Edith.

Benedict ignored her. 'It's impossible to work when I'm tired. My son is no respecter of my need to sleep and Edith hasn't yet got the hang of settling him.'

'He usually goes through the night now,' she protested, 'though he doesn't sleep so much in the day as he used to. I can't do more than a few sketches or a simple watercolour study while he takes a nap.'

'You need a nanny,' said Clarissa.

'Don't you start nagging me about that as well!' said Benedict. 'Edith knows she'll have to wait until I sell some of my work.'

'Now that I've sent my wildflower illustrations to *Nature Review*,' said Dora, 'I can mind Baby in the mornings sometimes while you work, Edith.'

Her face lit up. 'Would you? I'm desperate to start a new painting but it's impossible to give it my full attention when I'm with Jasper. I'm so jealous when I see Pascal working. He concentrates so fiercely he isn't even aware there's anyone near.'

'Oh, but I am,' said Pascal, his eyes smiling as he looked at her.

Edith's cheeks grew warm and she bent her head over Jasper. She hadn't realised Pascal knew that she watched him.

Dora said, 'Tell Clarissa about the gallery in Truro, Pascal.'

'They've sold a number of my seascapes,' he said. 'It has been an interesting year for me. I use quite a different palette here in Cornwall, cool blues, greys and greens instead of the hotter ochres and umbers of Provence. I am experimenting with colour all the time.'

'Despite my difficulties over the past weeks, I've had some success myself,' Clarissa said. 'While I was convalescing, I filled another sketchbook with designs. Once I was sufficiently recovered, I called on Madame Monette and she took all the sample pieces I'd had made. But first, I showed the samples to Marshall and Snelgrove as well as some small independent shops. I've had a few orders already and Madame Monette says she can sell more.' She rested a hand on her stomach and sighed. 'After all this is over, I'll return to London and see who else might be interested.'

'You can use this time to search for more sea glass and shells,' said Edith.

Clarissa nodded. 'I wondered,' she said, examining her fingernails, 'have there been any further difficulties with the Penroses?'

'Not directly.'

'What do you mean by that?'

'You remember that trouble over the Christmas goose? Since then, neither the greengrocer nor the coal merchant will give us credit. It seems Jenifry Penrose is determined to stir up trouble for us.' Edith sighed. 'After that row outside the post office, some of the villagers still think we're witches and most are convinced we live a life of moral turpitude. I stopped to pat a dog outside the grocer's the other day and its mistress pulled it away as if I carried the plague.'

'So it was all for nothing,' murmured Clarissa. 'I'd hoped the Penroses would leave you alone.'

Edith was surprised to see she looked utterly downcast.

'In any case,' continued her friend, 'I've made arrangements with St Catherine's in Truro for the nuns there to place the child with a suitable family. The adoptive father's a well-off stock-broker, so it's all perfectly respectable.'

'I don't know how you can bear it!' said Dora, her face stricken. 'Can you imagine what it would be like to grow up not knowing your real parents?'

'Actually,' said Clarissa quietly, 'I rather wish that were the case.'

20

February 1894

Edith stared at her canvas. There was something wrong with *Exploring the Ruins* but she couldn't put her finger on the problem. She knew her drawing skills were excellent but, nevertheless, the composition was lifeless. A business associate of Mr Rosenberg's had admired her three paintings of the Roman amphitheatre and she'd been thrilled when he commissioned a large canvas on a similar theme for his drawing room. She hadn't even started to apply the paint yet and it would be a race against time to finish it. Sighing, she rested a hand on her stomach. In a few weeks' time, she'd have another baby, only eleven months younger than her firstborn.

She peered through the half-open doorway to the other studio. Benedict was chatting to his new model and she wished he'd learn from Pascal and work harder. Merryn was a shy, pretty little thing, daughter of a local fisherman, who'd made it clear her father had forbidden her to pose naked. Benedict had almost completed a charming, if slightly sentimental, painting of her, supposedly looking out to sea as she awaited the return of the fishing fleet.

Edith went downstairs and found Dora in the sitting room playing pat-a-cake with Jasper.

'Has he been good?' Edith asked.

'Of course he has,' said Dora. She tickled him until his solemn little face became convulsed with giggles.

It gave Edith a pang of jealousy mixed with guilt to see how happy her son was in Dora's company but, without her help, Edith had little hope of working at all. Since Benedict wasn't earning a proper living as an artist, she simply had to make every effort herself. 'Have you seen Pascal?' she asked. 'I want him to take a look at my painting.'

'Isn't it the day he takes his art class in the village? He'll be back soon.'

Edith's spirits sank. She relied on Pascal to identify where she was going wrong. 'I forgot it was Tuesday. I'll take Jasper so you can get on with your own work now.'

'His cheek is pink. If he fusses, it'll be because he's teething.'

After Dora had gone upstairs, Edith dropped kisses on her son's nose until he chuckled and then put him on the rug with his bricks.

Clarissa opened the door, saw Edith making towers of bricks for Jasper and hastily backed out again.

Edith sighed. She'd imagined they'd support each other through their pregnancies but Clarissa avoided Jasper and refused to speak about her own child.

There was a sudden crash and the baby wailed. He'd crawled across the room while his mother was distracted and pulled over the coal scuttle. She soothed him and bent awkwardly to pick up the scattered lumps of coal. There were footsteps behind her and she glanced up to see Pascal.

'Edith, I will do it.'

'Thank you. It's hard for me to reach the floor now.'

He cleared up the mess and then sat down beside her, wiping coal dust from his fingers. 'Keep still!' He dabbed at her face with a corner of his handkerchief and showed her the black smudge. 'Now you are perfect again.' There was a warm smile in his brown eyes. Their gazes locked for a fraction too long and Edith realised she was holding her breath.

Then Jasper hauled himself up by Pascal's knees into a wobbly standing position.

'How clever you are, *mon petit!*' he said. 'He is growing so fast, Edith.' He lifted the little boy onto his lap and jiggled him up and down.

Edith felt like crying. Why couldn't Benedict show such interest in Jasper?

Frowning, Pascal peered at the child's face. 'His eyes have turned brown.'

'Hazel,' she said, quickly, 'like Benedict's.'

Unsmiling, Pascal studied her face.

Despite the trembling that seized her limbs, she stared straight back at him.

'Are you happy again, Edith?'

Some of her tension dissipated. 'Can't you see that I am?'

Jasper struggled to get down and Pascal sat him on the rug. 'I see you are a dutiful wife and a loving mother and that you are kind to your friends. I see you work very hard, always striving to make each painting better than the last. But I do not hear you laugh with simple joy as you once did — except perhaps when you are with your son. And I cannot forget the Edith who one day thought her world had ended and she would die of grief. Recollecting your sorrow on that day still distresses me.'

'I'm not talking about that!' She looked down at her knuckles, greeny-white as she clenched the arm of the sofa.

Pascal looked away. 'I carry the burden of my own dishonourable action every day. I am ashamed I wasn't strong enough to resist temptation. And yet I cannot regret that, for a few glorious moments, we were together. But because of what we did, I must ask you this.' His voice was quiet but insistent. 'Is Jasper my son?'

'No!' Her heart thudded so hard, she wondered if it would burst. 'Jasper was conceived at Spindrift House, on the day Benedict and I arrived here.'

Pascal scrutinised her for a long moment and then his shoulders sagged. 'When he was born so early, I was sure he must be my child,' he said in a low tone. 'I thought, I hoped . . . ' He rubbed his eyes as if they hurt him. 'I feel a *lien* . . . how do you say it? . . . a connection with him. Perhaps that is no surprise because of my feelings for you . . . '

'For me?' Heat flooded her chest and throat.

'Of course, for you! When you arrived in France, you shone so brightly it was hard for me to look at you. It was a *coup de foudre*, a thunderbolt, that first time I saw you.' He

209

pressed his fist to his chest. 'I couldn't sleep, knowing you were another man's wife and there was no chance to make you mine. So of course I hoped Jasper was my son. In that way, you would always hold a part of me close to your heart.'

Aghast, she stared at him. 'Pascal . . . ' She couldn't find the words, any words, to explain her tumultuous feelings. She wanted to make the pain in his eyes go away but, at the same time, wished he hadn't told her because it forced her to face the truth. She admired Pascal more than she did her own husband.

He held up his hand. '*Reste calme*, Edith. I shall not talk of it again. I am *désolé* if I have caused you pain or embarrassment.' He didn't look back at her as he strode from the room.

She slumped against the sofa cushions, feeling drained and tearful. In another life, if she'd never met Benedict, she might have loved Pascal. Closing her eyes, she imagined them as a family where Jasper would grow up secure in his father's love. It was immensely painful to her that Benedict appeared to consider the child little more than an inconvenience to him. But there was no other choice for her except to rebuild her marriage.

Jasper whimpered and she enfolded him in her arms so tightly he began to cry.

★ ★ ★

The following week Pascal disappeared to Truro for several days, for which Edith was thankful. She spent hours in the studio, staring at her

210

canvas, unable to summon the energy to finish it and anxious because time was running out. Pascal's confession churned endlessly in her thoughts. It disturbed her to know the intensity of his feelings for her. She was distressed that he was unhappy but she could never tell him the truth about Jasper.

Late one afternoon, she heard Benedict calling her from his studio. She went to find him, carrying Jasper on her hip.

He was studying his canvases, all propped in a row against the wall. 'Tell me which I should take to show the London galleries,' he said.

She studied them carefully. 'Definitely this one of Merryn looking out to sea,' she said. *Waiting for the Fishing Fleet* was technically competent, if not entirely original, but she believed it had commercial appeal. 'And then these three of Tamsyn.'

'You don't like the others, then?'

Jasper crowed in Edith's arms, reaching out to touch a canvas. Benedict slapped his hand away, making him whimper. 'Quiet!' he said.

Edith kissed Jasper's fingers. 'Three of Tamsyn are enough. They're all very similar. Didn't you do some pastel drawings of Merryn? And then there was that one of Dora.'

Benedict pulled the sketches out of his portfolio. 'Pastel smudges so. They'd need framing but I could arrange that in London if any of the galleries will take them. They won't raise as much as the oil canvases, though.' He laid out the sketches on the table and sighed. 'Edith, I'm worried.'

211

For ever-optimistic Benedict to say such a thing, it must be serious.

'I made investments in the stock market that haven't done as well as I expected and Aunt Hester's inheritance is dwindling at an alarming rate.' He rubbed the back of his neck and sighed. 'How I wish we could go back to that golden time when we first arrived in France. We had such fun together then, didn't we?'

A small, painful lump seemed to have become lodged in Edith's throat. 'It was a magical time,' she whispered, remembering. Could they ever recapture that magic again?

'I feel as if I've lost you, Edith. As if I've lost *us*.' He touched her swollen stomach. 'It simply isn't the same now you're a mother.' There was sadness in her husband's eyes and she knew then that something was irrevocably broken between them. 'We're trapped in a marriage that isn't making either of us happy.'

Cold with shock that he'd articulated what she'd refused to acknowledge, she buried her face in Jasper's neck. She would never again be the naive girl that Benedict fell in love with and he was no longer the god-like figure she'd once thought him.

'Jasper needs me,' she said, 'but when he's a bit older . . . '

'Then there will be the next child.' Benedict sighed heavily. 'And more expenses.'

'I'll speak to Mrs Jenkins about cheaper cuts of meat,' Edith said. 'And perhaps we should stop drinking wine?'

He nodded distractedly.

Edith took Jasper away to give him his bath but anxiety and a terrible feeling of sorrow gnawed at her. It was more important than ever now that she contribute to the household coffers. If it hadn't been so close to her confinement, she'd have accompanied Benedict to London and attempted to find a new commission.

That night, she pushed away all thoughts of Pascal and made an extra effort to be loving to Benedict. They had to make the best of things and rekindle their marriage. She massaged his back but, when she kissed and stroked him as a prelude to making love, he turned away irritably, saying he was tired. His rejection made her feel ugly and unwanted.

She couldn't sleep and lay stiffly beside him, her arms cradling her stomach as their baby moved restlessly within her.

★ ★ ★

Later that week, Edith waved goodbye to Benedict when he set off for London with his portfolio. She'd vowed to make a monumental effort to progress with her commission while he was away and went straight to the studio. Forcing herself to focus, she rubbed away part of the pencil drawing and started again.

It must have been hours later that she heard footsteps on the stairs. She stood up in a flurry, feeling guilty she'd left Dora minding Jasper for so long. 'Sorry!' she called out. 'I'll come down now.' Snatching up a rag, she wiped graphite from her fingers.

213

Pascal, bearing a sandwich on a plate, appeared in the doorway and she stopped dead, her pulse skipping.

'You're back,' she said.

He placed the sandwich on the table. 'Jasper is asleep and you don't need to come down. Dora is working beside him in the nursery.'

'She's so good to me!' Edith sighed. 'Will you look at this? It's not right and I keep redrawing it but I'm beginning to panic because I'm running out of time.'

He stood back from the canvas and studied it silently for several minutes before he spoke. 'The draughtsmanship is good but it has no soul. Sometimes hard work isn't the answer. Look at you! Your shoulders are tense and your eyes so worried. You must stop holding your breath in fear and enjoy your work again.'

The sight of the canvas, all smudged with pencil lines, made her uneasy. Could she produce a successful painting by giving up her usual precise way of working?

'Edith?'

'Mmm?'

'I am leaving Spindrift House.'

'Leaving?' She stared at Pascal.

Pulling at his shirt collar as if it were too tight for him, he said, 'I distressed you and embarrassed myself by talking of matters I should have kept locked in my heart. It is better if I go.'

'You're returning to France?' A dull ache began to grow inside her, as if she'd swallowed a huge crust of stale bread.

He shook his head. 'There is still much in

214

Cornwall to inspire me. A potter I met in the Truro gallery told me about a community of artists in Newlyn.'

'Is that where you've been?'

'I have found a room to rent in a house owned by another artist and I will share his studio. A carriage will arrive shortly to take me there.'

'So soon!' The words burst out of her before she could stop them. 'Must you go?' Panic fluttered under her ribs. 'I hadn't expected . . . Will you write to us?' She couldn't bear to think he'd disappear entirely from their lives. From her life.

'Perhaps. Edith, I must thank you and Benedict for your most kind hospitality. Will you tell him that when he returns?'

She hardly heard the words. She'd grown so accustomed to his quiet presence that for Pascal to be absent would make her feel as if her world had slipped awry.

'It is for the best, Edith,' he said, his voice gentle. 'Newlyn is not so very far away and, if you should have need of me, write and I will come. Dora has the address.' He lifted her graphite-stained fingers to his lips and, a moment later, he'd gone, leaving nothing behind but the faint scent of bay rum.

She waited by the window until a carriage rolled up. A moment later, Pascal walked briskly down the garden path, carrying his easel and suitcase. Dora followed with his portfolio. At the garden gate he kissed her on both cheeks.

All of a sudden, Edith was desperate to run downstairs and wave him goodbye, but she'd never reach him in time. She didn't know whether he caught a glimpse of her or if, somehow, he sensed her desperation, but he glanced up. He remained motionless for a moment, looking at her. She pressed her palm against the windowpane, gaze fixed upon his face. He mirrored her action by holding up his own hand. Then he climbed into the carriage and it drove away.

21

March 1894

Clarissa stared out of the bedroom window. Clouds raced across the sky and Cliff House up on the headland was alternately shrouded in shadow and lit up by sunlight. Feeling fidgety, she decided to go down to the cove.

The difficult descent to the beach was worth the effort, to feel the sea breeze blow the cobwebs away. She bent awkwardly to pick up a glistening pebble at the water's edge and the wind flapped her skirt in her face. She'd never imagined it would be so hard to see her feet over the mound of her stomach and hissed with annoyance under her breath when a wave caught her by surprise, foaming over her shoes.

A black dog splashed through the shallows towards her.

Clarissa glanced around in alarm, anxious Hugh might be nearby. She couldn't stand for him to see her, all bloated by pregnancy. Shading her eyes against the light, she saw a figure walking along the sand. It was Jenifry Penrose. The last thing she needed was another *contretemps* with that vile woman. Shaking sand and seawater off her shoes, Clarissa hurried towards the cliff steps.

It was as she hauled herself up by the rope

handrail that the niggling ache in her pelvis intensified. Panting, she bent over until it passed. She glanced down at the beach again. Jenifry Penrose was looking up at her with her hands planted on her hips. It was plain to see Hugh must have made up his differences with his wife very soon after he'd impregnated Clarissa. Jenifry was expecting again.

By the time she'd dragged herself back to Spindrift House, Clarissa's pains were coming every ten minutes.

Dora bustled about, full of suppressed excitement as she put a rubber sheet and clean linen on the bed before she went to fetch the midwife. Edith instructed Mrs Jenkins to set water to boil.

Clarissa's legs shook like a leaf and she clung to Dora's hand. 'I want it over and done with,' she said, 'so I can pick up the pieces of my life.' And then there was no time to talk because the contractions came so thick and fast there was barely a chance for her to rest between them.

The midwife, Mrs Bolitho, arrived and took charge. 'My, someone is in a hurry!' she said. 'You're almost there.'

Clarissa strained and groaned. Perspiration trickled down her forehead. The pains were worse than the cramps she'd had after Mrs Collins had tried to abort the baby. She'd had nightmares ever since then about what terrible damage might have been done to it. Would it be born deformed or bear dreadful scars? She wouldn't look at it when it arrived, she'd decided, and once it had been taken away she'd

218

never think about it again.

Half an hour later, she let out a terrified scream and the baby slithered into the world.

'It's a girl!' Dora, with tears of relief glistening on her eyelashes, stroked the damp strands of hair off Clarissa's forehead.

The midwife wrapped the baby in a clean towel, a smile on her round, country face, and went to put her in Clarissa's arms. 'Your lovely daughter, Mrs Fitzgerald.'

Clarissa turned her head. 'Take it away,' she said.

Dora gasped. 'But you haven't even looked at her, Clarissa.'

'I don't want to see it. Take it away!'

The midwife tutted under her breath.

'How can you be so heartless?' said Dora. She burst into tears and fled from the room.

After the midwife had gone, Dora returned with Edith.

In a corner, the baby wailed in her makeshift cot made from a drawer while Clarissa cupped her hands over her ears.

Edith picked up the infant. 'Mrs Bolitho said you refused to feed your baby. Whatever your feelings are, it's not her fault.'

'Can't you make it be quiet?' whispered Clarissa.

'She, not it,' said Dora.

'I won't allow cruelty to a defenceless newborn,' said Edith. 'If you wish to remain at Spindrift House, you must feed her. She's entirely your responsibility until you're fit enough to take her to the convent.'

219

Clarissa hung her head, shocked by Edith's implacable tone and struck dumb with terror at the prospect of being asked to leave.

Edith sighed. 'I'll show you how to nurse her. Rest her on this pillow.'

Clarissa flinched away from the warm little body pressed against her chest. Perhaps she could manage to feed it if she made sure not to look. It took a few attempts until the baby latched on and Clarissa's toes curled at the strange sensation. It was both painful and curiously pleasurable at the same time. She was relieved it had stopped crying but she still couldn't look at its face.

The gong sounded in the hall. 'Now you're settled, we're going downstairs for luncheon,' said Edith, 'but I'll bring you a tray once you've fed her.'

Clarissa experienced a moment of pure panic at being left alone with the baby. It still suckled, making strange little snuffling sounds, but she kept her gaze fixed firmly on the view out of the open window. On the headland, the windows of Cliff House glinted in the afternoon sun. Hugh was probably home by now, completely oblivious to the fact that he'd become a father again. Anger seethed inside her. The brief flare of triumph she'd experienced nine months ago after shattering his self-importance would never compensate her for what had happened. She couldn't believe how stupid she'd been not to seek a second opinion about her supposed lack of fertility. Men could take their pleasure where they chose but they never had to deal with the consequences.

The fierce grip on her nipple loosened and the

baby's head lolled sideways. In the silence, Clarissa remained motionless, listening. Was it breathing? She flicked a glance at the infant's face and froze in horror. Its head was tipped back and the eyes were half-open with only the whites showing. Her pulse began to race. It looked dead. What hideous damage had it suffered as a result of her selfish irresponsibility?

She dropped the baby on the eiderdown and shrank back against the brass bedhead. Closing her eyes, she breathed deeply to stifle her rising panic. What if the others thought she'd killed it; smothered it, perhaps, with the pillow? They'd put her in prison and then they'd hang her. She forced herself to look at the dead infant out of the corner of her eyes. It . . . she . . . had a fuzz of flaxen hair and a heart-shaped face. Her pink mouth was a perfectly drawn Cupid's bow and her eyelids, delicately blue-veined, were now closed. Asleep or dead? Tentatively, Clarissa prodded the baby's cheek with a trembling forefinger.

The corner of her mouth curved up into what seemed to be a smile. And then she opened her eyes.

Clarissa caught her breath, transfixed by the infant's steady blue gaze. The tiny creature waved a hand in the air as if greeting her and, unable to stop herself, Clarissa reached out to hold it. Each little finger was perfect, the nails like minute pearly shells.

Then the baby's face crumpled. She drew up her knees and yelled.

Alarmed, Clarissa stared at her. The noise

went on and on. It grated on her nerves, like chalk scraping a blackboard. The sound of such anguish made her ache inside until she wanted to weep, too. When she couldn't stand it any longer, she picked the baby up. Helplessly, she propped it against her shoulder and patted its back. The little head wobbled so she cupped it in one hand and found it fitted her palm as if it had been made for the purpose. Gradually, the ear-splitting wails turned to whimpers. Clarissa put the baby to her other breast and she began to suck again.

She stared down at her daughter's face. Poor little brat; as Edith had said, she hadn't asked to be born. One thing Clarissa was quite certain of was that she would never again risk bringing another unwanted child into the world. What future was there for this little one? She touched the baby's silky hair, hoping her new family would love her. She shivered, knowing only too well what it was like not to be loved.

Later, the door opened and Edith came in carrying a tray. 'You've settled her, then?'

Clarissa nodded.

Edith sat on the edge of the bed. 'She's such a pretty little thing.'

'Is she?'

'Of course she is; she looks exactly like you.' Edith caressed the baby's cheek.

A wave of wretchedness swept over Clarissa and a great sob welled up inside her. 'Oh, Edith, what have I done?' she wept. She rocked back and forth, the baby against her chest. 'I never meant there to be a child.'

Edith pulled her close, her arms encircling both mother and baby. 'No,' she said, 'I don't suppose you did but sometimes these things happen. And here she is.'

The baby yawned widely and closed her eyes.

'I suggest you doze while she sleeps,' said Edith. 'It's the only way to get any rest at all in the first weeks. Shall I put her in the cot and draw the curtains?'

Clarissa nodded. 'There's a letter on my dressing table. Would you post it for me?'

Edith picked up the envelope. 'St Catherine's Convent?'

'I was told to write to them as soon as I was delivered. They'll tell the parents and make arrangements for me to take the child there to hand her over.'

'Are you quite sure you still want to give her away?'

'Absolutely.' Clarissa handed the sleeping infant to Edith, all at once feeling strangely bereft.

★ ★ ★

The following week passed in a daze for Clarissa. Her friends tiptoed in to bring her meals on a tray and encourage her to brush her hair, or else to take the napkin bucket away. Her milk came in and it was easier to nurse the infant than to cope with the discomfort of binding her breasts. Night and day merged, almost as if she was in an alternate world where nothing existed but tending to the infant's needs. There was a physical hurt inside her when the baby cried and she learned how to calm her by resting her against her shoulder and pacing around. One night, while an owl hooted outside in the darkness, Clarissa surprised herself by realising she was humming a half-remembered lullaby.

A few days later, Dora came to sit with her. 'Shall I look after Baby while you rest?'

Clarissa cradled her daughter in her arms. 'She's quiet now,' she said.

'I saw that a letter arrived for you from the convent. Is there any news?'

'I've to take her there next week.'

'So soon!' Tears started to Dora's eyes.

Clarissa turned her head away, her lips clamped together. 'I don't want to discuss it.'

In silence, Dora left the room.

★   ★   ★

Clarissa's lying in was over and she was relieved to leave her room while the baby slept. She went to the studio and watched Edith working. Her draughtsmanship, as always, was excellent but the composition was a little too neat. It lacked spontaneity.

Edith sighed. 'There's something missing, isn't there?' she said. 'And I must deliver it to my client before my baby arrives.'

'Can you ask for an extension?'

'I don't want to look unprofessional.'

'But it's better to be happy with it before you send it.'

Heavy footsteps clattered up the stairs.

'Benedict must be back,' said Edith, a moment before he burst into the studio.

He caught hold of her hands and whirled her around. 'Guess what? I've made an excellent contact at a gallery in Mayfair,' he said, his hazel eyes shining. 'I'm to return in the summer with new work to show them.'

'That's very encouraging.' Edith stood on her tiptoes to kiss him. 'Welcome home. Did you see, Clarissa's had her baby?'

He looked Clarissa up and down. 'Have you? It's hard to tell in these voluminous painting gowns you girls wear. I had the most marvellous time. Parties and dinners almost every night.'

A tiny ember of rage began to glow inside Clarissa. 'How lovely for you.'

'I'm sorry to have left it all behind.'

'I'm almost recovered from the birth, thank you,' she said. 'Would you like to see my baby?'

'It's still here, then?'

'Until next week.'

'Splendid! I'll take a look at the little chap after I've had my tea.'

'She's a girl.'

'Jolly good.' He turned back to Edith. 'Dora tells me Pascal has left. What brought that on, do you think?'

Edith bent over her palette and began mixing another colour. 'He's looking for new experiences.'

'Can't blame him for that. Will you help me unpack?'

'Later. I'm snatching the chance to work while Jasper naps.'

Benedict sighed heavily. 'I wonder why I bothered to return. You'll be too busy with him when you've finished here to pay any attention to me.' He marched off downstairs.

Brush poised, Edith gazed at her canvas, her lips pressed together.

'He's very full of himself,' said Clarissa.

Edith dropped her brush on the worktable. 'How do other wives manage to keep their husbands happy without neglecting their children?'

'Domestic servants. And they have no ambitions for a career. They forget their own needs and wishes and make sure they're always welcoming in bed.'

'Benedict isn't interested in me in that way now and I will never give up my painting.'

Her friend looked so woebegone that Clarissa hugged her. 'Give it time and all will be well again.'

★　★　★

The following week, Clarissa sat on the end of the bed rocking her drowsy baby in her arms. This was the last time the little one would sleep in a drawer. She wondered if the adoptive mother had bought an expensive cradle and had been excitedly collecting together a layette for her new daughter. All Clarissa hoped for was that the baby would be loved. She kissed her downy head and felt as if something inside her was broken.

There was a soft tap on the door.

Dora came in, bearing a cup of cocoa. 'I

thought this might help you sleep,' she said. 'And I wondered if you'd like me to come with you to the convent tomorrow?'

Clarissa drew a shuddering breath. 'Oh, Dora, would you? I've been dreading it. All those sanctimonious nuns looking at me . . . ' She'd had nightmares about it.

'Of course I will. You shouldn't face it alone.' She sat on the bed and wrapped her arm around Clarissa's waist, watching the baby fall asleep. 'Her skin is as soft as silk and as white as a lily,' she murmured. 'That would be a pretty name for her, don't you think?'

'Lily?' Clarissa bent her head, despair rising inside her.

'Have I said something to upset you?'

Clarissa swallowed, determined not to let the tears fall. 'It's a lovely name but her adoptive parents will name her, won't they?'

'Lily suits her so well they might keep it. Even if they don't, you'd always have that name to remember her by.'

'I won't ever forget her,' whispered Clarissa.

There was a long silence and then Dora said, 'Have you changed your mind?'

'No. I have no choice.'

'There's always a choice,' said Dora. 'Making it wouldn't be easy, though, and the consequences might be testing.' She gripped Clarissa's wrist. 'But if you're having second thoughts, we'll work out a plan. Perhaps your parents might . . . '

'My father would send me to an asylum and Lily to an orphanage. You think I'm heartless but she's better off with people who want her.'

'Wouldn't your mother help?'

Clarissa shook her head. 'She won't stand up to Father. Besides, I'm not capable of being a good mother.'

'Of course you are! Since the shock of her birth, look how devoted to her you've been. It's obvious that you love her, even if you don't realise it yet. Love is what a baby needs, far more than fancy clothes and posh schools. Once you're back on your feet and earning, you might be able to manage.'

'You're so kind and good, Dora,' said Clarissa. 'I haven't always been nice to you and I'm so sorry for that.'

Dora's face lit up. 'We're friends, aren't we?' She stood up. 'Now, you get a good night's sleep and I'll see you in the morning.'

After she'd gone, the baby stirred and woke.

'Hello, Lily,' said Clarissa. 'Do you like your new name?' She gazed into her baby's eyes. Lily was perfectly calm, focusing intently on her mother's face.

Clarissa nestled her daughter against her shoulder, inhaling the delicious milky smell of her. Dora had put into words the thing she hadn't been able to face. Lily had stolen her heart. The prospect of giving her away was unbearable but she had no choice. No choice at all.

The following morning, Clarissa was heavy-eyed when she dressed Lily in the nightgown and shawl Edith had given her for the occasion. Whilst it didn't matter that the nightgown was second hand, she wished now that she'd made something special for Lily to wear. She wanted the adoptive parents to know that, even though she'd had to give Lily away, the baby was precious to her.

Edith, with Jasper on her hip, came to say goodbye while Clarissa and Dora waited for the carriage. Edith had tears in her eyes when she kissed Lily's forehead.

Clarissa welled up, too, when Jasper gently patted Lily's cheek.

The carriage arrived. Dora tucked a travel rug over Clarissa's knees and they set off.

★   ★   ★

Dora rang the convent bell and Clarissa shivered as they waited on the doorstep. Eventually a nun opened the door and indicated they were to follow her down a corridor. Their shoes squeaked as they walked over the highly polished floors. They were shown into a room containing only a table and chairs and asked to wait.

'It's all very clean,' said Dora.

A small fire burned in the grate but it wasn't enough to make Clarissa warm. Her stomach roiled and blood pounded in her temples. She wondered if she looked as whey-faced as Dora. Thankfully, Lily slept peacefully in her arms and Clarissa gazed at her, fixing the tiny face forever in her memory.

Footsteps approached and Clarissa tensed. There was the sound of hearty male voices, interspersed with a woman's nervous laughter. The door opened and admitted the Mother

Superior, two middle-aged men and an expensively dressed woman.

Mother Superior introduced Mr and Mrs Coates and Mr Galton, their lawyer.

Mrs Coates, her black hair curling out from under her hat, came straight over to Clarissa but she had eyes only for the baby. Diamonds sparkled on her fingers as she moved Lily's shawl aside to reveal her face. 'Thank goodness!' she said. 'Look, John. She's pretty.'

Mr Coates nodded in approval. His complexion was swarthy and his eyes as dark as his wife's. He wore a beautifully tailored suit and a heavy gold watch chain across his waistcoat.

'Let me have her,' said Mrs Coates, reaching out for Lily.

Unable to speak, Clarissa clutched the baby to her breast.

Mr Galton glanced at her and pulled some papers out of his briefcase. 'We'll finish the formalities first,' he said. He began to read the paperwork aloud but there was such a commotion in her head that Clarissa couldn't catch the words. She was deathly cold. Dora touched her arm and she started. 'Sorry?'

Mr Galton placed the papers in front of her and indicated a pen and inkwell. 'Mr and Mrs Coates have already signed, as you see. All you need do is to sign on the line below.'

Clarissa's fingers trembled as she dipped the pen in the ink. She signed her name but as she wrote the last letter, the nib crossed and splattered a blot.

'Never mind,' said Mr Galton, snatching the

papers from her, 'it's still legal.'

'My daughter is to be called Adelaide Margaret now,' said Mrs Coates. 'Give her to me, please.'

Clarissa kissed the flaxen down on Lily's head. Her baby was going to a new family where she wouldn't look like any of them. She'd always be the odd one out. A sob rose up in her throat. Dora touched her hand and Clarissa looked up and saw the question in her eyes.

The uproar in her head suddenly quieted and she clutched Lily protectively in her arms. 'My daughter's name is Lily,' she said in clear tones. 'And she's coming home again with me.'

'No!' whispered Mrs Coates.

Dora reared to her feet and plucked the signed papers from Mr Galton's fingers. Ripping them in half, she threw them on the fire.

Mrs Coates shrieked and fell to her knees by the grate, attempting to pull the charred scraps from the coals.

Dora caught hold of Clarissa's wrist and they ran helter-skelter from the room.

22

July 1894

Edith, Benedict and the children arrived at her parents' house in Bedford Gardens after a trying journey. Benedict had become increasingly short-tempered on the train, weary of Jasper's inability to sit still. Their beautiful three-month-old daughter, Pearl, was preparing to work herself into a screaming fit if she wasn't fed very soon and Edith's breasts ached.

They were shown straight into the drawing room where Edith bent to kiss her mother's cheek. 'The train was delayed,' she said.

'If you will live in the wilds of Cornwall, what can you expect?'

Benedict put Jasper down with a sigh of relief. 'Go and kiss your grandmama.'

Mama held out her hand to Jasper but he tottered off to investigate a potted palm instead. Ignoring her, he sat down to examine the pedals of the piano. Amelia's piano.

Edith hurried to distract him.

'Edith,' said Mama sharply, 'don't let him put fingermarks on it!'

'He's been so confined today,' she said, a note of apology in her voice as she lifted him away.

The piano, draped with an embroidered silk shawl, enshrined Amelia's memory with a forest of silver photograph frames capturing her likeness from bonny babyhood to the day before her death. In that last photograph her emaciated body was carefully displayed in a frilled white dress. Her dark hair was coiled into ringlets and tied with silk ribbons but nothing could disguise the deep shadows under her eyes or her sunken cheeks.

'Are you going to show me my granddaughter, then?' said Mama.

Proudly, Edith pulled back Pearl's shawl.

Mama caught her breath. 'But she looks *exactly* like dearest Amelia did at that age!' she said, reaching out eagerly to take her.

'She's damp. Let me change her first.'

'Grandmama doesn't mind that, does she, Pearl?' she cooed. 'Oh, what a little darling she is!' She pressed kisses onto the baby's plump cheeks and Edith was pleased to have done something to please Mama at last.

Pearl began to fret and then to cry. 'I could cuddle this precious little bundle all day,' said Mama, 'but I can see she needs Nanny to minister to her.' She passed Pearl back to Edith. 'Bring her back once she's fed and changed, won't you?'

'There's no nanny,' she said, 'only me.'

Mama's eyes widened in shocked surprise. 'You haven't brought your nanny with you?'

'We have no need of one,' said Benedict. 'Mother knows best. Isn't that right, Edith?'

'My friend Dora helps,' she said, patting Pearl's back as she started to yell in earnest. 'Otherwise I'd never have time to work.'

'Benedict,' said Mama, 'you must insist Edith

has a nanny. It's essential the children are guided into regular habits from the very beginning.'

'Dora has a way with babies,' said Benedict, leaning back in the armchair and crossing his legs.

'Children are far too important to trust to the attentions of an untrained person.'

'I must feed Pearl,' said Edith, making her escape to the guest room.

★　★　★

After dinner, Benedict and Edith's father lingered over the port, discussing the elections for the newly formed parish councils, in which some women were allowed to vote.

'It'll end in tears,' said Papa. 'Women have neither the will to vote nor the first idea about politics. Unless, of course, their husbands advise them.'

Mama pushed back her chair. 'Edith, shall we retire?'

In the drawing room, she poured the coffee. 'Tomorrow, we'll engage a temporary nanny,' she said. 'A husband needs his wife's full attention and prefers children to remain in the nursery. I shall make enquiries about a suitable applicant for a permanent position.'

'Benedict says we can't afford a nanny.'

Very carefully, Mama placed her cup back on the saucer. 'What do you mean?'

Edith shrugged, uncomfortable under her scrutiny. 'Our expenses have been greater than he thought.'

'He told your father he had a considerable private income. If he hadn't, we shouldn't have allowed you to marry him, especially since, as an artist, his income may be irregular.'

'Unfortunately, he made some poor investments. One of the reasons we've come to town is for him to seek advice from his father's stockbroker.'

'I see.' Frowning, Mama tapped a fingernail against her tooth. 'And you still have friends staying with you? House guests are expensive. You must send them away and make strict economies.'

'Clarissa pays for her keep.' She didn't mention how uncertain Clarissa's financial future was, now that she had a child to support. 'Dora helps to look after the children.'

'The Frenchman?'

'Pascal left us months ago.' Edith remembered her last glance of him with a pang of melancholy. 'While we're here, Benedict is meeting an art dealer. He's also going to show his latest work to a gallery that expressed interest before.'

'How many paintings has he sold since you married?'

'One or two.' She didn't mention they were sketches and he'd received very little for them.

'Have you had any more commissions?'

Edith nodded. 'I'm going to show my most recent work to my art dealer before I deliver it to the client.'

'Then you'll definitely need a temporary nanny while you attend that meeting.' Mama sighed. 'Papa will have to pay for it.'

235

Edith didn't say that she'd assumed Mama would mind the children while she was with her client and, clearly, it had never occurred to her that she might do so.

★　★　★

Two days later, Edith and Benedict left the children with a fearsome dragon of a nurse in grey uniform. They took a cab to Jermyn Street, where the dealer, a Mr Hutchinson, had his offices. Edith brought *Exploring the Ruins* with her, wrapped in brown paper. Benedict carried an expensive calfskin portfolio that had been a present from his mother.

A clerk asked them to wait while he enquired if Mr Hutchinson was available.

'He damned well better be,' muttered Benedict after the man had disappeared through a doorway.

The clerk returned and ushered them into the inner sanctum. Mr Hutchinson sported a paisley silk cravat instead of a tie and wore his hair artistically long. Despite his informal dress, he was briskly efficient. 'I haven't long,' he said. 'I'm meeting a client for luncheon so let's have a look at what you've brought, Mr Fairchild.'

Benedict opened his portfolio and laid out his portraits on a long table. 'I'm particularly interested in the female form, in all its wonderful variety,' he began.

'Yes, yes,' said Mr Hutchinson impatiently. 'A good painting needs no explanation; it speaks for itself.' He walked slowly along the table, looking at each canvas in turn. He paused beside *Waiting for the Fishing Fleet* and pursed his lips. 'I might find a buyer for this one,' he said. 'I've sold one like it that was afterwards used to decorate a tin tray. Can't be a house in the land that hasn't got one.'

'The nudes?' asked Benedict.

Mr Hutchinson waved a hand dismissively. 'Not for me.'

Benedict's jaw clenched and he ran his fingers through his hair. Edith knew he'd be in a sulk for the remainder of the day.

Mr Hutchinson looked at her brown paper-wrapped parcel. 'What have we here?'

She unwrapped her canvas together with a cardboard folio. 'I deliver this to the client today but I wondered if something similar might be of interest to you?' She lifted *Exploring the Ruins* onto the table.

He narrowed his eyes. 'This is your work, Mrs Fairchild?'

'It is. I trained at the Slade, like my husband.'

'A serious artist then, not a dabbler.' He took a monocle from his waistcoat pocket and leaned over to examine the painting more closely. 'Hmm. Interesting. But it lacks vivacity,' he murmured. 'Female artists are generally more suited to dashing off a pretty watercolour. Perhaps you might try doing that?'

Edith's cheeks flamed at his patronising remark but she didn't care to antagonise him. 'I also have a number of watercolour studies for paintings,' she said, handing him the portfolio.

He flicked through them and extracted two or

three. 'Leave these with me and I'll see what I can do.' He glanced at his pocket watch and shook hands briskly with them both. 'Record your details with my clerk,' he said.

Outside Mr Hutchinson's office, Benedict hunched his shoulders and walked ahead.

Edith sighed and followed him.

At their next appointment, she presented *Exploring the Ruins* to her client with some trepidation, especially since Mr Hutchinson hadn't thought much of it. The client made no comment when he studied the canvas and didn't commission her to paint a companion picture, as she'd hoped.

Benedict tucked the cash payment into his pocket for safe-keeping. Edith was deflated but at least she'd be able to buy Jasper new shoes and put something away for the coal merchant, ready for the autumn.

She visited two galleries with Benedict but neither was interested in his portfolio and he became increasingly tetchy. By then it was time for Pearl's feed so Edith left him to continue his visits and returned alone to Bedford Gardens.

As soon the front door opened, she heard Pearl crying.

The dragon in the nursery was feeding Jasper his lunch of boiled fish and mashed potatoes. He regarded his mother with solemn brown eyes when Nanny ticked her off because she was a few minutes late.

'It is imperative to adhere to a routine if Baby is ever going to be fit for polite society, Mrs Fairchild.' She fixed Edith with a steely gaze.

'Should Mother's social engagements regularly conflict with Baby's feed times, it is preferable to bottle feed.'

'Yes, Nanny,' Edith said meekly. She had no intention of telling her that, at home, she simply nursed Baby whenever she was hungry.

After Edith had fed Pearl, she said she'd take the children downstairs to visit their grand-mama.

'The proper time for that is after tea,' said Nanny. She took Pearl away to be changed. 'Master Jasper will have his rest now.'

Her tone brooked no argument so Edith went downstairs.

Her mother was in the conservatory, dozing with a book open on her knee. The French doors were open and sunshine pooled on the quarry-tiled floor. When Amelia became ill, the doctors had said she needed to spend as much time as possible in the fresh air. There had been talk of a clinic in Switzerland but in the end her bed had been moved into the conservatory. Edith could picture her still, eyes bright with fever and her poor wasted body wracked by violent spasms of coughing. Mounded with eiderdowns, she'd slept with all the doors and windows open, even when the glass was clouded with frost flowers and snow made drifts against her bed. She'd still died, though.

Edith sat down beside a potted palm and glanced at Mama, asleep in the rattan chair she always used to sit in, next to where Amelia's bed had stood for three long years.

Mama stirred and opened her eyes, staring

blankly at her. 'Amelia?' she whispered.

'It's Edith, Mama.'

'Yes . . . yes, of course it is.' Her voice was heavy with disappointment. 'I was dreaming.'

Edith related the morning's events, wondering if her mother would ever cease to mourn Amelia.

'So neither you nor Benedict actually secured any new commissions or sold any paintings?'

'It's early days. I'll begin another painting when I'm home again.'

Mama took her crochet out of her workbag to show Edith. There were pink rosebuds around the edge. 'It's a bonnet for Pearl.'

'It's very pretty. Thank you, Mama.' She flicked through the latest copies of *Country Life* while her mother hooked the bonnet. The silence pressed down upon her and Edith went to look out of the window.

'Do sit down, Edith! I can't concentrate with you fidgeting.'

'I'm used to having a painting to work on or the children to see to.'

'Go and practise the piano. Then you could play something to amuse us after dinner.'

'I never play these days,' Edith said. What was the point when, as Mama had so frequently told her, she could never be even half as good as Amelia?

'You look tired,' her mother observed.

'Pearl needed nursing three times during the night.'

'That's exactly why you need a nanny.' Mama sighed. 'And may I offer a word of advice? Jasper and Pearl were born less than a year apart. You really must take more care to prevent that happening again; you need time to recover your strength.'

Irritated and embarrassed that her mother should mention such a private matter, Edith spoke sharply. 'You told me on my wedding day that it was my duty to do my husband's bidding.'

'While that may be so, there's no requirement to be over-eager to do your duty. Since your financial position is precarious, I suggest you explain to your husband the advantages of restraint.'

Restraint wasn't a word Edith had ever associated with Benedict. Besides, she knew from experience what harm could be done to their marriage if she refused him.

The afternoon crawled by until it was time to feed Pearl again and then to play with Jasper under Nanny's watchful eye. After teatime, Edith brought the children downstairs to spend ten minutes with Grandmama.

Benedict still hadn't returned when Edith went up to change for dinner.

He didn't arrive until they'd finished their soup, which didn't endear him to Edith's father.

'I do apologise,' said Benedict, sounding not in the least contrite. 'I took my portfolio to the owner of a gallery in Mayfair. We're meeting for dinner tomorrow night while we talk about the possibility of my paintings being included in an exhibition.'

'But that's wonderful, Benedict!' Edith said.

'Isn't it?' He was in a good humour again and set out to entertain and charm her parents, reminding Edith of what had attracted her to him in the first place.

After dinner, they went into the garden at twilight to take the air. It was a still and balmy summer's evening. They sat in the rose arbour and listened to the street sounds drifting over the garden wall: horses' hooves clopping along the cobbles, cab drivers having a shouted conversation from opposite sides of the street, a snatch of music from a barrel-organ and the clatter of a dustcart.

Benedict lit one of his Moroccan cigarettes, the sweetish, aromatic smell of the smoke curling around them and the tip glowing orange in the growing darkness. He pulled Edith to him and she rested her head on his shoulder. Stubbing out the cigarette on the flagstones, he kissed her. His hand cupped her breast and he nibbled her throat, making her shiver. It was the first time since Pearl's birth that he'd given any indication he found her attractive again.

'I'm going to make love to you,' he said, his voice husky.

'Benedict, we can't,' she said, pulling away from him.

'Of course, we can; you're my wife.' His fingers trailed up her thigh.

'Supposing Mama and Papa come into the garden? Anyway,' she said, 'it's too soon to risk another child.'

'I want you, Edith.' He lifted her onto the grass.

'Benedict, no!' But if she refused him now, what further damage would it do to their marriage?

242

His mouth came down on hers and his hands were under her skirt, stroking her inner thigh. 'It's all right,' he said, 'I'll be careful.'

* * *

The following day, Benedict went to visit an old school friend. Edith passed the morning visiting an artists' supplier to stock up on paints and canvas. In the afternoon she took the children to visit Benedict's mother, returning to Bedford Gardens in time for nursery tea. Benedict dashed in, rather late, to change before meeting the owner of Armitage's Gallery for dinner.

'Edith, help me with this, will you?' He lifted his chin so she could adjust his bow tie.

She handed him his hat, gloves and cane. 'Very handsome,' she said.

He glanced at his pocket watch. 'Don't wait up for me, I may be late.'

* * *

Edith had already settled Pearl back to sleep after her two o'clock feed when Benedict returned.

'Still awake?' he said, pulling off his tie. Slightly unsteady, he plumped down on the bed to toe off his shoes.

'I was worried.' She didn't ask him if he'd been drinking because it was obvious from his breath and dishevelled hair that he had. Frowning, she noticed his shirt was incorrectly buttoned.

'Told you I'd be late, didn't I? We went on to the Café Royal after dinner.'

243

She wondered that a visit to such a place was necessary to sell his paintings. 'Was the evening successful?'

Benedict chuckled. 'You could say that.' Striking a pose, he said, 'Armitage's will take six to ten new canvases and half a dozen drawings for their November exhibition.'

Edith pressed her fingers to her mouth. Benedict usually took longer than a month to produce one canvas. 'Four months! However will you manage it?'

He shrugged. 'Can't you just be pleased for me, Edith? I'm going to be a bit pressed but I could hardly refuse. Think of how much money I'll make!'

'As long as you have time to produce your best work.'

He sighed heavily. 'It'll be fine as long as you keep the children quiet.'

She sat with her arms wrapped around her shins. It was excellent news but it was going to be harder than ever to find time for her own work.

Humming to himself, Benedict dropped his shirt on the floor. 'I hope,' he said, as he climbed into bed, 'that this will be the beginning of a long-term and very profitable relationship with Armitage's.'

'I hope so, too,' she murmured.

He pecked her cheek. 'G'night.' Yawning, he turned over and went to sleep.

She lay awake for some time, thinking. Then she slipped out of bed, picked up Benedict's shirt and held it to her nose. Tiptoeing to the window, she rested her hands on the sill and leaned out to take deep breaths of the night air. She'd thought she'd detected a musky perfume when Benedict kissed her and now she knew his shirt smelled of it, too.

But the perfume wasn't hers.

Undoubtedly Benedict had been with another woman. The question was, how far had it gone? The previous night he'd made love to her in the garden and, despite the risk, Edith had been jubilant that he'd wanted her. Surely he wouldn't have betrayed her only twenty-four hours later?

She remembered the perfume on his misbuttoned shirt and his tousled hair. Rage and humiliation boiled up inside her. There was nothing, absolutely nothing, she could do on her own to mend their marriage if Benedict persisted in ignoring their wedding vows. Except, perhaps, be grateful for the crumbs of his affection, should he deign to bestow them on her, and accept the slights and humiliations he inflicted without complaint. But could she do that and still have a life worth living?

23

Clarissa and Dora sat on a rug with four-month-old Lily between them in the dappled shade of the copper beech. Lily waved her tiny fists in the air, as if trying to catch the dancing shadows and Clarissa fell in love with her all over again.

Dora stroked the baby's cheek with her finger. 'I was remembering that awful day at the convent.'

Clarissa shuddered. 'Thank God you were there! I'd never have found the strength to tear up the adoption papers like you did.'

'I was terrified but I only had to look at your face to be certain it was the right thing to do.'

'You knew me better than I knew myself. If I'd given Lily away, I'd have regretted it for the rest of my life.' And perhaps that wouldn't have been very long if there'd been nothing left to live for.

Dora giggled. 'Do you remember Mr Coates and Mother Superior shouting and running after our carriage?'

Clarissa nodded. 'And my sheer terror at accepting permanent responsibility for Lily. I had no idea how I'd manage and you said, 'One day at a time.'' She shook her head. 'I've been living in a dream and it's time for me to wake up and act.'

'What will you do?'

'I'm kicking myself for not going to London

with Edith and Benedict this week. My savings are dwindling. I must see Madame Monette soon and visit some other shops about selling my jewellery.'

'It's a long journey with a baby.' Dora twirled a stray curl around her finger, a sure sign she was thinking. 'Why don't I come, too? I could help with Lily and visit my family. I was going to post my wildflower collection to the editor of *Nature Review* but I could deliver it myself.'

'I'd love to have your company.' Clarissa was surprised by how much she wanted it. Once, she'd had little time for Dora the Mouse but, now she knew her better, realised how arrogant and snobbish that had been. Spindrift House had been tranquil while Edith, Benedict and the children were away and Clarissa had used the time to consider the future and evolve a strategy. There was something unpleasant she must deal with in the next day or two, before her courage failed her, and then she'd go to London.

Wheels rattled down the lane and Dora jumped to her feet as a carriage came into view. It drew up by the front gate and Benedict descended, followed by Edith with the children.

Clarissa hurried to lift Jasper down and then hugged Edith. 'A successful visit?'

Benedict puffed up his chest. 'I've brought a case of Champagne to celebrate.'

'Is that what's in the heavy box?' asked Edith. 'I thought we had to make economies?'

'Don't *nag*, Edith!' He caught hold of Clarissa's hands. 'Armitage's Gallery in Mayfair is holding an exhibition of my work in November.'

Clarissa's eyes widened. 'An exhibition of your own?'

He waved his fingers vaguely in the air. 'There'll be a couple of other artists exhibiting at the same time but I intend to make my mark. I've even bought myself a new suit.'

'A new suit?' said Edith, frowning. 'And Champagne? You were annoyed with me for buying paints and a couple of brushes.' Her face blanched. 'Oh, no! Benedict, please tell me you didn't spend the money I earned from the sale of *Exploring the Ruins*?'

He shrugged. 'It's essential I look the part for the opening of my exhibition, to inspire confidence in the buying public. It's in our best financial interests.'

'How could you!' Edith shouted, trembling with outrage. 'You've two perfectly good suits already. Jasper desperately needs shoes, we've no coal for the winter and the sheets are so thin you can see through them.'

'I really can't concern myself with trivial domestic problems, Edith. Why must you spoil everything with a childish fit of temper? You're embarrassing our friends. Go and tell Mrs Jenkins to bring us some tea.'

Silently, Edith handed Pearl to Dora and set off towards the kitchen.

Benedict rolled his eyes heavenwards. 'She'll sulk for days now. I was only doing what I thought best for my family.'

Clarissa raised her eyebrows. Was he selfish or simply deluding himself? 'Perhaps you should have asked Edith first?'

'She'd have said no.'

'Exactly.' Selfish then. Clarissa said no more, in case she made it worse for Edith.

Jasper tottered towards his father and clung to his knees, crowing with delight.

'I'm going to change,' said Benedict, hastily loosening his son's grip on his trousers. The little boy bumped to the ground and began to wail. Benedict sighed and set off across the grass.

Dora laid Pearl, fast asleep, on a cushion next to Lily and lifted Jasper onto her knee. 'I can't believe Benedict has spent Edith's money.'

'You still have a great deal to learn about men,' said Clarissa.

Dora kissed the top of Jasper's head. 'You'll never behave like that, will you, Little Man?'

Edith returned and sat down on the rug beside them.

'Was your client pleased with his commission?' asked Clarissa.

'I think so but he didn't offer me another, as I'd hoped.'

Poor Edith, she looked as miserable as sin. Clarissa knew she'd worked hard to improve the canvas but, somehow, it had missed the mark. 'Are you all right?' she asked.

'I'm happy to be home. Mama is rather trying and Benedict found travelling with children tiresome.'

'And I expect his irritation made the journey exhausting for you?'

Edith gave a wan smile. 'It would have been ghastly if he hadn't been so thrilled about his exhibition.'

Mrs Jenkins arrived with the tea tray.

Clarissa watched Benedict stroll across the lawn towards them. Casually dressed in flannels and with the sleeves of his white shirt rolled to the elbows, he sat down on the lawn with the self-satisfied elegance of a cat. He stretched out on his back, hands behind his head, and chewed a blade of grass. The sun highlighted the golden hairs on his forearms. It was no wonder, she thought, that Edith had fallen for this god-like figure. What a shame he had feet of clay.

Sipping her tea, Clarissa eyed her friends from under her eye-lashes. Dora chatted to Jasper as he toddled about on the lawn. Benedict, sunny-natured again, wolfed down a piece of chocolate cake. Edith, her eyes soft with love but shadowed with exhaustion, held out her arms and called to Jasper. And then there was perfect little Lily, lying side-by-side with Pearl, just as if they were twins. Clarissa imagined for a moment what her life would have been like without her Spindrift 'family' and shivered.

★ ★ ★

Clarissa remembered how difficult the cliff steps had been for her when she went down to the cove on that windy March day of Lily's birth. This time was no easier, since she carried her daughter in her Moses basket and was terrified of slipping. At last she reached the bottom and then skirted around the cliffs to the cave. Inside, she carefully placed the sleeping baby on a wide, rocky shelf, tucking the shawl around her in the basket. Then she sat on a rock outside to wait.

It wasn't long before Hugh descended the steps from Cliff House. Clarissa stood up and made every effort to look composed, even though her heart was racing. To give herself courage, she'd corseted herself tightly and taken pains to dress her hair becomingly.

He walked unhurriedly across the sand, finally coming to a halt in front of her. 'Well,' he said, 'it was a surprise to receive your note!'

She looked him up and down appraisingly. His expression was guarded but Clarissa noted his eyes gleamed with excitement. 'I thought it was time we had another conversation.'

'Have you forgotten how insupportably ill-mannered you were to me the last time we were together? Perhaps you wish to apologise?'

She took a deep breath to prevent herself from slapping his smug face. 'Since Jenifry is in the family way again, I suspect she hasn't much time for you these days?'

Hugh grimaced. 'What is it about motherhood that makes her want to do nothing but read penny dreadfuls, eat violet creams and complain?'

'Oh, dear!'

'She says I have no idea what she has to endure but *she* was the one who wanted another child.'

Clarissa held out her hand. 'Shall we go into the cave? There's something I want to show you.' The anticipatory smile on his lips was enough to prevent her from feeling guilty about what she was about to do.

She led him inside, letting go of his hand so as to be able to lift Lily's basket from the rocky ledge. 'Hugh, I'd like you to meet your daughter. This is Lily.'

His face blanched. 'What preposterous lie is this?'

'No lie,' said Clarissa, with a calmness she didn't feel. 'You've had your fun and now it's time to pay up.'

'What utter rot! I'm not giving you a penny.'

'You'd let your own child starve?' She raised her eyebrows. 'You're even less of a man than I thought.'

'You can't prove she's mine. It was only once that we . . . '

'The hotel manager and the waiter at the Molesworth Arms will remember us. And the date we stayed will be in their register.'

'That doesn't prove I'm the father.' His lips curled in a sneer. 'It could have been anyone with a tart like you.'

She fixed him with a cold stare but inside she was trembling. 'I know with absolute certainty that Lily is your daughter and I shall do whatever is necessary to ensure her well-being. You will pay me a monthly allowance for her keep and there will be an agreement to that effect, drawn up by a solicitor.'

'I will not!'

'Then I have no choice but to tell your wife about Lily.'

'You wouldn't!'

'Oh, but I would.'

'That's blackmail!'

'All I want is a fair allowance for our daughter.'

Hugh's face seemed to crumple. 'Be reasonable! Jenifry is expected to give birth any day now and she'd never forgive me.'

'I *am* being reasonable. You planned my seduction in considerable detail but omitted to consider the risk when you took your pleasure,' said Clarissa. She tightened her grip on Lily, taking strength from her tiny body.

Hugh clenched his fists, his complexion turning an alarming shade of puce. 'You are a cold-hearted bitch!'

'And you are a sanctimonious hypocrite. You're no better than your father when he made Hester Tremayne his mistress. I wonder what your family and friends will say when they find out? Like father, like son?'

Lily whimpered and Clarissa rocked her. If Hugh didn't agree to her demands and called her bluff, she was lost. She could pretend she'd been married and widowed while she'd stayed in London but she couldn't possibly shame Hugh publicly. Once the local community knew, her daughter would forever be labelled a bastard.

'Can't you shut her up?'

She held Lily out to him. 'Why don't you try? She's as much your child as Noel or Timmy, after all.'

He took a hasty step backwards.

'Look, Hugh, this can be very simple or it can become horribly complicated,' Clarissa said. 'I shall visit a lawyer in Wadebridge, ask him to advise on a reasonable monthly allowance and have him draw up an agreement, which you will sign. You will then make a discreet arrangement with your bank to pay me the allowance until Lily is of age or until she marries. As long as I continue to receive the allowance, there need be no unpleasant accusations nor any further contact between us.'

Frowning, he looked out to sea.

Lily continued to fret and Clarissa fought with her own panic.

Hugh faced her again. 'How do I know you'll keep quiet?'

'You'll have to take my word for it but it's not in our daughter's interests for me to compromise the source of her allowance, is it?'

He kicked up a spray of sand. 'Damn you! Tell the lawyer to inform me when the agreement is ready.'

Clarissa nodded and dropped her gaze, in case her relief was too obvious.

'You can't know how much I wish I'd never set eyes on you,' he said, his teeth gritted.

'Oh, but I do.' But then, she thought, if she hadn't set eyes on him, she wouldn't have her precious Lily.

Hugh hunched his shoulders and hurried away.

Clarissa covered Lily's face in kisses, her own cheeks wet with tears. 'From now on, my darling, above all else, I vow to love you forever and to keep you safe, always.'

24

September 1894

Clinging unsteadily to the handrail, Edith descended the steps from Dr Hardwicke's front door in Dolphin Street. She turned into Temple Bar, an alley running between the cottages that was no more than a foot and a half wide in places. The alley always made her uneasy, even though she knew there was no likelihood of becoming trapped within its narrow confines. A moment later she emerged into Fore Street. Blinking in the dazzling sunshine, she walked onto the harbour beach. She needed a quiet moment before returning to Spindrift House.

The tide was out, leaving reeking heaps of bladderwrack stranded on the sand, together with lobster pots and driftwood. She picked her way between the fishing boats and men carrying boxes of salted herrings from the fish cellars to the waiting wagons bound for Newquay. At the water's edge, waves frilled around the toes of her boots, salt-staining the leather, but she was beyond caring. Picking up a stone, she flung it out to sea with all her might. Calm today, the sea glittered in the sunshine, oblivious to her angry apprehension.

How could she have been so foolish? It wasn't as if Mama hadn't warned her. She blamed herself for not speaking more firmly to Benedict about self-restraint. But here she was, pregnant again, with a new baby expected barely a year after Pearl. From the guarded hints the midwife had given her when Pearl was born, she'd thought nursing one baby would prevent conception of another.

Sighing, she started for home. She was crossing Fore Street when she met old Mrs Gloyne struggling with her shopping bags.

'May I help you carry those?' Edith said.

Mrs Gloyne looked at her with beady eyes. 'I'd be glad of it, Mrs Fairchild,' she said. ''Tis potatoes that's so burdensome.'

In a narrow cottage in Back Lane, Edith followed her into a neat little parlour and came to a sudden stop. Someone was asleep on a truckle bed under a mound of blankets.

'My sister,' said Mrs Gloyne. 'She fell ill not a month after I left Spindrift House. You'll stay for some tea?'

Edith hesitated. She longed to sit for a few minutes. 'I don't wish to intrude.'

'I'd welcome the company.' Mrs Gloyne gave her a shrewd look as she lifted the kettle onto the fire. 'You look as if you could do with a sit down.'

Edith perched on one of the rocking chairs beside the hearth and sipped the tea.

'Your guests from London never left then?' said Mrs Gloyne. 'Except, I heard the French-man went to Newlyn. You do know there's talk of ungodly goings on at Spindrift House? Some people don't care for artists.'

'There's nothing ungodly about us,' Edith

said. 'We live quietly and work hard. My husband needs new models but the trumped-up rumours have made it hard to persuade any young woman to come to Spindrift House.'

'There's been trouble between Cliff House and Spindrift House for years,' said Mrs Gloyne. 'Still, it's good there's children again at Spindrift.' She sucked at her gums. 'Three so far, isn't it?'

Edith nodded.

'And I warrant there'll be another in a few months.'

Edith stared at her and anxiety bubbled to the surface again. 'How did you know?'

'You've got that look about you. Not happy about it neither, I'd guess.' Mrs Gloyne patted her wrist. ' 'Tis God's will, Mrs Fairchild, though 'tis hard on a woman. A man won't be told and a babe won't wait.'

'That's very true.' Edith stood up. 'Thank you for the tea and I hope your sister recovers soon.'

'Come and see me again, if you're passing.'

Slightly fortified by tea and Mrs Gloyne's kindness, Edith set off up Roscarrock Hill, wondering how to break the news of the new baby to Benedict. She hadn't gone far when she saw a nursemaid, pushing a perambulator down the hill. Jenifry Penrose walked beside her, holding young Noel by the hand. Timmy and a new baby were both in the perambulator.

Edith nodded at the little party but Jenifry swept by without acknowledging her. Humiliated, Edith held her head high. It was fruitless trying to make friends with the Penroses.

When she arrived home, Dora was in the sitting room, painting a Bird's-Foot Trefoil. The previous month, she'd visited London with Clarissa and presented her wildflower illustrations to the editor of *Nature Review*, who'd commissioned her to make a new collection of illustrations of coastal plants.

Pearl was asleep in her bassinet and Jasper was on the rug, making marks with a pencil on a sheet of paper. He climbed to his feet and shouted, 'Mam-mam-mam!'

As always, her heart turned over with love for him. 'What a hive of industry!' she said, kissing his nose.

'Jasper's been ever so good since I set him to drawing,' said Dora. 'What's up with you? You're looking very glum.'

'I'm expecting again.'

'Hell's bells!'

Edith cupped her hands over her eyes. 'Why isn't motherhood enough for me? I feel so selfish but all I can think about is that it'll be harder than ever to find time to paint. I can hardly breathe at the thought of it. It's not that I don't love my children . . . '

'Anyone can see that!' Dora hugged her, stroking her hair as if she was a child.

'Benedict will be furious.'

'He should have thought of that before.'

Edith wiped her eyes. 'You sound like my mother.'

'Go and tell him.'

'Is he in the studio?'

She nodded. 'Tamsyn is modelling for him.'

'At least he's working! I've been worried sick he's not making enough effort to finish sufficient canvases for his exhibition. There's only two months left. Would you watch the children for a moment longer while I speak to him?'

On the top landing, Edith stopped dead in the studio doorway. Tamsyn, partially draped in a skimpy piece of muslin, was entwined in Benedict's arms. He was fully clothed but one hand cupped her naked breast as he kissed her.

Edith froze, not wanting to believe what she was seeing. A memory of Benedict and Delphine framed in another doorway flashed into her mind and she made a small cry of distress.

Benedict jumped and hastily disentangled Tamsyn's arms from around his neck.

'Put on your clothes and leave, Tamsyn,' Edith said. Her voice was icy, though white-hot anger seared her face and throat.

Tamsyn looked at Benedict, her head cocked. He shrugged. Tossing her black curls, she unwound the flimsy scrap of muslin, held it out at arm's length and dropped it to the floor. Stark naked, she sauntered over to the screen to dress, glancing back over her shoulder to smile brazenly at Benedict. Edith couldn't help noticing her smooth young flesh and narrow waist over full hips.

'Edith . . . '

'Quiet, Benedict!' she said. It nauseated her that, despite his promise to remain faithful after Delphine, he thought so little of her he'd philander with another woman here, in their own home.

259

Sighing, he wiped his paintbrushes on a cloth.

Edith clenched her fists to prevent herself from battering his chest and screaming at him like a fishwife. Her own chest rose and fell as she fought for self-control.

Tamsyn emerged from behind the screen, buttoning her dress. 'I'll be off then, Benedict,' she said. 'Usual time tomorrow?'

'You will not return to this house,' Edith said.

'Well,' the girl drawled, 'that depends on Benedict, don't it?'

'Cut along now, Tamsyn,' he said. 'I've almost completed this canvas and I shan't be needing you for a while.'

She sniffed. 'See myself out then, shall I?'

'You will not!' said Edith. She harried the protesting girl down the stairs, slammed the front door behind her then stamped back upstairs, her fury and wretchedness growing with each step.

Benedict was studying Tamsyn's half-finished portrait.

Edith threw the discarded scrap of muslin over the canvas. 'I can't bear to look at it.'

'I do hope you aren't going to make a dreadful fuss, Edith,' he said. 'Tamsyn is an impudent girl and likes to tease but there's no harm in her.'

'No harm?' she yelled. 'Even if that were the case, you're a married man, though you seem to have conveniently forgotten that.'

'I didn't do anything!'

'I suppose it was nothing to do with you that your hand was holding her naked breast?' She swept his pot of brushes off the table with the back of her hand, scattering them far and wide.

'I'm not *stupid*, Benedict! And it's not as if it's the first time you've been unfaithful.'

'For God's sake, Edith! Are you never going to stop harping on about one little indiscretion?'

Rage made her shake. 'But it's not only one so-called indiscretion, is it? What were you up to in London that night you went out? Don't think I didn't notice you came home reeking of another woman's scent and with your shirt buttoned incorrectly.'

'I don't care for these jealous accusations. Tamsyn is a bit free with herself and pressed up against me, that's all.' He gave her his charming, crooked smile. 'You've sent her packing and, to be honest, I'm relieved. She was beginning to take liberties, as you saw.'

'Don't you *dare* tell me you weren't enjoying kissing and fondling her. And what would have happened if I hadn't put a stop to it?'

He bent to pick up his brushes. 'Don't blame me, Edith! You're no fun anymore. You're always either working or minding the children.' His voice had taken on a distinctly peevish tone. 'You never have time for me.'

'Perhaps I would, if you didn't keep making me pregnant.' She was so tired and miserable she could have wept. Once, she'd loved him with all her heart and it cut her to the quick that he was so careless of her feelings.

'What do you mean?' Benedict's expression was wary.

'I've seen Dr Hardwicke this morning. I'm expecting again.' There was a long pause, while she watched horror dawning on his face.

'Are you sure?'

She nodded.

He let out a muffled curse. 'Are we never to have a life of our own? We'll be trapped by those children for years and years. It's an impossible strain on our financial resources.'

'It's not my fault! Nor is it the children's. If you kept your trousers buttoned and spent less time seducing other women, you'd have more time to produce saleable paintings.'

'God, but you're a shrew, Edith!'

'If I'm shrewish it's because I'm exhausted. You never get up in the night to tend to a baby or spend precious painting time changing the sheets or pacifying Mrs Jenkins.'

'But then,' said Benedict, 'your work is unimportant right now. *I'm* the one who has been given the opportunity to sell my work through an exhibition, not you. Besides, Dora helps you.'

'She has to work on her own new commission now.' Edith rubbed tears from her eyes. It was all too much.

Sighing, Benedict pulled her into his arms. 'I'm sorry about Tamsyn,' he said.

'You promised me,' Edith said, her lips trembling, 'you *promised* me, after Delphine, that nothing like this would happen again.'

'It won't. And we'll manage. Somehow.' He kissed her forehead. 'I'm bound to sell my paintings at the exhibition. If I work really hard perhaps I can complete ten canvases. Meanwhile, we'll just have to make economies.'

She didn't say they'd pared those to the bone already. 'I'd better see to the children.'

'Let's go down together,' said Benedict. 'What do you say we put them in the perambulator and take them for a walk?'

Still angry and upset, Edith daren't contemplate the consequences to their marriage if she refused his olive branch. But she knew that their quarrel was another nail in what she'd begun to realise was the coffin of their love.

★   ★   ★

Edith wiped her mouth. It was a month since Dr Hardwicke had confirmed her pregnancy and she was suffering badly from morning sickness. Sighing, she closed the lavatory door behind her and went down to the kitchen.

Clarissa had propped Pearl up in the Moses basket next to Lily and Dora was feeding Jasper fingers of toast.

Benedict looked up from his bowl of porridge. 'Better now?'

Edith nodded and poured herself a cup of tea.

'I was saying that I've completed two portraits of Merryn,' said Benedict, 'and I must find a new model.' He scratched his half-grown beard and his gaze slid away from Edith. 'I'll have to call on Tamsyn again.'

'Over my dead body!' she retorted. 'I'm not having that sly minx back in this house.'

He shrugged. 'I must have at *least* six good canvases for the exhibition. Widow Armitage is a terrible old tartar . . .'

'Widow Armitage?'

'The owner of the gallery. She likes to have

things her own way. If you're going to be difficult about Tamsyn, then you'll have to pose for me, Edith.'

'I can't,' she said. 'I've barely time to see to Jasper and Pearl, never mind work on anything myself.'

'You could pose on the bed with Pearl beside you,' he said. 'Pretend to be sleeping.'

She considered the idea. Morning sickness and overpowering exhaustion were wearing her down and she'd rather pose for Benedict than have Tamsyn in the house again. Sighing, she said, 'The children will still need attending to.'

He shrugged. 'You can rest and Jasper can play on the floor nearby. I'll bring my easel down to one of the spare rooms. There's that patchwork bedspread of Aunt Hester's and the blue-patterned ewer and bowl for the washstand. It'll be a comfortable, homely scene.'

Later, Edith lay against a pile of pillows, with Pearl dozing in the crook of her arm. She'd refused point blank to be painted in the nude. Benedict had compromised on a state of déshabillé and she wore her lace peignoir, loosely tied over her thickening waist, with her hair unpinned and falling over her shoulders.

A week later, she swore she'd never sit for Benedict again. *Edith, Sleeping*, as he named the portrait, tried them both. He became irritable if the children so much as whimpered. Pearl was fretful with nappy rash and when Edith had to change her, he shouted at her. She burst into tears, hugging the screaming infant to her breast, and Jasper clung to her, weeping as if his heart

264

would break. There was a horrible, nagging feeling in the pit of her stomach. She and Benedict had grown apart and there didn't seem to be any way to mend the rift. But what else could she do? She had no money to set up home with the children away from him.

Benedict threw his paintbrush on the floor and stormed out, slamming the door behind him.

Edith tried unsuccessfully to soothe the screaming children. 'I'm no good as a mother and useless as a wife,' she sobbed, when Dora came to help.

Dora put her arms around her. 'Of course you aren't! Benedict's gone out and I'm going to mind the children now while you rest.'

Speechless with gratitude, Edith hugged her. Her head throbbed and she curled up under the quilt and slept for two hours without stirring.

When she awoke, Benedict was sitting on the end of the bed watching her. Silently, she stared back at him, conscious they were both trapped in what had become an unhappy marriage.

'Sorry,' he said. 'I know you need to tend to the children but I'm anxious I won't have enough finished canvases for the exhibition.' He reached out to stroke her cheek. 'You looked so lovely lying there asleep.' He leaned over and kissed her, his fingers trailing down her throat to her breast.

She slid her arms around his neck. Perhaps this was the way to heal the discord between them? At least it wouldn't result in another baby this time.

'I've missed you, Edith,' he murmured, his

breath warm on her ear.

'Come back to me,' she whispered.

Hastily, he pulled off his clothes and pressed his nakedness against her, his skin so warm and the scent of him so familiar.

She closed her mind to all the hurt and recalled the passion there had once been between them. That memory was enough to make her arch her back when he buried his face in her breasts. Eyes shut, she concentrated on the sensation of his caresses and the tension within her rose. She gasped out his name and heard him groan as he shuddered to his own release.

Afterwards, he raised himself on his elbow to look at her. 'You look glorious with your cheeks all flushed and your eyes so bright. It's as if there's a light shining within you and I'm seeing you afresh. If I can capture that look, *Edith*, *Sleeping* is going to be a winner, I feel it in my bones.'

★ ★ ★

The following week, Edith settled the children for a nap one afternoon and went downstairs to the sitting room, where Benedict was reading the newspaper.

'If the rain stops, I'll take a walk down to the village this evening,' he said. He glanced at the empty grate. 'At least they have a cheerful fire at the Golden Lion.'

'There wasn't any housekeeping left to buy coal for the grates, only enough for cooking,' she said, biting her tongue to prevent herself from reminding him he'd wasted the coal money on his new suit.

Footsteps clipped along the passage and Mrs Jenkins knocked peremptorily on the door. 'There's a person to see you, Mr Fairchild,' she said, 'at the back door.' She sniffed.

Benedict rustled his paper, impatient at being disturbed. 'Who is it?'

'A Mrs Gloyne, she said.'

'Send her in, then.'

A few moments later, Mrs Gloyne stood before Benedict, her hands folded together. 'Mrs Fairchild mentioned you're seeking a model, Master Benedict,' she said.

'Are you offering your services, Mrs Gloyne?'

Alarmed, she took a step back. 'Oh, no, not me, sir!'

Benedict's eyes twinkled. 'Who have you in mind, then?'

'My neighbour Albert Cleave is a carter. He's broke his leg, poor soul, and can't work so his wife must. She's waiting outside.'

'Let's have a look at her.'

Edith experienced a qualm of unease when Mrs Gloyne brought in a fresh-faced young woman with copper hair and a slender figure. Would Benedict find her a little too interesting?

He studied Mrs Cleave through narrowed eyes. 'You'd do very well,' he said. 'Can you sit still?'

'I can, sir.' She lowered her eyelids. 'Mrs Gloyne has explained I would be required to . . . ' she hesitated and a delicate flush stained her cheeks ' . . . take off my clothes.'

'Indeed,' said Benedict.

'Yes, sir. Only, my husband said he'd wish to meet you first.'

'That's perfectly understandable,' said Edith, 'but I'm Mrs Fairchild and you may tell him that I shall be on hand *at all times.*'

'Will you start tomorrow, Mrs Cleave?' said Benedict, ignoring Edith's comment.

'Yes, sir.'

Edith supposed they'd have to cut back on the groceries again to find the money to pay Mrs Cleave. Still, hopefully, now Benedict would complete enough canvases in time for the exhibition.

★ ★ ★

Clarissa walked briskly along Trevanson Street to Trewin's the jeweller's. It was the first time she'd been apart from Lily for any length of time and she wanted to conclude her business and catch the coach home as soon as possible.

In the workshop, Mr Lobb bent over the bench polishing a gold bracelet. He rose to his feet and greeted her with a smile. 'You wrote to tell me you wish to have more samples made?'

Clarissa nodded. 'A while ago, I approached Marshall and Snelgrove, the department store in London, and they've sent me an order. It's only for a few pieces,' she said, 'but they want to see other ideas, too. It's really rather exciting. It seems I was right and there's a market for this type of costume jewellery.' She opened her portfolio. 'There are twenty new designs here. While I've designed settings for the best stones, I'd be happy to discuss ways to use the remainder.' Taking a velvet pouch from her bag, she poured the contents onto the table.

Mr Lobb, his gold-rimmed pince-nez gleaming, lifted a piece of sea glass up to the light and then a pretty striped pebble. 'This,' he said, 'could be wrapped in a spiral cage of silver or copper wire to make a pendant. Perhaps I might drill holes through these flat stones and thread them to make a bracelet?'

Clarissa laughed and picked up a pink granite pebble. 'I've already made a drawing in my sketchbook of a wire cage to encircle this stone. Our thoughts are in tune with regard to design.'

'I'm disappointed my skills aren't used for making good modern pieces. Mr Trewin doesn't care for anything contemporary.'

'Perhaps one day you'll have your own shop and will make whatever you choose,' said Clarissa.

He sighed. 'I have some savings but not enough to rent premises in the right part of town.'

Frowning, Clarissa examined a grey pebble sliced through with white that reminded her of the sea on a stormy day. 'I wonder,' she said, 'is it really a shop you need?'

'I'm not much of a salesman,' he admitted. 'I like working with my hands best of all but I couldn't sell the jewellery without a shop.'

She rolled the pebble around her palm, thinking. 'Tell me,' she said, 'what percentage of the cost of materials does Mr Trewin add for his profit?'

'I couldn't possibly tell you that!' Mr Lobb's expression was scandalised.

'I'm pleased you're loyal to your employer but that percentage must add considerably to the sale price. Let me ask you this. If your savings were sufficient to make a slightly risky little investment, would you consider entering into a partnership where you could have a workshop of your own and someone else whose job it was to sell the jewellery?'

'Like a shot!'

'I need some time to mull over an idea. Meanwhile, will you write to me with a manufacturing price for the first six designs?'

'I thought you said twenty?'

'All in good time!' Clarissa tied together the ribbons of her portfolio. 'I've enjoyed our discussion, Mr Lobb, and I'll look forward to seeing the finished articles.'

25

November 1894

'Edith, help me with this, will you? I can't get the damn thing straight and I'll miss my train.' Benedict held out his gold stickpin.

She took it from him and inserted it neatly into his silk tie.

He smoothed the moustache and neatly trimmed beard he'd grown in the past weeks and studied himself in the mirror. 'The beard gives me more *gravitas*, don't you think?'

He looked breathtakingly handsome. His shoes were highly polished, shirt starched, new suit pressed and a gold watch-chain tucked into his waistcoat pocket. Edith caught sight of her reflection behind him. Her hair was tangled, her face wan with morning sickness and there were paint stains on her shapeless painting dress. 'You look very dapper, Benedict,' she said.

'I do, don't I?

'Are you sure you don't want me to come with you?'

'I've already said, I'll be too busy to pay you any attention. There's the exhibition to set up and I must ensure my canvases are in the best positions. Mother's delighted she'll have me to herself for a while and has planned a visit to the opera for us.'

'I'm sorry to miss your exhibition,' Edith said, 'and I'd have liked to meet the gallery owner. You never know, she might take something of mine in the future.'

'As I said before, old Widow Armitage is a fearful harridan. Rather stout and a tongue like a rapier.' His expression showed an uncharacteristic touch of uncertainty. 'I hope to God she likes my paintings.' He'd made a tremendous fuss over packing the canvases but refused Edith's help. Thankfully, the carrier had collected them the previous day.

She handed him his hat and gloves. 'I'm sure it will be a great success.' She hoped she was right. Some of his work had been, in her opinion, too hastily executed.

He stroked his beard again, a worried frown between his eyebrows. 'It *must* be a sell-out success, Edith.'

Downstairs, his travelling case was already in the hall. The children were in the sitting room with Dora and Clarissa.

'Jasper, come and say goodbye to Papa,' said Edith.

Benedict ruffled his hair and Clarissa and Dora wished him good luck.

'I'll wait for the carriage with you,' said Edith.

They stood by the front gate. The November wind nipped their cheeks and there didn't seem to be anything to say to each other.

At last, the carriage hove into view.

'Send my best wishes to your parents,' Edith said, as he climbed inside. 'And good luck with the harridan.' All at once, she was overcome by melancholy and wished she'd found a way to go with him. 'I love you, Benedict.' She held up her face to be kissed. He pecked her cheek briskly and slammed the carriage door.

She watched the carriage lurch away along the lane, remembering how it had once been between them and thought of all the things they hadn't said.

★ ★ ★

'Edith?' Clarissa touched her shoulder.

She glanced up, blinking. 'Sorry?'

'What is it? You're completely lost in thought.'

The children were in bed and Clarissa, Dora and Edith sat in the drawing room.

'I was wondering what Benedict was doing.'

Clarissa laughed. 'Having a fine old time, I expect.'

'I should have gone with him.'

'He wasn't upset you didn't,' said Dora.

'Exactly.' Edith chewed at her thumbnail. 'Once, we couldn't bear to be out of each other's sight. And now . . . ' It felt as if there was a stone lodged in her chest. 'I looked in the mirror this morning,' she said, 'and I barely recognise myself as the girl Benedict married.'

'Men are shallow creatures,' said Clarissa. 'The question is, does Benedict still see you as a desirable woman or only as the mother of his children? Perhaps you should go to the exhibition? Arrive elegantly dressed and hang on his arm, looking up adoringly at him for the whole evening. Afterwards, make him take you

273

somewhere romantic for dinner.'

'How can I?' she said. 'The children . . . '

Dora glanced at Clarissa, who nodded. 'We can manage for a few days.'

'Three days,' Edith said, sitting bolt upright, her eyes shining. 'One day's travel each way and one to visit Mr Hutchinson and buy winter vests for the children. Then I'll surprise Benedict at the gallery in the evening.'

'Do it!' said Clarissa.

A prickle of excitement at her unexpected daring made Edith laugh aloud. 'I'll send Mama a telegram, saying to expect me.'

★ ★ ★

Two days later, the gas lamps were being lit in the streets when Edith presented herself, fizzing with excitement, at the Fairchilds' townhouse in Berkeley Square. The butler showed her into the drawing room and she anticipated Benedict's pleasure when he discovered his wife had come to support him, after all. Her hair was washed and perfumed with rosewater and her cheeks discreetly touched with Clarissa's rouge. Her mother's maid had laced Edith's expanding waist so tightly that her breathing was of necessity shallow, but it was worth the discomfort because, with the seams let out, she'd triumphantly squeezed herself into the pink costume she'd worn on honeymoon.

Mrs Fairchild, dressed for dinner, said, 'Edith! How delightful. I had no idea you were in town.'

'I wanted to surprise Benedict,' she said. 'We can go the opening of his exhibition together.'

274

'But Benedict isn't here.'

Nonplussed, she said, 'He's already left?'

'I gather he's staying with an old school friend. Mr Fairchild and I are visiting the exhibition, of course, but we're dining with friends first and calling in to see him later.'

'I see.' Edith twisted her wedding ring around her finger, wondering how she could have misunderstood. 'Then I'll go straight to the gallery.'

Benedict's mother directed her butler to wave down a hansom cab and they made small talk about the children until it arrived.

The cab reeked of stale cigars and Edith hoped it wouldn't make her clothes smell unpleasant. She peered out of the window, thinking about her visit to Mr Hutchinson that morning. A client of his had liked her watercolour study of the harbour in Port Isaac and had commissioned an oil painting. She couldn't wait to tell Benedict her exciting news.

Although it was dark, the streets were teeming with pedestrians. Carriages and cabs rattled past, their headlamps glowing. The racket of horses' hooves and the shouts of street vendors reminded her of how she'd grown to love the peace of the countryside.

The cab halted outside the gallery in Mount Street. Light spilled out through the open door and a chattering crowd milled around, waiting to go inside. Shivering, she stood on the fringe of the gathering, feeling awkward without an escort. The throng shuffled forward and finally she stepped over the threshold, only to be asked by the doorman for her invitation card.

'I'm the wife of one of the exhibitors,' she said. 'I can't let you in without an invitation.'

The people behind pressed against her and there was an unpleasant fluttery feeling in her stomach. She tried to take a deep breath but her corset was too tight. 'Perhaps you'd fetch Mr Fairchild so he can vouch for me?'

The young man glanced at the horde at her back, sighed and waved her in.

Once past the bottleneck, the crowd thinned and Edith took a glass of wine from a passing waiter. The gallery had a series of interconnected rooms and she made her way into the first and glanced at some gloomy pastoral landscapes. She couldn't see Benedict.

Weaving through the guests, she spied one of her husband's portraits of Tamsyn. The impudent little baggage stared back at her with a mischievous grin and Edith resisted the childish temptation to poke out her tongue. She moved on to the next canvas. Mrs Cleave's pale freckled skin, copper hair and slender body gave her a distinctly Pre-Raphaelite look as she gazed wistfully into the distance. Edith thought the canvas was one of Benedict's best.

And then there was *Edith, Sleeping*. In the gallery, her portrait looked different from how she remembered it in the studio. Her painted self, in apparent abandon, reclined on the bed. The loosely tied peignoir had slipped off one naked shoulder and her black hair was spread out over the pillows. She appeared vulgar and wanton, her eyes closed, cheeks flushed and her full lips suggestively parted. It looked as if she'd fallen asleep after an afternoon tryst and a blush rose up her throat as she recalled their unexpected lovemaking that afternoon. In his painting, Benedict had exposed the aftermath of that private moment to the public gaze. She couldn't look at it any longer and fervently hoped none of the guests would recognise her.

The gallery was hot, noisy and overcrowded. She went into the adjacent room and came to an abrupt halt. Facing her was the portrait of Delphine, the very one Benedict had promised faithfully he'd burned two years before. Wearing nothing but silk stockings and a choker of black velvet, she sprawled on a daybed, one arm raised above her head to shield her heavy-lidded eyes from the sun. Edith pressed her fingers to her mouth, reliving her shock and anguish at Benedict's infidelity.

A portly man, talking loudly to a friend, stepped back and jogged Edith's arm, causing her to spill red wine down her skirt. She stared at it in dismay.

'I do apologise,' he said, and offered her a none-too-clean handkerchief.

Over his shoulder she glimpsed Benedict. He was at the centre of a group of people, laughing and talking animatedly. A tall, flame-haired woman dressed in emerald green had her slender arm linked through his. Benedict smiled down at her and squeezed her briefly to his side. Then, almost as if he felt Edith watching at him, he looked up and met her gaze. His mouth fell open.

'I say,' said the portly man, 'aren't you the girl

in one of the paintings? The one asleep on the bed?' His face broke into a grin. 'Yes, it *is* you! Awfully jolly painting, what?'

'No! That is . . . ' Benedict was pushing his way towards her through the crowd. She thrust the handkerchief back into the man's hand and backed away. 'Excuse me, my husband is looking for me.'

A moment later Benedict reached her. 'What on earth are you doing here, Edith?' His lips were pinched together in annoyance.

Hurt, she said, 'I wanted to surprise you.'

'I *told* you I'd be busy.' His voice was low and aggrieved. 'Can't you see, I must be free to talk to potential buyers?'

'Like that beautiful redhead in the emerald silk?' Edith noticed the woman was watching them.

'Are you staying with your parents?' he asked, ignoring her question.

She nodded. 'And I have some excellent news. I met Mr Hutchinson today. He's found me a commission.'

'You're trying to steal my thunder, tonight of all nights, Edith?'

'Of course not! The money will be useful though, won't it?' Feeling uneasy, she glanced at the redhead again. She was still staring.

'I'll call you a cab and we'll meet up later. Or tomorrow, if it's too late.'

'But I've just arrived!' Dismay that her lovely surprise had caused them both embarrassment made her voice tremble.

'Edith, I want you to leave. Now.' Her

husband gripped her arm.

A flash of anger made her dig her heels in. 'I saw the painting,' she said, pulling herself free.

He became very still, his expression wary.

'Benedict, how could you?' Tears started to her eyes. 'You *promised* me you'd burn it. You said we'd make a fresh start . . .'

'Burn it?'

'The painting of Delphine!'

He exhaled. 'Oh, that! I needed more canvases and it's one of my best pieces. I couldn't possibly burn it. Don't worry. I'll sell it and you'll never have to see it again.'

'That isn't the point! You knew how hurt I was after you and Delphine . . .'

Benedict stepped away from her as the elegant redhead appeared at his side. Her features were fine, her skin creamy and her pouting mouth stained crimson.

She cocked her head at Edith's husband. 'Well, well, Benedict,' she drawled. 'This must be your fecund little wife up from the country?'

Stiffly, he performed the introductions. 'Isobel, my wife. Edith, Mrs Armitage.'

Edith stared at her. She wasn't more than thirty-five. She wasn't remotely stout or ugly and she didn't look like a harridan. A vaguely familiar perfume floated like a cloud around her. 'Mrs Armitage, the owner of this gallery?' she said.

'Just so. I recognised *you* from your portrait, though I believe Benedict must have used more than a dash of artistic licence to enhance your charms.' She looked Edith up and down and then leaned forward with a patronising smile. 'Did you know you have a ghastly stain on your skirt?'

Mortified, Edith was unable to find the appropriate words to respond. What she really wanted was to slap this woman's lovely disdainful face.

'That's why I'm about to put Edith in a cab,' said Benedict smoothly.

'In that case, I'll say goodbye.' Isobel Armitage looked back over her shoulder as she walked away. 'Don't be long, Benedict,' she warned, 'your public awaits you.'

It was then Edith remembered that night in London when Benedict returned after an evening out and his shirt had smelled of musky perfume. Isobel Armitage's perfume. Humiliated and close to tears, she allowed him to lead her through the gallery towards the entrance.

The man who'd caused her to spill wine on her skirt stepped in front of them and laid a hand on Benedict's sleeve. 'I say,' he said, '*Edith, Sleeping* is one of yours, I believe?'

Benedict nodded curtly.

'Well,' the man said, 'I'm going to buy it.' He gave Edith a lascivious look. 'It caught my fancy, don't you know?' He held out his hand. 'Lionel Forster.'

Benedict's frown disappeared and his face lit up. 'You are a man of very good taste, Mr Forster.'

The two men began to chat and Edith was unable to bear it. It had been a dreadful mistake for her to come to the gallery. She backed away and escaped into another room. A group of people were discussing a painting and, as she squeezed past them, she heard a man say, 'I must meet this Benedict Fairchild. He's definitely an up and coming artist if this canvas is anything to go by. There's a delicious delicacy in the brushstrokes and the sunlight on that glorious hair simply shimmers.'

Edith glanced at the painting and blinked, unable to believe her eyes. Entitled *Summer in Provence*, it depicted a willowy young woman dozing in a wicker chair in a sunny garden. There was a backdrop of terracotta roofs and cypress trees on land sloping steeply towards the distant sea. The young woman wore an ice-blue dress that matched her eyes and she had a fall of flaxen hair to her waist. It was the study of Clarissa that Edith had painted when she and Benedict were on their honeymoon. She peered at the bottom left-hand corner of the canvas. It was signed with a flourish: Benedict Fairchild.

Heat washed over her entire body, prickling her skin with red-hot needles. She turned so sharply she trod on a man's foot and he jumped back with a muffled curse. Forcing her way through the crowd, she returned to Benedict.

'I want to speak to you,' she said, through gritted teeth.

Exhaling, he refused to meet her accusing gaze. 'You've seen it then?'

'How could you?' she hissed. 'Of all your betrayals, this is the worst . . .'

'Shh!' He gripped her wrist, none too gently, pulling her towards the door.

Edith refused to budge, heedless of the faces

turning to look at the disturbance. 'I'm going to tell that 'old harridan' of yours what you've done . . . '

'Don't!' said Benedict, speaking in a threatening undertone.

A white-haired old gentleman stepped towards them. 'Do unhand the lady, there's a good fellow.'

Benedict, his jaw clenched, released her.

'May I assist you, madam?' asked her protector.

'Thank you,' she said, 'but my husband will escort me home.'

Benedict took hold of her elbow. 'Come outside and I'll explain.'

'There is absolutely no satisfactory explanation you could possibly give for stealing my work.' Her chest rose and fell rapidly with suppressed fury as he hauled her through the gallery.

Outside, they crossed the road in angry silence and entered Hyde Park.

Edith's evening shoes were totally unsuitable for a forced march in the dark and she sat down on the first bench they came to, in a pool of light under a gas lamp. She folded her arms. 'Well?' she said.

He sighed. 'Why did you have to come here and make a scene, tonight of all nights? I hope to God you haven't ruined everything.'

'I came to support you!' Her voice rose, incandescent with rage. 'How was I to know I'd find you making up to *poor, stout, old* Widow Armitage, while you tried to pass off *my* painting as your own?'

He looked at her, coldly. 'Sarcasm doesn't become you, Edith.'

'Your behaviour is totally unforgivable, Benedict. How could you?'

'It's imperative I keep Isobel sweet if I'm to sell my paintings.'

'But they're not all your paintings, are they?'

'At the very last minute, I decided some of mine weren't quite up to scratch,' he said, looking at his feet. 'I didn't think you'd miss that old one of Clarissa. Besides, we need the money.'

'I warned you,' she said. 'How often did I tell you to stop wasting time in the Golden Lion and concentrate on your work?'

'For God's sake, Edith, will you never stop badgering me?'

'I'm not! Any fool could see you simply weren't putting in the effort required.'

He reared up from the bench. 'I can't stand this any longer. By God, I wish I'd never married you.'

She pressed her hands to her chest, the pain as sharp as if he'd thrust a rapier into her heart.

'I've had enough,' he said. 'I was having a splendid time here until you turned up and spoiled it. I shall sell Spindrift House and return to London. Alone.'

Edith caught her breath in horrified disbelief. 'You can't!' She reached towards him with trembling hands. 'Benedict, I implore you, think of our children!'

'But they're the root of the trouble, aren't they?' He raked his fingers through his hair. 'I'm not talking about this now. I must hurry back to the gallery and try to repair the damage you've caused.' Ignoring her gasp of outrage, he drew a handful of coins from his pocket and thrust them at her. 'Find yourself a cab. I'll come and see you tomorrow morning.'

'Benedict, you can't walk away like this!'

But he did, without once turning back.

26

'I don't care what he's done,' said Edith's mama at breakfast the following morning. 'You made an unpleasant scene last night. It's your duty to support your husband. If Benedict is selling one of your paintings, it's a decision he's taken in the best interests of your family. You must beg his forgiveness for making a fuss about it.'

Edith pushed away her cup of coffee, the violent movement slopping brown stains onto the tablecloth. 'Forgiveness?' she shrieked. 'I haven't done anything!'

'Precisely.' Mama's expression was cold. 'If that's the kind of behaviour you display to your husband, I don't blame him for wanting to live apart from you. Clearly, you've made insufficient effort to be loving and supportive. Neither your father nor I will allow you to shame this family with an unsatisfactory marriage. Do not imagine, even for one moment, that there is a home here for you and your children. You must mend your marriage.'

'If we're talking about shame,' Edith said, 'then look to Benedict. He was unfaithful to me on our honeymoon. Our honeymoon! Then there was his Cornish model. And now, I'm sure he's embarked upon an affair with Isobel Armitage.'

'Edith!' Mama put her hands over her ears momentarily. 'Men do stray; it's a fact of life.

285

Why, even your father . . . ' She bit her lip. 'Once you're married, it's for better or worse. It's entirely up to you to make things work. There is no divorce for ordinary women, not if they wish to keep their children.'

Edith bowed her head. She'd walked the floor most of the night and was too exhausted and wretched to argue. 'After all that's happened, I'm not even sure if I love him anymore.'

Mama looked at her with amazement. 'Love has nothing to do with a successful marriage. Surely you understand that?'

'Benedict blames the children.'

'Children will entirely disrupt the household if not correctly managed. I warned you before about your refusal to employ a nanny.'

'Benedict can't afford one.'

'All the more reason for you both to show restraint. And here you are, expecting again. Utterly irresponsible!' She shook her head at Edith's shameless fecundity. 'I shall send a telegram to Cornwall to advise it's necessary for you to remain here another day while you repair the damage you have done.'

Edith buried her face in her hands.

'Consider your reputation, Edith. If you allow a separation, you'll become an outcast from society. I suggest you think about that while you're waiting for your husband. You may receive him in the drawing room, where you will be undisturbed.'

★　★　★

286

Edith had plenty of time to consider her position since Benedict didn't arrive until early afternoon. While she could not, would not, bring herself to beg him for forgiveness, she was painfully aware of her precarious situation. She'd dressed her hair carefully and put on a pretty dress but couldn't disguise the shadows under her eyes.

Benedict, hair scented with pomade and shoes shining, strode into the drawing room, acknowledged her with a curt nod and sat down.

She gripped her trembling hands together, suddenly struck dumb.

'I haven't long so we'd better get this over with,' he said. 'The truth is, I thought I'd be happy living in Cornwall but I'm bored to death with it. Hugh Penrose has made sure the neighbours aren't friendly and I'm tired of not having enough coal to keep the house warm and always needing to scrabble to cover the bills.' He sighed. 'And then there's us.'

'Yes,' she whispered. 'You never did love me as much as I loved you, did you?'

Benedict shrugged one shoulder as if brushing her comment away.

'If you really wish to return to London,' she said, 'then the children and I will come with you.' It made her miserable to imagine leaving Cornwall but she was prepared to make the sacrifice to save their marriage.

'Good God, no! I'm sorry but I can't and won't go on like this. Living with a houseful of children is intolerable . . . all that noise and disturbance. And you know we haven't been

287

happy for a long while.' He paused to examine his neatly manicured nails. 'I did love you, Edith, but now you're a mother you're no longer the girl I fell in love with. It was all a dreadful mistake.'

An icy wave of nausea washed over her. 'But . . .'

He shook his head. 'I want some fun again. I want a new life. This morning, Isobel offered me a position in her gallery for a few days a week. In return, she'll provide me with a small salary, accommodation and a studio in her townhouse overlooking Hyde Park as well as introductions to her society friends.'

Edith knew then that Isobel Armitage had bought him. There was cold determination in his eyes and, though she guessed it would be useless for her to beg, she did it anyway. 'Please! Our children need their father,' she said. '*I* need you!'

'Nonsense! Once I've sold Spindrift House . . .'

Aghast, her stomach lurched. 'Not that! Please don't sell the house, I beg you.' She wasn't frightened just for herself and the children. Spindrift was Dora and Clarissa's refuge, too.

He paced over to the fireplace. 'There are debts to settle and I intend to make a fresh start.'

'But we don't have debts,' she protested.

He shrugged. 'I need more canvases and paint. Then there's my wine merchant here in town, a few gambling debts, the tobacconist and my tailor . . .'

'But you used my earnings from *Exploring the Ruins* to buy your new suit!'

'It wasn't nearly enough to cover my future

requirements. I'm sick of grubbing around to find enough to live on in comfort. Once I'm free from all the baggage that's holding me back, London will give me far greater opportunities.'

Stung that he should think of her and the children as baggage, Edith tried another tack. 'Will Isobel still want you if I tell her you stole my painting and pretended it was yours?'

'I really wouldn't do that if I were you, Edith,' her husband said, his voice hard. 'That would ruin us all. Cornwall's cheap but I wouldn't even be able to rent a cottage there for you and the children if you destroy my artistic reputation.'

She buried her head in her hands. Weeping and railing wouldn't help. Lying awake during the night, she'd imagined the worst that could happen if Benedict abandoned them but she hadn't really thought he would. Now, she must bargain with him, aiming to keep what was most important for the children and herself while allowing him to think he'd got the better deal.

Drawing a deep breath, she faced him. 'You were so fond of your aunt Hester and your happiest childhood memories were of Spindrift House. Wouldn't you prefer to keep it?'

'I shan't be earning enough in the immediate future to support myself to a decent standard and to keep Spindrift House as well as you and the children.'

'Perhaps,' she said slowly, 'you don't need to.' Her thoughts whirled. 'If the children and I remain there, I could take in paying guests. Then you'd be relieved of the necessity of providing financial assistance for us.'

289

'That's all very well for you,' he said, 'but it doesn't allow me to sell the house and use the money, does it? You'd have to send me half the rent you receive from the paying guests.'

'Half! There are three of us, soon to be four, and only one of you!'

'London's expensive and the children are too small to need much.'

'And you have the proceeds from the sale of *Summer in Provence*.' She refrained from saying, 'the painting you stole from me'.

'You've always been a better painter than I.' He sounded aggrieved. '*Summer in Provence* has achieved an excellent price but it cut me up that everyone was raving about it.' Benedict pursed his lips momentarily and then smiled. 'I know! Send me three or four of your paintings a year and I might manage. Nudes wouldn't be any good; our styles are too different and I shall carry on with those. People admired the landscape in *Summer in Provence*. You can work up some of your sketches from our honeymoon.' He nodded decisively. 'Yes, that'll do. I'll say it's a new and alternative direction for my work.'

She hated her husband, then. He'd given her an agonising choice. Either she must betray her artistic talent by allowing him to take credit for her work, or she and her children would have no home and no financial support. It would mean the workhouse for them all. Of course, it was no choice at all.

'If you let us remain at Spindrift,' she said, 'I'll send you three canvases a year and you'll be free to live the life you want.'

'Make it four,' he said.

'Three, for the children's sake.' She held her breath.

He rubbed the back of his neck, plainly ill at ease. 'I'm sorry it's come to this, Edith but you have to admit the lustre's worn off our marriage.'

'I believed our love was special,' she said.

'Perhaps it was, once.' He smiled, that endearingly crooked smile that had once made her melt. 'Who knows, Edith? Maybe one day I'll come back. When the children are older and less demanding.'

A rush of scalding anger exploded inside her. She stared at her lap, where her fists lay so tightly clenched the nails pierced her palms. How did he *dare* to think he could abandon her to take his pleasure elsewhere, abdicating responsibility for the family, while at the same time keeping the door ajar in case he fancied returning at some distant date? It took a great deal of self-control for her to reply to him in a civil manner.

'All I care about,' she said, 'is that our blameless children do not suffer.'

Benedict nodded. 'I'll send them a box of chocolates now and again. Or a jigsaw or some such.'

She rose abruptly to her feet and rang the bell for the butler. 'No doubt Isobel is waiting for you.'

'Indeed she is.' Benedict came over to kiss his wife's cheek.

'Don't!' said Edith. 'Just don't.'

'There's no call to be so prickly!'

291

'Isn't there?'

He shrugged. 'As you wish.'

Edith watched him through the window as he strode down the street, swinging his silver-topped cane for all the world as if he were a schoolboy who'd just been let out of class.

One thing she knew for sure was that she'd be too ashamed ever to tell Dora and Clarissa that, in colluding with Benedict, she'd prostituted her own talent.

★　★　★

Dora and Clarissa were bathing Lily and Pearl in front of the kitchen range, laughing as the babies splashed the water with their tiny hands. Dora felt a draught and looked up to see Edith standing in the doorway.

Jasper dropped his spinning top and ran to his mother. She snatched him up and hugged him tightly. 'I've missed you so much!' She squatted down by the tin bath to kiss the babies.

'Welcome home,' said Clarissa.

Dora blew a damp curl off her forehead. She'd hoped Edith would return looking refreshed, especially since she'd delayed by an extra day, but she was bone-white.

'How was the exhibition?' asked Clarissa.

'Benedict has already sold two paintings. And I have a commission from Mr Hutchinson.'

'That's such good news!' Clarissa saw the expression on Edith's face. 'Isn't it?'

'Yes, of course.'

Dora lifted Pearl out of the water, wrapped her

in a towel and handed her to her mother. Edith was upset about something, she knew it. She dried Lily and sat her on Clarissa's knee to put her in a clean nightgown, all the while covertly watching Edith. 'Was Benedict surprised to see you?'

'He certainly was,' said Edith. 'I'll tell you all about it once the children are asleep.' She rubbed at her temples.

Dora glanced at Clarissa. Something was definitely wrong.

★　★　★

'You're unhappy, Edith,' said Dora, after dinner.

'Yes,' she said. 'Benedict has left me.' When she'd recounted the whole sorry tale, she said, 'Please don't say anything too kind or I shall burst into tears.'

'Benedict is a complete and utter bastard!' said Clarissa.

Dora was shocked by her language but she couldn't help agreeing. 'To leave you high and dry when you're expecting is despicable,' she said, her heart breaking for poor Edith. 'And how *dare* he steal your painting and sell it as his own? He shouldn't be allowed to get away with it.'

'No,' said Edith. 'I was never angrier in my life but I was forced to let it go because of his threat to sell Spindrift House. And I'll have to keep sending him enough money so he can live in the luxury he craves.'

'But how can you?' said Dora. 'You haven't got

any.' There was an empty feeling in the pit of her stomach, as if she were standing on the edge of a cliff. If Spindrift House were sold, she'd have nowhere to go. None of them would. And what about the poor children? Dora had grown to love them as if they were her own.

'I told Benedict I'd take in paying guests if we could stay.'

'But apart from us,' said Clarissa, 'where would you find them?'

'On the journey home, after I'd had a good weep,' Edith said, 'I spent the rest of the time thinking.'

'I'd have been planning my revenge,' said Clarissa, darkly.

Edith sighed. 'Who was it who said 'living well is the best revenge'? That's what I must do. I remembered Pascal talking about Newlyn, where artists live in a community. Suppose we build a similar artists' community at Spindrift House? There are outbuildings in the farmyard that could be turned into studios.'

'I don't like the idea of strangers here,' said Dora.

'No,' said Edith. 'The three of us are so close it could feel intrusive, but if we have only a few other people it might not be too awful.'

'The outbuildings are full of rubbish and broken furniture,' said Dora. 'And the roofs leak. Could you afford to mend them, Edith?'

She shook her head. 'Artists who want to rent a studio would have to pay for that themselves.'

'Most artists never have any money.'

'That's the problem,' said Edith. Her eyes

glistened with unshed tears. 'But I can't think what else to do.'

'Why don't you write to Pascal?' said Clarissa. 'He'd tell us about the community at Newlyn.'

Edith fiddled with her napkin, folding and unfolding it. 'I suppose he may know of someone looking for a studio.' She sighed. 'But our pressing need is to make savings. The winter's coming and we need coal and food. I don't know how long it will be before Benedict starts chasing me for money.'

'It's outrageous,' said Clarissa. 'He should be supporting you and the children.'

'Send Mrs Jenkins back to London!' said Dora. 'We could use her salary to buy coal. I'll teach you both to cook and we'll take it in turns. Perhaps sharing the housework should be a condition of joining the community?'

'Wouldn't that put people off?' asked Edith.

'If it does,' said Dora, 'they aren't the right sort. Only rich artists who like doing housework need apply.'

'That's all very well,' said Edith, 'but do such artists exist? And, if so, where can we find them?'

They sat in silence for a while, considering the problem.

'Of course,' said Dora, 'knowing how easily Benedict is distracted, he may grow tired of this Isobel woman and come home.'

'Then Edith would kick him straight out of the door,' said Clarissa.

'But I couldn't, could I?' she said, her voice cracking. 'This is his house. I'm his wife. I have no income of my own and soon I'll have three children to support. All I have is one new commission.'

She looked so pale and sick with worry that Clarissa put her arm around her. 'Look, we're in this together. We all want to stay at Spindrift House, not only because it's a handsome roof over our heads but because we've made ourselves into a family here.'

Dora sat down on Edith's other side. 'Somehow, the three of us together will make this work.' They had to. The alternative was unthinkable.

★ ★ ★

The following day, Clarissa looked at the shadows under Edith's red-rimmed eyes and asked her to come for a walk. 'The fresh air will bring the roses back to your cheeks. Also, there's something I want to ask you.'

They put all three children into the perambulator and set off along the lane.

'I still can't believe Benedict has abandoned us,' said Edith. Her face crumpled with the effort of holding back tears. 'I feel no desire to paint — cannot imagine it returning. Without that driving force, I'm in a deep, dark well with no way to climb out. It doesn't seem two minutes since we left the Slade, so full of hopes and dreams.'

'There's no point in looking back,' said Clarissa. 'You mustn't let him ruin your life.'

When they reached the five-barred gate, she led the way into Spindrift's abandoned yard. A barn, stables, cart shed, coach house, an open-fronted cowshed and attached dairy, all in different degrees of dilapidation, surrounded them. There were some ramshackle pigsties and chicken sheds, too.

Outside the old dairy, Clarissa put the brake on the perambulator.

Edith lifted Jasper into her arms and pushed open the door.

It was a small building with a rickety wooden staircase, barely more than a ladder, leading to a loft. The room downstairs had a brick floor, two windows and slate shelving running around the once-whitewashed walls.

'It's musty,' said Edith, 'and smells of ancient cheese.' She set Jasper down so he could explore. 'Why have you brought me here?'

'I'm thinking of going into partnership with my jeweller friend, Mr Lobb,' said Clarissa. 'It's expensive having my designs made up by Trewin's so my profit margin is too small. Would you rent the dairy to me and my partner, to use as a workshop?'

'But you hardly know him!'

'He's a good worker. There's something about him that makes me think we'd do well together.' Clarissa ran a finger along the slate workbench. 'If there's no expensive shop to maintain, only the materials to buy, we can share the profits.'

'Isn't this too dilapidated?'

'I'm hoping the rent wouldn't be too high. I have my earnings but Mr Lobb has savings. He'd have to pay for the improvements.'

'What about facilities?'

'There's the outside privy and the well in the yard.'

Edith lifted Jasper up to stop him climbing the broken ladder to the loft. 'A jewellery workshop could be the beginning for our new community, couldn't it? And I suppose three young women living alone here are vulnerable. You'd better bring your Mr Lobb to take a look.'

'I'll write to him today.'

'A week ago,' said Edith, 'I'd never have imagined I'd have to open my home to strangers so I could feed my children. It frightens me,' she whispered.

Jasper whimpered, sensitive to his mother's distress.

Edith soothed him until he wriggled to be put down again. 'Benedict might have stayed if I'd only had one child,' she said. 'But if the Devil offered me the chance to go back and live the past three years again, I'd still prefer to lose my husband and have the children. I love my babies so very much.'

Clarissa glanced at Lily, asleep next to Pearl in the perambulator. 'Life doesn't always turn out how you expect but now I could never wish that Lily hadn't been born.' She hugged Edith. 'It'll all work out in the end, you'll see.' And she really hoped that it would.

27

Edith gave Mrs Jenkins notice and, over the following weeks, the friends found comfort in eating in the warmth of the kitchen again, thereby making savings on their coal bill. Together, they evolved a routine of daily household chores.

In addition, Edith kept herself busy clearing out and burning rubbish from the outbuildings, procrastinating over beginning a canvas for Benedict. Eventually, she couldn't delay any longer and shut herself in the studio each night after the children were asleep. She daren't paint it badly but the joyless exercise resulted in a lacklustre painting. As soon as the oil was dry, she sent it off to him, relieved it wouldn't bear her signature.

She was suffused with an overpowering sense of failure both as an artist and a wife. Her emotions see-sawed back and forth between optimism, despair and intense grief for the love she and Benedict had shared. Married but separated from her husband, she'd never again feel the intimate touch of a man. A desperately lonely future stretched before her that almost made her wish she'd never savoured the secret delights of physical love. There was a strange relief, however, in that she no longer had continually to placate Benedict or worry that he'd find her unattractive now her waist was expanding so rapidly.

Dora gave Edith and Clarissa daily cooking lessons. After several disasters, Edith learned to cook a creditable stew, a sponge cake and, her favourite, a suet roll stuffed with bacon, onion and cabbage.

After church on Christmas morning, where they sat as far as possible from the Penrose family, they celebrated with a roast chicken and a bottle of excellent wine that Benedict had left behind. There wasn't enough housekeeping money to make a pudding or to give presents but they'd collected greenery from the garden and made newspaper paper chains.

After lunch, Dora bashed out comic music hall songs on the out-of-tune piano and they played charades. They ran out of coal and, wrapped in blankets, huddled together and took it in turns to read *A Christmas Carol* aloud.

'I wonder what Benedict is doing,' said Edith, imagining him in bed with flame-haired Isobel.

'He can't be enjoying himself as much as we are,' said Clarissa.

Dora kissed Pearl's soft cheek. 'But he should have sent his children a present.'

Benedict had sent an expensive box of candied apricots to Edith from Fortnum & Mason. He hadn't enclosed a note. She wondered if that was all she was worth to him now, a box of sweets? And then there was Pascal. It saddened her that he'd never responded to her letter. After the declaration of his feelings for her, she hadn't imagined he'd have forgotten her so soon.

* * *

In the new year, Mr Lobb, a polite, lanky young man with auburn hair and startlingly blue eyes, came to Spindrift House to be inspected over tea. He played pat-a-cake with Jasper and tickled Lily and Pearl until they chuckled. Edith and Dora decided they liked him and he was clearly enthusiastic about the opportunity to start his own workshop there.

They went to look at the old dairy and he walked around it, saying so little that Edith became anxious he thought it too much to take on.

'My father has his own building firm,' he said, at last. 'So I understand what's what here. It looks worse than it is. Once the slipped roof slates are replaced, I can whitewash the inside and it'll be as good as new.' He scratched his head absentmindedly. 'Cold, though, and we'll need a stove. I'll find lodgings in the village.'

'You could take a room here,' said Edith, thinking of the rent money.

He shook his head. 'Best keep work and home separate until we see how we rub along.'

'So you'll join me in the new venture?' said Clarissa.

Mr Lobb glanced at Edith. 'Is that agreeable to you, Mrs Fairchild?'

'It is.'

His eyes shone as he shook hands with Clarissa. 'Then I'll give in my notice to Mr Trewin tomorrow.'

301

'Lily and I are going to the village,' said Clarissa to Edith, one morning. 'If I take the perambulator, Pearl and Jasper can come too. You'd have an hour or two to work in peace.'

Once Clarissa had disappeared down the lane, Edith went to the studio. She shivered in the cold and stared uneasily at the stretched and primed canvas on the easel, nervous of spoiling its pristine newness. Her last paintings hadn't been a great success and she was nervous of trying again. Sighing, she looked at the watercolour study of Port Isaac harbour Mr Hutchinson had returned to her, picked up her pencil and made the first, tentative lines.

An hour later she stood back. There was a dull, leaden feeling inside her when she looked at it. She wondered why she'd ever made a study of that particular view as it didn't, now, appear to have anything to recommend it. And the whole time she was filled with dread at the prospect of having to paint yet another canvas for Benedict.

She heard a footstep behind her and turned, expecting to see Clarissa. She pressed a hand to her chest. 'Pascal!' She put down her pencil, her heart hammering. 'What are you doing here?'

He stared at her, his expression shocked. 'You wrote to me and so I came. I didn't know . . . ' His gaze dropped to her waist. Composing himself, he took one of her hands and lifted it briefly to his lips. 'You are so thin it seems as if a puff of wind might blow you away.'

Edith attempted a little humour. 'Except for

my enormous stomach.' She was conscious of her faded painting dress, stretched over her burgeoning abdomen, and her hair pulled back carelessly into a loose knot by a crumpled ribbon.

'Benedict is a fool. He had everything he could ever want here. How could he desert you? And at such a time. I'm so very sorry, Edith.'

Pascal held her hand still and his kind words made the tears that were never far away prick her eyes again. It had been over a year since they'd seen each other. There were fine lines etched around his eyes now, as if he'd spent a great deal of time squinting into sunlight, but his narrow face and aquiline nose remained as arresting as ever. Until she saw him again, Edith hadn't realised how much she'd missed him.

There was an awkward pause and then he said, 'I was in France for Christmas and did not see your letter until I returned to Cornwall this week.'

A small hurt inside her eased.

'I have brought a friend from Newlyn with me,' he said, 'a photographer. He is looking for a studio.'

She was instantly alert. 'Then we must go downstairs.'

'May I see Jasper and meet your new daughter? And Clarissa's baby, too?'

'She's taken them out but they'll be back soon.'

Julian Clemens was drinking tea in the kitchen with Dora. Taller than average and with a rangy figure, he had a firm handshake and a smiling mouth bracketed with deep lines. He was a little older than the rest of them and there were a few flecks of silver in his brown hair.

Edith shook his hand. 'Pascal tells me you're a photographer, not an artist.'

'Photography is the art of the future,' he said.

She gasped in mock horror. 'I hope not, or no one will buy my paintings.'

He laughed. 'There will always be room for excellence in both disciplines. I take studio portraits for my bread and butter but like to experiment with artistic images. I sell them as framed prints and as illustrations for books and magazines. I write articles on photography for periodicals, too.'

The back door opened then and Jasper ran inside. Clarissa followed with the babies. 'That wretched woman in the greengrocer's refused to sell me a cabbage . . . Pascal! What a surprise!'

He kissed her cheeks in the French fashion, exclaimed over the beauty of the baby girls and then crouched down to greet Jasper, who regarded him with solemn eyes and a shy smile.

Dora poured tea and cut a sponge cake into generous slices.

Jasper climbed onto the chair next to Pascal's and offered him a bite of his cake.

Pascal chatted quietly with him and there was a poignancy to the scene that made Edith want to weep.

'You must be proud of your children,' said Pascal.

'I am.' Edith poured Julian another cup of tea. She faltered slightly when she noticed his left hand bore livid scars and two of his fingers were bent like claws.

He held out his hand. 'Let me spare you the embarrassment of pretending not to have noticed. I burned it in a fire.'

'What a dreadful thing!' said Clarissa.

'It was,' he said, all traces of humour gone from his voice. 'I can't hide the damage but prefer not to talk of it.'

'May I see your new workshop, Clarissa?' said Pascal, filling the uncomfortable silence.

'And you shall meet Augustus, who is teaching me to make jewellery.'

'Julian,' Edith said, 'there are various outbuildings here that could be converted into studios. Some might have a sleeping space, but you'd have to fund any building works yourself.'

'Pascal explained that.'

Edith sighed in relief and they went outside to introduce him to Augustus. Soon, they were all discussing the various building options for a photographic studio.

Julian decided the cart shed would suit him. 'I'd whitewash it myself and make a darkroom. I'd use the apple loft for a bedroom.'

He walked with a limp and Edith hoped he'd manage the ladder to the loft. 'Before we all decide,' she said, 'we must tell you how this community works.'

'Members take an equal share in the chores,' said Clarissa. 'You might be expected to bring in the coal, peel potatoes, do some gardening or fetch groceries from the village.'

Julian nodded in agreement.

'Your rent would include your share of food,' Edith said, 'and simple, homely meals would be provided.' She looked at him with a challenging expression. 'Sometimes you might be asked to cook the dinner.'

'I'm not sure my cooking is up to much,' he said, 'but I can learn. If I'm offered a place, I'd be delighted to accept.'

Edith suggested Pascal and Julian should wait in the drawing room while she discussed an appropriate rental figure with the others.

'How do we know he'll fit in?' asked Clarissa.

'Don't you like him?' Edith was surprised. 'I thought he was very personable.'

Clarissa shrugged. 'Men are arch deceivers; you need only consider Benedict to know that.'

'I'm sure Augustus isn't like that,' protested Edith.

'Augustus is . . . ' Clarissa hesitated ' . . . different,' she said.

'Well, I like Julian,' said Dora, 'and you need the income, Edith.'

'I suppose we can always give him notice if it doesn't work out,' said Clarissa.

Julian agreed to their terms and Edith suggested that, since it was growing late, he and Pascal stay the night rather than take a room at the Golden Lion.

During dinner — a root vegetable hotpot with barley, and an apple pie prepared by Clarissa — Edith decided it was a good decision to invite Julian to join them. An amusing conversationalist, he brought a welcome additional viewpoint to their discussions. After they'd finished, it was her turn to wash the dishes and make the coffee while the others retired to the drawing room.

The scullery was chilly and she shivered as she poured a kettleful of hot water into the sink and added a sprinkling of soap flakes.

Pascal came to find her and picked up a tea towel. 'I shall dry the plates, like the early days here.'

'I'm relieved to have sent Mrs Jenkins away,' Edith said. 'She was dreadfully cross when I told her, which surprised me since she never liked us, but I wrote her a glowing reference. And cooking is interesting once you get the hang of it.' She knew she was prattling but his proximity disturbed her. 'You're happy at Newlyn?'

'I have made many friends there.'

She couldn't stop herself from asking. 'Do you have a special friend?'

'There is a potter,' he said. 'Her name is Naomi.'

'How lovely,' Edith forced herself to say. 'Tell me about her.'

'She is very skilful, bending the clay to her will to make the most astonishingly original works.'

Edith disliked her already. 'And you're close to her?'

He hesitated. 'For a while, I thought I would make her my wife.'

A wet plate slipped through Edith's soapy fingers and Pascal caught it and laid it carefully on the draining board. She knew it was unreasonable to be jealous but that didn't stop her. 'Why didn't you marry her?'

'Because ... ' His eyes were dark and

brooding as he met her faltering gaze. 'Because she wasn't you.'

'Oh, Pascal!' She was still a married woman and not free to feel flattered but it comforted her to know he valued her, even if Benedict didn't.

He shrugged. 'I cannot remain at Newlyn now, for Naomi's sake. I would like very much to rent a room and studio space in Spindrift House, if you will have me?' He held up his hand as Edith opened her mouth to speak. 'I promise not to talk to you again of passion. But your friendship makes me happy. We would have a . . . ' he frowned ' . . . how do you say it? A business relationship.'

Edith's disappointment to hear this was tempered by relief. 'Your old bedroom is waiting for you. Of course you must come back,' she said, her heart lifting at the prospect.

28

March 1895

Clarissa ran upstairs to the studio, full of excitement. Poor Edith was spending every free moment there, struggling with her landscape for Mr Hutchinson. 'Edith! Do come and see!'

Her friend, figure now cumbersome in her eighth month, appeared at the top of the stairs.

'Come down to the yard. Quickly!'

'I can't stop.'

'A break will do you good.' Clarissa held out her hand and led Edith downstairs.

Pascal and Julian had left the colony at Newlyn and arrived at Spindrift House the previous month. They'd worked together to clear the cart shed and then Augustus's father was sent for. His joiners replaced the tall double doors with a large window and a front door. They partitioned off a darkroom in one corner and inserted a window into the gable wall of the apple loft. Julian whitewashed the walls and Pascal helped him to carry in from the barn a bed and other furniture that had previously been in the servants' attics.

Clarissa hurried Edith down to the yard, where Dora and the three men were gathered around a sturdy brown and white pony with a shaggy mane decorated with yellow ribbons. He was hitched up to a trap freshly painted in dark green and trimmed with canary yellow. Jasper bounced excitedly up and down on the trap's seat.

'Has someone come to visit?' asked Edith.

'It's a surprise,' said Julian. 'Pascal and I found the trap among the detritus in the coach house. It seemed a waste not to repair it.'

Pascal ran his hand over the gleaming paintwork and polished leather seat. 'We painted it together.'

Julian patted the pony's neck. 'This is Ned. He's my gift to our community, to thank you for welcoming me here. The children can ride him when they're bigger and any of us can use the trap to go to the market or the station. And, don't worry, he'll remain my financial responsibility.'

Clarissa laughed as Edith's mouth fell open in surprise. 'Isn't it a wonderful gift, Edith?'

She stroked Ned's velvety nose, smiling as he nuzzled her hand. 'Thank you, Julian. I can see Ned will soon become part of our family.'

Clarissa noticed Julian smiling at her and it was impossible not to smile back.

★   ★   ★

The following week, Clarissa watched Augustus Lobb as he bent over the workbench, filing excess solder from a silver ring.

'There,' he said. 'You can polish it now. Start with the coarse grade and work up to the finest.'

Clarissa picked up a buff stick wrapped in

310

sandpaper and carefully worked in even strokes over the surface of the ring. Her once-manicured nails were chipped and ingrained with dirt, something she'd never have allowed to happen a few years ago, but she was more content now than she could ever remember.

She glanced across the workshop, a corner of which was penned off with a picket fence. Behind it, thirteen-month-old Lily was playing with her rag doll and wooden blocks. Augustus never complained when Clarissa brought her, and sometimes Pearl and Jasper too, to the workshop.

So far, the partnership was working well and they were on first-name terms already. Augustus was quiet and hard-working and she never once felt him looking at her in that calculating way so many men did. When she suggested she might become his apprentice, he'd readily agreed. In turn, she'd promised to take him with her on her next sales visit to London. That way, either one of them would be in a position to hold the fort should it be necessary.

The door to the workshop opened and Dora came in with Jasper in her arms and a worried frown on her forehead. 'I'm sorry to bother you,' she said, 'but we need to send for the midwife. Pascal is out painting so I can't ask him. Would you mind Jasper and Pearl while I fetch her?'

'The midwife?' Clarissa put down the ring. 'But Edith's baby isn't due for a month.'

'Why don't I go?' said Augustus. 'Then one of you can stay with Edith and the other can oversee the children?'

'Thank you! Mrs Bolitho in Middle Street,' said Dora. 'It's the white cottage with the slatestone porch.'

Clarissa picked up Lily and returned with Dora and Jasper to the house.

'Edith's waters broke, right in the middle of the studio,' Dora said. 'Her pains are coming thick and fast. It's going to be a month early, like Jasper was.'

Upstairs, Edith was sitting on the edge of her bed. She glanced up, her face pinched with pain. She leaned over the brass foot-rail of the bed as another contraction gripped her.

Jasper ran to his mother and hugged her knees. She stroked his hair but couldn't speak.

Dora took his hand and lifted Lily from her mother's arms. 'Shall we play a game, Jasper? And we'll see if Pearl is awake from her nap.' She led the children away, looking back over her shoulder to give Edith an encouraging smile.

Clarissa helped her into a nightgown and supported her back with pillows.

Edith's eyes were bright with tears. 'This couldn't have happened at a worse time. I haven't finished my painting.'

'The baby won't wait for your convenience,' said Clarissa. 'Can't you write to Mr Hutchinson and ask for extra time?'

'If I let him down, he's unlikely to find me another commission.'

'You can't worry about that now. Just think, in a little while you'll have another beautiful baby in your arms.'

'Should anything happen to me,' said Edith, 'if

312

it's a girl, she'll be Nell and a boy would be Lucien.' She drew in her breath sharply as another spasm gripped her.

'Nothing is going to happen to you,' said Clarissa in her firmest voice.

Mrs Bolitho arrived. She tied a starched apron around her broad waist and ignored Clarissa. Covered in shame, she guessed the midwife remembered how she'd rejected darling Lily after her birth. 'I'll go down and see the children while Mrs Bolitho examines you,' she said.

Edith caught hold of her hand. 'Come back, won't you?'

Later, Mrs Bolitho appeared in the sitting-room doorway. 'May I have a word? Mrs Fairchild tells me her husband is away.'

'He's in London.'

The midwife clicked her tongue in annoyance. 'He ought to be here.'

'I'm afraid he won't be coming back.'

'At all?'

Clarissa shook her head.

'I'd heard rumours. Are you members of Mrs Fairchild's family?'

'We're as close as sisters to her,' said Dora.

'I suppose that will have to do, in the circumstances. I've examined Mrs Fairchild and I'm almost certain she's having twins.'

Dora gasped. 'That's why she's so big this time!'

'Twins?' said Clarissa. 'Isn't that dangerous?'

'Possibly. One of the babies is breech. Will you send for Dr Hardwicke?'

After Mrs Bolitho had hurried upstairs again,

Clarissa said, 'Augustus can fetch the doctor.'

'Poor Edith!' said Dora.

'It's disastrous,' said Clarissa. 'She'll have no choice now but to give up her painting.'

'At the moment, I'm not sure she'd care,' said Dora. 'She can't seem to settle to it.'

In the workshop, Clarissa told Augustus what was happening.

He buttoned up his coat. 'I'll stay here afterwards until she's out of danger. Perhaps I can entertain the children? I'm used to helping with my sister's brood.'

The rest of the afternoon passed very slowly for Clarissa as she sat beside Edith while she laboured.

'I can't do this anymore,' Edith whispered at length. Her lips were dry and cracked.

Clarissa moistened them with a damp cloth. 'Of course you can!' But she was worried. Her friend had grown so thin over the last months and now she barely had the strength to lift her hand.

Dr Hardwicke arrived and Clarissa waited downstairs while he examined Edith. Dora was sitting on the rug beside Jasper and Lily amongst their scattered toys. Pearl was fast asleep in Augustus's arms.

Pascal returned from his painting expedition and stood by the window, silently staring out at the deepening dusk while his fingers nervously tapped the sill.

They ate bread and cheese for supper and spent the evening playing whist, at which Augustus proved to play a devilish hand, while waiting for news from upstairs.

Then came hurried footsteps on the staircase and Clarissa and Dora rose to their feet as Mrs Bolitho opened the door.

'Mrs Fairfield is asking for you,' she said, looking at Dora. 'It won't be long but she's a hard time in front of her. Will you sit with her while I assist the doctor?' She shook her head. 'What's the world coming to? Four children and no husband!' She gave Clarissa a pointed look. 'A child needs a father. Feckless, I call it.' Muttering to herself, she retreated upstairs.

Clarissa seethed but her having a set-to with the midwife at this point wouldn't help anybody.

Edith's cries of distress drifted downstairs and Pascal silently paced up and down.

Clarissa gripped her hands together in her lap as she relived Lily's birth. It was terrifying enough to have to go through that once, but the thought of giving birth to twins was hideous. The midwife's comment about a child needing a father gnawed at her. No child needed a father like hers, of course, but she'd had friends who'd adored their papas and who'd been loved in return. It distressed her that Lily would never know a father's affection. Feeling restless, she said, 'I'll go and make sure the children are still asleep.'

She tiptoed into the nursery and stroked Lily's hair, her heart clenching with love. The three children slept peacefully, despite Edith's cries and groans from across the corridor. They were all so small and vulnerable, Clarissa's greatest fear was that something might hurt them.

'One more push, Mrs Fairchild,' said the doctor, peering between Edith's thighs.

Dora held her breath as Edith let out a long groan.

There was a flurry of activity and then came the thin, reedy cry of a newborn.

Sighing with relief, Dora watched as the baby was wrapped in a sheet and shown to Edith, who then subsided against the pillows, eyes closed.

Mrs Bolitho handed the infant to Dora. 'Hold this one while we try and turn the other.'

Edith whimpered in pain while the doctor and the midwife kneaded her abdomen.

Unable to watch, Dora rocked the babe in her arms. She pulled aside the sheet. A little boy. 'Welcome to the world,' she said. Small but perfect. She wiped blood off the top of his head with a corner of the sheet and laid him in the waiting cradle.

'It's turned!' said the doctor. 'Right, Mrs Fairchild. Push again.'

'Too tired,' mumbled Edith.

'Come along now!' said Mrs Bolitho. 'Take a deep breath!'

Dora moistened Edith's lips with a wet cloth. 'You can do it, Edith!' Her voice was firm. 'You *must* push your baby out, right now.'

Edith drew a gasping breath and pushed.

A little while later the second twin was born. Smaller than her brother and a strange blue-grey colour, she didn't cry.

Dora held her breath while the doctor held the baby up by her ankles and slapped her bottom.

Silence.

'Is it all right?' whispered Edith through cracked lips.

The doctor smacked the baby's bottom again. Still, she made no sound. He chafed her limbs but she remained limp. After a long moment, he looked up at Edith, his eyes filled with sorrow. 'I'm so sorry to tell you . . . '

Dora let out a sob and buried her face in Edith's hair.

The midwife snatched the baby from the doctor's hands, laid her on the dresser and tipped the cold water from the ewer over her.

The infant gasped and let out a piercing shriek.

★   ★   ★

Half an hour later, the doctor left.

Dora washed Edith's face and hands. 'There's a clean nightgown for you,' she said.

Edith closed her eyes and murmured, 'Too tired. Where are my babies?'

'Quite safe in their cradle,' said the midwife. She turned to Dora. 'Perhaps a cup of tea would be restorative for Mother? Then she may hold the infants.'

Dora hurried downstairs to the sitting room and Clarissa, Pascal and Augustus rose to their feet, their faces expectant. 'One of each,' she said. 'We thought we'd lost the little girl but she's rallied.'

317

Clarissa pressed her fingers to her chest. 'Thank God!'

'And Edith?' asked Pascal.

'It's been very hard for her.'

Dora returned to Edith's bedside and propped her up with pillows while she sipped her tea.

The midwife dressed the babies in napkins and nightgowns and brought them to their mother.

Edith held a baby in the crook of each arm and murmured softly to them, stroking their cheeks and downy heads in wonderment. She looked at Dora with tears in her eyes. 'Aren't they beautiful? To think I might have lost Nell . . . '

'But you didn't, thanks to Mrs Bolitho. She's as right as rain now.' Dora smoothed strands of hair off Edith's clammy forehead. But she knew they'd never forget those terrible moments while they waited until Nell breathed.

Edith's eyes closed, her face pinched with exhaustion and her arms trembling with the effort of holding the twins.

The midwife returned the babies to the cradle. 'I must see them feeding before I leave,' she whispered to Dora, 'but Mother needs a nap first.'

'I can sit with her if you want to stretch your legs?'

She nodded. 'Where's the privy?'

Dora directed her to the bathroom and went to look at the twins. Her heart melted all over again when she saw how they slept with their foreheads and knees touching, their snuffling breaths mingling.

The grandfather clock ticked peacefully on the

landing, echoed by another small sound. A water leak? Dora tightened the washbasin tap, even though it seemed to be turned off. She listened again and turned her head. Staring in horror, she saw blood dripping from beneath the bedspread, forming a glistening red puddle on the floor under Edith's bed.

Snatching open the door, she yelled for Mrs Bolitho.

Edith still slept but Dora gently shook her shoulder until she stirred, moaning and plucking at the bedspread. Pulling back the bedclothes, Dora flinched at the sight of the sheet saturated in blood.

Edith shivered, semi-conscious and muttering nonsense.

The midwife burst through the door. Grimfaced, she pushed Dora aside. 'Send for the doctor and bring me clean linen and towels. Lots of them. Quickly!'

Dora flew downstairs and ran into Pascal in the hall.

He caught her in his arms. 'I heard you shout. What is it? Edith?'

'She's bleeding!'

Clarissa and Augustus appeared in the sitting-room doorway.

'Fetch the doctor!' said Dora.

'I'll go.' Augustus opened the front door and ran off into the night without even fetching a coat.

'And towels.'

'I'll bring them,' said Clarissa, hurrying away.

'Go back to Edith,' said Pascal. 'Tell her . . .'

319

He shook his head, his olive complexion bleached bone-white. 'Look after her, Dora.'

She nodded and raced back upstairs.

Edith, waxen-pale, moaned softly while the midwife firmly kneaded her abdomen.

'Towels?' snapped Mrs Bolitho.

'Coming,' said Dora. She swallowed. It was impossible not to remember Ma's frightening stories of women dying in childbed after bleeding that couldn't be stopped.

The midwife snipped and ripped a strip off the bedsheet and packed it tightly into Edith's birth passage.

Clarissa ran into the bedroom with an armful of towels, coming to a sudden stop when she saw the blood.

Mrs Bolitho snatched a towel and wadded it between Edith's thighs before massaging her abdomen again.

Edith didn't speak or move, except for the terrible trembling that had taken possession of her body.

Clarissa glanced at Dora with fear-filled eyes.

One of the babies began to cry.

'Fetch it here,' said the midwife, 'and put it to Mother's breast. It may encourage the womb to contract and stop the bleeding.'

Dora hurried to do her bidding. After a couple of false starts, little Lucien latched on. Mrs Bolitho changed the blood-soaked towel but Edith remained unconscious.

The doctor returned and pushed Dora and Clarissa out of the room with instructions to boil water.

Clarissa's hand crept into Dora's as they hurried downstairs. 'She won't die, will she?'

'I don't know.' Dora felt as though her heart was being squeezed in a vice. 'The children! Please God, don't leave them motherless!'

Downstairs, she boiled water and Pascal carried it up.

Afterwards, the four of them huddled round the range, listening for any indication there was even the slightest change in Edith's condition.

Pictures of her passed through Dora's mind: her dear friend who'd never made her feel she didn't belong; the glowing bride bursting with happiness; the talented and ambitious artist; the loving mother of Jasper and Pearl. And now Nell and Lucien lay in their cradle oblivious to the probability they might never rest in their mother's arms again. Dora's throat constricted and she began to weep.

Pascal put his arms around her. 'Edith's life is in God's hands,' he said, his voice breaking, 'but we shall send Him prayers to remind Him she is loved and needed on this earth until it is her natural time to depart.'

Dora nodded. She whispered words of supplication under her breath and heard the others, even Clarissa, murmuring their own prayers. Eventually, Dora's sobs slowed, then ceased.

'There's nothing we can do now but wait,' said Clarissa.

Augustus, ever practical, made tea. 'We must rest,' he said. 'The doctor will call us if there's a change and, no matter what happens, the children will need us tomorrow. It's only a couple of hours to dawn.'

Unwilling to retire separately, they settled down on the comfortable old sofas in the sitting room, leaving the door ajar.

Dora drifted off, holding Clarissa's hand, and dreamed of the Spectre of Death hanging over Edith, while her children looked on, weeping helplessly.

Dora's eyes flickered open. Clarissa was curled up beside her. Grey dawn light outlined the sitting-room curtains and Pascal stood between them, staring out at the garden. The hideous events of the previous night came flooding back.

She sat up, afraid to find out the latest news. It almost stopped her breath to imagine four precious children left without their mother to love them. Benedict had no time for them and Edith's ma was so cold. Without his wife here to protest, Benedict would sell Spindrift and turn them all out. The children might end up in an orphanage. It was unthinkable. But what if Dora went to Edith's ma and offered to be the children's nanny? If Mrs Hammond would give them a home, at least that way Dora could give the children the love they deserved.

Upstairs, floorboards creaked and then there was a step on the stairs.

Pascal spun around, taut with anxiety. His jaw was shadowed with dark stubble and his face creased by exhaustion.

Dr Hardwicke pushed open the door.

Augustus rose to his feet and Clarissa sat up.

The doctor wiped his face with his hand. 'The bleeding has stopped,' he said, 'but Mrs

Fairchild is extremely weak.'

'Will she live?' asked Pascal, his voice husky.

'I believe so,' said Dr Hardwicke. 'She'll need careful nursing and mustn't exert herself in any way. I shall visit tomorrow. Good day to you.'

Clarissa let out a sob and Pascal swayed and sat down suddenly.

All at once it was plain to Dora that, for all his careful attempts to hide it, Pascal, steadfast and loyal, was in love with Edith. How desperately sad for them both that Benedict had come along first and swept her off her feet with his false promises.

★   ★   ★

Later, Edith barely remembered the days that followed. Frequently, she fell asleep while feeding the twins under Dora's watchful eye. She swallowed sips of beef tea and, when she was a little stronger, endless meals of chopped liver to restore her strength. The midwife visited each day, sometimes accompanied by Dr Hardwicke.

Eventually she was able to sit up and Jasper and Pearl were brought to see her. Overawed, they kissed her cheeks and stared curiously at the twins. Feeling exhausted after they left, she leaned back against the pillows while Clarissa read to her.

Edith awoke one afternoon to find Pascal sitting beside her, holding her hand. Involuntarily, she smiled.

'You have a little colour today,' he said.

Dora sat in a corner of the room, rocking the

cradle and humming to the twins.

Cautiously, Edith sat up and found she was less dizzy than before. 'I shall be better soon,' she said. 'I must be ... I have to finish my commission.'

'There is time for that when you are well.' He kissed her fingers and stood up. 'You must rest. I shall see you tomorrow.'

After he'd gone, she began to fret. If she didn't complete her commission, Mr Hutchinson might not find her another.

Over the following days, her anxiety grew and eventually Dora, usually so patient, snapped and scolded her. 'Your milk will dry up and your babies will be hungry if you don't stop worrying!'

Edith sighed. 'I *will* stop worrying, if only I can finish the beastly painting.'

The following morning, Pascal carried the twins up to the studio and, whenever they slept in the nest of blankets by Edith's feet, she worked on her painting. Some days she was so drained it was as much as she could do to lift a brush.

Pascal worked silently beside her. When she burst into tears because she couldn't mix the exact colour she wanted, he calmly took the palette from her and mixed it himself. If the twins fussed, he rocked them in his arms.

A week later, Edith wept with relief when she made the final brushstroke. She was so fatigued she could barely see straight but Mr Hutchinson would have the canvas in time.

Augustus made a crate for the painting and

Julian arranged for the carriers to convey it to London.

Edith crawled back to bed.

29

The following weeks passed for Edith in an extraordinary merry-go-round of intense love, pride, elation and the most profound exhaustion known to woman. Some nights she didn't sleep at all. Often it took more than an hour to feed, change and settle one baby and then the other would wake, ready to start the whole cycle again. Some days she never managed to get dressed at all and she didn't know how she'd have survived without Dora and Clarissa to help mind Jasper and Pearl.

Early on the morning of Jasper's second birthday in May, Edith surfaced from the depths of a deep, dark pool of sleep as suddenly as a cork popping from a shaken bottle of Champagne. She reared up in bed, her limbs tangled in the sheets. She'd only closed her eyes for a moment but one of the twins was wailing — again. Stumbling over to the cradle in the pale dawn light, she hurried to pick up Lucien in the vain hope he wouldn't wake Nell but she began to whimper even before Edith had crossed the floor. Sighing, she laid her daughter on the other shoulder and padded back to bed.

Unbuttoning her nightgown, Edith closed her eyes while the twins suckled. Eventually, they finished their feed and she placed them in their cradle, face to face, bodies touching, in the way that was most likely to soothe them. Often, they slept with their tiny starfish hands entwined. Overwhelmed again by love for them, she watched them fall asleep.

Slowly, she washed and dressed, all the while attempting to shake off the fog of weariness that seeped into her very bones. On the day Jasper arrived she could never have imagined that, less than two years later, she would be the mother of four. Weary, even before the day began, she sank onto the nursing chair and closed her eyes, just for a minute, and immediately slipped back into the pool of darkness.

Clarissa awoke her with a cup of tea. 'Breakfast is ready,' she murmured, glancing at the sleeping twins. 'Dora's dressing the children.'

'You are both absolute saints,' said Edith, full of gratitude.

Clarissa hugged her. 'You saved my life once, by allowing me to live here. I'll never forget that.'

Jasper opened his birthday presents after breakfast. He showed a passing interest in the wooden train Edith had bought for him but it pleased her greatly to see his face light up at the sight of the tin of crayons and a sketchbook that was Pascal's gift. He immediately set about scribbling intently, trying all the colours, one by one. Pascal sat beside him, their dark heads touching as they bent over the sketchbook.

Pearl bounced up and down in her highchair, banging on the tray with a spoon until Dora set her on the floor. She crawled over to Julian and pulled herself up to a wobbly standing position.

Smiling, he took her hand and walked her across the room.

Pearl shook off his grip and, crowing with delight, took her first tottering steps towards Edith. Her little legs gave way and she collapsed onto her padded bottom, her eyes round with astonishment.

Edith laughed and picked her up. 'My clever little girl!' Her heart swelled. Even though Benedict had never responded to the telegram informing him of the twins' arrival, she had four beautiful children and a group of faithful friends. Despite the difficulties, there was much to be thankful for.

★ ★ ★

Clarissa and Lily usually visited Ned in the afternoons, bringing him an apple core or a tuft of grass. The door to Julian's studio was open one day and he ambled out to join them.

Clarissa lifted Lily onto her hip so she could pat the pony's nose. 'How are you settling in, Julian?'

He sighed contentedly. 'It's so peaceful. And I swam before breakfast today.'

'Are you finding inspiration here?'

'Oh, yes,' he said.

Clarissa gave him a sideways glance and saw he was looking at her. She hoisted Lily up against her chest, like a shield.

'Would you like to see some of my work?' he asked.

She nodded and followed him into his studio.

Julian opened one of the shallow drawers in a plan chest and spread out a number of photographs on the table.

She picked up an image of an ethereal scene: skeleton trees in a winter landscape. 'This is extraordinary.' She examined the others, mostly landscapes and one or two of the sea in swirling mist; they caught her interest every bit as much as a good painting would have done. Tucked beneath a photograph of a cornfield was a portrait of a small boy. Dark-haired, his clear eyes looked out with a direct gaze. His mouth was half-open, as if about to speak. 'What a lovely portrait,' she said.

'My son Will. He's three now. This was taken a month before . . . ' Julian took the photograph from Clarissa and replaced it carefully in the drawer.

'Before what?' she prompted.

His voice was so quiet she had to strain her ears to hear him. 'Before the fire that took his mother's life.'

Clarissa caught her breath. 'What happened?'

'I don't talk about it.'

She slid one hand inside the opposite sleeve, feeling with her fingertips for the old scars on the inside of her forearms. There were painful things she could never, ever speak of but maybe she could help him by listening. 'Perhaps you should,' she said. 'When you keep terrible memories bottled up inside you, it can only do harm.'

He was silent for some time, staring down at his twisted hand. 'The guilt eats away at me,' he murmured.

'Tell me.'

'Maybe it is time.' He gave a great sigh. 'I'd gone to meet friends. It was late when I returned and there was a light flickering in the downstairs window. Our maid was visiting her mother and I thought Sarah, my wife, had left the lamp to light me upstairs.' He rubbed his temples. 'I opened the front door and was hit by a wall of scorching air and smoke. The kitchen was ablaze and the hall floor glowed orange. I shouted for Sarah but there was no reply. The draught from the open door fanned the flames and thick smoke curled up the stairs. Will was crying.'

Clarissa hugged Lily tightly, imagining how she'd have felt if it had been her child in such danger.

'I ran upstairs,' Julian continued, 'and felt my way along the landing, shouting for Sarah. She was asleep. Smoke from the parlour seeped through the bedroom floorboards and the rug was smouldering. She went into a paroxysm of coughing and I snatched up a towel and made her hold it over her nose.' He paused, his own breathing ragged. 'I told her to run outside while I fetched Will.'

'Where was he?'

'In the back bedroom. It was full of smoke and he was struggling to breathe. He clung to me and the fire was roaring and the flames leaping as I hurtled down the stairs. The hall floor-boards had burned through. I jumped from one red-hot floor joist to another to reach the front door. I was never so relieved as when I made it outside.' He closed his eyes. 'But I couldn't find Sarah.

Our neighbour arrived and he took Will while I ran back inside. I'd barely gone through the front door when there was a hideous creaking and groaning and the drawing-room ceiling collapsed. I was thrown back by a blast of searing air and covered in a shower of orange sparks. And then came the terrible screams . . . '

Clarissa's heart ached for him as he buried his face in his hands. Awkwardly, she patted his heaving shoulders.

'I apologise,' he murmured.

'You have nothing to apologise for.' There were tears on his eyelashes but she resisted the urge to wipe them away.

He drew a steadying breath. 'I went back inside, of course.' He held up his damaged hand. 'My feet and legs burned, too, but I was too late. Sarah's screams had stopped. When the bedroom floor collapsed into the parlour, she fell with it. I torture myself with the knowledge that she must still have been in bed when I carried Will past her door.'

'You mustn't blame yourself,' said Clarissa fiercely.

'But I do.' He shrugged. 'And then, Will was so young and I couldn't give him the care he needed. He lives with Sarah's widowed mother in Launceston now. That's why I came to Cornwall, so I can visit him.'

A double bereavement. 'You must miss him dreadfully.'

'More than I can say.' Julian swallowed and composed himself. 'My recovery, mental and physical, took time and I lost my job at a bank. I

331

decided then that I'd make a fresh start and chose to learn more about my hobby of photography. So here I am.'

'I can't begin to imagine your suffering,' Clarissa said. 'I wish there were something ... anything ... I could say to make you feel better.' She sighed. 'Sometimes loneliness is nearly as distressing as the memory of an unspeakable event.'

He frowned slightly. 'You sound as if you speak from experience.'

'Oh, I do,' said Clarissa. She walked towards the door. 'Don't forget,' she said, 'I'm here if you need to talk.'

★ ★ ★

It was a warm and sunny June day and Dora laughed and clung onto her hat as they bounced over the potholes. Pascal, with Augustus beside him, drove the trap and she'd never travelled so fast before, except in a train.

Jasper squealed in delight, snatching fruitlessly at the foaming masses of cow parsley that lined the lane. Edith and Clarissa held the little girls firmly on their laps while the twins were nestled safely into a Moses basket between their feet.

The whole village would be at the inaugural opening of the new Port Isaac Road railway station. After the ceremony, vehicles would drive the three miles from the station to Port Isaac, to continue the celebrations there with swimming races, aquatic displays and a tea party. Rows of flags had been strung across the narrow streets and almost every house was hung with bunting.

A brass band was in full flow when they arrived at the station, adding to the general air of excitement. They pulled up alongside a number of other traps, carts and carriages. People dressed in their Sunday best gathered in chattering groups and shrieking children ran about playing tag.

Julian, who had gone on ahead with his photographic equipment, came hurrying across to say, 'You need to find a position straight away or you won't be able to see the ceremony.' He lifted Lily down from the trap and offered his hand to Clarissa.

A podium was set up in front of the entrance doors to the new station, with a semi-circle of chairs facing it.

Dora nudged Edith. 'The Penroses are here,' she said. 'Do you see? Sitting next to Reverend George's wife.'

'I'll stay in the trap,' said Edith. 'I can't manage all four children without the perambulator.'

'I'll stay with you then,' said Dora. She grabbed at Pearl's frilled pinafore as the little girl stood up on the seat to watch the goings-on.

Pascal came to sit beside them with his sketchbook. He made lightning sketches of the crowd while Jasper leaned against him, watching.

A carriage bowled up and a number of important-looking gentlemen descended. The band struck up a military marching tune and the crowd parted as the men made their way to the podium.

The speeches went on too long in Dora's opinion. The big-wigs from the North Cornwall Railway banged on about expansion and progress, the benefits to the fishermen in sending their catch to new markets and the expectation of bringing holidaymakers and new revenue to Port Isaac. At last, the ribbon securing the station doors was cut and they were ceremonially opened to a cheer from the crowd.

Clarissa and Lily returned to the trap and Julian set up his camera and took a group photograph.

Dora noticed half-a-dozen women were standing nearby, glancing over their shoulders at them. She knew that secretive, backward look. They might be fine ladies in posh hats but they were no different from common washerwomen, inciting each other to exchange nasty tittle-tattle. 'I don't like the look of that lot,' she said to Edith. 'They're talking about us.'

'Isn't that Reverend George's wife with Mrs Penrose?' said Edith. 'I hope there isn't going to be any trouble.'

But there was. Dora clutched Pearl tightly as the ladies walked purposefully towards Edith.

'Shameful!' said Mrs Penrose. 'Three women and three men all living together in the house you stole from my husband . . . and none of you married to each other.'

A lady wearing a lilac hat and an expression of moral outrage pointed her parasol at them. 'It's disgraceful you see fit to parade yourselves in public amongst decent, God-fearing people.'

Pascal reared to his feet. 'Such groundless

accusations dishonour only your own character, *madame*.'

Lilac Hat rapped the side of the trap with her parasol. 'It was only out of Christian duty that the midwife attended the recent births. Five children between you and no one knows who fathered them, least of all their mothers.'

Edith gasped. 'That's a dreadful lie!'

'And unwarranted,' said Julian, frowning. 'There's some misunderstanding.'

'Yes,' murmured Clarissa, 'and it's caused by Mrs Penrose's malicious lies.'

'Artists and foreigners have no moral compass,' said Jenifry Penrose. 'Who knows what wicked debauchery takes place in Spindrift House?' Her eyes gleamed with spite.

'None so wicked as that of your imagining,' said Clarissa. She scanned the crowd. 'Julian, would you go and ask that man,' she pointed at Hugh Penrose, 'to come and take his wife away before I inform the constable of her slanderous accusations?'

'I'm astonished any of you presume to show your faces in my husband's church,' said Mrs George, pressing a lace handkerchief to her lips. 'You're not morally fit to have the care of children.'

'Please, leave us alone,' said Edith. She was so ashen-faced Dora thought she might faint.

Pascal jumped down from the trap and stood before the vicar's wife. 'Enough! You must inform yourself of the truth before you accuse innocent people, *madame*.'

In the face of his anger, Reverend George's

335

wife stepped back, one hand pressed to her bosom.

Hugh Penrose hurried towards them and Clarissa descended from the trap with Lily in her arms. 'Mr Penrose,' she said, 'your wife has once again made false and vicious allegations about me and my friends. I must insist you curb her spiteful rumour-mongering.' She turned Lily to face him. 'Surely you'd no more wish this innocent child to suffer from your wife's lies than one of your own little angels? I'm warning you,' she said, 'restrain your wife or I shall be forced to make a complaint at the police station.'

Hugh Penrose looked as sick as a dog and, if Edith hadn't been so distressed, Dora might have laughed.

A few minutes later it was all over. Hugh took his wife's arm in a tight grip and shepherded all the women away.

Dora breathed a sigh of relief.

★   ★   ★

After that confrontation, none of them had felt like joining the village celebrations and they'd decided to go home. In the trap, Edith sat in uncomfortable silence all the way, conscious that Jenifry's accusations bore an unpalatable and shameful seed of truth that had made it impossible for her to refute them.

When they arrived at Spindrift House, a wagon had drawn up outside and a carter was lifting down a large parcel. 'Package for a Mrs Fairchild,' he said.

Pascal carried the parcel into the kitchen.

Edith put the twins in the perambulator outside the back door. Her spirits lifted a little as her friends crowded around the kitchen table, waiting for her to open the parcel. She glanced at Pearl, walking unsteadily across the kitchen, her skirt already grown too short. 'I hope it's from Benedict's mother,' she said. 'She sent nightgowns for the twins last time.' She tore open the brown paper. 'Oh!' she said. 'It's the canvas I sent to Mr Hutchinson. Why . . . ' She snatched up an enclosed envelope.

Not what was expected . . . disappointed my client . . . unlikely to find new commissions for you . . .

Silently, she handed it to Clarissa. Humiliation seared Edith's cheeks and she turned her back on the others to set the kettle to boil while she composed herself. Every brushstroke of that painting had been as painful to her as walking on broken glass and she'd hated it by the time it was finished. What had happened to her talent? Her vision blurred as she set out the cups and saucers.

'Oh, Edith!' Dora put her arms around her.

'I wish I hadn't wasted my time.' She swallowed. 'The awful thing is, I agree with Mr Hutchinson. It's not a good painting and, deep down, I knew it.'

'You're too hard on yourself,' said Clarissa. 'The twins were newborn and you were exhausted.'

'I'm always exhausted.' Jasper tugged at her skirt. She cut a slice of bread and set it in front of him at the table.

Pearl tottered after Lily, tripped over and began to yell.

Edith picked her up and she lurched off again, a determined expression on her face. 'The truth is,' she said, 'even if I wasn't overwhelmed by the children's needs, I'm too frightened to pick up a paintbrush again.'

'You can still paint,' said Pascal, 'but your confidence has suffered.'

Then Pearl banged her head on the table and her outraged screams made conversation impossible. She sat on the floor with tears rolling down her cheeks, refusing to allow either Dora or Edith to comfort her.

Pascal crouched down and made funny faces at her. Miraculously, the screams ceased. She rolled onto all fours and pushed her bottom into the air.

Wearily, Edith went to lift her up but Pascal caught hold of her wrist. 'Wait,' he said.

Slowly, Pearl pulled herself up by the table leg into a standing position. She laughed in triumph and staggered off again.

'Did you see?' said Pascal. 'Your brave daughter picks herself up each time she falls. She laughs in the face of misfortune.'

Silently, Edith watched Pearl. Perhaps there was something to be learned from her? Certainly she couldn't go on as she was. She straightened her back as she realised what she had to do. 'Will you all come with me? Please, bring the painting.' She put Pearl in the perambulator with the twins, held out her hand to Jasper and led

338

the small procession outside. In the walled kitchen garden, she collected newspaper from the shed, crumpled it up and made a pyramid of sticks over it on the ashes of the bonfire. Then she placed her painting on top and lit a match.

'But you can't!' said Dora. 'All that work . . . ' She snatched the canvas off the pyre.

Pascal shook his head and put it back. 'Wait, Dora!'

'I'm still determined that, one day, my work will be displayed in the Royal Academy,' said Edith. 'I wouldn't then want anyone to know I ever painted anything as poor as this, whatever my excuse.'

Flames licked the edge of the canvas, greedily feeding on the oil paint.

'It's been a horrible day,' said Edith. 'I can't change Jenifry Penrose but I can change myself. I adore my children but I can't work properly in brief snatches of time. I hadn't wanted more strangers at Spindrift but I see now it's essential I make this community into a proper commercial venture. Once there's more income, I'll find a girl from the village to help with the children. Then I shall start working properly again.'

'Augustus and Julian were strangers to us once,' said Clarissa, smiling at them. 'But they've turned out quite well.'

'They're part of our family now,' said Edith. She poked the fire vigorously with a stick and a shower of sparks flew into the air.

'I was cautious about fitting into such a tight-knit group,' said Augustus, 'but you've all made me most welcome.'

'Hear, hear!' said Julian.

Augustus waved a hand at the sheltering garden walls. 'There is more we can do to be self-sufficient,' he said. 'It's a waste not to grow vegetables here. If we all help to maintain it, I don't see why we shouldn't grow enough for our needs.'

'I don't know the first thing about growing potatoes but I can learn,' said Edith.

'And, if it's agreeable to you,' said Augustus, 'now we know each other, I'd prefer to rent a room here than in the village.'

'I'd far rather have you here than a stranger.' said Edith. 'If you'll pay the same rent as you do at present, you can move in as soon as convenient. Then I'll be in a position to look for a part-time nursemaid.'

'If you can find one,' said Clarissa. 'The whole village thinks we're depraved. They might not let their daughters come here.' She sighed. 'I'm finding it hard to work with Lily underfoot in the workshop. I can't keep her behind a fence now she's walking. The tools are sharp and there are the acid baths for cleaning the jewellery. I'm frightened she'll hurt herself.'

'The older children are running about all over the place,' said Dora with an anxious frown. 'Before long the twins will be on their feet too. Suppose the girl didn't watch them properly? There's the stream and the cattle pond at the end of the garden and, dear God, the cliffs . . . '

'But I *must* start painting again.' Edith poked the fire and the last of her painting crumbled into blackened ashes. 'Not only to make a living

340

but because it's everything I am.'

'What you and Clarissa need,' said Dora, 'isn't a part-time nursemaid but a full-time wife.'

Clarissa laughed. 'What an extraordinary thing to say!'

Dora's cheeks reddened. 'Is it? Fathers work to bring home the bacon but they never change Baby or cook the dinner. For you and Edith to bring home the bacon, you must be freed from domestic cares to use your talents.'

'If only Edith and I could find such a helpmate!'

'Why not me?' said Dora. She shuddered. 'After what I've seen of Benedict's antics, I'm doubly sure I'll never marry.' She looked away, blinking rapidly. 'But you can't know how sad it makes me that then I'd never have children of my own. I've wanted that beyond anything, far more than becoming a famous artist.'

'The children adore you,' said Edith, 'but it's too much to ask.'

'And I love them,' said Dora. 'You'd both still be their real mothers but I could take on the role of another parent to them.' She jutted out her chin. 'Let me *fully* share the joys and responsibilities of motherhood. I don't want paying, only my keep and to be part of this family.'

'You're already part of the family!' said Clarissa. 'There's no one else I'd trust as much as you to care for Lily.'

'Absolutely,' said Edith. 'I'd much prefer to pay you than a girl from the village.'

Dora beamed. 'My sister Annie is fifteen now,' she said. 'She's a good girl and a hard worker. If she came to help me — and she wouldn't need much more than board and lodging — I'd put aside my artistic career for a few years, to keep house and mind the children for you both.'

Sudden, hopeful euphoria made Edith catch her breath.

'And if you'd consider supplementing the twinnies' feeds with a bottle, Edith,' Dora continued, 'we could share the night feeds.'

'Oh, Dora,' breathed Edith, 'I can't remember when I last had an unbroken night. If only I could sleep, I think I could paint again.'

'Then that's settled.'

Tears welled up in Edith's eyes. 'You'd really sacrifice your work for the children?'

'Oh, yes,' said Dora, 'with all my heart.'

30

The postman brought a number of responses to Edith's newspaper advertisements seeking artists to join their community. She scanned replies from several painters, a potter, spinster sisters who designed and printed fabrics, and a sculptor. The group invited the most suitable applicants to visit Spindrift House.

Augustus gave notice to his landlady in the village and moved in, taking on another share of the heavier chores.

Edith heaved a sigh of relief when Dora completed her series of illustrations of coastal plants and posted them to *Nature Review*, leaving her free to take over the household management. Her sister Annie arrived a week later and Edith liked the girl's open, smiling face at once. Annie set to work with a will, scrubbing floors and cleaning under the furniture without complaint. Like her sister, she had a natural fondness for children.

Early the following morning, Edith opened the bedroom window and leaned over the sill. Mist wreathed the garden and, at the horizon, the sky dissolved into the sea. She breathed a sigh of pleasure. For the first time in a long time, she yearned to paint and, today, she'd have several hours to do exactly that.

After breakfast, she waved goodbye to the

children and walked to the village, feeling as free as the air. The sun was already hot and the mist had burned away. She spent a happy morning sitting by the harbour making rapid watercolour studies. A number of holidaymakers came to peer at her sketchbook and she remembered Pascal suggesting summer visitors might buy some of the community's work as souvenirs.

Finally, hunger made her stomach growl and she packed away her paint box. On her way home, she called in at the baker's. The sight of a whole tray of glistening saffron buns made her mouth water.

The woman before her in the queue murmured to another, who glanced over her shoulder at Edith.

The shop bell jangled and Mrs Gloyne entered. 'Good afternoon, Mrs Fairchild. No little 'uns with you today?'

Edith was relieved to see a friendly face. 'I came to buy saffron buns for their tea. Are you well, Mrs Gloyne?'

'Fair to middling.'

Edith forgot the suspicious glances as she and Mrs Gloyne chatted until the other customers had left. Edith went to the counter then and asked for nine saffron buns.

'All gone,' said the baker's wife.

'But there was a whole tray a moment ago!'

The baker's wife shrugged.

'I'll have two white loaves, then.'

'Everything left is spoken for.'

Edith looked at her mulish expression and knew it was useless to argue. She nodded at Mrs

344

Gloyne and left, a pulse of anger beating in her temples.

Further along the street she heard someone call her name.

Mrs Gloyne was hurrying after her, holding out a small twist of paper. 'Two ounces of yeast,' she said. ''Tis terrible the mischief-making in this village and I daren't buy you bread.'

Edith's vision blurred. 'That's very kind, Mrs Gloyne.'

Back home, as she served vegetable soup for lunch, Edith bemoaned what a good job Jenifry Penrose and Mrs Bolitho had made of turning the villagers against the Spindrift community.

'On a more positive note,' she said, 'I had an idea when I was painting by the harbour. Several summer visitors came to look at my sketchbook and were so interested. It occurred to me that if we made a gallery in one of the outbuildings here, then there'd be somewhere holidaymakers could buy our work.'

'I like that idea,' said Clarissa.

'If we work hard this winter, we'll have enough to display in our gallery next summer.'

After lunch, Edith and Pascal went to the studio. Setting out her morning's watercolour sketches, she chose one to be the inspiration for her new canvas. As she started to draw, her thoughts kept drifting back to the women in the bakery. Too agitated to concentrate, she went to stare out of the window.

When she returned to her easel, she could see her drawing was all wrong. She rubbed it out and began again. Her shoulders were tense and the pencil felt awkward in her hand. All her confidence of the morning dissipated. After a while, she dropped the pencil with a sigh.

Pascal looked up from his easel. 'Trouble?'

'There was some unpleasantness at the bakery this morning and now I can't concentrate.'

He rinsed his brush. 'Shall we take a walk?'

'I *must* start the new canvas today.' She knew she'd have to face up to painting another canvas for Benedict before long. The thought of explaining their agreement to Pascal and the others was unbearable. She'd never imagined she'd compromise her artistic ideals in this way and it made her ashamed.

'We shall go to the cove and come straight back,' said Pascal.

Ten minutes later they walked along the water's edge, the waves lapping gently onto the sand.

'Look at the sea, Edith!' said Pascal. 'Sometimes it is calm, like today, and at others wild and stormy. It was here yesterday and it will be here tomorrow. You must learn to weather the storms in the certain knowledge that painting will bring you pleasure again.'

'I *was* excited this morning. Jenifry Penrose and her gossip ruined that.'

'Forget her! Look ahead to what you wish to achieve. It may be a grand ambition like an exhibit in the Royal Academy or simply to finish a sketch to your satisfaction. Don't try so hard. Allow yourself to dream as you work. Forget how little time you have and feel your way into the work with your pencil.'

346

'I'm not sure I understand?'

'Don't attempt a finished drawing straight-away. Let the pencil make the marks while you look for the main lines of tension in the drawing. Search for the patterns of light and dark — and suddenly your haphazard scribbles will come together.'

'I was taught to make sure the under drawing was perfect before adding colour.'

Pascal shrugged. 'But that way isn't working for you. Now you must try something different.'

Edith walked beside him, lost in thought. Her usual method was to concentrate fiercely and make each pencil line as perfect as she could as she went along. Her drawing skills had been learned through sheer hard work and perseverance and she didn't know if she could work in such a loose way. Dream your way into your work, indeed! Whatever did he mean by that? She sighed. But Pascal's paintings were vivid and lively so there must be something in his suggestion.

They returned to the studio. 'I work better after a walk,' he said, 'and you will too.'

Edith studied her sketches of the harbour and chose a different view. There was an exuberant freshness about it. When she'd painted it, she hadn't worried about anyone else judging it, attempting only to capture the scene with the intention of using it as a basis for a more polished future work. She summoned up the memory of the sun warm on her shoulders that morning, the salty breeze in her hair and the fishing boats bobbing about on the water. Holding onto that moment, she took a deep breath and picked up her pencil. Pascal had said, *Don't try so hard. Allow yourself to dream as you work.*

An hour later she stepped back from the easel. She'd sketched the main lines of the composition, feeling her way into the relationship between the shadows and the sunlight. There was a delightful energy about the drawing and her former excitement in her work throbbed through her veins again. She had Pascal's advice to thank for that.

★ ★ ★

Edith arranged for the five most promising applicants who were interested in joining the community to visit Spindrift House. One wasn't financially able to take on the repairs required to convert a stable workshop. Another had a manner so dictatorial that Edith's hackles rose. He made the foolish mistake of pressing his opinions on Clarissa and the resulting spat was so sharp he stormed off without saying goodbye.

Gilbert Ryan, a sculptor, was a different kettle of fish entirely. A great big bear of a man with a bushy red beard, he was enthusiastic about the vegetable garden and asked if he could bring his bee hives. A childless widower in his fifties, he wrote poetry in his spare time. His jovial and enthusiastic manner endeared him to the others.

The remaining applicants were elderly spinster sisters, Maude and Mabel Ainsley. Tall and lanky, they resembled a pair of storks. Almost entirely beige themselves, with mousy hair and pale eyes, they wore shapeless dresses of homespun wool, but created wonderfully colourful and intricately detailed silk scarves and embroidered wall-hangings. Their dear departed father had left them a substantial income. All three new applicants cheerfully agreed to share the rota of chores.

A great weight lifted from Edith's shoulders. The children needed new clothes, the cost of provisions for the growing community was frightening and there were slipped slates on the roof. Even with new members, they'd still have to live frugally because of how much had to be paid to Benedict. Still, the extra income would ease some of the worries and, hopefully, bring the additional benefit of new ideas.

Knowing her children were lovingly cared for while she worked, allowed Edith finally to regain her strength and find pleasure in painting again. She finished her canvas of the harbour. It depicted a bright and breezy summer day. The blue of the sky was reflected by the sea, fishing boats sailed gaily upon the water and a group of children paddled in the rock pools beside fishermen mending their nets. It was a million miles different from her previous canvas of the harbour that she'd burned.

Her work had taken a new direction and she was determined to refine it into something quite different from her original style. She'd leave that behind now for Benedict to pass off as his own. Meanwhile, if she worked hard enough, she might complete a canvas good enough to submit to the Royal Academy the following spring.

31

March 1896

Dora smiled fondly at Jasper. Now almost three, he worked with an expression of intense concentration. Wielding a rake twice as tall as himself, he was spreading clean straw in the chicken shed.

Pearl and Lily carried in more armfuls of straw. Pearl threw hers into the air with a mischievous shriek. Lily copied her and soon they were laughing so much they fell into a heap like a tangle of puppies.

Out in the yard, a cart came to a halt.

'That sounds like Mr Mellyn,' said Dora.

The farmer waved cheerily and lifted down a small boy with tousled fair hair. 'This is Tom,' he said, heaving a crate off the cart. 'Where do you want them?'

'In here,' said Jasper.

'Good lad! Lead on, then.'

Inside the chicken shed, the farmer lifted a dozen pullets from the crate. 'Buff Orpingtons,' he said. 'Keep 'em in for a fortnight so they know where to roost at night. As the days lengthen, they'll start to lay.'

'Look, children! Aren't they lovely?' said Dora. 'And soon we'll have fresh eggs for tea.' She watched Tom and Jasper stroking the chickens' soft feathers. 'It's the twins' first birthday today,' she said to Mr Mellyn. 'Would Tom like to stay for tea? There's chocolate cake and pink blancmange.'

Tom tugged his father's sleeve. 'Please, Pa?'

Mr Mellyn ruffled his son's hair. 'Enjoy yourself, then.'

'Tell Mrs Mellyn I'll walk him home afterwards,' said Dora. Unlike the other villagers, the farmer's wife had been friendly when Dora went to buy milk and eggs at their neighbouring farm.

'Better be off then — pigs to muck out.' Mr Mellyn tipped his hat and drove away.

Dora held out her hands to the children. 'Shall we wake the twins and lay the table?'

As they walked across the yard, Gilbert Ryan, ghostlike in a covering of white dust from his latest sculpture, called out, 'I've a pot of honey for the birthday tea.'

'What a treat!' said Dora. 'Will you join us?'

'Best get on,' said Gilbert. 'I took time off to finish digging the potatoes this morning.'

Dora touched her skirt pocket and heard the crackle of the letter inside. She'd had some delightful news and had hoped the whole community would be together at teatime. She thanked Gilbert for the honey and then knocked on the door of the adjacent studio.

Maude Ainsley opened the door, her eyes red-rimmed and streaming.

'Oh! Have we called at a bad time?' asked Dora.

'Not at all, my dears. I've been peeling pounds

of onions to boil up the skins and dye a new batch of wool.'

Mabel appeared, wiping her stained hands on a cloth. 'Onion soup for lunch tomorrow.'

'Don't forget the birthday party,' said Dora.

'How could we?' said Mabel, a smile in her faded eyes. 'It's the highlight of our social calendar.'

Half an hour later, the twins were sitting in their highchairs and the girls wore clean pinafores. Jasper and Tom squabbled amicably under the table as they played marbles.

Edith came down from the studio.

'You've got that faraway look in your eyes again,' said Dora.

Edith blinked. 'Sorry. Planning a new painting.'

Dora thought she looked tired. During the last twelve months, she'd turned out so much work, all top quality. She'd submitted ever such a pretty canvas to the Royal Academy and they'd all been watching for the postman ever since. Meanwhile, everyone was preparing work to hang in the new gallery they'd made in the barn. They planned to open in June.

Clarissa, Augustus, Julian and Pascal wandered into the kitchen, chattering and laughing. They gathered around the table, which was set out with a chocolate birthday cake, bread and butter spread with honey or sprinkled with coloured sugar strands, egg sandwiches, fairy cakes and a moulded pink blancmange.

Dora sighed. Benedict should have been with them. Of course, he'd never even bothered to meet the twins and, though they were too small to notice his absence, it broke her heart for their sake that he hadn't sent them so much as a present.

Once Maude and Mabel arrived, Annie poured the tea while Dora passed around the sandwiches. Edith lit the candle on the birthday cake and each child took a turn in blowing it out while everyone sang 'Happy Birthday'.

Dora pulled the envelope from her pocket. 'I have some interesting news,' she said. 'Wilfred's mother is going to remarry.'

'No!' said Clarissa.

Pascal whistled. 'My mother will be very happy for her sister.'

'The wretched woman kept him tied to her apron strings for as long as it suited her,' said Dora, 'but now she's taken up with her new neighbour. So,' she looked at Edith in happy anticipation, 'Wilfred's asked if he might join the Spindrift community?'

'Another man?' said Maude, looking concerned.

'My cousin,' said Pascal.

'Wilfred trained with Dora, Clarissa and me,' said Edith.

'Oh, dear me, no!' Mabel shook her head. 'It's the *facilities*, you see. The single privy in the yard really isn't enough.'

'Particularly when it's shared with so many of the male sex.' Maude pinched her lips together. 'It's *indelicate*, especially when there's a queue during the morning rush.'

'You did say we all had to agree to any new

members, didn't you?' said Mabel.

'Yes,' said Edith. She glanced helplessly at Dora. 'I did.'

Dora's shoulders drooped. She'd been so excited and hadn't imagined encountering any objection. Now she'd have to write and tell Wilfred he wasn't wanted.

Augustus smiled sympathetically at her. 'You're disappointed.'

Dora nodded. Clarissa spent so much time with Augustus, and Edith and Pascal were always discussing their work, which left her a bit lonely for adult company. She and Wilfred had been such good friends at the Slade.

'I'm sorry,' Edith whispered. 'Perhaps we could invite Wilfred to visit us?'

'That's like offering him a box of Belgian chocolates,' she said, 'and then telling him he can look at them but can't eat any.' Still, she mustn't sulk; it would set a bad example to the children.

After tea, they trooped outside to Julian's studio for a group photo to commemorate the occasion.

Dora became helpless with a fit of the giggles when she and Annie tried to make the little ones sit still. 'It's like herding cats!'

At last the children were all facing the same way and Julian, chatting to keep their attention, held up the flash tray. 'Ready for the bright light?'

There was a blinding flash and Lucien began to shriek, followed, as always, by Nell. Once the twins had been soothed, Julian took their photograph sitting on a wing chair against a

354

backdrop of draped satin. This time, neither of them cried at the flash. The rest of the children were photographed one by one, bribed to sit still with the promise of a spoonful of honey.

'We'll look at the photographs in future years and be reminded of this happy day,' said Clarissa.

'I wondered,' Julian said, 'if I might take some artistic portraits of Lily for my portfolio? Have you heard of Pictorialism?'

'Vaguely,' said Clarissa. 'Something to do with photography as Fine Art instead of simply using the camera to document what the photographer sees?'

Julian nodded. 'Exactly. I attempt to emphasise the beauty of the subject, whether an object or an individual, through focus, tonality and composition. It's interesting to experiment with creating atmospheric effects in Nature, too.'

'What about Pearl?' asked Dora. 'She's pretty.'

Julian nodded towards Edith, who was trying to catch hold of Pearl as she chased after Jasper and Tom. 'She's delightful but, unlike Lily, she can't sit still. Lily's fair and delicate features will suit the photographs I have in mind. Dressed in diaphanous muslin, she'd make an excellent fairy in a misty landscape setting.'

'There is something a little fey about her,' said Clarissa.

Edith snatched a wriggling Pearl into her arms and smothered her in kisses.

'What a little mischief she is!' said Maude.

Mabel tickled the little girl's chin. 'But so very sweet.'

'We'd better leave Julian in peace to develop his photographs,' said Edith.

They followed her into the courtyard and Maude and Mabel opened their studio door.

'Before you go, ladies,' said Augustus, 'I have a suggestion concerning Dora's friend Wilfred. If Pascal, Julian and I build a second privy for the men, in addition to a new one at a discreet distance for the sole use of the ladies, would you agree then to Wilfred joining us?'

'What a good idea!' said Edith. 'Mabel, Maude, what do you think?'

'In that case,' said Mabel, 'Maude and I can have no objection at all.'

Dora laughed. 'Thank you! I'll write to him straightaway.'

Annie took the older children into the sitting room to play with the spinning top and Dora and Edith went to the kitchen to do the washing up.

Up to her elbows in suds, Edith said, 'Thank you for making such a lovely birthday party, Dora. I love my children more than I can say but motherhood seems to come naturally to you in a way it never did for me. I can't thank you enough.'

'I couldn't love them more if they were my own flesh and blood.'

It was true, Dora reflected, as she dried the plates. Nell sat on the tartan rug by her feet, watching Lucien shuffling along on his bottom. It was hard work keeping house and mothering five children, even with Annie to help, but her reward was the children's love. They always wanted a hug from Auntie Dora if they bumped themselves, or one of her bedtime stories before they settled. There had been one or two sticky moments when Edith accused her of being too soft with them, probably because she'd been brought up by a strict nanny herself. Dora smiled, remembering her own mother's haphazard mothering. Nevertheless, she reckoned she'd turned out all right.

★ ★ ★

In April, Clarissa took Augustus to London on a sales visit. They'd arranged to meet Wilfred at the station afterwards so as to travel back together to Cornwall. She caught sight of Wilfred through the jostling crowd and waved.

Elegantly attired in dove grey, he sauntered along the platform to greet them. 'How delightful,' he said, kissing Clarissa's cheek. 'You are as beautiful as ever, my sweet. Do introduce me to your handsome companion.'

'Augustus Lobb, my business partner.'

The two men shook hands as the engine emitted a blast of steam.

'We'd better find our seats,' said Augustus.

Once they were settled, Clarissa said, 'How was your mother's wedding, Wilfred?'

'A happy affair.' His eyes twinkled. 'Especially for me. I am freed from my gilded cage at last. And you? What have you been up to in the big city?'

'I introduced Augustus to our buyers. We had dinner with Madame Monette and agreed on a

357

collaboration. As she says, the New Woman on a budget wants to look chic but doesn't always know how to put the right items together. Her new collection of evening wear will consist of fully accessorised outfits. We shall make the jewellery.'

'You astonish me, Clarissa,' said Wilfred. 'I never thought of you as a businesswoman.'

'I've astonished myself,' she said.

'I was at a rather smart party the other day when I ran into Benedict,' said Wilfred. 'It's become quite the thing in some circles to have your portrait painted by Benedict Fairchild. He was absolutely shameless in admitting he was on the prowl to charm another rich woman into letting him paint her. Apparently, he seduces them, then captures their expression at the moment of rapture for their portrait.'

'What a swine!' said Augustus.

Wilfred nodded. 'He is, rather. Dora's tearstained letters to me when he upped and left Edith were heartbreaking. How is the poor girl now?'

'She suffered a crippling loss of confidence,' said Clarissa, 'and couldn't paint for a while but now she's producing excellent work again. Pascal has encouraged her greatly.'

'It seems a lifetime ago since we were all in France,' said Wilfred, 'but I wondered then if my cousin had a hankering for her. Sometimes it's what he doesn't say that gives him away.'

'Edith's never given any indication she has romantic inclinations towards him,' said Augustus.

'Besides, she's married to Benedict and there's nothing she can do about that,' said Clarissa.

'She had another setback last month,' said Augustus. 'A canvas she'd submitted to the Royal Academy for their summer exhibition was rejected.'

'Most of them are, so it's not surprising.'

'Still, it'll make the centrepiece of her exhibition when we open the Spindrift Gallery in June,' said Clarissa.

'A gallery?' Wilfred's eyebrows rose. 'Tell me more.'

The long train journey passed pleasantly as they caught up on the news. Clarissa watched Augustus laughing when Wilfred related a particularly scandalous tidbit of gossip, pleased they seemed to like each other.

Pascal met them at Port Isaac Road station, his face wreathed in smiles at the sight of his cousin.

Back at Spindrift, Dora came running out of the house to greet Wilfred. 'Come and meet the others. Everyone is here except for Julian who's gone to Launceston for a few days.'

Clarissa smiled inwardly at Dora's obvious pleasure as she prattled non-stop. Wilfred seemed as pleased to see her as she was to see him. Such an unlikely friendship but perhaps it worked because they were so different?

After tea, Clarissa and Dora took Wilfred to see his room.

He hung his coat in the wardrobe and looked out of the window down to the harbour. 'I feel as if I've come home,' he said.

★ ★ ★

The following day, Clarissa pinned Madame Monette's sketches and fabric swatches onto the wall, along with the first of her jewellery designs, and stood back to study them. Each evening dress was skilfully cut to flatter with no other adornment save for the jewellery. A little thrill ran through her. Already, she knew this collection was going to be something special.

Augustus was bent over the bench, soldering a bracelet. It had been a felicitous decision to take him on as her business partner. Diligent and thoughtful, he had a good eye for design, tempered by sound commercial sense. Their business was successful, in that it provided each of them with an adequate income, friendship and work they loved. And she never worried that he might make advances to her. She guessed that, like Wilfred, Augustus's inclinations lay in another direction.

Wilfred and Julian rapped on the door then and she greeted them with a smile. 'Julian, you're back! How was your journey? I see you've met Wilfred.'

'Dora introduced us,' he said.

'She's gone to the cove with the children but left this for us,' said Wilfred. He placed a jug of lemonade and four glasses on the workbench.

Augustus turned off his blowtorch and plunged the bracelet into an acid bath, where it hissed and steamed.

'It was hot and crowded on the train,' said Julian. 'I'm going for a stroll by the sea before I start work. Any of you care to come?'

'That sounds appealing,' said Clarissa.

'Far too exhausting,' said Wilfred, brushing back a lock of hair from his forehead. 'I'll take a minute or two to sit and chat with Augustus before I return to my labours.'

A little while later, Clarissa and Julian stood at the top of the cliffs marvelling at the deep blue of the sea below, spread out like a bolt of crushed silk trimmed with lace where it swirled around the rocks. The tide was out and, down on the beach, the children were shrimping in the rock pools. Dora and Tamara Mellyn, the farmer's wife, sat on the sand, watching over their charges. Dora and Tamara had been friends ever since Tom had attended the twins' birthday party.

Clarissa and Julian clambered down to the cove and Lily came running to show them a bucket with a tiny crab in the bottom of it before skipping off again.

'She's a delight,' said Julian.

'I was walking along this beach on the day she was born,' said Clarissa. 'I was frightened and didn't want to be a mother at all. But today my heart nearly bursts with love for her.' She glanced at Julian. 'How was Will?' she asked.

'His grandmother adores him but she fusses over him endlessly.' Julian passed a hand over his face. 'He's not a baby anymore and we're drifting apart.'

'Could he come and live at Spindrift?'

'He's too young to be left to his own devices and I need to work. Besides, after all he's suffered, it would be cruel to tear him away from the grandmother he loves, to suit my own selfish feelings.'

They walked in silence for a while, their hair ruffled by the breeze.

'I had some good news,' he said. 'Those photographs I took of you and Lily have been accepted by the *London Illustrated News*.'

'Well done! Which ones?'

'The one of Lily in the fairy wings dancing in the stream, and the other is the close up of the two of you in profile in drifting mist. The editor wrote that he hopes to see more of my work.'

'They were beautiful,' said Clarissa. 'So otherworldly.' She'd enjoyed learning more about how he brought artistry to his photography. He'd taken her into his darkroom and she'd been very aware of his nearness in the darkness as he wrought chemical magic on the photographs. Julian was serious about his work and as an artist herself Clarissa respected that. 'I wondered,' she said, 'about suggesting to Madame Monette that you might take photographs of the new collection of evening gowns and jewellery we're working on? I could model them.'

'An interesting thought,' he said. 'It would be a new commercial avenue for me.'

'Why don't you come to London with me next month and show her your portfolio?'

'I'd like that.' He nodded decisively and gave a warm smile. 'There's a periodical, the *New Age*, that promotes literature and the arts so I could combine the visit with a meeting there.'

That night Clarissa lay in bed anticipating the

362

forthcoming visit to London with pleasure. She recalled Julian's attractive smile and felt something soften inside her. Lily liked him, too, and he was infinitely patient with her, frequently making her laugh with funny stories. But it would be all too easy to become involved with him and she'd vowed never to risk putting herself in such a dangerous position again. Men, even decent ones like Julian, must be kept in their place. If you showed them any weakness, they hurt you. No, her iron rule now was to keep all men at arm's length forever.

32

May 1896

'*Parfait!*' said Madame Monette. She closed Julian's portfolio. 'Your photographs are exquisite, Mr Clemens. It will be of benefit to all three of us to work together and I will inform you when I have made the sample gowns. Our business is concluded for now, Mr Clemens, but Miss Stanton and I have much still to discuss.'

He shook her hand and said to Clarissa, 'I shall come to Gunter's at half-past four, as agreed.'

After he'd gone, Madame Monette raised her eyebrows coquettishly and said, 'Your Mr Clemens is most charming.'

A blush raced up Clarissa's throat.

Once they'd finished their meeting, she hired a hansom cab. The traffic was heavy, which gave her plenty of time to re-read her mother's letter. Thankfully, Father appeared to have washed his hands of her and she'd heard nothing from him recently. Over the years, Mother had written several times imploring her to visit but her most recent letter had sounded desperate. Now she was a mother herself, Clarissa understood how painful it must be when your only child turned a deaf ear to your entreaties. Guilt had prompted her to write and suggest they meet for tea; on condition her mother didn't mention the meeting to Father.

The cab pulled up outside Gunter's and Clarissa stood in the doorway until she saw her mother, sitting alone at a corner table.

She gripped Clarissa's hand. 'I'm so happy you came.' She'd become painfully thin.

A waiter came to take their order then Clarissa said, 'I don't have long. I'm meeting a friend.'

Mother sighed. 'I don't know where to begin.'

Clarissa hesitated. 'Has Father been unkind to you again?' She tried to forget all the times she'd heard Mother weeping behind closed doors, reappearing a few days later with a black eye or a split lip.

She gave a sad little sigh. 'I hardly remember a time when he was kind to me.' She fumbled in her handbag and withdrew a folded piece of paper.

The waiter arrived, making a great show of positioning the sandwiches and the cake-stand and setting out the cups and saucers.

Clarissa waited impatiently, eyeing the paper in her mother's trembling fingers and wondering what had disturbed her.

At last the waiter bustled away and she pushed the paper across the table.

Clarissa's heart began to bang like a drum. It was a page torn from the *London Illustrated News*. And there was Julian's photograph of Lily and Clarissa's identical profiles, artistically wreathed in mist. After a long moment, she said, 'It's rather good, don't you think?'

'Tell me about the child, Clarissa.' Her

mother's eyes bored into her.

'Why, that's Edith's little girl,' she said, a guileless smile on her lips.

Mother sighed, rummaged in her bag and brought out another page. 'I wish you wouldn't lie to me.'

Clarissa smoothed out the folds in the cutting of Lily, dressed as a fairy, dancing in the shallow water of a stream. Her mouth was so dry she couldn't form words.

'She's the image of you at that age.' Mrs Stanton dabbed her eyes with a handkerchief. 'You'd have told us if you'd married so I assume the worst. One of your artist friends is her father, I suppose?'

'No.' Clarissa cleared her throat. 'You're mistaken.'

'Whatever you may think of me, Clarissa, I'm not stupid.' Her mother's voice softened. 'My granddaughter is so beautiful. What's her name?'

'Please,' Clarissa whispered, 'you can't tell Father about her.'

'Of course not! He'd only blame me and I don't care for another beating.' She pressed her fingers to her lips. 'There! I've always been too ashamed to admit it before but now we both have shameful secrets.'

'I'm not ashamed of Lily!'

'Lily?' Mother clasped her hands to her breast. 'Such a pretty name. May I meet her?'

Clarissa pushed back her chair and rose to her feet. 'I daren't risk that.'

'Clarissa, please . . . '

She rushed out of the tea rooms, straight into

366

the street, and barrelled into Julian, knocking the wind out of them both.

He caught hold of her shoulders. 'Whatever's the matter?'

'I must get away!'

He hailed a passing cab. As they drove off, Clarissa saw her mother looking wildly up and down the street.

'Was that your mother?' asked Julian.

Clarissa leaned back against the seat. 'I don't care to discuss it. Please will you take me back to Aunt Minnie's?'

Julian took one look at the resolute set of her mouth and said, 'Yes, of course.'

The cab dropped them in Devonshire Place. Aunt Minnie greeted Julian with every appearance of delight, insisted he stayed for tea and then grilled him about his life and work. He answered her probing questions with good humour. Apparently satisfied, she said, 'How very opportune, Mr Clemens! We've been invited to a soirée tonight but the hostess was lamenting the lack of sufficient men for the dancing. It's only a small affair, thirty or so guests. Do say you'll come!'

He glanced at Clarissa and she nodded. 'I'd like that very much,' he said.

Julian returned to his hotel to change and Aunt Minnie pulled Clarissa into her dressing room. 'I have an apricot silk dress with a low décolletage that would suit you, or a sapphire velvet gown to bring out the blue of your eyes.'

'Really, Aunt Minnie,' Clarissa protested, 'I'm perfectly happy to wear my pink dress.'

'Nonsense! You've had that for years. Your Mr Clemens is clearly in love with you and . . . '

'He is not!'

'Don't be ridiculous, Clarissa! You only have to see the softening in his eyes when you speak to know that, even if neither of you seems to be aware of it as yet. It's about time you found a father for my darling little great-niece.'

'You know I'll never marry.'

Aunt Minnie sighed. 'Sometimes you are more like your father than you know. Pigheaded. Obstinate.'

'You don't understand . . . '

'I understand that a delightfully agreeable man with charming manners is very interested in my favourite niece. For goodness' sake, Clarissa, that terrible time before Lily was born is over. You must look to the future.'

'I told you . . . '

'Try on these dresses! And don't forget to dab your wrists with the Persian Rose perfume I gave you.'

★   ★   ★

At eight o'clock, Julian presented himself, looking handsome and debonair in his evening clothes. His eyes widened at the sight of Clarissa in close-fitting sapphire velvet.

Despite her best intentions, she couldn't help but bask in the warmth of his admiration.

'We shall walk,' said Aunt Minnie. 'It's a fine evening and my friend's house is only a step away.'

They arrived at an elegant townhouse in Chester Gardens. Circulating amongst an interesting array of poets, authors and artists with a glass of Champagne in her hand, Clarissa began to relax. A small orchestra played and the large reception room had been cleared of furniture and the floor chalked for dancing.

After an extravagant buffet supper, couples took to the dance floor. Julian held his hand out to her with a smile.

Clarissa liked the way he held her, firmly but without pressing himself unpleasantly against her. She felt light as thistledown pirouetting around the dance floor in his arms. 'I didn't want to come tonight,' she murmured as they circled around in a waltz, 'but now I'm here, it's all rather fun. It's like revisiting a forgotten, glamorous life after our informal habits at Spindrift.'

'Nevertheless,' said Julian, 'I'll be content to leave the noisy bustle of London behind and return to the peace of Cornwall.'

She laughed in agreement.

Later, Aunt Minnie came to tell them she had a headache.

'We shall escort you home,' said Julian.

'Absolutely not,' said Aunt Minnie. 'Freddie Ireton has already offered, so you young things must stay. You'll see my niece returns safely, won't you, Mr Clemens?'

'Absolutely.'

As Aunt Minnie left on her friend's arm, she glanced back over her shoulder. Clarissa wasn't sure but she thought her aunt winked at her.

The room heated up as the dancing, fuelled by

liberal glasses of Champagne, became more energetic. Julian, despite his limp, whirled her around the floor and Clarissa became breathless from their exertions.

'Shall we catch a breath of air?' he suggested. His cheeks were flushed and his eyes glittered in the gaslight.

Clarissa wondered if he'd always looked so full of life before that terrible fire.

Light from the windows spilled into the small garden, illuminating the darkness. Bursts of laugher came from groups of chattering guests, mingling with the music drifting from the house.

Clarissa and Julian sat in the arbour. 'The honeysuckle smells so sweet,' she said.

'Not as sweet as you,' he murmured.

She glanced at him, her pulse fluttering in the most peculiar way, and found herself uncharacteristically speechless. There was a tension in the air that vibrated between them and she hardly dared move in case it broke the spell.

At last, he said, 'Would you like to dance again?'

She shook her head.

They thanked their hosts, collected their coats and went out into the night. While they strolled along Albany Street, horse-drawn carriages clattered by, the streets still busy even at that late hour. A drunk lurched out of the dark into a pool of light shed by a gas lamp and Julian took Clarissa's elbow and steered her away. He spoke little but all the while she was conscious of the warmth of his arm tucked through hers. Once or twice, when pressed together to allow other pedestrians to pass on the narrow pavement, his thigh brushed lightly against hers, sending a *frisson* down her spine.

They turned into Devonshire Place and stopped outside Aunt Minnie's apartments. Reluctant to end the evening, Clarissa, took her time finding the door key. 'Thank you for escorting me,' she said, suddenly shy.

'It was my very great pleasure.' Julian took the key from her and unlocked the door to the hall.

'I'll say goodnight, then.'

'Goodnight.'

She held her breath but he didn't step towards her. Crestfallen, she stepped towards the door.

'Clarissa?'

She turned.

'May I?'

And then his hands rested lightly on her shoulders and he touched his lips, very gently, to hers.

She returned his kiss, chastely at first but then her knees trembled and he pulled her against him, kissing her more deeply. A sweet ache rose inside her and she wanted to press herself shamelessly against him but she dared not.

Drawing back, she whispered, 'Goodnight,' and went inside.

★ ★ ★

At breakfast the following morning, Aunt Minnie took one look at Clarissa and prescribed a dose of bicarbonate of soda. 'It's just the thing to settle the stomach after too much Champagne,' she said.

371

'I didn't drink too much,' protested Clarissa.

Aunt Minnie raised her eyebrows. 'You have black circles under your eyes.'

'I couldn't sleep.'

'You looked ravishing. Mr Clemens must have kissed you goodnight?'

'You know I don't intend to encourage him. Or any man for that matter.'

Aunt Minnie made a moue of disappointment. 'Then more fool you!'

Clarissa sipped her coffee, hoping it might revive her. She'd sat by the guest room window staring down at the street for most of the night while she relived the evening. Until now, she'd never experienced a yearning to be held in any man's arms and Julian's kiss had awoken such tumultuous emotions that it frightened her.

An hour later Julian came to take her to the station. He was unusually cheerful and asked solicitously after Aunt Minnie's headache.

Clarissa kissed her aunt goodbye and allowed Julian to guide her into the waiting cab. At the station, he bought newspapers and flowers for her before finding their seats. Their carriage was almost full. At Camelford, the last remaining fellow passenger alighted.

'Alone at last!' said Julian. 'Last night was the most marvellous evening, wasn't it?'

'Lovely.'

Julian's smile slipped at the flatness in her tone. 'Didn't you enjoy it?'

'I may have had a glass or two of Champagne too many.' Clarissa mentally braced herself for what had to be said. 'I shouldn't have allowed you to kiss me like that.'

'Why not?'

'I don't want to complicate matters.' She studied her fingernails. 'I enjoy your friendship but . . . '

'I see. I hoped so much that you returned the great affection I feel for you. Damn it, Clarissa, can't you see I've fallen in love with you?'

'Don't!' she said. 'I can't love any man. I'm simply not capable of it.'

'Why would you imagine you're not capable of love?'

'Because men always hurt me.'

'I would never hurt you, Clarissa.' He tried to take her hand but she snatched it away. 'Was it Lily's father that made you distrust men?'

She shook her head. 'That was all a dreadful mistake although, now, I suppose I'm grateful to him. He gave me Lily, otherwise I'd never have known what it is to love anyone. My daughter is everything to me. I'm sorry if I gave you false hopes, Julian.' She turned resolutely to the window so he wouldn't see her face working as she fought back the tears.

33

June 1896

'He did *what*?' Clarissa's voice rose in anger.

'There was no stopping him. He tore that poster off the wall and trampled it underfoot.' Mr Curnow, landlord of the Golden Lion, turned up his palms and shrugged. 'Mr Penrose is a very determined gentleman and I don't care to cross him. He called you lot up at Spindrift a gaggle of debauched libertines and an evil influence on decent society.'

'Absolute rubbish!'

'The Penroses are important in Port Isaac.'

Clarissa sighed. 'I've brought more posters about the Spindrift Gallery with me.'

'I don't know . . . '

'Please, Mr Curnow.' She flashed him her most winning smile. 'There's a longstanding disagreement between the Penroses and Mr Fairchild but he doesn't live here now. We've never caused any difficulties and it's unfair of Mr Penrose to prevent us from making an honest living. Our gallery will become a great attraction for the summer visitors and bring you more custom, too.'

The landlord rasped his chin with his fingers. 'There is that.'

She struck while the iron was hot. 'Thank you

so much, Mr Curnow.' Before he could change his mind, she unrolled Wilfred's poster and pinned it to the wall.

After she'd left the Golden Lion, Clarissa fumed when she found further evidence of Hugh's high-handed behaviour in the shops where she'd previously placed posters. She replaced most of them before calling upon Mrs Gloyne. She, Edith and Dora often visited the elderly housekeeper with little gifts of a slice of cake or a piece of apple pie. The old housekeeper opened the door, her wizened old face breaking into a smile. 'Come in, my dear.'

'I'm in a hurry, I'm afraid,' said Clarissa. 'I came to tell you the Spindrift Gallery is having its official opening tomorrow.'

'I saw the posters.' Mrs Gloyne clucked her tongue. 'Mr Penrose has been saying very nasty things about you people at Spindrift House.' She leaned forward to whisper. 'Acts of immorality, he says.'

Clarissa drew in a steadying breath. 'Thank you for warning me. There'll be a celebration tea at the gallery tomorrow. Mabel and Maude have been baking seed cake, shortbread and scones, so please come. We want the villagers to see what we do at Spindrift, in the hope they'll tell the summer visitors about the gallery.'

'They might not come after what they've heard . . .'

'I hope sheer curiosity will still bring them. And every room in the Golden Lion is booked from June to September with summer visitors so some of them may visit, too.'

'The new station is bringing them in fast and no mistake. Some of the fishermen are taking them on boat trips and their wives are offering cream teas. The holiday trade should bring money to all who live here,' said Mrs Gloyne.

Clarissa said goodbye. Fury with Hugh made her mutter under her breath with every step she took. She marched all the way up to Cliff House, knocked on the door and asked to see Mr Penrose. The maid invited her to wait.

Two minutes later, Hugh hurried into the hall, gripped Clarissa by her upper arm, hustled her out of the front door and into the lane.

'Let me go,' said Clarissa, 'or I shall scream. Loudly.'

'What the hell are you doing here?' hissed Hugh. 'How *dare* you come to my home?'

'What the hell are *you* doing,' she countered, 'tearing down our posters and slandering the Spindrift community all over Port Isaac?' She took a threatening step towards him and he recoiled, snagging his coat on the hawthorn hedge. 'I'm warned you before, Hugh, if you or your wife continue to denigrate us and attempt to prevent us from making an honest living, it will be the worse for you. Next time, I'll come to your house and tell your wife about our daughter.'

Hugh's face grew purple with rage. 'You wouldn't dare.'

'Wouldn't I?' Clarissa fixed him with an unwavering stare. 'You've spread unfounded rumours of promiscuity amongst the Spindrift community. Unfounded, that is, except where

376

you're concerned. Your wife and the congregation of St Endellion's would be very shocked to hear that you're the father of the only illegitimate child at Spindrift House, don't you think?'

'It's my word against yours.'

'I'll tell them about that mole on your buttock.'

He stared at her, his Adam's apple bobbing up and down.

'Be very careful, Hugh!' Clarissa glared at him and said, 'Your allowance for Lily was a week late this month. Don't ever let that happen again.'

Still simmering, she strode off along the lane.

Her anger had dissipated by the time she arrived at Spindrift. The great doors to the barn were open to the fresh air. Sunlight illuminated even the darkest recesses of the soaring, beamed roof and dust motes drifted lazily on the air.

The community had enthusiastically adopted Edith's suggestion for a summer gallery and during the winter they'd cleared the barn of abandoned farm implements, broken furniture and heaps of musty straw. They lit a glorious bonfire one evening and baked potatoes in the ashes for supper.

Augustus's father sent one of his men to clamber, monkeylike, over the roof to replace loose slates, and clerestory windows had been installed for additional light. Pascal and Julian had fixed panelling to the rough-sawn walls to provide a smooth surface for displaying their work.

When Clarissa arrived, Mabel and Maude's

vast wall-hanging opposite the entrance made an imposing first impression. They'd arranged silk-screened scarves in a colourful array, together with children's pinafores appliqué-ed with apples and trains. Dora had a small exhibition of illustrations: wildflower paintings and decorative paperweights made from painted stones. Gilbert had heaved his vast sculpture of Medusa into the centre of the space and arranged a number of smaller pieces on a side table. He rubbed his bushy ginger beard while he studied Medusa through narrowed eyes, turning her this way and that until the light fell on her in the most flattering way.

Edith was whitewashing the last section of panelling.

'It's looking good!' said Clarissa.

Pascal, halfway up a ladder, hanging a seascape, gave her a mischievous grin. 'Edith has a great future as a painter before her.'

She laughed. 'Once I've washed the whitewash off my hands, could you spare a minute to look at my exhibition, Clarissa?'

First she went to see if Augustus needed help. They'd bought a glass-topped display cabinet and he was arranging an assortment of pendants, hatpins, bracelets and rings on sapphire velvet inside it.

'The sea glass and beach pebbles should appeal to the summer visitors,' said Clarissa. 'They're well priced, too.'

Augustus nodded across the gallery to where Julian was setting out his photographic display. 'He was asking where you were.'

Clarissa watched Julian for a moment as he worked. Her heart ached. It had hurt her to reject him but she knew it would be worse in the end, for both of them, if she hadn't. She studied his artistic portraits of the Spindrift community alongside photographs of fishermen mending their nets or hauling in their catch, the train arriving at the station wreathed in clouds of steam, and a series of ethereal images of Lily. Samples of studio portraits and *cartes de visite* were arrayed on another panel, together with a notice stating that portrait photographs would be taken in his studio by appointment and delivered to any address in Port Isaac the following day.

'Very impressive, Julian,' she said.

He climbed down the steps. 'I've developed two portraits of you and I wondered if you'd choose the one you prefer.'

She selected the one that showed her looking up from her sketchbook.

'That's my favourite too,' said Julian. 'Your Mona Lisa smile is intriguing.' He gazed at the photograph for so long, she became uncomfortable.

'I promised to look at Edith's exhibition.' Clarissa could feel his gaze following her as she crossed the barn.

Edith straightened one of her canvases and stood back. 'What do you think?'

Vivid and colourful, her work had gained new energy over the past year. The central piece, *Picnic in Tregarrick Cove*, was the largest canvas, the one rejected by the Royal Academy. It depicted the Spindrift 'family' lolling on the sand, enjoying an idyllic picnic on the beach, while wisps of cloud floated in a cerulean sky and boats sailed by on a sapphire sea.

Edith was watching her intently, waiting for her reaction.

'I've seen your paintings before,' Clarissa said at last, 'but looking at them all together takes my breath away. I simply don't understand why the Royal Academy rejected this one.'

'I can't deny I was disappointed,' said Edith, 'but I always knew the odds were stacked against me.' She sighed. 'I'll keep trying, year after year.'

Clarissa hugged her. 'Meanwhile, don't forget how far you've come in the last twelve months.' She glanced around. 'This gallery is a terrific achievement for each one of us.'

'Did you see Dora's display? She worked on it every night after the children were in bed, bless her.'

'I did. Each item is small but they should be just right for souvenirs.'

'All we have to do now is to pray people will come and buy our work.' Edith sighed. 'I do hope Jenifry Penrose hasn't poisoned *everybody* against us.'

34

April 1897

Edith finished priming a new canvas and propped it up by the studio window to dry. Outside, Dora walked across the lawn with the twinnies trotting along beside her. At the sight, Edith's heart filled with gratitude. In the two years since Dora had become a second mother to the children, it had been possible for Edith to immerse herself in her work and to hone her talent.

She remembered the crisp and bonfire-scented October afternoon the previous autumn when she'd stood by the same window and watched Annie and Dora in the garden playing with the children. They'd waded through drifts of russet leaves, snatching them up in armfuls and throwing them into the air. The delight on their upturned faces as the leaves drifted down like a snowfall had entranced her. She'd grabbed her sketchbook, experiencing that inner thrum of exhilaration that meant she'd found the right subject for a new painting. She'd used a canvas the same size as *Picnic in Tregarrick Cove* and, when *Autumn Leaves* was finished, she had the idea of producing winter and spring subjects to complete a Four Seasons Quartet.

On Pascal's advice, she'd presented them to

the gallery in Truro and they took on the Quartet on a sale or return basis. Afterwards, she began a new canvas, *Sunday Morning in Port Isaac*, intended for submission to the Royal Academy. When it was finished, a sense of peace descended on her. Even if the judges rejected it, she knew it was her best work to date. Since then, she'd worked flat out. There'd been the miserable task of the paintings she was obliged to send to Benedict. She loathed deceiving her friends and worked on them only when Pascal wasn't in the studio. Once she'd smuggled them out of the house, she sent them to the London address Benedict had given her. On a happier note, she'd also completed a number of smaller canvases ready for the re-opening of the Spindrift Gallery in June.

The previous summer, the locals had come to the opening day out of curiosity and for the free tea party, which served its purpose in getting the gallery talked about in Port Isaac. Mr Curnow at the Golden Lion had sent his guests along and dear Mrs Gloyne had sat on the harbour wall, chatting about the gallery to the holidaymakers. Business had been pleasingly brisk. Pascal's seascapes sold more quickly than he could paint them, Edith received a new commission and the community felt their effort was worthwhile. At the end of the season, they heaved a collective sigh of relief at being able to close the gallery and peace descended once again at Spindrift.

Edith went downstairs. The dining-room door was open and she stopped to chat with Wilfred. Dressed in a crisp white artist's smock and a velvet beret, he was painting a mural of voluptuous, semi-naked ladies reclining upon silken cushions with winged cherubs attending. His execution of the bold shapes and flowing lines was sublimely poetic.

'I'll finish by the end of the week,' he said. 'And then I'll start on the landing.'

'How is it you always look so elegant,' Edith said, 'even when you're working?'

He smoothed his long hair out of his eyes. 'It's a question of standards.'

She groaned. 'You sound like my mother.'

'A lady of exquisite taste, I'm sure.'

'Don't you need to be working on something you can sell?'

'I'm not entirely immune from commercial considerations, Edith.' He softened his words with a smile. 'Julian has promised to photograph my finished masterpieces and I shall exhibit them in the gallery. I rather fancy decorating the homes of the rich. It would be an amusing and potentially lucrative sideline.'

'I'll let you get on. I'm on garden duty this afternoon.'

Narrowing his eyes, Wilfred studied one of his naked ladies. 'I shall have to paint her face again,' he murmured. 'There's something positively bovine about her expression.'

A short while later, Edith walked across the yard with the egg basket over her arm and Jasper and Pearl running beside her.

In the yard, the children scattered grain and vegetable peelings for the hens. Edith lifted the nesting box lid and Jasper carefully extracted an egg, holding it out to her with a wide smile.

'Me too!' said Pearl, pushing her way between them and grabbing at the eggs.

Edith caught her hand. 'Careful! You're always so impatient, Pearl.'

They entered the walled garden, where Pascal was hoeing between the seedlings. Edith paused to watch him working, his lean body moving efficiently along the neat rows. He had his sleeves rolled up to expose brown forearms. His welcoming glance made her heart somersault. He handed her a hoe and filled watering cans from the butt for the children, who then skipped off to water the seedlings.

Edith and Pascal worked side-by-side.

'I have learned weeds grow faster than carrots,' he said, digging up yet another dandelion.

Then Pearl screamed, frightening Edith into dropping her hoe. The little girl had fallen headlong and her pinafore was caked with mud. 'Look at you!' Edith scolded.

Pearl wriggled out of her grip and ran off again.

The sun was warm on Edith's back and she was filled with a deep contentment. There were always financial worries but, at last, everything was beginning to come right. Children's laughter drifted from behind the compost heap.

An hour later she put down her garden fork. 'I'd better take the little ones in for their tea, Pascal.'

'Must you? I like it when you work beside me.'

'It doesn't feel like a chore when we're working together, does it?' She cupped her ear and listened. 'The children are suspiciously quiet.'

Thrusting his fork into the earth, he hurried over to the compost heap, with Edith close on his heels. He began to laugh.

The children had stripped themselves naked and Jasper had finger-painted Pearl's entire body and face with decorative whorls of mud. She was attempting, without success, to replicate the patterns on his stomach. Edith couldn't help but laugh, too. She gathered up their muddy clothing and the basket of eggs and shepherded them back to the house.

Opening the kitchen door, she called out to Dora, 'Is there enough hot water for the children to have a bath?' Her skirt and hands were smeared and she dropped the mud-caked clothes in a heap by the door.

Pearl and Jasper pushed past her and ran into the kitchen, shrieking with laughter.

Dora's face was fixed in a rictus smile. 'Edith,' she said, 'your ma has come to visit.'

And there, standing behind her, was Mama.

'What is this disgraceful exhibition?' she said, her mouth pinched with distaste.

For a split second, Edith forgot to breathe.

Jasper and Pearl, nervous of the severe stranger, hid behind her, clutching her skirts with muddy fingers.

'What are you doing here, Mama?'

'Surely you received my letter?'

Mutely, Edith shook her head.

'I was expecting to be met at the station. Instead I had to find a public carriage to convey me here. To cap it all, I'm accosted by two of my grandchildren who appear to have been raised as savages.'

'Merely a mishap in the garden,' said Edith, 'followed by a little artistic expression with some mud.'

'Don't be impertinent, Edith! I shall take my tea in the drawing room and wait for you to attend me there once you and the children are bathed and appropriately dressed.' She swept out of the kitchen.

Dora and Edith stared at each other and then they were stuffing their fists in their mouths to stifle their whoops of laughter, while the children watched them, wide-eyed.

'It's not funny!' said Edith, at last, tears of mirth rolling down her face.

'Make her some tea,' said Dora. 'I'll get these little scallywags clean.'

Edith washed her hands, put the last slice of Mabel's seed cake onto a plate and carried the tea tray into the drawing room where Mama waited, poker-backed, in the armchair.

'How is Papa?'

'Perfectly well.' Mama sipped her tea but pushed away the cake. Edith hoped she'd leave it; gardening always made her hungry.

'I met Benedict at the opera the other day,' Mama said. 'He was very charming. There was a woman with auburn hair on his arm, dressed in the latest Paris fashion.'

Edith's stomach clenched. 'Isobel Armitage, I expect.'

'I'm disappointed in you.' Mama looked her

386

up and down. 'Clearly, you've made no proper attempt at a reconciliation.'

Edith was all too aware of her shabby dress, loose hair and rough hands. 'I'm dirty because I've been digging carrots to feed the children since Benedict doesn't provide for us. He never responds to my letters and I'm working too hard to chase after him in London.' She flashed a brittle smile. 'My only recent communication from him was a note ten days ago demanding money again. He's run up large bills with his tailor and wine merchant and, yet again, has threatened to sell the roof over our heads if I don't send him enough money to settle his debts.'

Mama stared at her. 'You can't mean that?'

'Oh, but I do.'

'How can you let him?'

'How can I stop him?'

'Don't raise your voice to me, Edith!'

'No one ever stops Benedict from doing what he intends to,' she said.

Mama shook her head in despair. 'Living like this, you'll never be accepted in polite society. What can you and the children hope for in such circumstances? Amelia would never have made such a dreadful misjudgement of a man's character.'

Riled, Edith snapped back, 'That's easy to say, isn't it? Dear, sainted Amelia was nothing like as perfect as you imagine. All I can do is to manage as best I can in extremely difficult circumstances. Excuse me, I'll fetch the twins. I expect you'd like to see them before you leave?'

Without waiting for an answer, she fled the room. Would her mother never stop comparing her with Amelia? If she only knew about Edith's sister's capricious and petty acts of cruelty or how she'd frequently mocked their mother behind her back, perhaps then Mama would stop placing her eldest child on a pedestal.

The tin bath in front of the range was full of muddy water and the children were protesting loudly as Dora hurriedly buttoned them into fresh clothes.

'Now listen,' Edith said, pulling Pearl and Jasper into her arms, 'Grandmama has travelled a long way and she's tired and cross so I want you to be very good. I expect she'd like you to give her a kiss and tell her you're happy she's come to visit.'

'Shall I ask Annie to bring the twinnies to the drawing room?' asked Dora.

'Please. But check they're clean first, won't you?'

Edith led Jasper and Pearl into the drawing room.

Pearl, all bronze curls and dimples, ran to her grandmother and hugged her knees. 'I so happy now,' she said.

Mama's frozen expression melted as she bent down and the child wound her arms around her grandmother's neck, smothering her cheeks in kisses.

'The little angel!' murmured Mama, lifting Pearl onto her knee. 'She's the image of Amelia.'

Edith watched, made uncomfortable by seeing the naked grief displayed on her mother's face as she gazed wonderingly through her tears at Pearl.

'Say hello,' Edith whispered to Jasper, but he gripped her hand and stared shyly at the floor. It didn't matter since Mama had eyes only for Pearl, even when Annie brought in the twins to see her.

In Mama's honour, dinner was served in the dining room. Her face paled at first sight of Wilfred's mural so Edith seated her with her back to it. Dinner was not a success. Pascal had shot a few rabbits and there was a hearty stew, with cabbage and mashed potatoes, which everyone except for their visitor ate with apparent enjoyment.

Mabel and Maude attempted to engage the visitor in conversation but she could only gaze in horrified fascination at their homespun gowns draped with myriad bright silk scarves that slipped and trailed about their persons. Pascal, as a foreigner, and Dora, who cared for the children, were naturally beneath her notice but Clarissa, Augustus and Wilfred managed to elicit a few clipped responses to their conversational overtures. Mama stared, aghast, at Gilbert when he arrived late for dinner, with thick white dust frosting his bushy beard and ragged work clothes.

'Welcome, dear lady!' he said, shaking her hand briskly.

Silently, she wiped marble dust from her fingers with a lace handkerchief. When the jam roly-poly arrived, she pushed back her chair.

'I have a headache,' she said. 'If you will

389

excuse me, I shall retire.'

'I'll come up with you to see if there is anything you need,' said Edith.

'Please don't,' her mother said. 'I shall lie quietly in a darkened room and hope to feel better tomorrow.'

When the door closed behind her, they all let out their breath. Carefully, no one looked at Edith or passed comment.

★ ★ ★

The following morning, she took a cup of tea upstairs to her mother. She'd slept in Edith's bedroom, while her daughter tossed and turned on a truckle bed in Dora's room.

'I thought you might prefer a quiet breakfast today, Mama.' What that meant was it would be too awful for them to have to share another meal with her. 'Shall I bring it to you in about an hour?'

Silently, her mother inclined her head and Edith escaped.

Breakfast in the kitchen was the usual noisy affair. Pearl had a tantrum because Clarissa had cut her bread into triangles instead of soldiers and Nell and Lucien squabbled over a cup of milk. Dora had to scold them and mop the floor.

Edith found one of Aunt Hester's dainty tray cloths in the back of the dresser drawer and laid a tray with a pretty rose-patterned cup and saucer. She slipped outside to gather a few daffodils for a posy.

The postman was coming up the path and

handed her a letter. She opened it and her stomach turned a somersault. This was the news she'd been waiting for but what if it wasn't the answer she hoped for? She read it and gave a great sigh. Forgetting the daffodils, she hurried back inside.

Wordlessly, she handed the letter to Pascal to read.

Clarissa gave her a sharp look. 'Is it . . . '

She nodded.

'*Merveilleux*!' Pascal shouted. He grasped Edith by her waist and lifted her up to kiss both her cheeks.

And then they were all laughing and hugging her.

'I *knew* you could do it!' said Dora.

'My painting is to be hung in the Royal Academy's Summer Exhibition,' Edith said, shaking her head in disbelief. '*My* painting.' Her knees trembled so much she had to sit. 'I was thrilled when the Truro gallery sold my Four Seasons quartet but this . . . I've dreamed of this for so long.'

'It will be the first of many acceptances, I'm sure,' said Pascal, his eyes shining.

Edith felt overwhelmed with love for her friends. There was no hint of jealousy at her success, only happiness for her.

Half an hour later, she carried her mother's breakfast upstairs, feeling full of excitement. At last, she'd achieved something that would make Mama proud of her.

'Mama, I have some wonderful news . . . '

'Sit, Edith,' she said. 'There's something I

wish to say to you first. While my visit has not been enjoyable, it has clarified my thoughts. When you sent me photographs of your children, it was immediately apparent to me that Pearl still bears the close physical resemblance to Amelia that I noted when she was an infant. Yesterday, I was touched by her considerable show of affection for me.'

Edith deemed it imprudent to say that Pearl was affectionate to everyone. She kissed the postman, the coalman and Ned the pony, quite impartially.

'I cannot condone this dreadful Bohemian way of life you have chosen,' continued Mama, 'though it makes Benedict's decision to absent himself all the more understandable.'

'But . . . '

'Do not interrupt! I shall ease your deplorable situation by taking Pearl back to London with me and bringing her up as my own. And I'll send you a small allowance for the other children.'

'You've decided to take Pearl, without even discussing it with me?' Edith could hardly believe her ears.

Mama smiled regally. 'She'll have every advantage and you will be in a financially improved situation.'

'How dare you!' There was a pounding in Edith's head. 'You want to *buy* my daughter because you imagine she bears a resemblance to Amelia? Let me tell you, I will *never* sell any of my children! Thankfully, Pearl is a loving and joyous little girl and as different from my duplicitous, spiteful sister as it's possible to be. I wouldn't in a million years let you bring her up and encourage her to become like Amelia.'

Mama rose to her feet, her cheeks mottled with rage. 'Don't you dare tell vicious lies about my precious Amelia. She was worth two of you!'

Edith's chin quivered. 'So you've told me, many times. Amelia was a talented pianist but you spoiled and petted her, choosing never to see or curb her spite. It was cruel she died so young but what kind of a mother were you, to vent your grief and disappointment on me?'

'I did not!'

'You believed Amelia's malicious tales about me, never, ever, questioning if her comments and accusations were in fact true.' Edith felt she couldn't bear to be near her mother a second longer. 'I shall convey you to the station in ten minutes.' She barely resisted slamming the door behind her as she left her mother to gather her things.

Pascal came into the stable while Edith was attempting to hitch Ned to the trap, tears of fury and frustration blinding her as she struggled with the buckles.

He took the leather traces from her shaking hands and put his arms around her. 'Edith!' he said.

She clung to him, weeping and sniffing. 'Mama thought she could buy Pearl from me!' she sobbed.

He tipped up her chin and wiped her tears away with his thumb. 'Your *maman* can no longer tell you what to do and that has shocked her. I shall drive you both to the station and she will not say unpleasant things to you while I am there.'

She buried her face in his coat. 'What would I do without you, Pascal?'

His arms tightened around her for a second, then he released her. 'You don't have to be without me,' he murmured, then busied himself harnessing Ned.

She watched him covertly, his long fingers adroitly managing the buckles. Somehow, he was always there when she needed him and she could no longer imagine a world she'd want to live in if he weren't there beside her. For a long time, she'd taken pleasure in his calm presence and depended on him for friendship and advice. It was strange how she'd refused to recognise that love had stalked her for years. Now it had ambushed her and knocked her sideways when she least expected it.

35

The sun was shining so Dora had made a picnic and taken it down to the cove for the children. Wiggling her bare toes in the sand, she breathed the intoxicatingly briny air deep into her chest. Life was good. At the water's edge, she and her charges made a boat of sand and dug a channel around it, ready for the incoming tide.

Pearl came running towards her, laughing and with her arms held wide. Now three years old, she nearly knocked Dora flying when she barrelled into her knees.

Dora lifted the little girl up and kissed her warm neck, tasting the salty, fresh-air tang of her skin. How she loved this quicksilver child! She'd never once regretted her decision to mother the children. She'd had to give up her dream of becoming a successful illustrator but had been repaid a thousandfold by the love they all gave her. And there was always the future. Meanwhile, she kept her hand in with her drawing whenever she could snatch a few minutes. Smiling to herself, she thought about her latest project.

'Mama!' yelled Pearl.

Edith was descending the cliff steps. Pearl ran to her and they walked hand-in-hand towards Dora.

'It's such a glorious day,' said Edith, 'so I've put down my paintbrush and come to share the picnic.'

'Will you play with us, Mama?' said Pearl. 'Please? The pirate ship is about to sail and Auntie Dora is Queen of the Pirates.'

'We'd better hurry, then, or we'll miss the tide.'

Moments later, Edith was hard at work digging a moat around the ship under the direction of Theodora the Pirate Queen.

Nell and Lucien, on lookout duty as the tide came in, yelled with glee as waves foamed over their knees.

'All aboard!' shouted Dora. She put on an eyepatch and distributed newspaper hats decorated with a skull and crossbones. 'I didn't know you were coming, Edith,' she said, 'so there isn't a hat for you. You'll have to be the ship's cat.'

Edith laughed, feeling the wind in her hair, and it gladdened Dora's heart that she looked so young and carefree again.

Dora stood in the prow looking out to sea with a newspaper telescope while the children scrambled into the ship. 'Right, my hearties. A big wave is coming. Row as fast as you can and look out for sharks!'

Later, the Pirate Queen and the ship's cat were rowed ashore to a desert island while the children were sent to forage for food, in the shape of the picnic.

'I'm exhausted,' Edith said. 'I don't know how you do it all day, Dora.'

'I love to see them happy,' she said.

'You're a far better mother to them than I could ever be.'

'You'll always be their true mother,' said Dora. She sighed. 'They're growing so fast. It's hard to believe Jasper was four last month and the twinnies are already two.' Her smile was determinedly bright but she felt tears glistening in her eyes. 'One day I'll wake up and they won't need me anymore.'

'But they'll always love you.'

Lucien, closely followed by Nell, brought them egg sandwiches. Their chubby little fingers were liberally dusted with sand. Nell hugged Dora and her mother before trotting off after her twin again.

Dora bit into her sandwich and felt sand crunch between her teeth.

'Do you ever wish you were still painting?' Edith asked her.

Dora glanced at her sideways. 'Oh, but I am.'

'Really? You've kept that very quiet!'

'It's something a bit different and it's such fun. The children are so involved with this pirate game. We play it all the time so I'm writing the stories down at night and illustrating them, too.'

'How wonderful!'

Dora couldn't contain her smile. 'Theodora the Pirate Queen is my alter ego. She's so brave and clever. When I'm pretending to be her, there's nothing I can't do.'

'May I see your illustrations?'

Dora smiled. 'Come and listen to the bedtime story tonight.'

*　　*　　*

Two weeks later, Edith set up her easel next to Pascal's in the gazebo and they worked in companionable silence. He hadn't spoken again of his feelings for her but there was a new tenderness in his eyes and his frequent small acts of kindness made her love him more. She daren't think about it too much, afraid that this sweet, forbidden love would be snatched away from her.

The day she'd gone down to the cove to play pirate ships with Dora and the children had inspired her to start a new painting, *Catching the Tide*. She'd made mental notes then of how the sun highlighted their hair, sparkled on the water and shimmered over the sand. It was a beguiling scene, simply begging to be captured in paint. Her canvas depicted downy clouds drifting across an azure sky on a blithely sunny day. White horses pranced across a restless sea and the onshore breeze ruffled the marram grass. It gladdened her heart to capture the joyful concentration on her children's faces as they built their ship of sand and dreamed of desert islands. When a painting was going well, there was something immensely uplifting about the way energy flowed through her fingers and into the brush, painting the canvas with life.

Pascal peered over her shoulder. 'This is very good, Edith.'

She felt the warmth of him radiating from his chest onto her back. 'It's a happy painting, isn't it? I hate to sell it, even though it should command a good price. It reminds me of that wonderful day with my children.'

'Then you must keep it,' he said, his brown eyes serious.

It hadn't occurred to her not to sell *Catching the Tide* but now she could see it was absolutely the right decision. She'd treasure it forever. 'You always cut to the heart of the matter, Pascal.'

As lightly as a feather, he rested his hand on her shoulder, one finger caressing the curve of her neck. 'I want you to be happy,' he murmured. 'Always.'

Her pulse was like a drumbeat in her ears. Holding her breath, she turned around to face him. She touched a hand to his cheek and he caught it and pressed his lips to her palm. With her gaze meeting his, time seemed to stretch into infinity. Edith's mouth softened in anticipation of his kiss.

As he bent his head towards her, a yell came from the garden and they sprang apart.

The children raced across the lawn towards them, chased by Annie.

Jasper ran straight to the gazebo. 'Save me, Mama!' He thundered up the steps and hid behind Edith's skirt. 'Annie wants to wash my face.'

Pascal examined the boy's cheek closely. 'Chocolate cake?'

Jasper nodded, his eyes alight with mischief. 'Auntie Maude lets us scrape the bowl.'

'Every pleasure in life must be paid for,' said Pascal. He snatched up his painting rag and wiped away the chocolate smear from Jasper's face before he could wriggle away.

'Off you go,' Edith said. 'And make sure you listen to Annie!'

Jasper laughed and ran back to join his siblings.

That moment of breathless expectation between Pascal and herself had vanished. Perhaps it was as well.

★ ★ ★

Edith felt truly honoured that *Sunday Morning in Port Isaac* was one of the ten per cent of submissions accepted for the Royal Academy Summer Exhibition. She'd let Mr Hutchinson know of her success and the dealer had written back by return to say he'd be pleased to see her at the preview party. She'd written to her parents, inviting them to meet her there, but Mama sent a brief reply, saying they were previously engaged.

'I hoped she'd be proud of me at last,' Edith said to Clarissa, who'd found her weeping over the letter. 'That's what drove me on through all the hard times to achieve this success. She hasn't even invited me to stay with her while we're in London.'

'Don't dwell on it,' said Clarissa, hugging her. 'I shan't see my parents either. Lily and I will stay with Aunt Minnie. Your mama is living a half-life, trapped in her grief for Amelia. You'll never change her.'

'But she should be happy for me. She's my *mother*!'

'In my experience, mothers provide more

disenchantment than encouragement. Tell her to go to Hell! Work hard for your *own* pleasure and benefit and make sure you're a better mother to your children than she ever was to hers.'

Wiping her eyes, Edith determined to accept Clarissa's sage advice.

★　★　★

Pascal, Wilfred and Clarissa accompanied Edith to the Royal Academy preview party. She wore her pearls and had trimmed her hat with new feathers. Walking through the hallowed doors of Burlington House sent a tingle of excitement down her spine.

'I feel like an imposter,' she whispered to Pascal.

He shook his head. 'Not at all. You have worked for years for this.'

The exhibition was overwhelming, every inch of wall space crammed with canvases, cheek by jowl, right up to the ceiling.

'I feel sorry for that poor blighter,' said Wilfred, pointing to a small portrait high up in a dark corner.

Edith was relieved to find *Sunday Morning in Port Isaac* hung at eye level, in reasonable light.

They spent several hours studying the paintings and, as Pascal said, there was plenty to learn from them. Mr Hutchinson came to congratulate Edith, shaking her hand warmly and inviting her to have tea with him the following day.

It was as they were leaving that she felt a tap on her shoulder. She turned to see a suave, bearded man smiling confidently down at her. A gold watch chain gleamed across his impeccably cut waistcoat. 'Benedict!' she said. Her pulse began to race uncomfortably. He looked older. Sleeker.

'Well, well, Edith,' he drawled. 'So you've achieved your ambition. I always knew you were a better artist than any of us.'

Lifting her chin and looking him in the eye, she said, 'I've worked for my success.'

'You've changed your style.' It sounded like an accusation.

'It was time to try something new, something less *constrained*.' Something different from the paintings he forced her to paint for him.

'You always were an ambitious little thing. That seriousness was part of your charm.' His bold gaze eyed her appreciatively. 'Along with your other undeniably attractive assets.' Beside her, Pascal stiffened, his outrage almost tangible.

'You look so prosperous, Benedict,' said Clarissa, 'but we haven't heard anything about your work at all.' She smiled sweetly. 'Or perhaps your lady friend is keeping you in the style you believe you're entitled to?'

There was a warning twitch of anger in Benedict's expression, hastily concealed. 'You always were a tease, Clarissa. Once upon a time, we had such fun together. There's nothing quite so delightful as a romantic assignation in the afternoon, is there?'

Clarissa grew very still and then her face flushed an unbecoming shade of crimson.

In that moment, Edith knew. Clarissa's

sideways glance at her confirmed it and she reeled from the shock of this disclosure. She'd thought Clarissa was her friend but she'd betrayed Edith with her husband.

'Things to do,' murmured Benedict, 'parties to attend.' He turned to Edith. 'May I call on you after breakfast tomorrow? There's something urgent we need to discuss.'

The last thing Edith wanted was to see him again. Reluctantly, however, she gave him the name of the hotel in Bayswater.

He inclined his head to Wilfred and Pascal. 'Delightful to see you. Goodbye, Clarissa . . . Edith.'

Edith's ribcage felt too tight and she couldn't catch her breath. How could she ever have loved him? How could she have trusted Clarissa?

Pascal, with jaw clenched, murmured, 'Do not let him distress you, Edith. He is nothing.'

Wilfred sighed. 'Shall we go somewhere amusing and have tea? I think we need to wash that nasty taste away.'

Clarissa, her head bowed, avoided Edith's accusing gaze.

But what had upset her most of all was that Benedict hadn't even enquired after their children.

* * *

What should have been a celebration tea at Gunter's was a subdued affair. Pascal and Wilfred made a manful effort to keep the conversation cheerful, congratulating Edith on her success and

403

speculating on the possibilities of further commissions from Mr Hutchinson.

Edith couldn't forget the spark of malice in Benedict's eye when he'd revealed his affair with Clarissa.

She was silent and withdrawn, her gaze downcast.

After tea, Pascal volunteered to find a cab to take them to their hotel before conveying Clarissa to her aunt's apartment.

'Wilfred,' said Clarissa, once Pascal had gone outside, 'would you find me a separate cab? Aunt Minnie is minding Lily and I want to return to the apartment straightaway.'

As soon as he'd left their table, she said, 'Edith, let me explain . . . '

'There's nothing to be said.' Edith cupped her hands over her ears. 'I trusted you, Clarissa! You betrayed me.'

'It wasn't like that!'

'You deny you had an affair with my husband?'

Clarissa shook her head. 'No, but . . . '

'You can't change the facts.' Edith crossed her arms tightly over her chest. 'I gave you a home when you were desperate. If I'd known, I'd have sent you away.'

Clarissa caught her breath. 'I wish I could turn back the clock but . . . '

'I'm not discussing it!' Edith pushed away her chair and fled outside.

★ ★ ★

404

At ten o'clock the following morning Pascal escorted Edith to the hotel sitting room to wait for Benedict.

'Shall I stay?' he asked.

Edith shook her head, anxious in case her husband might ask for more of her paintings to pass off as his own. She was deeply ashamed to be involved in such a contemptible scheme and didn't ever want Pascal to learn of it.

Benedict didn't arrive until an hour later, by which time Edith was seething with nervous anticipation.

He breezed in, smiling good-humouredly at an elderly gentleman reading a newspaper and two ladies sharing a pot of coffee. He greeted his wife and sat down in an adjacent wing chair, tweaking the creases in his trousers perfectly straight over his knees.

'What is it you have to say to me?' she said, unable to wait any longer.

Benedict sighed. 'You could have made everything so much easier for both of us, if only you'd agreed to your mother's idea of adopting Pearl.'

'It wouldn't have been easier for me,' she snapped. 'I love Pearl far too much to subject her to Mama's influence.' She frowned. 'How did you know about that?'

'She took me to lunch at the Savoy and offered me generous remuneration if I'd declare the children were neglected and you were living a ramshackle and immoral life. As she reminded me, a husband has complete control over his wife and children and, in such circumstances, I'd have every right to take them from you.'

Edith gripped her hands together and felt the hair lift on the nape of her neck.

'She suggested sending you, indefinitely, to a secure nursing home for your nerves. Her doctor would declare you of unsound mind, she said.'

Fear made Edith's voice shrill. 'None of that is true! And I'm not mad.'

Benedict sighed. 'A pretty cold fish your mama, isn't she? And I'm not as wicked as you may think I am. But it was a lot of money . . . I can't deny, I had to think twice about it.' He gave her one of his most charming smiles. 'Besides, if you were banged up in a lunatic asylum, whatever would I do with the other children?'

She forced herself to breathe slowly, unable to comprehend how any mother could have dreamed up such a cruel plan. 'What do you want?' she asked harshly.

Benedict shifted in his chair. 'Ah, well,' he said. 'My circumstances have recently changed. Isobel has become exceedingly tiresome so I'm looking for alternative accommodation.'

Edith guessed Isobel had realised how lazy he was. Foreboding made her blood run cold.

'Therefore, my financial needs have increased and I find myself obliged to sell Spindrift.'

'No!' Her stomach contracted sharply. 'We had an agreement! I've stuck to my side of it and sent you my paintings and every penny of spare money.'

'The alternative, of course, is for me to return to the bosom of my family.'

That was unthinkable! Pressing down her

panic, Edith tried to think clearly. This was all about money, of course. 'How much do you need?'

He grimaced. 'More than you have. My bookmaker is making unpleasant threats. The thing is,' he ran a finger round the inside of his collar, 'I've been in touch with Hugh Penrose.'

'Hugh Penrose!'

'Strange, isn't it?' Benedict shook his head wonderingly. 'He wrote to me via my solicitor and made an offer for Spindrift House.'

'But you hate each other.'

'Undeniably so but Hugh wants Spindrift with a passion. And I . . . ' he turned his palms up and shrugged ' . . . need the money.'

Edith's mouth was dry. 'And what about your responsibilities to your wife and children?'

'I daresay there might be something left over to rent a cottage for you.'

She fought back a wave of nausea. It was inconceivable that she might lose Spindrift House. The community, her family, would be forced to separate. Everything they'd worked for would collapse in ruins. Nothing would ever be the same again.

'I need to settle my debts, Edith.'

Benedict's voice was hard but she detected something else in his tone. Regret? He'd loved Spindrift House, once. How could she make him forget the idea of selling it? An appeal to his greed was the only answer.

'Now we have the train station, do you know how many summer visitors come to Port Isaac every summer?' she said.

'How is that relevant?'

'Spindrift House is bound to increase considerably in value in the future. It's not in your long-term interest to sell it. Already, some of the fishermen's cottages have been sold for holiday homes at surprisingly high prices. How much has Hugh offered you?'

'What's that to you?'

'Everything,' Edith said crisply. 'Here's an idea that will suit us both. Suppose you sell a proportion of the house to the Spindrift community?'

Laughing, he said, 'You're joking! You don't have two ha'pence to rub together.'

'Will you give me a month to see how much we can raise before you sell to Hugh?'

Frowning, Benedict rubbed the back of his neck. 'I don't want him to have it.'

'It's a perfect scheme,' she said, elation coursing through her veins, 'you'd have some money but keep an interest in the house while it increases in value. You wouldn't have to rent a cottage for the children and me either.'

He stared at her. 'When did you grow a business head on those pretty shoulders? One month then.' He sighed. 'I daresay I can put up with Isobel's nagging for that long. I'll speak to the land agent about valuing the house. And, if you can't raise the funds, I can still sell to Hugh. Send your offer to me via my solicitor.' He stood up to leave. 'There's one other thing I wanted to say.'

'Yes?' Edith heartily wished he'd go.

He hesitated. 'I apologise. I shouldn't have

said anything about Clarissa and me when we were at the Royal Academy yesterday. She always did know how to plant one of her barbs where it hurt most. She made me angry but I'm sorry if my comment hurt or embarrassed you.'

Amazed, Edith watched him walk away. Then she slumped back in her chair, the momentary euphoria evaporating. What had she been thinking? It would be an impossible task to raise enough money to buy even part of Spindrift. And in one month, the community would lose their home.

★ ★ ★

The following days passed in a whirlwind. Edith had several pre-arranged meetings with art dealers and one at a publishing house. She met Mr Hutchinson for tea. He treated her completely differently now her work had been exhibited at the Royal Academy. Enthusiastic about the new direction her painting had taken, he promised to see what he could do about finding her fresh commissions. Afterwards, she went shopping for essentials for the children and art supplies not easily obtained in Cornwall, then took her mother's pearls and the earrings Benedict had given her to a pawn shop, where she sold them.

Wilfred treated Edith and Pascal to a performance of Two Little Vagabonds at the Princess's Theatre. When they returned to the hotel, there was a note waiting for Edith from Clarissa. Still angry and shocked, Edith returned it, unopened. It was a relief that Clarissa and Lily had planned to stay with Aunt Minnie for the next few weeks. Edith had more than enough to worry about without agonising over her so-called friend's betrayal and whether she could bear to let her remain at Spindrift. But then, very soon, perhaps none of them would be able to stay.

She debated until late into the evening with Pascal and Wilfred on how they might raise enough funds to secure their position at the house.

'I shall touch Mother for a loan,' said Wilfred. 'She's disgustingly happy and bound to agree.'

Edith, full of desperation, didn't allow herself time to reconsider but called upon her father at his office.

He sat on the other side of his desk and studied her over his steepled fingers. 'Despite what your mother thinks, Benedict has let you down. She's not well, you know. Never recovered from your sister's death. I took her to a physician in Harley Street. He said she's suffering from temporary insanity due to her age. Apparently it's perfectly normal for women in later life. All very awkward.' He sighed. 'I'm not of a mind to cross her but I'm uncomfortable about your state of affairs. When it's time, I'll pay for the boys to go to a decent school.'

'That's kind of you, Papa.' Edith swallowed. 'Unfortunately, we'll all end up in the workhouse first if we can't remain at Spindrift. It's *now* that I need a loan.'

He pursed his lips. 'I don't care for the idea of a loan.'

'I promise I'd pay you back as soon as I could. I'll take in washing if I have to.'

'For Heaven's sake! Have you no pride, Edith?'

'Not if my children are starving.'

'I'm not lending you money.' He picked up his pen and wrote on a piece of paper.

Edith's chin quivered. Was that it? Was she dismissed? She barely knew Papa but had hoped Mama's poisonous influence wouldn't prevent him from helping her.

He leaned over the desk and proffered the piece of paper. 'Take this to the bank in Wadebridge.'

Her eyes widened when she saw the sum written on the cheque. It would make a very substantial contribution to the Spindrift fund. Throwing dignity to the winds, she ran to her father and hugged him.

Patting her back, he said, 'What a fuss!' but she noticed the tips of his ears had grown pink.

'I can't thank you enough, Papa.'

'For God's sake, don't tell your mother!'

She almost skipped out of his office. The community still needed a great deal more but it was a start and she couldn't wait to tell Pascal and Wilfred.

It wasn't until they were on the train to Port Isaac that Edith had a dreadful thought. Clarissa had been in Cornwall when Lily was conceived but there'd been no sign of any suitor. It was no wonder she'd refused to reveal the name of Lily's father. It had to be Benedict.

411

36

Aunt Minnie took Lily to the zoo in Regent's Park, leaving Clarissa to work on her third collection for Madame Monette. Despite the lack of distractions, she drooped over her sketchbook, full of self-loathing and unable to concentrate. It had been two weeks since the Summer Exhibition preview and the look of naked hurt on Edith's face when Benedict exposed their affair still haunted her. The explanatory letter she'd sent to her friend had been returned unopened and, although she'd called twice at the hotel, Edith wasn't in on either occasion.

It had frightened her when Edith had said that, if she'd known, she wouldn't have allowed Clarissa to stay at Spindrift while she was pregnant with nowhere to go. The community meant more to her than her family and the jewellery business was based there, too. What if she and Lily were expelled? Clarissa's shameful past had caught up with her again and, this time, it might cause her downfall.

A fly buzzed at the window, banging against the glass. She opened the sash to let it out. All at once, she was desperate to be outside, too. Stuffing her sketchbook, purse and an apple into her carpet bag, she informed Aunt Minnie's maid she was going out.

As she left the building, someone called her name and she was surprised to see Julian limping along Devonshire Place. A momentary impulse of pleasure made her smile but then she wondered if Edith had sent him to tell her she was no longer welcome at Spindrift.

'What are you doing here, Julian?'

'I had business in town,' he said. 'May I walk with you?'

'I'm going to the park.'

They sat on a bench by the boating lake and watched children and their nursemaids sailing wooden boats.

'Did Edith send you?' Clarissa said.

'Not at all.' His gaze followed a small boy as he ran past bowling a hoop. 'Pascal did.'

'He told you what Benedict said during the Summer Exhibition?'

Julian nodded.

Ashamed, Clarissa turned her face away. 'Is the whole community talking about me?'

'No one else, apart from those who were there, knows what occurred. Pascal mentioned it because I asked him why Edith was so unhappy. I'd imagined she'd be euphoric after seeing her work exhibited.'

'What should have been the most wonderful day for her was ruined. And I'm to blame.' Clarissa massaged her temples.

'It was unnecessarily cruel of Benedict to say anything, especially then. Come back home! Unless you and Edith discuss the situation, you will never be able to resolve it. Besides, another matter is causing us anxiety. Benedict's selling

Spindrift to Hugh Penrose.'

She stared at him, incredulous. 'He'd never do that.'

'I'm afraid he would. Money problems. Edith's won a month's grace by persuading him to consider selling a share of Spindrift to the community instead. We're all scrabbling around seeing how much we can raise, though I doubt we'll find enough to satisfy him.'

Clarissa squeezed her eyes shut. So, regardless of her affair with Benedict, she and Lily might lose their home anyway. The new life she'd built for them at Spindrift was going to come tumbling down. Unable to prevent herself, she let out a low moan.

'Clarissa!' Julian stroked her hand. 'I hate to see you unhappy. Our friendship is so important to me.'

'And to me, too,' she said, knowing that was so much less than the truth.

Julian shot her a sideways glance. 'I can't help it,' he said. 'I've tried not to but I still love you.'

'Don't!' She turned away to look at the lake. Oblivious to her wretchedness, the water sparkled in the sunshine. 'It's not you,' she said, feeling as if her heart was breaking. 'I told you before: I can't love any man.' She drew in a deep, sobbing breath. 'I only wish I could.'

'Oh, Clarissa!' He caressed her hand. 'I wish you'd tell me what it was that made you so distrustful of men. Someone you loved must have made you very unhappy?'

'I can't talk about it.' Her throat was tight from choking back sobs of despair.

414

Tentatively, Julian put his arm around her. 'Was it . . . ' He hesitated. 'Was it your father? I know your relationship with him is strained.'

A sob welled up from deep inside her then and she pressed her face into his shoulder.

'Why don't you tell me?'

Resting her head against his chest, she heard his heartbeat, steady and strong. She was tired, so tired of the terrible burden she'd carried for so long. Perhaps it was time to share it, as he had shared his own burden with her?

She ran her finger over the scars on the inside of her forearm. 'When I was a child,' she said, her voice hesitant, 'Father used to force me to drink whisky from his hip flask before he . . . ' She swallowed. 'Even now, the smell of whisky takes me back to those times he made me do unspeakable things with him.'

Julian drew in his breath sharply but he didn't look at her with revulsion.

'For as long as I can remember,' Clarissa said, 'he used to come to my room in the night. And every time, after all the terror and the pain, he'd kiss me tenderly and tell me I was a good girl. It took me years to realise this wasn't how fathers should behave with their daughters. And when I asked him to stop, he held me down and forced me. When he hurt me inside so badly that a doctor didn't think it was possible for me to bear children, I threatened to tell Mother. He only smiled and said that if I made such a terrible accusation, he'd confine me in a madhouse.'

Convulsively, Julian wrapped his arms around her. 'He's the one who is insane! How any father

415

could do that to his own child . . . '

She heaved a great sigh. 'What Father did damaged me in more ways than anyone knows. I'm ashamed of things I've done and I know I'm not the woman you'd like me to be.'

'There's nothing you can tell me that will stop me loving you.'

'You don't know that!' Clarissa pulled herself away from him and took a deep breath. 'I can't look at you while I speak of it.'

He held out his hand to her. 'Come on. We'll stroll beside the lake together.'

Walking calmed her a little. 'I'm sick of secrets and the harm they do,' she said. 'You know about Benedict but he wasn't the only one. I've had many lovers.' She braced herself for Julian's disgust.

'Whatever happened in the past shall remain in the past,' he said. 'It doesn't change how I feel about you.'

She risked a glance at him and her heart leaped at the warmth in his eyes when he looked at her. 'It's hard to explain. Father did terrible things to me and I couldn't make him stop but, when I grew up, I discovered that my body gave me the power to control other vain and arrogant men. *Someone* had to pay for what I'd suffered. I'm ashamed to tell you I did everything I could to make men like that want me. Once they fell in love with me, I cast them off in the cruellest ways and revelled in their pain.'

'I'll wager it didn't make you feel better for very long?' said Julian.

'No, it didn't.' She could hardly believe he

wasn't revolted by her.

He hesitated. 'There's one thing I must ask you. Is Lily your father's child?'

'No, thank the Lord!'

The tension in Julian's expression eased.

'No one else knows,' Clarissa said, 'but Lily's father is Hugh Penrose.'

Julian whistled in surprise and said, 'I'd never have guessed that!'

'He's a sanctimonious hypocrite,' said Clarissa. 'I didn't believe it was possible for me to conceive and seducing Hugh gave me a hold over him. I used that to force him into curbing his wife from continually denigrating the Spindrift community. And I blackmailed him into contributing to Lily's upkeep.'

'Is that the last of your secrets?'

She nodded. 'There have been no lovers since Lily arrived. She changed everything for me. She taught me how to love and I'm doing my utmost to be a good mother to her.'

'You *are* a good mother.' Julian pressed her hand to his lips. 'This has been a terrible secret for you to bear alone for so long. None if it was your fault and you mustn't ever blame yourself for what your father did to you. Whatever happened in the past must end here.' Gently, he tucked a loose strand of her hair behind her ear. 'You helped me so much when you encouraged me to tell you about my own guilt. Please, Clarissa, will you let me support you now?'

The pain she'd carried inside her for so long eased, just a little, and the first tentative shoots of happiness blossomed in Clarissa's weary heart. 'I need time,' she whispered, 'but I'll never shut you out again.'

37

July 1897

'It's monstrous!' said Edith, after the land agent had been to value Spindrift House.

The whole community, except for Clarissa and Julian, who were in London, gathered around the kitchen table after dinner.

Gilbert scratched his head reflectively. 'So the renovations we paid for to convert the outbuildings have increased the market value of the property?'

'To be fair,' said Augustus, 'we always knew we didn't own Spindrift. Even if we have to leave, the rent's been very reasonable so we haven't really lost out.'

'But I don't want to leave!' Maude's faded eyes glistened with alarm.

Mabel put her arm around her sister. 'Spindrift is our home and all of you are the nearest to family we have.'

'I wonder how much Hugh offered?' said Augustus.

Pascal sighed. 'It is more important to find out how much Benedict would accept.'

'If he accepts my proposal and sells a proportion of the property to the community,' said Edith, 'I'm sure he'll want to keep more than fifty per cent, so as to maintain control.'

419

'There's only two weeks left,' said Dora, her face pinched with anxiety.

'We must find somewhere to go when we have to leave Spindrift,' said Edith, sick at heart. 'Meanwhile we'll beg, borrow or steal whatever we can.'

Wilfred tapped his fingers on the table. 'Let's sleep on it. Tomorrow we'll put figures together for whatever we can scrape up. Benedict might be content if we raised forty per cent of the valuation figure between us.'

'I should jolly well think he would,' said Augustus.

There was a chorus of gloomy goodnights.

Edith and Dora went upstairs and tiptoed into the nursery. They kissed the sleeping children then softly closed the door.

'It isn't right,' said Dora, mouth twisting as she dabbed her tears away. 'It's so unfair on the little ones. None of it's their fault.'

'No, it's not.' Edith kept a tight grip on her own emotions. Once she started to weep, she knew she wouldn't be able to stop.

'And why isn't Clarissa here? She should be helping us.'

Edith refused to think about her. 'Julian will have told her what's happening. She'll have to come back and collect her belongings if . . . '

'But where can we all go? None of us has another home.'

Edith's eyes were gritty with exhaustion. 'I can't think about it anymore now. Goodnight, Dora.'

Wearily, she undressed and went to bed.

Julian returned from London looking remarkably cheerful. He and Pascal set off in the trap for several days running to search for a house to rent, large enough to accommodate them all, only to return downcast in the evenings.

Wilfred made a list of funds the community could raise. Maude and Mabel offered almost all their substantial inheritance from their dear, departed father. Pascal had squirrelled away earnings from his seascapes. Augustus had some savings and went to visit his father, who agreed to make him a loan. Edith had the money from her pearls and Papa's cheque. Wilfred's mother had come up trumps in recognition of his past devotion to her. Julian and Gilbert volunteered what savings they had and Annie put her name down for the few shillings she'd saved.

'I feel bad,' said Dora to Edith. 'I have a few pounds but it isn't much.'

'Of course it isn't,' said Edith, 'because Clarissa and I can't pay you much, but your worth to my children and the community is incalculable.'

At last they'd all done what they could. They totted up the entries and the final sum was just over thirty per cent of Spindrift's value. Edith wrote to Benedict's solicitor with their offer and they all tried to keep busy whilst waiting for a response.

★ ★ ★

The Spindrift Gallery had been busy all morning while Edith and Julian were on duty. Edith had encouraged a summer visitor to buy one of Pascal's seascapes and was wrapping his purchase when quick footsteps ran into the gallery.

Dora, her cheeks very pink and her hair falling out of its pins, rushed up to her and flung her arms around her neck. 'Oh, Edith! Thank you, thank you!'

The customer, bemused, tipped his hat and left with his parcel.

'Whatever is it?' Edith asked.

'A letter!'

Edith caught her breath. 'From the solicitor?'

Dora shook her head. 'Sorry, it's not that. It's Pettigrew and Alleyn.' Her face was luminous with delight. 'They want to meet me to discuss publication of my stories. You never told me you'd been to see them.'

'I didn't want to get your hopes up in case it came to nothing.'

Julian sauntered towards them then. 'What's going on?'

'I borrowed some of Dora's illustrations,' said Edith, 'together with a couple of her stories about Theodora the Pirate Queen. I took them to a publisher when we were in London and they kept them to discuss at their next board meeting.'

'I looked everywhere for those stories and blamed the children for losing them,' babbled Dora.

'Oh, dear! I'd hoped you wouldn't miss them,' said Edith.

'I'm to meet Mr Pettigrew and must write to him straight away.' She chewed her lip. 'Would you look after the children for a few days while I'm away, Edith? Annie will help.'

'Of course. Now go and write that letter!'

Edith and Julian stood in the doorway, watching Dora hurry back towards the house.

'She deserves success,' Edith said. 'It would have been impossible for me to continue to paint if she hadn't cared for my babies. I hope it's her turn for some recognition now.'

*　*　*

A few days later, the children sprawled on the studio floor, drawing on sugar paper with coloured chalks, while Edith and Pascal stretched a new canvas.

Edith had hoped the simple task would distract her from her wretchedness but, so far, it had failed. The lawyers had written to say the community's offer for Spindrift House had been refused. Mr Fairchild, however, would give both them and another interested party an additional ten days to increase their offer. Edith knew they'd reached their limit and their days at Spindrift were numbered.

They'd looked at a house on the outskirts of Wadebridge but there were only enough bedrooms for Edith, Dora, Clarissa and the children. The Laurels had a high hedge that made the inside gloomy. The kitchen reeked of mice but there was a garden. They'd each have to work in their own room and, of course, there was nowhere for a gallery. And then there was the other question of whether Edith could bear to continue

423

living with Clarissa. She hadn't decided yet.

Meanwhile, Wilfred was scouting for cottages to house the rest of the community. The prospect of everyone being scattered was depressing.

She felt Pascal's gaze on her and glanced up.

He gave her his lovely slow smile. 'There is pleasure in simple tasks,' he murmured, 'when you share them with someone you cherish, don't you think?'

She paused, the tack hammer held in mid-air as a blush flooded her cheeks. 'I enjoy these tasks when I'm with you.' Sighing, she said, 'However will we manage without a studio?'

Pascal shrugged.

Childish laughter and footsteps clattered up the stairs and then Lily burst through the doorway.

'Auntie Edith, I've been on a train with Mama, and Auntie Dora and Uncle Julian came to meet us with the pony trap.'

Edith bent to hug Lily, feeling the child's silky hair brush her face. 'I missed you,' she said as the little girl clasped a pair of slender arms around her neck.

'I've brought you a present.' Lily held out a small glass globe with a tiny model of the Tower of London inside. 'You can make it snow!'

Pearl and Jasper joined in the excitement, taking turns to shake the snow globe. Then Dora arrived, looking smart in a new hat. Jasper and Pearl hurried to kiss her.

'Well?' Edith asked.

Dora's face broke into a grin. 'Please meet Dora Cox, author and illustrator,' she said. 'I

424

have a contract for *The Adventures of Theodora the Pirate Queen*.'

Pascal let out a shout of triumph.

'And,' said Dora, looking decidedly smug, 'if it sells well, there will be a series.'

'I'm so happy for you!' said Edith, hugging her.

Dora's freckled cheeks turned bright pink. 'Better still, I have an advance payment so now I can contribute properly to the fund!'

'Bless you, Dora! It's worth a try. Benedict's given us a few more days, almost as if he wants us to succeed so he doesn't have to sell to Hugh.'

Lily and Pearl's heads were close together as they played. Lily's delicate features and flaxen hair made her a carbon copy of Clarissa. Pearl, with her bouncing bronze curls, bore no resemblance to Lily but that wasn't proof Benedict hadn't fathered them both. What upset Edith wasn't Lily's paternity. She knew Benedict was like a tom cat sniffing round any female who caught his fancy. No, it was Clarissa's disloyalty that caused her such anguish. She'd been a loved and trusted friend, much more to Edith than a sister. Would it ever be possible to rebuild that trust?

She glanced at Pascal as he helped Jasper with his drawing. Perhaps it was unfair of her to blame Clarissa for concealing the identity of her child's father when that was exactly what Edith herself had done. None of what had happened was Lily's fault and she shouldn't have to suffer from her mother's banishment from the community.

Edith sighed, still unsure what to do.

During dinner, Wilfred refused to allow any talk of leaving Spindrift and Pascal opened a bottle of wine to toast Dora's success. Afterwards, feeling slightly tipsy, she played rollicking music hall songs on the out-of-tune piano, while Gilbert accompanied her in his rich, deep baritone. Augustus brought out his banjo and Wilfred pretended to be a sailor and sang a ribald sea shanty that made Dora dissolve into giggles.

Clarissa fidgeted on her chair. Then she caught Edith's eye. 'May I have a private word?' she murmured.

Edith nodded and they slipped outside into the dusk. They could hear the strains of 'Down at the Old Bull and Bush', thumped out on the piano and accompanied by raucous singing, as they crossed the lawn to the gazebo.

The bench seat creaked as they sat down together.

Edith glanced at Clarissa, twisting the chain of her silver pendant around a finger. 'There's something I must say to you.'

She hunched over, folding her arms across her chest. 'You're going to ask me to leave,' she said, her voice dull.

'I was going to,' Edith said, 'but I've changed my mind.' She heard Clarissa's sharp intake of breath. 'Lily came to see me when you returned this afternoon,' she said. 'I love her dearly and she's almost a sister to my children. The Spindrift community is a family in all but name and families have their ups and downs. I've come to understand it doesn't really matter that Benedict is Lily's father or that you betrayed me with my husband. We need each other. So, do stay, Clarissa.'

'What?' Clarissa stared at her. 'Edith, you're wrong! *Benedict* isn't Lily's father.'

Edith frowned. 'You admitted you had an affair with him.'

'But that was years ago, before you and Benedict even knew each other!' There was no guile in Clarissa's expression. 'I shan't tell you who Lily's father was. He was married and the affair, such as it was, meant nothing.'

Could Edith believe it?

'I'd never want to hurt *you* but Benedict was so very full of himself, just like my father, that I wanted to teach him a lesson. I planned to make him fall in love with me and then I was going to ditch him.' Clarissa sighed heavily, remembering how she had failed. 'But Benedict has only ever loved himself.'

'I learned that lesson, too,' Edith said, her voice bitter. The garden was perfumed with honeysuckle and the briny scent of the sea drifted on the breeze. 'What was it you wanted to say to me?' she asked.

Clarissa gave a soft laugh. 'I was going to save you the bother of expelling me from Spindrift. But now everything's different. I don't care where we live, as long as we can all be together, but I'd much rather stay here, wouldn't you?'

'If only we could.'

'I have some money set aside,' said Clarissa. 'Ever since Lily was born, I've been receiving an

427

allowance for her from her father. I've hardly touched it, intending to give it to her when she's twenty-one. I've realised how very important the community is to us . . . to her, and I want that money to be added to the community fund, along with Dora's advance.'

'It might be enough to make the difference,' said Edith. Hope flared in her heart. She stood up and held out her hand. Shrieks of laughter drifted from the sitting-room window, followed by the third chorus of 'Roll Out the Barrel'. 'Let's go and join the others.'

They walked arm-in-arm across the dew-laden grass towards the house.

Clarissa stopped suddenly. 'What's that?'

There was a strange orange glow visible at one end of the gallery. Edith stared, frozen by dread. Then a shower of sparks shot into the air, galvanising her into action. 'Fire! My God, Clarissa, the barn is on fire! Run for the others. Fetch water!' She gathered up her skirts and hurtled across the lawn.

In the stable yard, she grabbed a bucket and filled it from the well. It thumped against her legs as she ran, slopping water onto her skirt, and she snatched up a broom that she saw leaning against a wall.

The clapboard cladding at the back of the gallery was alight. Edith hesitated. To reach it, she'd have to go into the dark and smoky passage between the barn and the high wall of the vegetable garden. There was no way out at the other end. But the gallery contained the fruit of hundreds of hours of their labour. She couldn't let the flames ruin them. Holding her breath, she ran into the passage and threw the water at the source of the flames. The stench of paraffin came from a pile of burning rags at the foot of the wall and several lit pieces had been stuffed into gaps in the clapboard. Smoke belched upwards. Coughing, she beat at the blaze with her broom.

She glimpsed movement at the dead-end of the passage and then a man ran past through the swirling smoke. 'Hey!' Edith yelled. She stuck out the broom handle and he tripped, then scrambled to his feet. She flailed at his legs with the broom.

He thumped her in the chest with his outstretched hands, sending her sprawling to the ground. His face was briefly illuminated by the flames as he ran off.

A man's voice shouted, 'I've got him!'

Pascal appeared through the smoke and anxiously pulled her to her feet. 'Are you hurt?'

She shook her head. 'It was Hugh Penrose!'

Pascal threw a bucketful of water at the glowing timber. 'Go!' He thrust the empty bucket at her and picked up the broom to beat out the flames.

Gilbert had imprisoned Hugh in his brawny arms and carried him, thrashing and kicking, towards the stables.

Dora and Clarissa filled buckets at the well and the men ran with them to the barn. Maude and Mabel came to help. Edith found a spade and hurried back into the passage. She stood at Pascal's side, battering the flames while the choking smoke made her eyes stream.

Julian took her place and she went back to the well. She lost track of time but her palms were blistered and stinging by the time the fire was reduced to charred timber and acrid smoke. Several of Pascal's paintings, part of Julian's display of photographs and one of Mabel and Maude's wall-hangings had burned but the damage was less than it might have been.

In the kitchen, Mabel and Maude made tea and boiled water for them all to wash the soot from their faces. Dora applied salve to their burns.

'Where is he?' asked Edith.

Gilbert rubbed his hands together. 'Tied up nice and tight in the stable. Reeks of paraffin.'

They trooped outside and Gilbert unlocked the door to one of the looseboxes. Hugh Penrose was sitting on the ground, trussed up with his hands behind his back and his ankles hobbled. He glowered at them.

'Why did you do this?' Pascal asked. 'Why would you burn down part of the property you're about to buy?'

Hugh struggled against his bonds. 'Untie me!'

'I hardly think you're in any position to make demands,' said Wilfred.

Hugh heaved a sigh. 'Fairchild agreed to sell Spindrift House to me but then he changed his mind and accepted an offer from you lot. If I couldn't have it, I was damned if you were going to!'

'But Benedict turned down our offer,' said Edith.

430

Hugh snapped his head around to look at her. 'What?'

'He wanted more money than we had.'

Hugh gave a howl of rage. 'That double-dealing son of a . . .'

'Quite so,' said Wilfred, drily.

'It's not only the damage to the building that concerns us but you've destroyed some of our work,' said Augustus. 'I'm going to fetch the constable from the village.'

'No! Don't do that.'

'Give us one good reason why we shouldn't,' said Clarissa. 'Burning our work deprives us of our living.'

'No, please!' Hugh attempted, and failed, to stand. 'I'll pay for the paintings.'

'Not good enough,' said Clarissa. 'Pay triple the price for each work of art and the cost of repairing the barn and we might have something to talk about.'

'There must be adequate compensation,' said Edith, 'not only for our distress and the risk we took in putting out the fire, but for the continuing loss of business at the height of the season whilst repairs are undertaken.'

'Don't be ridiculous!'

'I'll fetch the constable then,' said Augustus.

Clarissa laughed mockingly. 'I wonder if your wife will dare to attend church on Sunday, while her husband is in jail awaiting trial for arson.'

'God damn you! I'll pay.' Hugh's face was scarlet.

'In that case,' said Edith, 'you will sign a confession and an agreement to recompense us

431

for the damage. Bring us the money tomorrow morning, in cash, and we'll return the signed confession to you.'

Gilbert, none too gently, pulled Hugh to his feet. He took a penknife from his pocket, cut the rope and bundled him towards the house.

In the kitchen, Edith sat at the table and wrote out the confession and the agreement. She placed it before Hugh, together with pen and inkwell.

He scanned the paper and gasped when he realised the sum he was expected to pay. 'It's too much!'

'Not at all,' she said. 'It's your choice. But if you refuse, we shall pursue you very publicly through the courts.'

'Whatever would your friends think of you?' said Clarissa, handing him the pen.

Hugh swallowed. Slowly, he dipped the nib in the inkwell.

Then there was silence, except for the scratching of pen on paper.

'A sensible decision, given the alternative,' said Clarissa when he'd finished. He shot her a look of acute dislike and she laughed softly.

Edith picked up the agreement and checked the signature. 'Gilbert, would you see our guest safely home?'

'Certainly.'

After Hugh had gone, they breathed a collective sigh of relief.

Edith handed the agreement to the others for them to see the sum she'd negotiated.

Augustus whistled and Dora gasped.

'I believe that this,' Edith said, 'combined with Dora's advance and Clarissa's savings, will enable us to offer Benedict forty per cent of the value of Spindrift House.' She felt laughter bubbling up inside her. 'There's a certain irony in making Hugh pay us so much that our offer is more attractive than his own, isn't there?'

'Oh, yes,' said Clarissa, laughter dancing in her blue eyes. 'He'll never know just how much he's contributed.'

38

September 1897

'Summer is nearly over,' said Pascal at breakfast. 'Shall we declare a holiday and take a picnic lunch to the cove?'

Edith, Mabel and Maude spent the morning baking gingerbread, jam tarts and apple and blackberry pies. Clarissa made lemonade and sandwiches. Dora organised the children into collecting driftwood and Pascal and Julian built a fire on the beach. Wilfred walked down to the harbour to buy fresh mackerel, while Gilbert set up a game of skittles. Augustus tuned his banjo ready for a sing-song.

It was an afternoon Edith would never forget, full of laughter and fun. Everyone, even Mabel and Maude, played skittles and rounders. Julian herded them against a backdrop of the cliffs to take a group photograph, smiling and dishevelled from their exertions. When the tide went out, Dora scratched hopscotch squares in the wet sand and they fell about in gales of laughter watching Gilbert play the clown.

Little Lucien lay on his stomach for hours watching crabs and anemones in the rock pools, while Nell, his ever-faithful twin, sat beside him humming happily. Edith bunched up her skirts and paddled in the shallows, watching Pascal patiently teaching the older children to swim. She felt blessed that, although her beautiful children didn't have a father to guide them, Pascal had taken on the role of their mentor and friend. And, one day, she would tell him that Jasper, the boy he loved, was his son.

After a picnic of mackerel roasted over the fire, hunks of crusty bread and home-grown tomatoes, they sat in a circle, spellbound, listening to Dora spin another yarn about Theodora the Pirate Queen. Later, the fresh air and the warmth of the sun caught up with Mabel and Maude and they nodded off, the twins asleep on a blanket beside them.

Clarissa and Julian meandered along the water's edge, ostensibly gathering shells, but Edith had seen their secret smiles and sideways glances at one another. She truly hoped Clarissa had found peace and love at last.

Pascal dozed on the sand beside Edith. She studied the sweep of his eyelashes and the dark stubble shadowing his jaw and resisted the impulse to lean over and kiss him. Carefully, so as not to disturb him, she rose to her feet.

He opened one eye and caught her hand. 'Where are you going?'

'To fetch my sketchbook. It's such a perfect day, I want to record it so I never forget it.'

He smiled lazily and kissed her palm. 'Don't be long.'

She trudged through the soft sand and marram grass towards the steps. At the clifftop, she leaned against the ancient standing stone to catch her breath. Before her was endless blue sky melding with the sea at the horizon and, on the beach below, all the people she loved most in the world. Smiling in contentment, she set off for the house. The gate creaked as she let herself into the garden but otherwise everything was quiet, sleepy in the golden sunshine.

The sheltering stone walls of the house were aflame with autumnal Virginia creeper and bees buzzed lazily about their business. Her sketchbooks were filled with happy memories of Spindrift House: the children in the tin bath by the range, Pascal hoeing the vegetable garden, a view of the sea from the landing window and the Spindrift family chatting and cooking together in the kitchen. At last, it seemed their future here was secure. The previous month, Benedict had accepted the community's offer and sold them a forty per cent share of Spindrift House.

Halfway across the lawn, a gust of wind lifted the brim of Edith's sunhat. Glancing up, she frowned to see dark clouds chasing each other across the sky. And was that flickering sunlight catching the uneven glass or had a shadow moved behind her bedroom window?

The chickens pecked peaceably in the courtyard as she opened the kitchen door. She stood still in the hall, listening, but all was quiet except for the sonorous ticking of the grandfather clock on the landing. Upstairs, she peered into her room. Dust motes drifted, undisturbed, in a shaft of sunlight and she shook her head at her fanciful imaginings.

Outside, a billowing cloud raced in front of the sun, plunging the house into shadow.

436

Impatient to return to the cove, her footsteps resounded as she hurried upstairs to the studio. She caught a hint of aromatic smoke in the air as she rummaged about on her worktable, gathering together a sketchbook and pencils. Pearl's rag doll lay abandoned beside her sketchbook and she picked it up too, relieved to have discovered it before bedtime.

'Hello, Edith.'

Yelping, she dropped the doll and spun around, pressing one hand to her throat.

Benedict slouched against the doorway, smoking and watching her with smiling, indolent eyes.

'What are you doing here?' she stuttered.

'That's not very welcoming!' he said. 'Still, you're looking well. Blooming, in fact.' He unfolded himself from the doorway and sauntered into the studio. 'I've taken a look around while you were all larking about in the cove. A gallery in the barn, workshops in the stables, every room in the house let, a kitchen garden and even chickens. Quite a little business. I have to say, your inventiveness has impressed me.'

Her skin crawled to know he'd been poking about while they weren't there.

'I'd forgotten how lovely Spindrift is at this time of year.' He took a step closer. 'Now I'm rid of Isobel, perhaps I should come home?'

Horror-struck, she was speechless.

'Don't look at me like that, Edith! Don't you remember how it was between us at the beginning?' Benedict's voice was low, cajoling. 'I thought I was the luckiest man alive when you agreed to marry me. I yearned for you so much

437

that I couldn't sleep. And on our wedding night, my dreams came true. My wife was not only beautiful and talented but as passionate as any man could desire.'

'I loved you with my heart and soul, Benedict,' she whispered. 'But you threw it all away.'

He sighed. 'It's a fault in my nature that I'm easily bored and driven to flit, like a bee, from one honeyed flower to another.' His shoulders drooped and Edith was amazed by the sadness in his eyes.

'Your irresponsibility has hurt us all,' she said, 'but you have been the greater loser by forgoing the joys of fatherhood.'

'I regret that,' he said, 'and that I've been a disappointment to you. The excitement of living with Isobel soon wore off. She's a hard woman and it didn't take me long to realise I missed you.' He reached out and captured her hand. 'Edith, if I were to come home, couldn't we try again?'

For a split second she looked into his hazel eyes and considered it, if only for the sake of the children. But it would never work.

Footsteps sounded on the landing and Pascal appeared in the doorway.

Edith slipped her hand out of her husband's.

'Benedict,' said Pascal, 'this is unexpected.' His tone was mild but his fists were clenched at his sides.

Benedict's gaze raked over Pascal, taking in the rigidity of his posture. 'I was discussing with my wife whether I should return to the marital bed.'

438

'Is that what Edith desires?' asked Pascal, his voice expressionless.

'She's my *wife*,' said Benedict.

Pascal moved to stand at Edith's side. 'But you deserted her.'

She took a small step closer to him, so that their arms were touching.

Benedict's eyes widened momentarily. 'So that's how it is between you! I never imagined . . . '

'Let her go, Benedict,' said Pascal. 'If you care for her at all, allow her to be happy in the new life she has made without you.'

Edith held her breath.

Benedict picked up the rag doll from her worktable and then gently put it down again. 'I'd intended to come back to Spindrift. On balance, however, I'll be happier to return to the freedom of a bachelor's life in the bright lights of London.'

Edith swayed. She leaned against Pascal and felt the tension in his body soften.

Benedict gave them a hard stare. 'The thing is,' he said, 'although I've cleared my debts, I underestimated how much I need for day-to-day living. Hugh Penrose has offered to buy my sixty per cent of Spindrift House. He's so desperate to have it that it's made me curious about what you've done to annoy him?'

'We made him pay for the damage after he set fire to the barn,' Edith said.

Benedict roared with laughter.

'It wasn't funny!'

'He has some notion of building a dividing wall and putting in tenants to squeeze you out.'

'No! You can't let him!' An icy wave of dread made Edith shudder. She'd thought the community was safe.

Benedict cracked his knuckles. 'I'd rather keep Spindrift out of Hugh's greedy hands so I might be persuaded not to sell. I'd want thirty per cent of the rents received and three of your paintings a year, Edith, as before. Oh, and ten per cent of everything sold in that gallery of yours.'

'Three paintings a year?' said Pascal. 'What is this?'

'It's our little secret, isn't it, Edith?' said Benedict. 'It's the price my wife agreed to a couple of years ago, to persuade me not to sell Spindrift. The canvases are signed with the name of Fairchild, except that the initial is a B and not an E.'

Pascal caught hold of Edith's wrist. 'You agreed to that?'

'I had no choice.' Mortified, she evaded his searching look.

'Oh, Edith! *Now* I understand why you found it hard to paint.' His voice was choked with emotion.

Benedict strode across the studio. Picking up one of Edith's canvases, he held it at arm's length. It was *Catching the Tide*, her precious painting of the children playing pirates.

She ached to snatch it from him but forced herself to keep her expression impassive.

'It's very good,' Benedict said. 'You've come on considerably, Edith.' He scowled. 'It's always irked me that my work is never as well received as yours. Still, signed by me, this canvas should serve to restore my reputation. Perhaps I'll forget portraits for a while and copy your new style.'

'You can't!' she said. There was a lurching, falling sensation in her stomach. 'Please,' she pleaded, 'not this one! It's special to me. Don't you see, it's our children?'

'Is it more important to you than Spindrift House?'

Mute with misery, she gave a small shake of her head.

'There!' he said. 'That wasn't so hard, was it? You'll paint other pictures, my artistic career will be revived — and Hugh can grind his teeth all he likes.'

Numb and sick-feeling, she watched Benedict tuck her painting under his arm.

'By the way,' he said, 'I'll want to see the accounts of all the little businesses you're running here, so don't try to cheat me.'

Goaded beyond endurance, Edith shouted, 'I'm not the cheat here!'

He moved abruptly towards her and she flattened her back to the wall, fearful of angering him further.

Pascal stepped between them, one hand pressed firmly against Benedict's chest.

'Don't provoke me, Pascal,' warned Benedict, 'or I'll change my mind and you and the rest of the raggle-taggle band can go hang!'

Pascal remained where he was, immovable.

Benedict dropped his gaze and checked his pocket watch. 'Time I went.' He took a step back and Pascal let his hand drop. 'Good afternoon to you both.' At the doorway, he paused and looked back at Edith.

441

She thought, for a moment, that there was regret in his eyes. And then there was only the sound of his retreating footsteps.

Pascal's jaw was rigid with anger. When he wrapped his arms around her, he was trembling with rage. 'You have made immense sacrifices for our community,' he said, 'but I tell you this: Benedict will *never* become a successful artist. And if he imagines he will assume the mantle of greatness by copying your work, then he is fooling himself.'

'I thought it was all over and we were safe.' Edith buried her face in his shoulder, breathing in the salty scent of his skin.

'I was so afraid he was going to return to living here,' murmured Pascal into her hair. 'Somehow, we will keep paying him to stay away. And you will make new paintings of your enchanting children, even better than *Catching the Tide*.'

She took strength from the feeling of his arms around her. His heartbeat was steady and strong. He was right; she could, and would, paint other, equally treasured, canvases.

Pascal cupped her chin. 'I will never understand how Benedict could abandon you so easily. How could he not see how very special you are?'

She looked deep into his eyes. The stillness in the room felt thick, echoing with the pounding of her blood. Tentatively, she touched his mouth with her forefinger.

Pascal captured her hand and kissed her fingers. 'I love you so much it hurts, Edith,' he said, his voice husky.

She clung to him, delight tinged with the

heartbreak of knowing she was still another man's wife. 'I love you, too,' she whispered, 'but I'm not free . . . '

'We cannot marry' he said, 'but you must know that we belong together?'

'Yes,' she breathed. 'I do.'

'Then that must be enough for us. I had far rather live in joy at your side, our souls entwined but separated by law, than merely exist in a world without you.'

Her heart swelled with love, secure in the knowledge that he knew the best of her and the worst of her and still he loved her completely.

Then he kissed her.

For as long as Edith lived, she would never forget the sweetness of that kiss.

Historical Note

When I was a child, my maternal grandmother, born in 1892, came to live with us. I loved to look at her photograph albums and listen to her family stories. She had eight siblings and on the death of her forty-two year old father, she went to live with an uncle at a manor house in Gloucestershire. What fascinated me was how vividly her stories brought to life her siblings, school friends, cousins and 'the Aunts'. I met some of the relatives Granny mentioned, others died before I was born, but it's only now I appreciate that those people were *Victorians*. Victorian and Edwardian history may seem a long time ago to my grandchildren but, to me, I feel almost as if I could reach back and touch it.

There have been great changes in society's attitude to women during my lifetime. Young women today may feel women are still oppressed but Victorian women had very few rights. Most women didn't have the vote until 1928. Spinsters, unless they were rich, had little social standing and a married woman's assets became her husband's upon their marriage. Divorce was almost unheard of and only applied to the rich since it required an Act of Parliament. The Married Women's Property Act of 1882 improved matters by allowing a woman to hold her wages and any inheritance up to £200, independent of her husband.

Felix Slade founded the Slade School of Fine Art in 1871. He envisaged a school where fine art would be studied within a liberal arts university and the education of female students was to be on equal terms with male students. Many, subsequently famous, female artists passed through the Slade at this time, including Kate Greenaway and Evelyn de Morgan. Evelyn's early work was in the popular Neo-Classical style favoured by artists such as Alma-Tadema and Lord Leighton.

During Queen Victoria's long reign, England was involved in imperialist expansion in Africa, the Orient and the Middle East. At the end of the 19th century, Britain was the foremost European power and possessed considerable material wealth. Through the varied global contacts of the Empire, there were many opportunities for intellectual and cultural enrichment. The Victorian era is noted for its romantic painting, photography and crafts.

William Morris, poet, painter and social reformer, founded the Arts and Crafts Movement. He strived to demonstrate that art should be both beautiful and functional and his ideas were strengthened by his friendships with Edward Burne-Jones and Dante Gabriel Rossetti of the Pre-Raphaelite Brotherhood. Their artistic influences are still to be seen today.

Artists had long been attracted to Cornwall for the dramatic landscape and the extraordinary quality of the light. In the 1880s the railway network extended from London into Cornwall and brought artists who congregated in colonies in St Ives and Newlyn.

The Newlyn colony comprised mostly English artists. They painted outside to capture the light and, before the turn of the century, used a muted palette in a predominantly French Realist style. At this time, the mining and fishing industries were failing and many of the artists set out to capture scenes of a fast disappearing way of life for the British public. Several artists had trained in Paris and they displayed their work not only in their studios but also sought sales and recognition from exhibiting at the Royal Academy. St Ives, on the wild and rugged Atlantic coast, became popular with English and international landscape and marine artists, who regularly showed their work at the Royal Academy and the Paris Salon.

The Light Within Us, the first of a trilogy, explores the lives, loves and female friendships of the fictional Spindrift artists' community near Port Isaac on the north Cornish coast. Spindrift House was inspired by a real house but the characters and the cove are entirely dreamed up out of my own imagination.

Acknowledgements

The Light Within Us is the first book of a trilogy and a slight departure from my previous novels. It has been an interesting and, sometimes complicated, exercise to plan a story that spans three books, while still making each one complete in itself. I'd like to thank both my lovely agent, Heather Holden-Brown and my enthusiastic new editor, Eleanor Russell, for their kind and patient support while I came to grips with it all. Lynn Curtis copy-edited the manuscript in her usual sensitive and careful way.

I'm very lucky to have word-wrangling friends, who have allowed me to ramble on about character arcs, plot holes and 'would she really have done that?' crises. My excellent writing group, WordWatchers, read the entire first draft and spent an evening or two discussing it in detail. Liz Harris, Carol McGrath, Deborah Swift, Jenny Barden and Henri Gyland, author friends met through the wonderful Romantic Novelists' Association, also gave me the benefit of their comments and advice. Thank you to all of you.

Thanks and love to my husband, Simon, who drove me to Cornwall for my research and provided encouragement and cups of tea while I was chained to my laptop.

The Light Within Us is dedicated to my mother, who passed away at the age of ninety, during the time I was writing the book. A wonderful painter, her creativity in everything she did inspired me from my earliest moment. She remained interested and supportive of my writing right to the end and I miss her gentle presence more than I can say.